every last breath

Jennifer L. Armentrout

Recycling programs
for this product may
not exist in your area.

ISBN-13: 978-0-373-21114-2

Every Last Breath

HARLEQUIN®TEEN
™ www.HarlequinTEEN.com

Printed in U.S.A.

Praise for The Dark Elements series by #1 *New York Times* bestselling author JENNIFER L. ARMENTROUT

Every Last Breath

"*Every Last Breath* has solidified The Dark Elements as my favorite YA paranormal romance series. Jennifer Armentrout delivers a knockout ending to the trilogy—steamy, smart and satisfying."
—Wendy Higgins, *New York Times* bestselling author
of The Sweet series

Stone Cold Touch

"Armentrout balances suspense and romance, spicing it up with Roth's one-liners and Layla's wry inner commentary, all adding welcome humor.... Demonic fun."
—*Kirkus Reviews*

"An absolutely phenomenal, edge-of-your-seat thrill ride.... [This] just might be the prolific author's best series."
—*RT Book Reviews* (Top Pick)

White Hot Kiss

"Armentrout works her magic with swoon-worthy guys and a twist you never see coming."
—#1 *New York Times* bestselling author Abbi Glines

"With this first title in her new Dark Elements series, powerhouse author Armentrout delivers another action-packed, believably narrated ride... Intense, well plotted, and very readable, this title should fly into the hands of every paranormal reader out there."
—*Booklist*

"Well-paced and peppered with intriguing details that allow both Romeo-and-Juliet swoons and a zombie apocalypse to have their turns."
—*Publishers Weekly*

"Constantly entertaining...the narrative sizzles with as much tension as romance."
—*Kirkus Reviews*

**Don't miss any of The Dark Elements series from
JENNIFER L. ARMENTROUT
and Harlequin TEEN**

Bitter Sweet Love (ebook prequel novella)
White Hot Kiss
Stone Cold Touch
Every Last Breath

Other books by Jennifer L. Armentrout

Shadows
Obsidian
Onyx
Opal
Origin
Opposition
Oblivion
Daimon
Half-Blood
Pure
Deity
Elixir
Apollyon
Sentinel

**Look for
the first book in Jennifer's brand-new
young adult series
from Harlequin TEEN**

The Problem with Forever

This is for every Zayne and Roth fan, everyone who rooted for Layla and wanted their very own Bambi, and for everyone who passionately rallied behind their favorite guy and voted for which one they'd like Layla to choose. Thank you for taking this journey with me.

one

I STOOD IN STACEY'S LIVING ROOM AS MY ENTIRE world crashed around me once more.

Sam was the Lilin.

Acute horror held me immobile, seizing the air in my lungs as I stared at what used to be one of my closest friends in the whole world. Because of the demonic familiar, Bambi, and being unable to see souls while she'd bonded to me, I'd never seen what had been right in front of my face this entire time. None of us had, but it was Sam—he'd been the one to cause the mayhem at school and all the recent deaths. Instead of stripping souls with a single touch, as I'd known a Lilin could do, he'd taken his time, taking a little here and there, playing with his victims and playing with us.

Playing with me.

Except what was standing in Stacey's house was—was basically wearing Sam's skin, a perfectly crafted costume, because the real Sam... He was no more. The pain of knowing that my friend was dead, had been dead for a while without any of us knowing, cut deep into me, making misery of my bone and tissue.

I hadn't been able to save him. None of us had been able to, and now his soul...his soul had to be down below, where all souls that were taken by a Lilin would go. My stomach cramped.

"You cannot defeat me," the Lilin said, his voice identical to Sam's. "So join me."

"Or what?" My heart pounded like a jackhammer in my chest. "Or die? That's not incredibly cliché or anything."

The Lilin tilted its head to the side. "Actually, I wasn't going to say that to you. I need you to help free our mother. The rest of them can die, though."

Our mother. Before I could dwell on the ick factor of being related to the creature that had killed my friend and inflicted so much carnage, Zayne shifted into his true form, distracting me. His shirt ripped up the back as his wings unfurled and his skin deepened to the dark granite of the Wardens. Two horns sprouted, parting his wavy blond hair as they curled back, and his nostrils flattened. When he parted his lips to let out a low growl of warning, fangs appeared. He stepped toward Sam, his massive hands curling into fists.

"Don't!" I shouted. Zayne halted, his head swinging sharply toward me. "Do not get close to him. Your soul," I reminded him as my heart raced. Or what was left of Zayne's soul, considering I'd accidentally taken a nice little bite out of it not long ago.

Zayne backed off, his stance wary.

I turned my attention back to the evil masquerading as Sam. Whatever the thing was standing in front of us, we did share the same flesh and blood. Only recently had I learned exactly how I'd come to be part demon and part Warden. I was the daughter of Lilith and this…this thing truly was a part of me. It had been born out of Lilith's and my blood, and it was just as evil as Lilith. It wanted her freed? Impossible. If Lilith ever ended up topside, the world as we knew it would irrevocably change.

"I'm not going to help you free Lilith." I was so not referring to her as our mother. Yuck. "That's never going to happen."

The Lilin smiled as it watched me with dark, inky eyes. "Get as close as you want." It ignored my statement, taunting Zayne. Heck, taunting all of us. "She's not the only one in this room with a taste for a Warden's soul."

I sucked in a sharp, stinging breath as Stacey let out a whimper. In the space of a second, her relationship with Sam flashed before me. They'd been friends forever and only recently had she recognized that Sam had always, *always* been in love with her. But she hadn't started paying real attention to him until Sam had begun to change…

Oh God.

Stacey had to be breaking wide-open, seeing the boy she finally loved become worse than the monsters that prowled the streets at night, but I couldn't afford to take my focus off the Lilin. It could make a move at any moment, and three of us in this room were vulnerable to the worst kind of attack it could deliver.

"There's nothing like taking a pure soul, but you'd already know that, Layla. All that warmth and goodness goes down as smooth as the richest chocolate." The Lilin tipped its chin up and let out the kind of groan that normally would've caused my ears to burn. "But taking your time, savoring the *taste* is so much more decadent. You should try it, Layla, and stop being so greedy when you feed."

"And you should try shutting the Hell up." Heat rolled off the powerful demon standing beside me. Roth, the reigning Crown Prince of Hell, hadn't shifted yet, but I could tell he was close. Fury dripped from his words. "How about that?"

The Lilin didn't even spare a glance in Roth's direction. "I like you. I really do, prince. Too bad you're going to end up dead."

My fingers curled in, nails biting into my palms as anger flushed through my system, hot and bitter. My emotions were all over the place. On top of everything else that had gone wrong recently, I was standing here between Zayne and Roth, which was about a thousand times awkward on a normal day, but now, after Roth…

I couldn't focus on any of that right now. "You're very brave, making threats when we outnumber you."

One shoulder rose in a gesture so quintessentially Sam it sent a slice of pain through me. "How about I'm just intelligent?" it queried gamely. "And how about I know more than all of you about how this will end?"

"You talk a lot," Roth growled, stepping forward. "And I mean a lot. Why is it that the bad guys always have to give disgustingly long and boring monologues? Let's just get to the killing part, all right?"

The Lilin's mouth formed a lopsided grin. "So eager to die the final death, aren't you?"

"So eager to be done with you running your mouth, more like," Roth retorted, moving so that once again he stood directly beside me.

"It's been you this whole time?" Stacey's voice trembled

under the weight of the pain she must be feeling. "You haven't been Sam? Not since…"

"Not since Dean displayed his fists of fury. That was fun." The Lilin laughed as those dark eyes slid in her direction. "Sam hasn't been home in quite some time, but I can assure you, I enjoyed…our time together as much as I'm sure he would've. You know, if that's any consolation for you."

She clapped her hands over her mouth, muffling the words as tears streamed down her pale face. "Oh my God."

"Not quite," it murmured silkily.

I stepped closer to Stacey, drawing the Lilin's attention from her. I was sick for her, absolutely repulsed. "Why?" I demanded. "You've been around us for weeks. Why haven't you attacked any of us?"

The Lilin sighed heavily. "I'm not all about violence, death and gore. I discovered rather quickly that there are a lot of fun things to do topside, things I've thoroughly enjoyed." It winked at Stacey, and I saw red.

My skin tingled like a thousand fire ants were marching all over it. "Don't look at her. Don't talk to her or even breathe in her general direction, and don't even think about touching her ever again."

"Oh, I've done more than that," the Lilin replied. "Lots more. Everything your Sam wishes he could've had the balls to do. But you know, he's not really concerned about those things at the moment. You see, I consumed him—his soul in its entirety. No part of him remains on this plane. He's not a wraith like the others who crossed my path. I didn't play with my food when it came to him, taking tiny bits of him. No, he's gone. He's in—"

Several things happened all at once.

Stacey shot toward the Lilin, her hand rising as if she was about to knock the mocking smile off his face. The Lilin drifted toward her, and while it hadn't taken her soul yet for whatever reason, I now knew there were no guarantees. The Lilin was unpredictable. It had exposed what it truly was, and I sensed it was done playing around. It was within arms' reach of her and I—well, I sort of lost it. Rage lit me up from the inside.

The change came over me without even trying. Like shedding a sweater, I let go of the human form I'd worn for so long, and in a way, had desperately clung to. It had never been this easy before. Bones didn't break and reknit. Skin didn't stretch, but I felt mine harden, become resilient to most knives and bullets. The roof of my mouth tingled as my fangs dropped, teeth designed to cut through even a Warden's skin, and most definitely a Lilin's. Just below the base of my neck and on either side of my spine, my wings broke free and unfurled.

There was a sharp inhale from someone in the room, but I wasn't paying attention.

Moving as quick as a cobra striking, I grabbed Stacey's arm and shoved her behind me. I got between her and the Lilin. "I said, do not touch her. Do not look at her. Do not even breathe in her direction. You do so, and I will rip your head from your shoulders and punt-kick it out a window."

The Lilin jerked, dancing a step backward. Its pitch-black eyes widened. Shock splashed across its face and then its lips curled back. "That's not playing fair."

What in the world? Was that fear I saw in its face? "Do I look like I care?"

"Oh, you're going to." The Lilin backtracked, moving toward the door. "You're so going to care."

Then the Lilin was gone, spinning right around and exiting the house with a quickness that left me standing there, staring foolishly at the empty doorway. I didn't understand. The Lilin hadn't batted an eyelash at Zayne or Roth, but I'd shifted forms and it had tucked its tail and run away?

Uh.

"Well, that was…anticlimactic." I turned around slowly, tucking my wings back. The first one I saw was Zayne.

He'd returned to his human form. Zayne always, even when he appeared exhausted, could've stepped out of a *Town and Country* magazine. His good looks went beyond all-American and straight into swoonville, population every girl on the planet. He looked like I imagined angels would. Vibrant blue eyes and near-heavenly features, but he stared at me with his mouth hanging slightly open. His absolutely gorgeous face was pale, which made the unforgiving shadows under his eyes stand out starkly. He stared at me like he'd never seen me before, which was bizarre, because he'd grown up with me. I felt like some kind of specimen.

A trickle of unease ran down my spine as my gaze switched to the couch. At some point, Zayne had moved closer to where Stacey had landed. I expected to find her rocking in a ball, but she too gaped at me, her hands pressed against her cheeks, and any other time I would've laughed at that expression. Not now.

My heart rate kicked into overdrive as I swung toward the back of the room, where Roth was standing. My gaze collided with eyes the color of amber. His were wide, his pupils vertical. Even so, he was a sight to behold.

Roth was—well, there was no one that walked this earth that looked quite like him. Probably had to do with the fact that he was in no way human, but he was stunning. Always had been, even when he'd styled the black hair into spikes. I preferred the lesser look he rocked now with his hair falling over his forehead, brushing the tips of his ears and the arches of equally dark eyebrows. Golden eyes were slightly slanted at the outer corners. He had cheekbones and a jaw you could cut glass with, a face any artist would die to sketch—or touch. And those full, expressive lips were parted.

His tawny skin wasn't pale and he didn't gape at me like I belonged under a microscope, but he was watching me in astonishment just as Zayne had.

The unease turned into balls of dread, settling heavily in my stomach. "What?" I whispered, glancing around the room. "Why are you all staring at me like…like there's something wrong with me?"

It couldn't have been because I'd told the Lilin I'd rip his head off. Yeah, I was a little less violent on most days, but in the past week or so, I'd thought I was the Lilin, had been kissed by Zayne and nearly took his soul, was subsequently chained and held in captivity by the very clan that had raised me, was almost killed by that same clan—deep breath—was then healed thanks to Roth and a mystery brew provided by a coven of witches who worshipped Lilith, and now I'd just discovered that my best friend was dead, his soul was in Hell, and the Lilin had taken his place. You'd think a girl could be cut a little slack.

Roth cleared his throat. "Shortie, look…look at your hand."

Look at my hand? Why in the world would he be asking me to do that in the midst of all the cray?

"Do it," he said quietly and too gently.

The dread exploded in my gut like buckshot, and my gaze dropped to my left hand. I expected to see the weird marbling of black and gray, a mixture of the demon and Warden that existed inside of me and a combination I'd become almost familiar with by now. My nails had lengthened and sharpened, and I could tell they were hard enough to cut through steel, as hard as my skin, but my skin…it was still pink. Really pink.

"What the…?" My gaze traveled to my other hand. It was the same. Just pink. My wings twitched, reminding me that I had shifted.

Zayne swallowed. "Your…your wings…"

"What about my wings?" I almost screeched, reaching behind me. "Are they broken? Did they not come out—" The tips of my fingers came into contact with something as soft as silk. My hand jerked back. "What…"

Stacey's watery eyes had doubled in size. "Um, Layla, there's a mirror above the fireplace. I think you need to look in it."

I met Roth's gaze for a second before I spun around and all but ran to the fireplace I was sure Stacey's mom had never used. Clutching the white mantel, I stared at my reflection.

I looked normal, like I did before I shifted…like I was going to class or something. My eyes were the palest shade of gray, a watered-down blue. My hair was so blond it was almost white, and a mess of waves that went in every direction like usual. I looked like a colorless china doll, which was nothing new, except for the two fangs jutting out of my mouth. I wouldn't show them off at school, but that wasn't what caught my attention and held it.

It was my wings.

They were large, not as massive as Zayne's or Roth's, and normally they were almost leathery in texture, but now they were black…black and feathered. Like legit *feathered*. That soft, silky thing I'd felt? It had been tiny feathers.

Feathers.

"Oh my God," I whispered at my reflection. "I have feathers."

"Those are definitely feathered wings," Roth commented.

I whipped around, knocking over a lamp with my *feathered* right wing. "I have feathers on my wings!"

Roth cocked his head to the side. "Yeah, you do."

He was absolutely no help, so I turned to Zayne. "Why do I have feathers on my wings?"

Zayne shook his head slowly. "I don't know, Layla. I've never seen anything like this."

"Liar," hissed Roth, shooting him a dark look. "You've seen that before. So have I."

"I haven't," mumbled Stacey, who, by this point, had tucked her legs against her chest and really looked like she would be rocking at any given point. Until recently, Stacey hadn't known what Roth really was. She hadn't even known about me. This had to be too much for her.

"Okay. How and why have you seen this before?" I demanded, dragging in air too fast. "Am I going to have to shave my wings now?"

"Shortie…" Roth's lips twitched.

I raised my hand, pointing my finger at him. "Don't you dare laugh, you jerk-face! This is not funny. My wings are freaks of nature!"

He lifted his hands. "I'm not going to laugh, but I think you should leave the razors alone. Besides, lots of things have feathers in their wings."

"Like what?" I demanded. Were there still more supernatural creatures I was unfamiliar with?

"Like…like hawks," he answered.

My brows furrowed. "Hawks? *Hawks?*"

"And eagles?"

"I'm not a bird, Roth!" Patience leaked out of me. "Why do I have feathers on my wings?" I shrieked, this time at Zayne. "You've seen this before? Where? Someone tell me—"

Underneath me, the floor began to tremble, cutting me off. The shudder increased, traveling up the walls, shaking the mirror and rattling the framed pictures. Plumes of plaster puffed from the ceiling. The house quaked and a loud rumble became deafening.

Stacey popped up from the couch, grabbing Zayne's arm. "What's happening?"

Wings forgotten, I exchanged a look with Zayne. Something about this was all too familiar. I'd felt this before, when—

Blinding golden light streamed in through the windows and the tiny cracks in the wall and from between the wooden boards of the floor. Soft, luminous light crept along the ceiling, dripping downward. I jumped to the side, narrowly avoiding getting hit with the splatter. I clearly remembered what had happened the last time I'd been stupid enough to touch the light.

My kind never could. Neither could Roth.

"Shit," he muttered.

My heart stopped as the rumble was cut off and the beautiful glow disappeared. In a flash, Roth was beside me, one hand curled around my upper arm.

Stacey sniffed the air. "Why does it smell like we're being suffocated in dryer sheets?"

She was right; a new scent permeated the air. To me, it was musky and sweet. Heaven…heaven smelled like whatever you wanted it to, whatever you truly desired most in the world, and it was different for everyone.

Zayne shoved Stacey behind him, and I had a feeling Roth was about to drag our nonangelic butts out of there, but a fissure of power radiated throughout the room. The sweet aroma that filled me with yearning was replaced by clover and frankincense. Warmth traveled down my back, and I knew we were too late to make an escape.

Oh no.

Stacey gasped. "Oh my…" Her eyes rolled back in her head and her knees gave out. She folded like an accordion. Zayne caught her before she smacked into the floor, and I didn't really have time to worry about her.

We weren't alone.

I didn't want to turn around, but I couldn't help it. I had to, because I wanted to see *them*. I had to see them before they wiped me off the face of the planet. Roth must've felt the same, because he also turned. There was a soft glow reflecting off his cheeks. He squinted and I looked toward the doorway.

Two of them stood there like sentries, nearly seven feet tall or possibly even bigger. They were so beautiful it was almost painful to look upon. Hair the color of wheat and their skin shimmered, catching and absorbing the light all around them. They were neither black nor white nor any shade in between, but somehow all colors at once, and they wore some kind of linen pants. The orbs of their eyes were pure white—no irises or pupils. Just white space, and I dimly wondered how they could see. Their chests and feet were bare. Their shoulders were as broad as any Warden's and their wings were magnificent, a brilliant white spanning at least eight feet on either side of them.

Their wings were also feathered.

Unlike mine, though, those feathers had hundreds of eyes in them, actual eyeballs. Eyeballs that did not blink, but roamed constantly and seemed to take in everything at once.

Each of the creatures held a golden sword, a real freaking sword—a sword that looked like it was the length of my leg. The whole combination was possibly the freakiest thing I'd ever seen, and I'd seen a lot of freaky things in my seventeen years of life.

They were here, the ones that ran this little show called life, who'd created the Wardens and who, to demons, were the equivalent of the boogeyman. Never in the history of ever had they been in the presence of anyone with a trace of demonic blood in them without ending their lives immediately.

I felt my wings—my *feathered* wings—tuck close to my back. I don't even know why I tried to hide them at this point, but I was a wee bit self-conscious. However, I wasn't willing to shift into my human form, not in the presence of these beings.

I couldn't stop staring at them. Awe and fear warred inside me. They…they were *angels* and their feathered wings practically glowed, they were so bright. I'd never been allowed anywhere near them, not even when they came to the Wardens' compound to meet with Abbot, the clan leader. I'd always been forced to leave the premises, and I never thought I'd ever see them.

An irresponsible urge to go to them hit me hard in the chest, and it took everything in me to ignore it. I breathed in deeply, and they smelled *wonderful*.

Roth jerked suddenly, and my heart lodged somewhere in my throat. Fear poured into me. Had they done something to him? Then I saw it. A shadow drifted off him, spilling into the air in front of us. I'd also seen that before. It happened whenever the tattooed familiars came off his skin.

I knew it wasn't Bambi or the kittens, because this shadow came from the general vicinity of his...well, pretty much where the belt on his jeans was. Only one tattoo existed there, the only one I'd never seen.

The dragon familiar that Roth had warned only came off his skin when the shit hit the fan or he was seriously pissed.

The Alphas were here, and Thumper had finally come out to play.

two

BRACING MYSELF FOR THE APPEARANCE OF A large and very destructive dragon, I tensed and held my breath. We all were going to die horrible, burning deaths.

The shadow was huge as it shifted into thousands of little black dots that spun together in the air, like a mini cyclone, taking shape and form. Seconds passed as iridescent blue and gold scales appeared along the belly and the back of the dragon. Deep red wings sprouted, as well as a long, proud snout and clawed hind legs. Its eyes matched Roth's, a bright yellow.

It was a beautiful creature.

But...the dragon was about the size of a cat—a really small cat.

Not exactly what I had been expecting.

Its wings moved soundlessly as it hovered to the left of Roth, its tail whipping around. It was so tiny and so...so cute.

I blinked slowly. "You...you have a...a pocket-size dragon?"

Zayne snorted from somewhere behind me.

A heavy sigh came from Roth.

Even though all our lives were in danger and we were all

probably going to die, there was definitely no love lost between Roth and Zayne.

The dragon swiveled its head in my direction, opened its mouth and let out a tiny squawk. More like a meep. A cloud of black smoke puffed out from it. No fire. Just dark wisps that smelled faintly of sulfur. My brows flew up.

"Remove the familiar from our sight," an Alpha demanded, causing me to wince. The one who spoke was standing to the right of the door, and his voice was impossibly deep, reverberating through both the room and me. Part of me expected my eardrums to rupture.

I was surprised that the Alphas hadn't immediately tried to take out Thumper, but then again, it wasn't like the pocket dragon was that much of a threat.

Roth's stance appeared casual, but I knew he was coiled tight, ready to spring into action. "Yeah, that's not going to happen."

The Alpha's lips formed a sneer. "How dare you speak to me? I could end your existence before you take your next breath."

"You could," Roth replied calmly. "But you won't."

My eyes widened. Smack talking to the Alphas wasn't what I'd consider a smart move.

"Roth," muttered Zayne. He sounded closer, but I didn't want to take my eyes off the Alphas to check. "You might want to chill out a bit."

The Crown Prince smirked. "Nah. You want to know why? The Alphas could end me, but they're not going to."

Across from us, the Alpha who had spoken stiffened but didn't interrupt.

"You see, I am the favorite Crown Prince," Roth continued, his smirk spreading. "They take me out when I haven't done anything to warrant it and they'll have the Boss to contend with. They don't want that."

Surprise flickered through me. They couldn't just end Roth because of who he was? I'd always thought they could simply do as they pleased.

The Alpha who had been silent up to this point spoke. "There are rules for a reason. It does not mean we have to like them, so I'd suggest you do not push your luck, *Prince*."

Then Roth did the unthinkable. He raised his hand and extended his middle finger. "Does this count as pushing it, Bob?"

Crap on a cracker, he'd flipped off an Alpha! And he'd called the Alpha *Bob*! Who did that? Seriously?

My jaw hit the floor while the miniature Thumper coughed out another cloud of smoke. "I'm not blinded by your glory," Roth said. "You sit on your lofty clouds passing judgment on every living creature there is. Not everything is black-and-white. You know that and yet you recognize no gray area."

Sparks of electricity crackled from the Alpha's all-white eyes. "One of these days, Prince, you will meet your own fate."

"And I'll do so quite spectacularly," he quipped back. "Looking damn good while I do it, too."

I briefly squeezed my eyes shut. *Oh my God…*

The Alpha on the right shifted, his large hand tightening on the hilt of the sword, and I had a feeling he wanted to shove it clean through Roth. I figured it was time to pry my tongue off the roof of my mouth. "You're here because of the Lilin, right? We will stop him." I had no idea how we would do that and I probably shouldn't give such an promise to beings who could obliterate me in a heartbeat, but I didn't see a choice. Not only because I needed to distract them from Roth, but because the Lilin did need stopping. Anything with a soul now was in danger. "I promise."

"The Wardens will take care of the Lilin. That's what they were created for—it's their job to protect mankind. If they don't, they will pay the ultimate price right along with the demons," the Alpha who'd spoken first replied. "But we're here to deal with you."

My heart stopped again. "Me?"

The Alpha Roth had dubbed Bob narrowed his eyes. "You are a sacrilege of the highest order. Before, you were an abomination that should have been dealt with, but now you're a perversity we cannot allow to continue."

Roth cocked his head to the side as Zayne rushed forward. "No!" Zayne said, his wings tucking back. "She has never done anything to—"

"Oh, really?" the other Alpha replied drily as his wings arced high. Those feather-embedded eyes swiveled around the room and then all of them—hundreds of them—focused on me. "We see all, Warden. Justice must be served."

Bob raised his sword, and before I could do anything, Roth's arm flew out. He caught me just above the chest, shoving me into Zayne. I bounced off his hard chest, and would've toppled right off if Zayne hadn't steadied me with his arm across my waist.

Thumper, still circling near Roth's shoulder, let out another squeak—

—which turned into a roar that made the house shake even more than it had when the Alphas showed up.

Roth lowered his chin, grinning. "As I've said before, size does matter."

Thumper began to grow at a rate I couldn't even track, sprouting legs the size of tree trunks and claws the length of hooks. The dragon's bright blue and gold scales appeared bulletproof and its hind legs stretched down to the floor, cracking the wooden boards. One crimson wing hit the ceiling, smacking straight through the drywall. Plaster fell in thick clouds as his other wing knocked over the recliner.

The Alpha shouted something, but it was lost amid the dragon's low, humming growl. It lurched forward, swinging its massive spiked tail along the floor. Furniture flew into the wall, demolishing a portrait. A window shattered and cold air from outside poured into the room. Thumper came to a stop in front of us, facing the Alphas as he drew back, huffing sparks of flame out of his nostrils. The fire darkened what was left of the ceiling as Bob called out again.

"You take one step toward her and I'm going to fry myself up some Alpha." Roth's voice was low and deadly calm. "Extra-crispy style."

One Alpha stepped back, but Bob looked like he would blow a gasket. "You dare to threaten us?"

"I dare a lot more than that." Roth's skin seemed to thin, his face becoming sharp angles. "I will not stand for one hair on her head to be harmed. If you want her, you're going to have to come through me."

Bob smiled widely at that, and my stomach plummeted. Roth was bound and determined to get himself killed because of me. He'd sacrificed himself to the pits, come back from that, and then gone against his Boss and saved my life. There was no way I could allow him to stand between me and danger again. "Stop!" I broke free of Zayne's hold, but

Thumper shifted. His tail swung back, stopping not even an inch from my hips.

I could go no further. My panicked gaze darted from Roth to the Alphas. "Whatever problem you have, you have it with me. Not them. So can we—"

Even as I spoke, Bob the Alpha moved toward Roth, lifting the fiery sword, and Thumper didn't like that. Rearing back, he stretched out his long neck and opened his mouth, revealing fist-size fangs. The scent of sulfur increased, and then a burst of fire shot out of Thumper's mouth.

A pain-filled shriek ended abruptly, and where Bob once stood was just a charred pile of ashes.

Everyone stood perfectly still. No one spoke or even appeared to breathe. And then, "Make that *extra*-extra-crispy style," Roth said, studying the mess.

My knees went weak as I lifted my hands helplessly. Thumper spun on the other Alpha. There was a series of sickening crunches, and then the dragon looked over its shoulder, its golden eyes finding mine as it opened its mouth. A shimmery blue liquid stained its teeth as it huffed out a sound that really sounded like a throaty chuckle.

Bambi had eaten a Warden.

Thumper had eaten an Alpha.

These familiars were really low on manners.

More important, I hadn't known anything could actually kill an Alpha, much less eat one.

"Oh—oh!" Stacey shrieked, and I turned sideways, just in time to see her all but squeeze herself into the two back cushions of the couch. "There's a dragon in my house! A dragon!" Guess she was still too out of it from fainting to remember there'd been angels in her house, too.

"Thumper," Roth called. "Return to me."

The dragon belched out a thick cloud of smoke and turned around. I jumped out of the way of its tail, as did Zayne. The fireplace wasn't as lucky. That lethal tail smacked into it, knocking a handful of bricks loose. They hit the floor, breaking into pieces. Thumper shifted his heavy weight from side to side.

Zayne frowned. "Is it...stomping its feet?"

Roth rolled his eyes. "He doesn't get out much."

"For obvious reasons," Stacey mumbled.

Thumper lifted his tail and slammed it down, cracking what was left of the floor and earning a sigh from Roth. The dragon shook its head, then shuddered before shrinking back down to its cute, pocket-size form. Thumper finally returned to Roth, settling on the side of his face as a small shadow that quickly raced down his neck and under the collar of his shirt.

I was struck absolutely silent and was barely aware of shifting back into my human state. My thoughts raced from one bad situation to the next. Sam as the Lilin. My feathered wings. Alphas popping in. Thumper—

"Mom is so going to kill me," Stacey whispered, clutching a beige throw pillow to her chest. She looked up. "How am I going to explain this?"

Roth pursed his lips. "Gas-line explosion?" Stacey repeated the words dimly as he continued. "I can torch the place, make it a little more authentic. Won't damage the upstairs if you don't want me to."

"Had a lot of practice with this, have you?" Zayne asked drily.

"Ah, when Thumper comes off, it's always good to go with

the old gas-line excuse. It's handy." Roth turned to me. "You okay over there?"

Was I okay?

Anger mixed with fear—fear for him. I stared for a moment and then I shot toward him. "What were you thinking?" Hauling back, I smacked his chest. "You threatened an Alpha!" I smacked him again, harder this time, enough to sting.

"Ow." He rubbed his chest, but his eyes twinkled. He thought this was funny!

Zayne walked over to where the pile of ashes remained. "More than just threatened. He let Thumper eat them."

"Hey, technically Thumper fried one and ate the other," Roth corrected, patting his stomach, where Thumper now rested.

"Oh my God!" This time my hand connected with his arm. "You're going to be in so much trouble, Roth! So much trouble."

He shrugged a shoulder. "Defended myself."

"Defended myself." I mimicked him, bopping my head back and forth. "You can't just go around killing Alphas, Roth!"

"You killed those angels?" Stacey asked, so I guessed she did remember them.

He sent her an innocent grin. "Well, *I* didn't, but..."

"Roth!" I shouted, backing away before I started choking the ever-loving life out of him. "This is not a joke. You—"

He was damn fast when he wanted to be. One second he was several feet away from me and the next he was there, clasping the sides of my face. He lowered his head so he was eye level with me. "There are rules, Shortie."

"But—"

"Rules that even the Alphas have to abide by. They cannot attack me without *physical* provocation. If they do, they tick the Boss off, and then the Boss retaliates in a way that makes what the Lilin could do look like child's play. I'm not just some random demon. I'm the Crown Prince. They took a swing at me, and I defended myself. End of story."

But he had provoked them—maybe not physically, but he wasn't an innocent bystander in this. As the shock ebbed, there was a different kind of bitter pill to swallow. What if Roth had gotten his rules wrong? What if more Alphas were even now on the way to avenge their brethren?

"I'm going to be okay." His eyes held mine as he stepped closer, lining his booted feet up with mine. "Nothing is going to happen to me. I promise."

"You can't make that promise," I whispered, searching his gaze intently. "None of us can."

His hands slid back and he curled his fingers in my loose hair. "I can."

Those two words were like throwing down a gauntlet to the whole universe. I lowered my gaze as he dragged my hair back, tucking both sides behind my ears. It was then, as he slowly withdrew his hands, that I remembered we were not alone.

I jerked back and my gaze collided with Zayne's. For a moment, I let myself really see Zayne. I hadn't almost killed him. I had almost done something much, much worse than that. When a Warden lost their soul, they turned into a horrific creature. I knew that for a fact, because I'd seen what had happened to a Warden after their soul had been taken from them. I'd almost done *that* to Zayne, and he was still here, standing by my side.

A hole opened up in my chest as I saw the keen wariness in his stare. My stomach twisted something awful and I opened my mouth, but I didn't know what to say. My heart and head were suddenly tearing in two very different directions. Fortunately, I didn't get the chance to say anything.

"I leave you alone for a few hours, and you let Thumper fry and eat an Alpha."

Yelping, I spun around as Stacey screamed. Cayman stood in the center of the destroyed living room. He'd come out of nowhere. Poof. There. He wore dark trousers and a white dress shirt he appeared to have gotten bored with when it came to buttoning it up, and his blond hair was loose around his angular face. When it came to the demon pecking order, Roth had once explained that as an Infernal Ruler, Cayman was middle management. He was kind of like the demon-of-all-trades, and I had a feeling he was more than just a...um, coworker of Roth's. Whether Roth claimed it or not, they were friends.

"That was quick," Roth commented, folding his arms across his chest.

Cayman shrugged. "It's a sign of the times, man. It'll probably be on some Alpha's Facebook wall within the hour."

Alphas had Facebook accounts?

Stacey was holding the throw pillow to her mouth now, and all that was visible were her huge, dark brown eyes. When she spoke, her voice was muffled. "Who is that?"

I started to explain, but Cayman bowed in her direction, extending his arm with a flourish. "Only the most handsome and smartest and downright most charming demon there is. But I know that's a mouthful, so you can call me Cayman."

"Um." Her gaze darted around the room. "Okay."

Zayne's skin had darkened in a clear indication that he was close to shifting again, and I hoped he kept it cool. Cayman was a friend, and the last thing we needed was the two of them getting into it. "Is Roth in trouble?"

"Shortie, I'm—"

I raised my hand, cutting him off. "Shush it. Cayman, is he in trouble?"

Cayman grinned. "I think the better question is—when is he not in trouble?"

Narrowing my eyes, I had to admit that was a good point. "Okay. Is he in more trouble than he normally is?"

"Ah..." His gaze shifted toward Roth, and then his grin spread into a devilish smile. He was thoroughly enjoying himself. "Let's just say that the Boss is not pleased with what just went down here. Actually, the Boss is ticked off about a lot of things, and if Roth goes down below anytime soon, he probably won't be leaving for a while. Like for a couple of decades."

I gasped. "That's not good." So much for the Boss being on Roth's side.

"Could be worse," Roth said, smirking.

Cayman nodded. "If you want the truth, I think the Boss secretly *was* pleased with what Thumper did, but you know... politics." He sighed while I raised my brows. "Ruins everything fun."

My temples were starting to ache. "Today has been..."

"Unbelievable?" offered Stacey. Dropping the pillow, she pressed the palms of her hands under her eyes. Her expression was pale and strained. Her hands shook as she wiped beneath her eyes.

I nodded slowly as I turned around. My gaze met Roth's and then Zayne's. Both of them stared at me, waiting. I wanted to pretend that I didn't know what they were waiting for, but that would be a lie.

And that would also make me a coward.

Weight landed on my shoulders as I rubbed my fingers along my temples. There was so much we needed to figure out. "We need to take care of this." I gestured at the ruined room. The scent of sulfur lingered, and part of me was grateful to have something immediate to focus on. "So Stacey doesn't get in trouble."

"Much appreciated," she said, and when I glanced at her, I saw her dragging her hands through her hair.

Roth stepped up. "Why don't you guys head down to the Cakes and Things bakery while I take care of this. You can do that?" The question was directed at Zayne, who nodded.

"I will keep them safe," Zayne replied in a level tone.

Roth hesitated, and then he took a deep breath. "If other Wardens show—"

"I will protect both of them from whatever or whoever may come at them," Zayne assured him. He drew in a deep breath. "Even…even if it is my clan."

"And I can also protect myself," I threw in, earning an amused glance from Roth. "What? Trust me. Any of my…my old clan comes in my direction, I'm not going to open my arms to hug them." I ignored the wave of dread that surfaced with the thought of coming face-to-face with them again. "Well, except Nicolai and Dez. I think they kind of—"

"Shortie," Roth said.

I sighed. "Whatever. Let's go." Turning to Stacey, I walked over to gently pry the pillow she'd picked up again loose from her white-knuckle grip. "You okay to go out there?"

She blinked once and then twice. "What are my options? I stay in here while Roth torches the place? No, thank you."

Good to see that even after the day we'd had, Stacey could still be a smart-ass.

Roth strode up to Cayman, placing his hand on the other demon's shoulder. "I want you to keep an eye out, okay?"

The list of things that Cayman would be keeping an eye out for was astronomical.

"Word." Cayman disappeared. Poof. Gone.

Shaking my head, I refocused on Stacey. Tears filled her eyes as she peered up at me through damp lashes. "Sam's... He's dead, isn't he?"

I placed the pillow on the couch beside her and knelt down. A burning knot of emotion formed in the back of my throat. "Yeah. He is."

She squeezed her eyes shut as a tremor rolled through her. "I remember you all talking about the...the Lilin and what it does to people. If Sam's dead, then his soul..."

His soul was in Hell. I knew that. Stacey already knew that. Everyone in this room knew that, and there could be nothing more horrific than being trapped in Hell. He didn't deserve all the horrifying things that happened to souls there.

Wrapping my hands around Stacey's, I squeezed them tight. "I promise we will get Sam's soul out of Hell. I promise."

three

"YOU SHOULDN'T HAVE MADE THAT PROMISE," Zayne said quietly the moment Stacey hit the girls' bathroom at the bakery several blocks from her house. I'd tried to go with her, but she stated quite firmly that she needed a few moments alone.

I sat in the booth closest to the window, watching the people rushing outside, their auras a dizzying wash of colors. It was so weird to see the auras again. A part of me had gotten used to not seeing them while Bambi had been on me, and I'd forgotten how distracting they could be. "Why not?"

Zayne slid in across from me. Concern pinched his features. "How are you going to get Sam's soul out of Hell, Layla? Roth may be the Crown Prince, but I seriously doubt that is something that he can ask for, even if he was on good terms with them. Hell isn't just going to hand Sam's soul right over."

"I hadn't gotten that far in my plan." Actually, I'd been hoping that it was something that Roth could help us out with. After all, being the Crown Prince meant he could just go around letting Thumper fry and eat Alphas. "But it's something we have to do. Zayne, he's my best friend." My voice cracked, and I felt my tenuous control over my emotions start to slip. "Even if he wasn't, I couldn't leave him there. He didn't deserve this. God, Zayne, Sam did not deserve this."

"I know." Zayne dipped his chin, his gaze never leaving mine. "I'm not suggesting that we forget about him."

"We have to do something," I reiterated, drawing in a deep breath as I leaned back against the booth, resting my hands on the smooth table. I glanced back toward where Stacey had disappeared. She'd asked for time, but it was so hard to give it to her. Considering everything that had happened, I was surprised that we could sit here and talk normally. "And then we need to figure out what to do about the Lilin, and then we—"

"Hey, slow down for a second." Zayne reached across the table, folding his hand over mine. I studied him as my heart turned over heavily. Anytime I looked at him now, I saw the smudges under his eyes, and I saw the dulled aura around him. I couldn't *un-see* that. "I know a lot of crazy stuff just went down, but you've been through a lot. We need to talk about it."

I really did not want to talk about any of that, because there was a good chance I couldn't handle it.

Zayne had other ideas. "Do you know how hard it is for me to sit on the other side of this booth and not reach across and pull you against me? Just to make sure you really are alive?" he asked, and my breath caught at the raw honesty in his words. "What happened wasn't your fault. You need to know that. My clan—*our clan*—and my father never should have done what they did."

I dropped my gaze to his hand, the one that held mine and had held mine for so many years. I closed my eyes and immediately saw Zayne lying on the floor of my bedroom, pale and still. I remembered the way Abbot, the Warden that had raised me, had looked at me when he found his son, stared at me like I was a monster he had helped create. Pressure clamped down on my chest as I recalled the panicked flight through the compound, my desperate attempt to escape and the failure.

Failure that had ended with me being caged and drugged, left alone in the dark with no hope of ever seeing the daylight again. I could still smell the musty scent that had lingered in the basement of the compound, feel the chains that had bound me when I'd been moved to the secret warehouse.

"Layla?"

A shudder rolled through me as I reminded myself I wasn't in that cage anymore. I opened my eyes and forced those dark thoughts out of my head.

"I appreciate you saying that. You're right. What they did to me was wrong. I get that they thought I was the one causing trouble around the compound—heck, even I thought I was a danger to everyone, but they went too far."

My words kind of surprised me. I'd always defended Abbot, but I couldn't make excuses for his actions or those of the majority of my clan. All the soul-searching I'd done after waking up from the blow, the wound delivered to me in front of Abbot, had changed who I was at the very core. There was no doubt about that. "They acted as the jury with some really crappy circumstantial evidence, and then they became the judge and the executioner. I could've died. I would've died if it hadn't been for Dez—and by the way, how much trouble are he and Nicolai in?"

Dez and Nicolai had risked everything by alerting Roth to what was happening. If they hadn't done that, I wouldn't have been sitting here right now.

Zayne's lashes lowered as his expression contorted. "At first, there were talks of casting them out," he said, and I sucked in a breath. Casting them out meant they'd be disowned from the clan, which was horrible enough for a single male, but Dez had a mate and two little babies. "But once we realized that it was Petr wreaking havoc around the house, Abbot began to see the light. Nicolai and Dez are safe."

With everything that had happened, I'd forgotten that Zayne had told me they'd discovered Petr's wraith, caught on camera. Relief coursed through me. I'd... I'd killed the young Warden in self-defense when he attacked me, carrying out his father's orders. Elijah. Who'd also turned out to be my real father, so that meant Petr, who'd been the worst kind of boy there was, was my half brother. That still sickened me. Since I'd sucked out Petr's soul, he'd become a wraith.

"You could've died, too. I could've taken your whole soul," I continued, keeping my voice low. That was the gift my mother, Lilith, had left me with—the wonderful ability to suck out souls with a single kiss. Anyone who had one was in danger if they got anywhere near my mouth, which up until recently had put a real damper on the whole dating business.

But then Roth had shown up, and as a demon, he was in the no-soul category. At first, I'd loathed his very existence, and looking back, it had a lot to do with how his words and actions made me question everything the Wardens had taught me. By nature, demons weren't something you'd invite in for dinner, but not all of them were the wretched creatures I'd been conditioned to abhor to a near-fanatical degree. They had their purpose, too. Every second I'd spent with Roth, I'd fallen a little harder for him, and I'd shared so much with him before he'd sacrificed himself to save Zayne from the fiery pits of Hell. I'd thought I'd lost him then, but he'd returned—only things had been different between us when he had. Roth had distanced himself, to protect me.

To shield me from Abbot.

Then there was everything that had happened with Zayne. I'd been raised with him, spent years idolizing and loving him from afar. For the longest time, he'd been my everything, but he'd been a Warden and I'd only been half Warden—and worse, half demon. Between his soul and my genetic background, he'd been off-limits. A friendship with him, the bond we shared, had been a glimpse of a future that every female Warden was assured of but that was never on the table for me. That knowledge had done nothing to stop my growing feelings, and when Roth had returned from the pits, pushing me away, he'd pushed me right into the arms of Zayne, the boy I never thought would return my affections.

I'd been wrong about that.

I'd been wrong about a lot of things.

Zayne's eyes flew open. "But you didn't."

"Barely." That pressure returned, weighing on me as I felt again the horror of the night I realized I'd been feeding on Zayne instead of…instead of kissing him back. "I can see where I've taken some. I can tell in your aura."

"I'm fine—"

"No thanks to me. The only reason I'd been able to…to kiss you before then was because of Bambi. When she was on me, I could control my abilities." I slipped my hand free, pressing my lips together as I shook my head. "You can't overlook what I did to you, and I know you can't be a hundred percent okay."

Zayne stared at me, and then he lifted his hand, thrusting his fingers through his hair. "You stopped in time. Other than feeling a little tired and...grumpier than normal, I am fine, Layla-bug."

My heart squeezed at the use of my nickname. "Grumpier than normal?"

His brows knitted and for a moment, I didn't think he was going to answer. "My temper is easier to ignite nowadays. I don't know if that has to do with what happened between us or if it's the natural result of everything else going on lately."

I think I knew the answer to that. When someone's soul was stripped away, even a tiny piece, it changed who they were in some way. Maybe it made some more prone to mood swings, others more reckless and others violent.

And apparently for Zayne, he'd lost a bit of his kindness, a little of what made him absolutely wonderful, and I had done that to him. While it hadn't been on purpose, neither of us, especially me, had shown any level of common sense by trying to be together. Neither of us had delved too deeply into why all of a sudden I could do things like kissing without taking a soul.

Then again, as Zayne had pointed out once, there was a lot more that we could've done that hadn't involved our mouths touching.

Strangely, sitting across from him, I realized I didn't feel the longing to feed. It was the first that I'd noticed its absence. Since my clan had turned on me, I'd been staying with Roth and Cayman, and as neither owned a soul, I hadn't even thought about feeding on one—something that I'd spent seventeen years fighting the urge to do.

Now, though I was once again surrounded by souls, the urge simply wasn't there.

Maybe today's events had shocked me bad enough that even that was affected.

"I'm sorry," I said finally, flipping my gaze to the street beyond the window. It was the second week of December, and the skies above Washington, DC, were gray and the wind brisk, carrying the scent of snow in the air. "I'm so sorry, Zayne."

"Don't apologize," he was quick to say. "Don't ever apologize to me. I don't regret anything that happened between us. Not a moment."

Did I?

"Anyway, it's not me I want to talk about. Are you okay?" he asked. "What they did—"

"I'm fine," I said, and it felt like a lie. "I was healed by the witches. You know, the ones who worship Lilith. They gave Cayman something for me to drink and it worked." Which reminded me of the fact that Cayman had to promise something in return and none of us knew what bargain he'd struck yet. "I have no idea what they gave me."

"That's kind of concerning," he replied wryly.

My lips twitched, and when I looked up, our gazes met, and then held. He leaned in, placing his elbows onto the table. "Layla, I—"

A shadow fell over our table, and when I looked up, I saw Stacey's aura first. It was a faint, mossy green. A common color. Pure souls were rare, and the darker the shade of the aura, the more likely it was they had sinned. Stacey's blotchy face broke my heart. I slid over, sending Zayne a glance. The look he wore promised that we weren't done with the conversation.

"How are you doing?" I asked, knowing it was a stupid question.

"I'm okay." She didn't sound okay. "I just needed a moment or five." It was more like ten, but she could have as many moments as she needed. She paused, smoothing the back of her hands over her cheeks. "I'm okay, right?"

My smile was weak as tears burned the back of my eyes. "Yes." I reached over, slipping my arm over her shoulders. "But if you're not, that's okay, too."

A tremor coursed through her as she leaned in, resting her head on my shoulder. Usually it was hard if someone got this close, but again, the urge that existed deep within wasn't gnawing at my insides. "He's dead," she whispered.

I squeezed my eyes shut and forced myself to take deep, even breaths to loosen the messy knot in my throat. All I wanted to do was hold on to Stacey and break down, because Sam... God, Sam was gone, and it was like a thousand razor blades were churning in my stomach, but I had to pull it together for Stacey. She'd known Sam a lot longer than me, since grade school, and she had fallen in love with him. Her pain was a priority over mine.

Keeping my arm around her, I didn't say anything, because I didn't know what to say in situations like this. Even when I'd thought Roth was gone, I had hope that he was still alive. This was different. There would be no surprises. Sam would not reappear one day. No one close to me had ever died before, and I knew my mind hadn't fully processed the reality of him being gone. So I just held her as I stared at the door, blindly watching the people streaming in and out. At some point Zayne got up and returned with two cups of hot chocolate. I barely tasted the sweetness.

I don't know how much time passed before I felt the tingle of awareness alerting me to a demon's presence. Across from us, Zayne stiffened, but when the door closed, it was Roth. He strolled to our table, and Zayne scooted over. Normally, I would've burst out laughing seeing them sitting side by side.

Neither of them looked exactly comfortable.

There was a woodsy scent that clung to Roth's clothes, as if he'd been near a bonfire. "Took care of it," he told Stacey. "Your downstairs is pretty much shot. The fire department is already on the way. Just remember you didn't go home after school. You came here to meet Layla and Zayne."

Swallowing hard, she nodded as she circled her hands around the cup of hot chocolate. "Got it."

Roth tilted his head to the side, his brows furrowed as he studied her. "You're going to do fine with this."

When Stacey nodded again, he reached across the table, his hand veering to the left. He snatched up my cup of hot chocolate. Taking a sip, he didn't even look in my direction.

"Help yourself," I muttered under my breath.

His lips twitched. "So what's the game plan, Stony?"

A muscle twitched along Zayne's jaw. He hated that nickname. "Game plan in regards to what exactly?"

"The Lilin," Roth replied, as if the answer should be obvious.

I stiffened. "I don't think now is the time to discuss this."

Golden eyes drifted from me to Stacey. There was a pause. "Good point."

"No," Stacey said, twisting toward me. "This is the perfect time."

"But—"

"That thing in my house wasn't Sam. It wasn't him," she said, her voice rising. A couple by the door glanced over at us with frowns on their faces. "So when you talk about it, the

Lilin, you aren't talking about Sam." Her voice caught. "That thing is not Sam."

Zayne shifted forward in the booth. "Are you sure, Stacey?"

"Positive," she whispered.

Chest aching, I glanced at the boys, and then nodded. "Okay."

Roth placed my cup back down in front of me and then leaned back against the cushioned seat, turning his head toward Zayne. "Sounded like the Alphas might've already spoken to the Wardens, and if that's the case, I find it a wee bit interesting you haven't said anything."

"When would I have had the time to say something even if that was the case?" Zayne retorted, voice clipped. "Between seeing Layla and when the Alphas actually showed up?"

Roth lifted his brows. "Are you getting snappy with me?"

"What does it sound like?" Zayne returned.

"I don't know." A slight smile formed on his lips as he threw his arm along the back of the cushion. I sighed, because I knew that look. "But you catching a tone with me is about as interesting as reading up on the benefits of a water purification system."

I stared at him. Only a handful of hours ago, Zayne had thanked Roth for saving me. They had actually been polite to each other. I guessed I shouldn't be surprised that hadn't lasted very long. "Roth."

"Hmm?"

My eyes narrowed. "Knock it off."

The smile spread until there was a flash of white teeth. "Anything for you, Shortie."

Oh Lord.

Zayne moved his gaze to me, and I couldn't decipher what I

saw in his stare. "I don't know if the Alphas have spoken to my father yet. I haven't really been...talking to him recently, and they haven't showed at the compound while I've been there."

"What I don't understand is why the Alphas would think that your kind would be the ones to stop the Lilin. You have souls, therefore you have a major vulnerability." Roth was eyeing what was left of my hot chocolate. "My kind doesn't."

"Not something to gloat about." Zayne exhaled loudly, and I resisted the urge to bang my head against the table. "Look, I'll check in and see if I can find anything out."

"Fine, but we have a bigger problem," Roth warned.

Stacey looked up from her cup. "We do?"

I wanted to echo that statement, because I wasn't sure exactly what could be bigger than taking down a creature that could inflict so much pain and destruction.

"What are the Wardens going to do once they realize Layla is alive and well?" There was a low rasp to Roth's voice that resembled a growl. "That's what I'm concerned about."

Zayne's lips thinned. "They will do nothing. They know she's not the cause of what happened—"

"That doesn't undo anything they've done," Roth cut in.

"I didn't say that it did." The hand Zayne rested on the table started to deepen to a granite color. "I'm not going to allow them to touch her."

I opened my mouth to point out again that *I* wasn't going to allow them to touch me, but Roth got right up in Zayne's face. "And I'm not going to forget a single thing that was done to her," he warned. "I haven't forgotten how she came back to me with claw marks on her face."

Sucking in a sharp breath, I leaned back against the cushion as Stacey turned to me. "You were clawed in the face?"

I clamped my mouth shut as I stared at her, refusing to look at Zayne or even Roth, but I didn't need to spare even a brief glance in their direction to know the two had locked eyes. When Zayne had kissed me, and I had inadvertently started to feed on his soul, he'd begun to shift and had clawed me in an attempt to break the connection. There was not a single part of me that thought he'd meant to truly hurt me. Roth had to know that, too.

Stacey's eyes searched mine, and she must've seen the truth, because as impossible as it seemed, an even greater sadness filled her gaze.

"I will never forgive myself for that." Zayne's quiet voice broke the terse silence, and I whipped around to face him.

Roth tipped his chin down. "Neither will I."

"Stop it." I clenched the end of the table. "Talking about that isn't getting us anyplace. It doesn't matter."

"It does matter," Roth replied. "Because no matter what, I would never, ever hurt you."

Zayne jerked back as if he'd taken a fatal blow.

"But you have." My knuckles were starting to ache. "You have hurt me."

Maybe not physically, but Roth had hurt me in the past. Words could cut just as deep as sharpened claws, and while the skin could heal, the wounds words left behind never faded as quickly. He might've been trying to protect me, but that hadn't lessened the sting one bit.

Roth's gaze met mine, and then his thick lashes lowered, shielding his eyes. Silent, he sat back and folded his arms across his chest. Zayne stared at the tabletop, a lock of blond hair falling in his face. Tension seeped from both of them, and my skin felt like it was stretched too thin.

Stacey's phone rang and she dug it out of her bag with a shaking hand. She started to stand. "It's Mom." Glancing at me with watery eyes, she looked years younger. "I can do this."

"You can do this." I reached out and squeezed her arm through her sweater. Her eyes had a wild, panicked look about them.

I heard her answer the phone as she walked over to the entry door and slipped outside. My gaze tracked her as she started to pace behind an empty bench. I just wanted to crawl under the table and rock for a little bit. I figured that couldn't be too much to ask.

Zayne cleared his throat. "You know this, but you can't go back to the compound. There're places that you can stay, where you will be safe."

"I have a place to stay," I told him, taking a sip of my now-lukewarm hot chocolate.

His jaw hardened. "With him?"

Surprisingly, Roth remained quiet, which made me feel like I needed to check if he was alive. I set the cup aside and rested my arms on the table, more than just exhausted. More like weary to my very core. "It's a place that's safe," I said. "And yes, it's with Roth and Cayman."

Zayne opened his mouth, and then closed it. Several seconds passed and they felt like the tick of eternity. "What are you going to do, Layla?"

The question carried a lot of weight, because I knew it went beyond just where I was staying for the night or the next couple of days. There was so much I didn't know the answer to. School was up in the air. Where I would be living was completely undecided. How we could defeat the Lilin or save Sam's soul still unknown. I had no idea what was going on when I shifted today. And there was more—there was Roth and Zayne, two very different guys that I had loved and fallen in love with.

Stacey returned, saving me from having to answer the question. Her mom was in hysterics, as expected, and Stacey needed to go to her aunt's house.

The four of us headed out into the chilly air. Stacey and Roth walked ahead, but I stopped and turned around. With my heart beating fast, I walked back to where Zayne stood behind the bench Stacey had paced near. Stretching up, I wrapped my arms around him. There was a moment of hesitation, and then he returned the embrace, holding me so tight that my cheek pressed against his chest.

The hug felt good, more than good. It was like coming home after a long day, and it was hard to break away from that.

"When will I see you again?" he asked, his voice thick.

"Soon," I promised.

His arms tightened around me. "Please be safe, Layla. Please."

"You, too."

"Of course, Layla-bug."

I looked up into his eyes. "I never blamed you for the claw marks, so please don't blame yourself for something that I don't even need to forgive you for."

Roth and I didn't talk on the drive back to the house across the river, in Maryland. I still had no idea how they'd come into possession of the McMansion, only that Cayman had acquired it at some point, and I figured it was best that I didn't ask too many questions.

I'd spent several hours with Stacey and her mom and little brother at her aunt's ginormous home while Roth lingered outside doing…demon things or whatever. It was late, almost midnight, by the time we'd left her house and made it back to this one.

I didn't know why Roth was so quiet, but I appreciated it, because I didn't have the brainpower to hold a conversation or to really think about anything.

Roth parked the vintage Mustang in the garage, and the house was dark and silent when we walked in. The place was toasty warm, but there was no sign of Cayman. I climbed the spiral staircase and dragged myself down the hall to the bedroom I'd woken up in after they'd first rescued me from the Wardens.

When I reached the closed door, I tucked my hair back behind my ear as I glanced over my shoulder at Roth.

He stood a few feet down the hall, leaning against the wall with his hands in his pockets and the back of his head pressed against the wall. "I'll take the room here," he said, not looking in my direction. He'd stayed with me while I'd been healing, but now there really was no reason to be...bunking together. "If you need anything, the door will be unlocked."

My hand tightened around the doorknob. "Thank you."

I had no idea if he knew what I was thanking him for, but he nodded. Neither of us moved for a long moment. He continued to stare at nothing while I stared at him. Finally I pushed out, "Good night, Roth."

He didn't respond.

Turning the knob, I pushed open the door and immediately headed for the bedside lamp, flipping it on. The room was huge, the master suite, and furnished with stunning antiques.

I'd never felt more out of place as I gathered up the pajamas Cayman had brought me a few days ago and quickly changed into the cotton bottoms and loose shirt. At least the nightwear was nothing like the other clothing he and Roth had picked out for me. I was half surprised that they hadn't given me a skimpy nightie. I padded barefoot into the bathroom, one much larger than the bathroom attached to my bedroom back in the Wardens' compound. Well, my old bedroom. Definitely not mine anymore.

Nothing in that house was mine anymore.

The light in the bathroom was harsh and bright as I brushed my teeth and washed my face, leaving little puddles on the marble basin and droplets on my shirt. I was so messy when it came to these things. More than once I'd ended up with toothpaste in my hair and looking like I was entering a wet T-shirt contest.

As I turned off the faucet, I looked up and saw my reflection in the mirror. But I didn't see myself. Not really. When I closed my eyes, I saw the same thing—the same image.

I saw Sam.

I saw Sam smiling. I saw him laughing. I saw the skin around his eyes crinkling, and as I stepped back from the sink, I could hear him spouting off some random, obscure piece of knowledge like how a frozen banana could act as a hammer. I could see him fiddling with his glasses and gazing at Stacey, unable to pull his eyes off her even when she'd been completely oblivious to his attraction. I could see him so clearly, as if he really was standing in the bathroom with me.

"Oh God," I whispered, and my face crumpled.

There was no one in there to see me, but I slapped my hands over my eyes as I pressed against the wall. A shudder rocked me as the tears I'd been fighting all afternoon and evening finally broke free.

Sam was gone.

The knowledge was like getting hit by a speeding snowplow, and then getting stuck under the wheels and dragged down a bumpy road. Tears poured out of me as my shoulders shook with the force of them.

I remembered the first time I'd met him. We shared a history class my freshman year, and I'd been such a big goober, too nervous about my first foray into public school to find the pens in my bag, so he'd given me one of his while explaining that an average of one hundred people a year choke on pens.

A strangled laugh escaped me. God, how did Sam know all of that stuff? Who knew that kind of stuff? Sam did, but I'd never know the answer to that question and that hurt.

Trying to pull it together and failing, I slid down the wall and tucked my knees against my chest. Pressing my face against my leg, I screamed it out, all the pain, the anger and the sadness. The sound was muffled, and it did very little to ease the storm of emotions swirling inside me. I wanted to scream again, to rage.

I didn't hear the bathroom door open, but suddenly an arm circled my shoulders, and then Roth was sitting on the floor beside me. He didn't say anything as he hauled me into his lap, and I was incapable of uttering a single word as I buried my face into his chest, inhaling the unique musky scent and soaking up his warmth. The tears fell faster and harder. There was no gaining control in any of this. Roth held on, one arm wrapped around me, the other hand buried in my hair, curving around the back of my head. He didn't whisper words of comfort, because there was absolutely nothing that could be said. My heart had cracked wide-open and it was raw, painful. It was unfair.

I cried it all out in the bathroom of a house that didn't belong to me, held in the protective arms of the Crown Prince of Hell. I mourned the loss of my best friend.

four

SITTING CROSS-LEGGED IN THE CENTER OF THE king-size bed, I keyed Zayne's and Stacey's numbers into the cell phone Cayman had deposited outside my room this morning.

I had terrible, horrific luck with cell phones. I'd left behind a graveyard of cell phones, piles of phones that simply had the misfortune of ending up in my hands, but like I had with every one before it, I really hoped this time was different.

Like the last phone Zayne had picked up for me, it was a nifty smartphone, but this one an even newer and fancier version. Oddly, no matter which way I positioned my finger over the little button, it wouldn't read my fingerprint.

Technology.

Sigh.

Dropping the phone on the bed in front of me, I blinked bleary eyes. I'd cried so much last night, my eyes now felt like sandpaper was taped to the back of my lids. I'd cried until I fell asleep on a bathroom floor, in Roth's arms. He must've carried me to bed, but I didn't remember that, though I did remember how good it felt to be held by him. He was gone when I woke up and I hadn't seen him or Bambi at all today. I guessed she was on him.

I tried not to panic about their absence, but it was hard. The way things were going there was a good chance that Cayman and Roth had underestimated the extent of their Boss's reaction to Roth's actions yesterday with the Alphas and Thumper.

My thoughts roamed from Roth to Zayne and then back to Roth, forming an endless circle before Sam and Stacey broke the cycle. The loss of him was going to hurt something horrible for a long time to come, but as badly as I felt, it was nothing compared to Stacey's pain.

If losing Sam had taught me anything, it was to seize life— seize everything it had to offer, including the tears, the anger and loss, but most of all, the laughter and the love.

To just seize life.

Because it was fleeting and it was fickle, and no one, not me or anyone I knew, had another day, let alone another second promised to them.

Scooting off the bed, I grabbed the phone and made my way downstairs. The closer I got to the kitchen, the stronger the scent of paradise grew. Bacon. I smelled bacon. My stomach grumbled, and I picked up my pace. I found Cayman in the kitchen, making eggs on the stove. Sure enough, bacon sizzled on a griddle beside them.

"Morning," he said without turning around. His hair was pulled back in a hot pink clip with a bedazzled butterfly attached to it. A small smile crept onto my face. "You like your eggs scrambled or what?"

"Scrambled is fine." I hopped up on the bar stool positioned at the large island.

"Good. My kind of girl." He flipped the bacon, and then headed to the fridge, twirling the spatula as he walked. Opening the door, he reached inside and grabbed a small bottle of OJ. Turning, he tossed it in my direction, and I caught it before it smacked me in the face. "Picked some of these up, too."

I glanced down at the bottle. "How did you know?"

He lifted his brows, and then shook his head, turning back to the stove. Bacon snapped and popped as I set the bottle down. Roth had to have told him that the OJ helped with the cravings, as did anything sweet. When I'd woken up, the familiar burning sensation in the pit of my stomach was there, even though it had been absent yesterday. Still, it was minor compared to what I was used to.

"So, what are you planning to do today?" Cayman asked, scooping up the eggs and dropping them on two plates.

"I don't know." Dragging my still-damp hair over one shoulder, I twisted it with my hands. "I was going to check in with Zayne later and see if he'd heard anything about the Alphas, and then call Stacey. I'm... I'm worried about her."

"She'll get through it. Seems like a strong girl."

"She is," I agreed. "But losing someone is..."

"I imagine it's hard, but I really don't know. I haven't loved anything or anyone other than myself," he replied, and I lifted a brow at that. At least he was honest. "Got to suck to lose that."

"It does." I screwed off the lid of the OJ, feeling the heaviness in my chest. I had no idea how long it would take for that to fade. I thought back to when Roth had sacrificed himself; there had been moments where the burden of pain eased, but it had always resurfaced with a bitter vengeance.

Cayman gathered up the slices of bacon, spreading them

out on our plates before joining me at the island. If someone told me a year ago I'd be eating scrambled eggs and bacon made by a demon, I would've laughed in their face and told them that crack was whack.

Times had most definitely changed. I picked up a piece of bacon.

"What's going on with you and Zayne?"

I nearly choked on the bacon. My eyes watered as I grabbed the OJ and took a huge swallow. "Excuse me?" I croaked.

A half smile formed as he forked up some eggs. "You and Zayne, the gorgeous gargoyle. What's going on there?"

"How do you know something's going on?"

Cayman rolled his eyes. "Honey-child, a blind person could see there's major tension. What's the scoop?"

Heat blasted across my cheeks. Well then. "I…" I had no idea how to answer that question, because I wasn't even sure myself. "I don't know."

He sent me a long look. "Ah, I think you totally know, but you're just not ready to put it into words."

Shoving another slice of bacon into my mouth, I eyed him. "Oh, do you now?"

"Yeah. Your shit is complicated. I got you, but I know what's really going on there, so I'm about to go all come to Jesus with you." Setting his fork down, he leaned over and whispered the "truth" in my ear.

I jerked back, his words echoing—no, actually taunting me—and anger rose in me swiftly. I glared at him, my hand tight on the fork. Something about what he said was so true I wanted to kick it back in his face. "I don't want to talk to you about this."

He chuckled. "Whatever floats your boat."

Ignoring him, I devoured the rest of my breakfast, then I got up and dumped the plate and silverware in the dishwasher. When I faced him, he was still grinning. I crossed my arms. "Where's Roth?"

"He's out."

I waited and there was no answer. "Doing what?"

"Things," he replied. "Demon duties."

Sighing, I leaned against the counter. "You're real helpful."

Winking, he held up his empty plate between two fingers. Air crackled, and then flames sparked off the tip of his fingers, climbing the plate. My eyes widened as I watched the fire completely obliterate the plate. The fork went up in flames next.

"Well, that's one way to clean up," I murmured.

"Just a little trick of the trade." He wiped the ashes off his hands. "But going back to the not being helpful part, I'll have you know I'm very helpful. Ask me how you can get Sam's soul back."

I blinked. "What?"

He sighed. "Ask me how to get Sam's soul back from Hell. You know, so you can make sure he goes where he's supposed to, which I'm assuming is beyond those big pearly gates in the sky."

Slowly, I unfolded my arms. "You know how to get Sam's soul?"

"Yep. Though I think Roth would prefer that I didn't tell you. Now get that look off your face that makes people think a bird just crapped on your head."

My brows flew up. That's how I looked?

He continued, "Roth might know a way, but I don't think

that's where his head is right now. Honestly, I'm not sure if I even want to know where his head is at the moment."

Unease blossomed in my belly as I inched toward the kitchen island. Cayman watched me closely. "So here's the deal. There is one being who watches over the souls down below and only that being can release a soul. At least, most of the time. If the person is not completely dead and is hovering in the in-between, then both the Boss and the big guy in the sky get the choice of either releasing the soul or pulling it back."

"Pulling it back?" I leaned in, placing my hands on the cool granite surface. "As in bring them back from the dead?"

He shook his head. "We don't like to use that particular phrasing. More like pull them back from the brink of death."

"Okay," I murmured, but hope sparked and burned bright. I knew it was crappy of me to only be concerned about Sam's soul when there were others who had also ended up unfairly in Hell, but I was also smart enough to realize that I wasn't going to be able to go in there and save everyone. Or maybe I could. My spine stiffened. I could at least try. "Semantics," I said.

"You say semantics and I say the balance of the universe."

I stared at him a moment, and then moved on. "Can we bring back Sam since—"

"No, sweet and incredibly naive child, you cannot bring him back." Propping his elbows on the counter, Cayman rested his chin in his hand. "Sam is dead. As in dead, dead."

Disappointment crushed me, but there was still something to grasp onto. If we couldn't bring Sam back, we could make sure his soul was in the right place. "How does it work? Getting a soul back and making sure it's in the right afterlife?"

"Well, when a person dies, the Alphas decide where their soul goes. Typically the soul goes where it belongs. There is no negotiation, begging or whining. If it's meant to go down below, that's where it goes." He paused. "Unless their soul is stripped away by a Lilin…or someone like you. In those instances it only goes in one direction. Sucks. Totally unfair, but that's just the way it is."

Someone like you.

Normally the reminder of what I was would've been a smack in the face, but that…that ability was a part of me. It didn't make me evil.

Sitting back down on the stool, I picked up the OJ. "How do we get his soul back, Cayman?"

"You go to Grim."

I felt my lips pinch. "Grim?"

Cayman grinned and said nothing.

It took a moment, but then I got it. Rocking back on the stool, I was surprised I didn't fall right off. "Grim, as in the Grim Reaper?"

"He doesn't like to be called that since that's the bastardized version of his name." Cayman spun on his bar stool, a complete circle. "You couldn't even pronounce his real name, so let's just go with Grim. He's cool with that. He's the guardian of the souls down below and he's the only one who can release them."

I mulled that over for a moment. "Is he nice?"

Cayman stopped midspin and threw his head back, laughing long and hard. "No, incredibly sweet and naive child, he is not. He's as old as time and has the temperament of someone who shit the bed and has been rolling around in it all day."

My nose wrinkled. "Ew."

"On the plus side, it's actually pretty simple to get down to the fiery pits in the first place. You just take one of the elevators in the Palisades," he continued, referencing the apartment building Roth normally lived in, which also housed a demonic club. "But you can't take Roth with you. The Boss is still pissed, and so are some of the other Upper Level demons. They get their hands on him, they are going to delay him."

"So...so I'd have to go alone?" A shiver danced down my spine. "To Hell?"

"Most likely. I'd go with you, but... Yeah, I really don't want to talk to Grim."

"Your support means the world to me," I muttered, and then took a drink of the OJ. "All of this seems too easy. I just take an elevator down to Grim and ask for Sam's soul?"

Cayman laughed again. "I'm beginning to think your darling naïvete is actually adorable idiocy. You're like the cute version of the village idiot."

"Wow." I scowled. "You really know how to stroke a girl's ego."

He spun on the stool again and the butterfly clip slipped in his hair. "What can I say? Guys are more my field of expertise. But back to the topic at hand—no, getting Sam's soul won't be as easy as you make it sound, but lucky for you, you'll have some time to plan your strategy. Grim isn't down below right now. He's...off, kind of like vacationing."

"The Grim Reaper vacations?" Disbelief dripped from my voice.

"If you'd been doing a job for two thousand-plus years, you'd need a vacation, too." His knees knocked into mine. "Okay. He's not really vacationing, but he *is* someplace much more pleasant than the pits at the moment. He pulls double occupancy."

"What does that mean? And don't call me an idiot again. I'm not familiar with all your demon lingo."

Cayman glanced up at the ceiling and then down to the floor. "You get it?"

"He's up there?" I pointed at the ceiling. "And down below, too? He goes both places?"

"Of course. He's the Grim Reaper, which means he's actually a— Oh, it's like a game of Taboo. I'll give you examples and you guess what he really is." Cayman clapped his hands together like a seal. "He has wings and—"

"An angel." I cut him off. "He's an angel."

Cayman's expression fell. "You're no fun."

I didn't know a lot about all the different kinds of angels, but I was guessing Grim was actually an angel of death, maybe the original one, so I supposed it made sense that he divided his time between Heaven and Hell. Honestly, I didn't even care. What was important was that there was something we could do for Sam, and maybe if I was lucky, for all those the Lilin had sentenced to Hell.

"He's back soon, next Friday our time." Cayman leaned over, tweaked my nose, and then laughed when I smacked his hand away. "Because that's your only option, going *down* there. You ain't going *up* there."

Well, duh. But Friday was six long days away. I swallowed hard. "I don't know if I can wait that long. Sam's soul…"

"You don't have a choice, Layla." The playfulness slipped away. "No one else can release his soul but Grim, and there is no way for you to enter the heavens to talk to him. None whatsoever, especially now."

My ears perked. "Especially now? How is today any different than yesterday? I never thought I could enter Heaven before—wait. Do you know something about my wings, why they're *feathered*?"

His lips twitched. "You say *feathered* like it's a bad hairstyle. Then again, feathered hair is really bad."

"Cayman," I griped, losing my patience.

"Why worry about your awesomely superior wings when you have a Lilin who's going to quickly realize that there is no way in holy Hell that Lilith will be getting free and that's no joke. The Boss has her on lockdown. She's going nowhere, my little frosted cupcake."

My lips pursed. His terms of endearment were less than endearing.

"And what do you think that Lilin is going to do when it realizes mommy dearest is not getting free and there's nothing that it can do?" He raised his arms and wiggled his fingers. Total jazz hands. "Chaos will ensue, and what do you think will happen when chaos ensues? The Alphas will step in, and there will be so many of them that Thumper would get an upset stomach trying to eat them all. We don't want that. For realsies."

I opened my mouth.

"And why worry about your sleek-ass feathered wings when you have an entire clan of Wardens who just found out in the last twenty-four hours that you're really not dead? Because trust me, they know. Zayne wouldn't have to tell them. The Alphas would have. Some aren't gonna be happy about your survival. Oh no, sugar bear. Then there's the whole witch thing, and don't *even* ask me what they wanted in return for saving your butt, because I am not gonna be the bearer of that bad news bears."

I snapped my mouth shut. Goodie gumdrops, I was really starting to feel super stressed out.

He wasn't done. "And why stress over wings in general when you're going to break someone's heart?"

"What?" I snapped.

Cayman popped off the bar stool, all grins. "Let's stop playing around, my own personal Beanie Baby. Zayne's in love with you. Roth's in love with you."

I inhaled sharply, but the air caught in my throat.

"Both would do anything for you—live, breathe and die for you, but you can't have both of them, Layla."

My hands fell to my thighs and I whispered, "I know that."

"And you know which one is the real deal," he continued, eyeing me intently. "You know, the forever kind of love, so why are you dragging this shit out?"

"I'm not dragging anything out," I protested. "I was kind of out of it, you know, what with the whole being held prisoner and then nearly killed by my own clan thing. Then I was holed up here recovering, and then yesterday happened." Frustrated, I jumped off the stool and stalked around the island. "And maybe I don't think it's the right time for me to be with either of them. Did you ever think about that?"

Cayman cocked his head to the side. "When is there ever a right time to fully give your heart to another? There are always going to be obstacles. You just have to decide which ones are worth it."

"Whatever." I crossed my arms.

He mimicked my stance. "Don't be a coward."

"Excuse me?"

"A. Coward," he repeated, and I briefly considered picking up the vase in the center of the island and throwing it at him. "Not making a choice is the coward's way out. You love both of them. I get that. But you don't feel the same kind of love for both of them, and the sooner you accept that, the better."

"Why are we talking about this again? And why do you even care?"

Cayman smiled. "Because I'm a caring sort of demon."

"Ugh," I groaned, throwing up my hands as frustration and panic fought their way through me. Cayman made it sound so easy, like I wasn't going to lose one of them, but I was. Call me selfish, but the idea of not having both of them in my life terrified me. "You can be so annoying."

"Don't hate," he said, grinning. "Procreate."

Now I just glared at him.

"Procreate with the right guy," he added. "Just wanted to clarify that."

"Oh my God," I moaned, leaning over and placing my forehead on the counter.

I stayed like that even after I felt Cayman exit the room— and probably the entire house, because after a few moments, I didn't sense a demon.

The granite countertop really was cool and smooth, and felt good against my flushed face. Maybe I'd stay like this all day. Sounded like a plan. Better than...

No, not better than listening to what Cayman had said about Zayne and Roth. He was right. Oh God, he was so creepily right. I did love both guys. I really did, and the idea of hurting one of them or losing one of them made me want to hurl, but Cayman was also right about a few more things.

I couldn't have both of them.

And what I felt for them was different.

There was no hiding that. It had always been that way. Both made me happy. Both made me laugh. Both filled me with longing and made my girlie parts all kinds of happy. But only one really made me…

Well, there was only one that I knew I would always be happy with, one that I would always laugh with. One that I did more than long for, but *yearned* for, and each second that passed ignoring it was a second I wouldn't get to spend with him—a second I wouldn't live life with love in it, *real* love in it, the kind that did have lasting power.

Despite what Cayman said, I wasn't sure that both of them were truly in love with me. I wasn't in their heads, but the way they felt didn't matter when it came down to it. It was how I felt, and I wouldn't settle. I also didn't expect them to settle.

My forehead was starting to stick to the granite.

For the first time in days, I let myself really think about Roth's words, the ones I thought I'd hallucinated before I had passed out from my wounds and whatever the witches had given me.

I love you, Layla. I've loved you since the first moment I heard your voice and I will continue to love you. No matter what. I love you.

Roth had pretty much confirmed that I had in fact heard those words spoken with such sweet urgency, but there was this part of me that just couldn't believe it. Or maybe I didn't want to, because when I thought about what Roth said, I also remembered what Zayne had said when he'd seen me standing in Stacey's living room.

I would know if a part of my heart was gone.

My entire being felt like it was squeezed to the point of pain. There were all the secrets that Zayne had told me, how he had waited...for me. Still, I had spent years wanting him and it never seemed possible that I would ever have him.

Maybe I was just scared out of my mind to finally—

Lost in my own thoughts, I didn't recognize the awareness that seeped into my skin, alerting me to another presence in the house until a deep voice rumbled throughout the kitchen.

"What in the world are you doing, Shortie?"

Jerking back, I lifted my head as I pressed my palm against my chest. Heart pounding, I watched Roth walk toward the island and stop. He was dressed much like he had been last night, except he was wearing a white thermal today that really complemented the golden hue of his skin.

"I was... I was thinking," I said, smoothing my hands over my hair. "Thinking about stuff."

He propped a hip against the island. "Was the countertop helping you think about stuff?"

I pressed my lips together. "Maybe."

Roth's gaze dipped, and then slowly slid back up to my face. There was a pleased heat in his gaze that wrought a very different kind of shiver out of me. "That's an odd way to do some thinking, Shortie."

"Yeah, I know. Cayman...um, he made breakfast." Toying with my hair, I wrapped the edges around my fingers as Roth started walking again. He was coming closer to me. "And got me a phone."

"I told him to get the phone for you," he replied, his tawny eyes aglow. "The breakfast, though, was nice of him. All his idea."

"It was nice." My heart had not slowed down, and it didn't help when he got closer still. "Where have you been?"

He stopped in front of me. "Checked out Sam's house.

Thought it would be a good idea." Reaching between us, he got his fingers in between mine and tugged them away from my hair. "It's not good news."

"It's not?"

Roth shook his head as he held my hands in his. "His family was dead. In their beds." His expression grew tight, somber. "And they'd been dead for at least a couple of days. Since I didn't see any wraiths, it doesn't look like their souls had been stripped. There was a…a mess left behind."

Squeezing my eyes shut, I couldn't suppress the shudder. I didn't need to ask what constituted a mess. "Why would the Lilin kill without taking a soul?"

His thumbs smoothed over the insides of my hands. "Because it can. No other reason than that."

"God." The only silver lining was that Sam's family would go where they belonged since they still had their souls.

"I kind of expected it, to be honest. I thought about it last night, but didn't want to leave until I made sure you were okay." His warm hands spread up to my wrists, and when I opened my eyes, he was staring down at me. "I hate to have to bring that news to you."

I hated the fact that more innocent lives had been lost. I'd met Sam's parents a few times. They were pretty cool, as random and adorable as Sam. "Wait. Sam has a sister. She's younger and—"

A muscle flickered in his jaw as Roth dropped his gaze, and then it hit me. Roth hadn't said his parents. He'd said *his family*. The eggs and bacon churned in my stomach, and I wished I hadn't eaten anything.

"I made an anonymous call to the police. They're probably already at the house. Even though what looks like Sam is up and walking around, with his family…deceased, that's going to force the Lilin out of school and away from the students there. It's going to have to be careful. Not that it would be easy to arrest, but I doubt it wants that extra hassle."

My chest ached so badly as I murmured, "That was really smart."

He stepped even closer. "I figured that for Stacey…and for you, it would be easier if either everyone assumed he was dead or, well, a murderer now rather than later. If the Lilin is allowed to roam around school as Sam, it means Stacey would have to go through that loss all over again."

My gaze flew to his. "That was very considerate."

Roth mouthed the word *considerate* like he'd never heard it before or didn't really understand what it meant. "I'm going to be honest. Okay?"

"All right?"

"I like Stacey. Don't get me wrong. That girl's got a lot of bad in her, the fun kind, but I was really thinking about you." His eyes held mine. "After seeing it tear you apart last night, knowing it's still tearing you apart, I don't want you to feel all of that again when you've just started to heal."

Oh.

Oh wow.

"So don't give me credit for something I am not," he finished, dropping my hands.

As he stepped back, I leaned into the island, absolutely shaken. "I don't think you give yourself enough credit, Roth."

He looked over his shoulder as he turned away. "I know what I am."

That was the thing. I didn't think he had a clue about what

he was, not what existed deep inside him, what really mattered.

Cayman's words, the whispered ones, echoed among my thoughts again, and I looked away. There was so much going on right now and so much was a mess. I had to start somewhere to sort all of this out, though, and I knew where. "I need to do something."

Roth went to the fridge and pulled out a bottle. He didn't turn around, but there was a suspicious hissing sound as he popped off the cap.

I took a deep breath and forged on. "I need... I need to see Zayne."

His shoulders tensed, and then hunched as he lifted the drink to his lips. "I figured as much," he said, and I stared at the rigid line of his back.

"Roth—"

He didn't let me finish. "I'll summon Cayman back. He'll take you where you need to go." Then he faced me, and my breath hitched. There was a vulnerability in his expression I'd never seen before, a great and terrible sadness that dampened the brightness of his eyes. "I know you trust and...and care for Zayne, but I don't trust the rest of them. Plus, there're the issues with the Alphas. Cayman goes with you."

Before I could say any more or even protest, Roth was gone. In the blink of an eye, he'd disappeared and I was left staring at the space where he'd stood.

five

IT WASN'T UNTIL LATER IN THE AFTERNOON that I could meet up with Zayne, and then I had to wait for Cayman to play chauffeur. He didn't seem annoyed by the new requirement imposed on him. He chattered on as we drove, but I was too anxious and distracted to pay attention to what he was saying, so I stared out the window, checking out all the garlands strung on the lampposts and the lights that would soon twinkle on. I squirmed the whole way to the coffee shop Zayne and I used to visit every Saturday, my mind stuck on the way Roth had stared at me in the kitchen.

I didn't get it. He'd gone from—from touching me to completely withdrawn. Not just distant, but *pained*. I didn't even have the chance to explain anything. Now my heart was pounding crazy fast, like I was about to go toe-to-toe with a Hellion, and it had nothing to do with seeing Zayne.

Maybe Cayman and I had completely misjudged Roth's... um, interest, but even if we had, it didn't change what I was about to do. It couldn't.

Cayman eased the Mustang to an idling stop along the

parked cars outside the shop. As I reached for the door, he tapped his fingers against the steering wheel. "My number is entered in your phone already, under Awesome Sauce. Text me when you're done."

"Okay." I opened the door, wincing as the wind smacked me in the face.

"Don't wander off. You have Alphas and who knows what else potentially gunning for your ass," he continued. "And I really don't want to go back to the house and have to explain to Roth that I lost you somehow."

I resisted both the urge to point out that I wasn't sure how Roth would even feel about that at this point and the desire to roll my eyes. "Yes, *Dad*."

He grinned. "Do me proud."

Shooting him a look over my shoulder as I climbed out, I slammed the car door shut and hopped up on the curb. The wind was brutal as I dashed around the people hurrying up and down the sidewalk. An array of auras greeted me, buttery yellows and soft blues and pinks. I kept an eye out for anyone who was missing one, a sure sign of a demon in our midst, but everything appeared to be business as usual.

The frosted wreath hanging on the door jingled as I stepped inside. Before I even stepped through the doorway, I knew Zayne was there. I sensed him as the warm air washed over me. The coffee shop was a total mom-and-pop kind of store, not one of the big chains, but it smelled like sweet baked goods and coffee beans. Espresso-colored booths lined the walls and I spotted Zayne's white glow immediately. He was sitting toward the back of the shop, in one of the comfy booths, facing the door.

Before I joined him, I took a few moments to get my head

on straight and ordered a peppermint mocha. Then I carried the warm cup over to him. He immediately rose to his feet, and the closer I got, the more I could see that the tired bruises under his eyes had faded a bit. For that, I was grateful.

The shop was packed with people in business suits and others carrying shopping bags, but when Zayne took the cup out of my hand and placed it on the table, no one else was there. Before I could speak a word, he wrapped his arms around me and held tight, lowering his cheek to mine. I froze up, because he was too close to my mouth, but Zayne—oh, he'd always been so incredibly reckless with me.

"This was what I wanted to do yesterday," he rasped, his voice low in my ear. "When I first saw you standing in that house, *this* was all I could think about."

I squeezed my eyes shut as I hugged him back. Emotion already clawed at my insides.

"The clan knows you're alive now," he went on, and I felt the muscles in my back tense. Cayman had said as much, but hearing it confirmed was a whole different story. "Danika wanted to come with me. She wanted to see for herself that you're okay."

A strangled, surprised laugh escaped me, and I felt Zayne's cheek rise against mine when he smiled. Danika and I had a very strange relationship. The entire clan expected Zayne to mate with her. In other words, get down to business and produce a lot of Warden babies, and because of that I'd always been extremely jealous of the full-blooded Warden. Danika was stunningly gorgeous and rather badass, unlike most Warden females. She was not okay with sitting around and popping babies out for the good of mankind. And she also had been interested in Zayne. In short, there were plenty of reasons to hate her, but she and I had finally formed an unlikely alliance.

I did miss her in a weird way, like one missed shoveling the snow during a heat wave. When Zayne reluctantly let go, I all but fell into the seat as I struggled to gain control of what I was feeling, of what I was about to do.

Zayne returned to the seat across from me. "You okay, Layla-bug?"

The concern in his voice was evident. "Yeah." I cleared my throat and took a sip of the minty mocha. "Last night was a little rough. I got to thinking about Sam…" I shook my head and kept my voice low. "Roth went to his house this morning. His family was gone—dead. It didn't look like their souls were taken."

"Damn." Zayne dragged his fingers through his hair.

I nodded slowly, casting my gaze to the lid on my cup. "He called it in to the police, which was pretty smart. That's going to force the Lilin to lie low for a little while since the police will be looking for…for Sam. At least, we hope. Did you find out anything about the Alphas?"

Zayne's stare was intense, and I realized he'd been staring at me like that since I sat down. "Yeah. Some of them paid the clan a visit at roughly the same time the other two showed up at Stacey's place. From what I could gather from Nicolai, the Alphas knew there was a Lilin, always did."

I hadn't missed the fact that he'd said he'd spoken to Nicolai instead of his father, but I was distracted by the last part. "They did?"

"Yeah, apparently they couldn't get involved for their own celestial reasons. They believed we'd figure it out."

Anger sparked in my chest as I stared at him. All those

weeks when I'd thought I was somehow responsible for the death, destruction and mayhem both at school and at home, and the Alphas had known the truth from the start. "They knew this entire time and never thought to tell any of us? Why?" My voice was rising, but I couldn't help it. "Because of some bullshit rules?"

"I know," he agreed softly.

I wanted to punch an Alpha in the face! Like fists of fury types of punches. "We could've saved lives. I can't even…" I took a huge gulp of the mocha, hoping that would calm me down. It really didn't. "What else did they say?"

He rested his arms on the table and leaned in. "My father was able to negotiate some time from them. They're giving us until the New Year to deal with the Lilin, unless the Lilin does something that has the risk of exposure. We have Wardens out now searching for it."

My brows flew up. To be honest, I hadn't thought they'd give us any time. I could easily see them giving us two hours. I wasn't surprised to learn of the whole exposure thing, though. The Alphas had decreed long ago that humankind could never have real, hard-core proof that a Heaven and a Hell existed, that they must believe in a higher power based on faith alone. I didn't understand that then and I still didn't get it now. All I knew was that the Wardens went to great lengths to keep the existence of demons a secret from humans everywhere. "What happens if we don't have it under control?"

"Nothing pretty. They threatened to wipe us all out. The same thing if the Lilin goes too far." He exhaled roughly while I wondered what "too far" would look like. "They seem to understand that tracking the Lilin down and killing it isn't going to be easy, but that's not all that they talked about."

"What else did they talk about? How cool it is up on their lofty perch?"

He stared for a moment, and then said, "Uh, no. They... Well, there's no easy way to say this. They're not happy with you, Layla-bug."

Maybe a few weeks ago, I would've flipped out and tossed myself in a corner to rock away all my troubles. Now? I snorted, and then took another drink. "Big surprise there."

Zayne's gaze drifted over my face. He didn't speak for a long moment. "Roth did say something true yesterday. I have seen black, feathered wings before."

I was doing my best not to think about my weird wings, but I set the cup down. "Where?"

A muscle under his eye twitched as he dropped his gaze, and my stomach tightened. Not a particularly good sign. "I've only seen one demon with them. Felt like an Upper Level one. It was a brief glimpse. I thought I was seeing stuff, but they were like yours."

"Oh," I murmured, unsure of how to feel about that. Zayne and Danika had already confirmed that I smelled like an Upper Level demon. That was why the Warden Tomas had attacked me. So this was nothing new, not really, but it still didn't explain why my wings were suddenly feathered and why I hadn't fully shifted like a Warden or a demon would. "Do my wings have something to do with why the Alphas suddenly don't like me? Well, not that they ever liked me in the first place, but what gives now?"

"All they said was that you were an abomination. That's not right. You—"

"I know. It's not right. There are worse things kicking

around than me. I know that. And if they don't know that, it's not my problem."

Zayne raised a brow.

"Well, okay, it is my problem if they try to come after me again, but I know I'm not an abomination," I repeated, dragging my finger along the rim of the cup.

It had taken a long time for me to get to that point, to not let the words of the Alphas or my own clan members cut me down. Or even the words of the girls at school, like Eva Hasher and the Bitch Pack, as Stacey referred to them, who used to have me doubting everything that I was. I don't even know what exactly flipped that switch for me. Maybe it was the long and dark hours I'd spent in that horrible cage below the compound or maybe it was almost dying. Either way, it was a wake-up call.

In more ways than one, and now I had to seize one of those other ways.

I glanced at Zayne, my closest of friends since I was a little girl, my everything for so very long, and found that I couldn't look away. This…this was going to hurt. Holy granola bars, it was going to sting like a swarm of wasps. And it was so scary, because there was no safety net for this decision.

Zayne inclined his head. "Hey…" He reached across the table for my hand, but I pulled it back, clasping mine together. His eyes flew to mine. "Layla?"

I thought about what Cayman had whispered in my ear that morning.

Stop being a coward and let go of the past. Embrace the future, because they are two very different things.

Cayman had been right. I'd been a coward, afraid of letting go of the past, of all that familiarity, because there was safety there, a simplicity in its comfort. The past was like going home, and it was sweet and warm, and perfect in its own right. It wasn't any less than the future, but I'd been terrified of embracing the unknown, of the potential of losing what I'd always counted on.

Because there was only one set of eyes I saw when I closed mine at night and when I reopened them in the morning.

"Layla?" Zayne's voice was soft.

I squared my shoulders as I drew in a stuttered breath. "You said we needed to talk yesterday and you were right. We do."

His gaze searched mine as I forged on. "I know there's a lot going on right now, so many things up in the air, and a lot of it is crazy."

"But...?"

There was a golf-ball-size knot currently lodged in my throat and I wanted to close my eyes. I wanted to look away, but I forced myself not to hide anything. "You know that you mean the world to me, always have, and that I care about you so much. I love you—"

"But you're not *in* love with me?" His eyes shut as his faced tensed. "Is that what you're saying?"

"No. I mean, I'm not saying it like that. I do love you, but—"

"You've got to be kidding me." Zayne opened his eyes as he leaned back against the booth, shaking his head. "Just stop."

I opened my mouth.

"Stop. Just for a second," he said again, eyes open and not missing a thing. He shook his head, staring at me in the worst kind of wonderment. "Is it because of what happened when I kissed you last time, or because of our clan? I trust you, Layla. And I know you trust me. We can make this work."

Oh God, that golf ball had turned into a softball. "I know you trust me, but that's not the reason. It's really not." Those words were truer than I'd realized until that moment, and it made saying what I had to so very important, because even if he and I could have made it work, in the end, my heart—my heart would've belonged elsewhere. "We could have made it work without…without the kissing and we could've been careful. And I trust you, but this isn't about trust. Zayne, you're important to me and I—"

"You love Roth," he continued for me. "You're in love with him."

My eyes met his bright blue ones. "Yes," I whispered, my lower lip trembling. "It's him. It's always been him. I'm sorry. I do love you. I care about you so much, and in so many ways, being with you was a dream come true, but it's not the same."

He drew back, as if I'd reached across the table and slapped him. "Please don't expect me to sit here and listen to a speech that makes me feel like a damn runner-up in some kind of contest."

I sucked in a sharp breath. "That's not how I want you to feel."

Zayne's brows lowered as he stared at me. "How in the Hell did you expect me to feel?"

Tears burned the back of my eyes, because I'd never, ever wanted to hurt anyone. Especially not him. "I don't know."

"Of course you don't." He thrust his hand over his head, clasping the back of his neck. A moment passed as tension tightened the lines of his mouth. "I love you," he ground out, a muscle thrumming along his jaw. "I'm *in* love with you. I *waited* for you, Layla. And none of that—none of that matters."

I didn't know what to say. It did matter—mattered a whole

lot, but how could I say that? Because in the end, even if I went back to the house and Roth laughed in my face, it didn't change anything.

Anger flashed over his face. "What was going on between us? Was it just passing the time for you?"

"Oh my God, no!" A woman with a faint pink aura glanced in our direction from the coffee line, and I struggled to keep my voice low. "It wasn't like that at all. God, it was perfect and it was like every fantasy I ever had come to life."

"Really?" Disbelief flooded his face. "Because how it seems to me is that you were just fooling around until you could be with him."

"Until I could be with him?" I repeated dumbly. "I don't even know—"

"Don't you dare say you don't know that he loves you. Don't play stupid by acting stupid," he spat, and I jerked back, stunned by the rancor in his tone. "Dammit," he muttered, dropping his arm.

"Zayne—"

"No more," he ordered, and I squeezed my eyes shut. "Just no more."

Zayne didn't say anything else as he got up, and I didn't try to stop him as he strode out the front door. Dropping my elbows on the table, I planted my face in my hands. My insides twisted and burned. Even when Zayne had been rightfully upset with me before, he'd never spoken to me like that. Not that I blamed him. I deserved this. I hadn't been careful with my own actions or with his heart. I didn't regret anything we shared, but I'd messed up and I shouldn't have allowed myself to get involved with him, because what I'd said a few moments ago had also been true.

It had always been Roth; from the moment he swaggered into that damn alley where I'd been unsuccessfully fighting off a demon, it had been him for me. Maybe I'd been too blind to see that after he returned from the pits. Maybe I had been too angry with him after the way he initially acted. Maybe I had played around with Zayne, even if that hadn't been my intention. I didn't know.

All I did know was that I had lost the boy I'd grown up with. If I'd had any doubts about that, the fact that he'd left me here alone told me all I needed to know. As protective as Zayne was of me, there was no way he would have left me unchaperoned with a Lilin still on the loose. Not unless staying away from me was more important than keeping me safe.

I don't know how long I sat there, but eventually I felt an unnatural warmth spreading along the back of my neck, alerting me to the presence of a demon. Expecting to find Cayman when I lifted my head, I looked around the coffee shop. My gaze drifted over the soft shades of auras until I found a young man standing toward the front of the shop with nothing around him.

There was my demon and it wasn't Cayman.

Grateful to have something to focus on other than the fact that I'd just shattered Zayne's heart to smithereens, I studied the man at the front of the store as I shifted my hair forward, shielding my face. Due to my dual heritage, demons had never been able to sense me, which made the hunting I'd done in the past easy-peasy. Once again, the mixture of Warden and demon had given me a unique ability to tag demons. One touch and they'd turn into a neon light, leaving a trace on them that the Wardens could easily track.

I hadn't tagged demons since...well, not since Roth had entered my life, showing me that even demons had a purpose in life. From him I'd learned that some demons weren't all that bad, like Fiends, who tended to just mess around with things like telephone poles, construction sites, anything electronic, and were a bit prone to being firebugs.

This demon didn't give off a Fiend vibe and I was willing to bet he also wasn't a Poser, a demon whose bite turned a human into something that would resemble an extra on the set of *The Walking Dead*.

No, this demon was giving off the Upper Level kind of vibes, meaning he could be a Duke or a King or any other variety of elite baddie. They weren't supposed to be topside because the kind of stuff they could pull off could really wreak some nasty, bloody havoc.

I frowned.

Which, apparently, meant that maybe *I* shouldn't be topside, either. I kept forgetting that I now smelled like them and sort of resembled some of them. Sigh.

The demon tilted his head to the side, and a lock of shocking white-blond hair fell across dark brows that stood out in stark contrast. He had a rocker look to him, like if the silver chain he wore broke, his skinny jeans would fall right off him. Scanning the coffee shop, he looked me over, kept going, and then his gaze darted back to me.

I froze.

The demon froze.

Uh-oh.

Demons couldn't sense me, but he was staring directly at me like I'd sprouted a third arm out of the top of my head.

His face paled to the color of his hair as he jerked back a

step, bumping into a woman with a pale blue aura. She nearly dropped her bag and coffee as she tried to step around him.

Then he spun on his heel and shoved an older guy out of the way. The man shouted, but the demon reached the door. I wasn't thinking as I stood. Curiosity and surprise had a hold on me. I hurried across the shop, leaving what was left of my mocha behind. I was a few steps behind the demon when he burst through the door, out onto the sidewalk. He sent a panicked look over his shoulder in my direction.

I skidded to a stop under the awning of the shop. "Uh…"

The demon picked up speed, racing down the sidewalk, disappearing around the block, lost in the sea of muted auras.

"Um," I murmured, glancing behind me and half expecting to see a pack of Alphas, but it was just me, myself and I, and that meant only one thing.

The Upper Level demon had run away—from me.

six

I DIDN'T TELL CAYMAN ABOUT THE RUNAWAY Upper Level demon, and he didn't ask how the talk went with Zayne, which I was totally cool with. After a near-silent ride, he dropped me off in front of the house.

"Have fun with *that*," was all he said, and then he zoomed off.

Turning to the McMansion, I had no idea what Cayman was referring to, but figured I was going to find out soon enough.

The house was dark, but not quiet when I walked in the front door, closing it behind me. The sharp riff of a guitar, quickly lost in the pounding of drums, drifted from the second story.

Frowning, I made my way toward the stairwell, and about halfway up I found something odd. I bent and picked up an empty bottle of beer. Looking up, I realized there was one on each step, all the way to the top. Ten empty bottles.

Oh dear.

My eyes widened as I placed the bottle back on the stair.

There was no way I could gather them all up without getting a bag and the last thing I wanted to do was go down to the pantry. I picked up my pace, hurrying to climb the rest of the steps.

Like a bread-crumb trail, bottles had been periodically dropped along the wide hall, leading to the bedroom Roth had stopped in front of last night when I had continued on to the master.

My heart jumped in my chest as I reached his room. The door was ajar, the music heavy and thrumming. Soft light crept out of the gap. Taking a deep breath, I pushed open the door—and came to a complete stop just inside the massive bedroom.

Nothing in this world could've prepared me for what I was seeing.

Bambi was bopping and weaving across the hardwood floor. She stopped, twisting her usually graceful body toward me. Those red eyes were glossed over, unfocused. Her forked tongue darted out, and then she went about her business, slowly making her way to the window seat. There, she shifted half of her six-foot-and-then-some frame onto the seat and promptly slid right off, flopping onto the floor.

Concern flooded me, but as I took a step toward Bambi something else caught my eye. On the bed, Roth's black-and-white kitten familiar was attempting to pounce on the all-white one, which appeared to be passed out, sprawled on its back, its little arms and legs spread wide. The black-and-white one, adeptly named Fury, jumped toward the sleeping Nitro, missed by a block and landed on the pillow. The kitten turned into a furry black-and-white tumbleweed as it rolled off the pillow, smacking into Nitro.

My mouth dropped open.

The third kitten, an all-black one named Thor, sat on a dresser, eyes narrowed into thin slits. As I stared at Thor, it swayed side to side. It spotted me and opened its mouth most likely to hiss at me, because those kittens were little bastards, but a rather human belch emanated from it instead.

Oh my God, the familiars were *drunk*.

A laugh bubbled up from me, but the door slammed shut behind me, stealing away the wild giggle. One second I was standing there and within the next breath, my back was against the door. A hard, warm and very bare chest was flush with mine, and hot breath skated over my cheek as two hands hit the door, on either side of my head.

"What are you doing here?" Roth demanded, and my heart slammed against my ribs, then doubled its beat as his lips brushed the curve of my jaw. He inhaled deeply. "Hell, you smell good. Like peppermint and…and the sun."

Um. I had no idea how to respond to that.

"I let you go," he went on, dipping his head to my neck, and a shiver swept through me. "You were right yesterday. I hurt you. Not like him. Worse. I let you walk out of this house so you could be happy with him. Wasn't that what you wanted? But you're here. I let you go and it *killed* me to do so, and you're here."

Oh my God.

Roth was rambling, but my heart imploded as his words stirred something deep and fierce inside me. The look on his face this morning when I told him I needed to talk to Zayne suddenly made sense. If he had just given me the chance to explain what I was doing he wouldn't have thought that I was leaving him, that I was choosing Zayne.

But Roth had let me go so that I could be happy. The

Crown Prince of Hell, who claimed to be the most selfish of all demons, had let me walk out that door when he believed I'd be happier with someone else. Words were lost as a different kind of tears filled my eyes. He'd stepped aside to protect me once before, and he had done so again so that I could be happy with someone else. There wasn't an ounce of selfishness in any of those actions. Actually, quite the opposite, and the revelation stitched the frayed crack in my heart, repairing the painful splinter. It didn't heal the scar tissue left behind when I let Zayne go, though. That would never fade.

I squeezed my eyes shut.

He slowly lifted his chin and rested his forehead against mine. He whispered, "Why are you here, Layla?"

"I'm here… I'm here because *this* is where I'm happy, with you."

Roth didn't move, and I wasn't even sure he breathed. There was a good chance my words didn't get through the haze of all the alcohol he'd obviously consumed, which was a good indication that this conversation needed to happen later. I placed my hands on his chest, about to point that out, when he moved.

His arms went around me and he held me tight to him. I liked it like this—more than liked. Every part of our bodies touched as he buried his head in my neck, dragging in a deep breath. My pulse was pounding and my hands trembling. A deep shudder rose through him and he shook in my arms, and then he moved.

Clasping my cheeks in his large hands, he said something too low and too quick for me to understand as he tilted my head back and kissed me. There was nothing soft about it. His mouth was on mine, the metal ball in his tongue clanking off my teeth as he pressed me into the door. He tasted of something sweet and the bitter tang of alcohol was still on his tongue. Little shivers of pleasure raced through my body as I moaned into the kiss. My hands slid up to his shoulders and my fingers dug into his smooth skin. The kiss was doing crazy stuff to my senses, obliterating my common sense when the lower half of him pressed against mine.

And it felt like it had been forever since I felt *this*. The sweet wildness that came from a single kiss and the release and freedom of finally letting go, of complete and utter acceptance, of having what I wanted, what I yearned for. The immediate and absolute rush of desire so potent it clouded my thoughts, and the nervous energy and elation that came from tasting love on the tip of my tongue. Nothing compared to *this*.

Roth broke the kiss, breathing heavily as he cradled my face. "Say it again," he ordered roughly. "Say it again, Layla."

I could barely catch my breath. "I'm happy here with you. I..." I dragged my hands up his neck, smoothing my thumbs along his jaw. There was more I wanted to say, but he grasped my wrists and just held them in his hands, staring down at them, saying nothing. My heart pounded fast, but my blood felt sluggish.

A lock of black hair fell into his face and when he finally lifted his chin, the vulnerability was in his gaze again. His beauty was unreal, almost too perfect, but in that moment, he looked more human than he ever had before. "I've... I've been drinking."

Not exactly what I had been expecting him to say. "I can tell."

Letting go of my hands, he took a step back and turned, giving me a rather nice view of his toned back. I was happy to see when he twisted sideways that Thumper was on him—a drunk not-so-pocket-size dragon would've been no laughing matter. I was also happy to see all the dips and planes of his stomach.

Really happy.

Those pants hung so low it was almost indecent. Almost. He picked up a bottle off the dresser. He shook it. "I got myself so drunk that I became literally incapable of going after you and stopping you." He studied the empty bottle he held, frowning. "But did you know that intoxication works differently for us? It only lasted for maybe an hour and then I just felt like shit, so I had to drink some more. Aaand I might be a little drunk still..." ·

I pressed my lips together to stop from laughing. "I'll say."

One side of his lips quirked up as he cast a sidelong glance at me. "I know I shouldn't be drinking. It makes me a naughty, naughty boy."

"Yeah, and apparently it also makes your familiars drunk." I gestured at Bambi, who was slumbering where she'd fallen, a pathetic snaky heap on the floor. "Maybe you don't get as intoxicated because your poor friends there soak up all the effects."

Roth tipped his head to the side. "Huh. Live and learn." He turned back to me, and there was a recognizable heat in his gaze. "I want to kiss you again."

Even though there were parts of me that were like, all aboard the Roth train, I knew this was not going to happen tonight, for so many reasons. "As you pointed out, you're drunk."

He faced me with his chin dipped low and his full lips

slightly parted. "I still want to kiss you. I want to do other things. A lot of it involves touching, with and without clothes."

My cheeks heated.

Tipping his head back, he sighed heavily. "But yeah, drunk. Sorry."

"Roth." I took a cautious step toward him. Even plastered, he was fast. "How long have you been drinking?"

One shoulder rose as he turned to the bed. "Since you left? If I didn't, I would've gone after you and possibly let Thumper eat Stony, and you wouldn't be okay with that."

"No," I whispered. "I wouldn't be."

"Maybe I shouldn't have drunk this much. You don't… Yeah, you deserve better than this." He stopped at the foot of the bed, staring at me as he scrubbed his fingers through his messy hair. "Are you really here? Or did I manage to become the first demon ever to have alcohol poisoning?"

Part of me wanted to burst into laughter, but there was a tight knot of sadness deep in my chest. It was formed by a bitter, rancid guilt. My actions had such a ripple effect. Of course, I hadn't held those bottles to Roth's mouth, but I'd never even seen him drink before.

"I'm really here," I told him.

He looked like he was about to say something as he went to sit on the foot of the bed. I started forward, already seeing that he'd misjudged the distance, but it was too late.

Roth hit the floor in front of the bed, smack on the rear. He tossed his head back, laughing loudly as I clapped my hand over my mouth. I hadn't been sure what I was coming back to after leaving the coffee shop. There had been this fear— albeit irrational fear—that Roth was just going to pat me on my head and send me on my way. Then there was a part of me that thought he'd sweep me into his arms, professing his undying love for me. Either way, finding him drunk hadn't even been in the realm of possibilities.

He settled down, resting his hands on his thighs as he looked over at me. "So, you really came back?"

I nodded, then said yes for extra bang.

His gaze dropped and he sighed heavily. "I bet you're regretting that now."

"No," I replied without hesitation as I walked over to where he sat. "I don't regret it."

He lifted a brow, but it didn't erase the lost look he wore. "Really?"

Easing to the floor beside him, I shook my head. "You're drunk. Big deal. I mean, you probably shouldn't be *this* drunk, but you're not even…human. And you're like the Crown Prince of Hell. I don't think consuming alcohol is a deal breaker where you come from."

"Nah, I guess not." He bent one leg at the knee as he wet his lips. "You… I don't want you to look back and think, wow, that was a terrible decision, because he would've—"

"Stop," I said. Pleaded really. "I'm not going to regret my decision even if you end up running for the hills screaming to get away from me."

"I don't think that's going to happen," he said drily.

I scooted closer and stretched out my legs next to his. "What I'm trying to say is that I made my decision. I'm not going to regret it. No matter what happens between us." Biting down on my lip, I watched an array of emotions creep across his striking face. "Look, I don't think we should talk about this right now. It can wait. It needs to wait, because I… I think I really hurt Zayne tonight. No. I know I did. And you're not in the right frame of mind." I halted again, because wow, I sounded so mature I kind of wanted to pat myself on the back. "This can wait. We have tomorrow."

Roth didn't respond as he studied me, and I had no idea what he was thinking in that head of his, but then he leaned over. He put that head in my lap, like he'd done that night I'd woken up after being healed by the witches' brew, but this time, I didn't hesitate. My hands didn't linger for a second. They immediately went to him, one threading through the silky, black strands and the other curving around his shoulder.

He curled onto his side and closed his eyes. Thick lashes framed his cheeks. Several moments passed in silence, but I knew he wasn't asleep. His muscles were too tense. "I've… I've done some really crappy things, Layla."

My chest squeezed as I stared down at him, and in that moment, I wasn't thinking about the Lilin or my wings or even Sam or Zayne. I was 100 percent focused on Roth, and the world around us and all the problems it kept serving up faded to the wayside. "I kind of figured that you have." And that was true. He was a full-blooded Upper Level demon—a Crown Prince at that. I'd never fooled myself into believing he was a saint masked as a sinner.

"Really shady things," he murmured.

"Got it." My lips twitched.

He managed to get one of his arms curled around my leg. "The…first time I was sent topside by the Boss was only a year after I was created. I was to find a Duke who was no longer heeding the Boss's summons," he continued as I gently worked my fingers through his hair. I didn't dare speak, because Roth had never really talked openly about what his Boss had him doing. "The Duke had found a woman, a human. I don't think she knew what he really was. Not that it mattered. The Boss was calling him back, but he wouldn't leave her."

Biting the inside of my cheek, I had a feeling that this story wasn't going to end with a happily-ever-after.

"There were others with me, who'd gotten called in." His arm tightened around my leg. "Things got…messy."

I closed my eyes, heart aching.

"That wasn't the only time. There were other…situations like that. And these situations, well, they never weighed on me before. It's not in my genetic makeup to feel guilt." A wry grin flashed across his face and quickly disappeared. "Not until you. Now I think about these things and I wonder if there is any…goodness in me. Or what you could possibly see."

Oh gosh, my heart was breaking all over again. I didn't know what it was like to be Roth, to be something that was just the latest in the long line that came before him. Other Princes that the Boss had grown tired of, destroyed in one way or another, before creating *this* version of Astaroth. And I didn't know everything Roth had done in his past, but in all honestly, I didn't care. Who was I to judge? Being that I was nowhere near perfect and was also part demon, myself, I'd done things I wished I hadn't, and I knew there would be things in the future that I'd want to take back. But Roth had spent eighteen years keeping the Boss of Hell happy. None of his darkness surprised me.

It just saddened me.

Leaning down, I kissed his cheek, and as I straightened, he turned wide amber eyes on me. "I see what you don't." I ran my hand up and down his arm. "You're not selfish, even if you have moments of acting like it. We all do. You're not evil, even if you were created by the greatest evil of them all.

You've proven to me and yourself that you have free will, and you've made the right decisions time and time again."

As I dragged my hand up his arm, he shuddered. "You've accepted who and what I am from the beginning. You've never tried to change me or...or hide me. You've always trusted me, even when you probably shouldn't have." I laughed at that, thinking of the time he'd left me alone in the Palisades club with explicit instructions not to roam off. "You've...you've celebrated what I am, and very few can claim that. Like I've said before, you're more than the latest Crown Prince. You're Roth."

For a moment, he didn't move or blink. Then wonderment filled his expression as he stared up at me, and finally, the tension eased out of his muscles. "And I'm yours."

seven

AT SOME POINT, I MANAGED TO TUCK ROTH into bed and Bambi eventually followed. That was quite the spectacle to witness, a blitzed demonic anaconda attempting to slither onto a bed. I had to step in and lift her back end, and then I'd *carefully* scooped up the kitten passed out on the dresser and placed it on the bed, as well. I could only hope Bambi wouldn't eat little Thor if she woke up in the middle of the night with drunken hunger pains.

Then I set about cleaning up the bottles. I stopped counting the ones that had been in the bedroom and took the rattling bag out to the trash. Afterward, I made myself a sandwich and checked in on Stacey.

She was doing as well as could be expected, and she also confirmed that Roth had indeed made an anonymous call. "The police came by this afternoon. Mom thought it was about the house fire, but it was…it was about Sam."

Sitting in the living room, curled up against the back of an oversize cushion, I closed my eyes. "His family…"

"I know." Her breath was shaky through the connection.

"They told me. They also asked if I'd seen him. I went with the last time he'd been at school. Yesterday."

"That was smart."

A pause, and then, "God, Layla, how did any of this happen? Two months ago, I would've never seen any of this coming— Hold on," she said, and I heard a door closing. "My mom has been following me around ever since the police showed up. She's worried and scared. The police think that Sam…that he snapped and wiped out his family. It's going to be all over school tomorrow, and it's not right. You know? That people are going to believe that Sam did something like that."

"It isn't," I agreed, opening my eyes. There was a painting hung on the wall across from me. A picturesque road with autumn on full display, but the bright oranges and reds were dulled. "Sam didn't deserve any of this."

"None of us do." There was another deep inhale on her end. "Okay. I need to be distracted, because otherwise I'm going to lose it again. I've been losing it about every hour, on the hour. Okay? Distract me."

"Um…" My brain emptied. Real helpful there. "Ah, I suck at this."

She laughed hoarsely. "What's Roth doing?"

"Well, he's… Yeah, he's kind of incapacitated right now." I cringed, knowing how that sounded.

"Really?" Interest perked her tone. "Why?"

I glanced at the wide archway. "I told him this morning that I needed to talk to Zayne, and I guess he thought that meant that I was going to tell Zayne I wanted to be with him. So he might have gotten a little drunk."

A strangled giggle came through the phone and my heart lifted at the sound. "Are you serious?"

"Yep. And his familiars? They're drunk, too." I paused, grinning a little. "It was quite the show."

"I can imagine. Nope. Wait. I can't. You need to go get pictures of this for me."

I smiled even though that was not going to happen.

"So…you don't want to be with Zayne? You've been obsessed with him since I met you."

"I wouldn't say *obsessed*." It felt really wrong talking about this with Stacey, but she'd asked to be distracted, so I would do whatever she wanted. "You know I love Zayne. Always have and will, but Roth? He's…"

"He's the one," she said quietly.

"Yeah. As much as he annoys the ever-loving crud out of me, I kind of love that he does. I know that sounds twisted, but it's true." I unfurled my legs and stood, curling one arm around my stomach as I started to pace the length of the room, wearing a little path in the Oriental carpet. "I… I love him, Stacey. I really do."

"I'm not surprised," was her response.

I started to grin again as I made my second pass in front of the couch. "Oh, really?"

"Nope. I've seen the way he looks at you. Seen the way you look at him. It was always different with Zayne. Not knocking him. You know I'd give up my left ovary for a shot at that—God, that's kind of really bad form right now, isn't it? Like too soon even as a joke?" She sighed heavily. "I'm a terrible person."

"No! Oh, gosh no! Don't think that at all, and you're not a terrible person."

"Can…can I ask you something? And you'll answer me honestly?"

I stopped in front of the painting. "Of course."

"Promise," she whispered.

"Promise."

A moment passed before she spoke. "I've been thinking about this a lot. I never really started paying attention to Sam until he started changing, you know? When he started dressing differently and styling his hair. When he started getting confident..."

Oh no.

"And this whole time, all of that, it was never Sam." Her voice cracked a little. "That was that thing pretending to be him. Does that mean I fell for that *thing*, Layla? And not Sam? And what does that say about me?"

"Oh, Stacey...don't go down that path. The truth is, I think you always liked Sam, it just took you a while to recognize it. You didn't fall for the Lilin."

"You sure?" Her voice sounded tiny and so very young.

"I'm sure of that, and look at it this way. The Lilin, it acted like Sam so much that none of us could tell the difference. You thought it was Sam. I thought it was Sam—a version of him that finally figured out how to use a comb."

Stacey's laugh was a pleasant shock to my ears. "Yeah. Okay."

Tiny knots formed in my belly. "You get what I'm saying, right? You don't think that about yourself."

"No. I mean, I just... I needed to hear you say what you said. That's all," she promised, and I hoped she was telling the truth. "When can I see you so I can get the deets about you and Roth in person?"

I wasn't sure what details I could give her since we really

hadn't talked, at least not when both of us were sober. "You going to class on Monday?"

"Probably so. What about you?"

My shoulders slumped. "I really want to, but right now we've got to figure out how to take care of the Lilin, and I've missed so much time."

"Oh, Layla."

I shook my head, not wanting to dwell on that at this moment. "Once everything is squared away, I'll figure something out. Anyway, I can try to come see you after school. Depends on what we do."

We made plans to text each other, but before I got off the phone, she stopped me.

"Layla?"

"Yeah?"

Her sharp inhale was audible. "Promise me that you will help Sam. That we can make this right for him."

My free hand squeezed into a fist, until the tips of my nails dug into my palms. "I promised you I would. I'm not going to break that promise."

Once night had fallen and a quick check assured me that Roth was still asleep, surrounded by snoring familiars, I grabbed a quilt off the foot of the master bed and stepped out onto a balcony that faced some kind of nature reserve.

A small, misty cloud of visible breath parted my lips as I tipped my head back. The night was clear, full of stars that twinkled like a thousand tiny, distant diamonds. I walked to the railing, pulling the blanket closer to me.

My mind wouldn't shut down. So much was cycling over and over. The conversation with Stacey replayed, lingering on her fears. I ached for her, wishing there was something more that I could do, but the only avenue left to me was to free Sam's soul, so I would do it. I already knew where to start—with Grim. I just needed to wait until next week, and that sickened me, because who knew what would happen to Sam's soul between now and then.

We needed to deal with the Lilin, because I knew it wasn't going to go underground for very long, but my thoughts shifted to the demon who'd run from me today and then to my feathered wings. Inevitably, that made me think about the Alphas and why they thought I was such an abomination now, when I'd been entirely tolerable for seventeen years.

I was guessing it had something to do with the wings and the way I shifted.

A star broke away from the masses, shooting across the sky and drawing my attention. When I was younger, I used to think they were angels coming down. Zayne knew better, but he'd humored me and made up stories about how they were guardian angels arriving to protect their charges.

Squeezing my eyes shut, it hurt when I drew in my next breath. I don't know how long I stood out there, but my nose was cold and my lips felt numb by the time I headed inside. Dropping the blanket on the bed, I changed into my pajamas but stopped before I could climb into the bed.

Heart speeding up, I wheeled around and left the room. I didn't give myself time to really think about what I was doing as I walked to the room Roth slept in. Opening the door, I slipped inside and quietly approached the bed.

Roth was lying on his side, facing the door. His lips were slightly parted and his hair was a messy tumble across his forehead. The blanket was shoved down to his lean waist, and I could see that Bambi had found her way back to him. She rested in tattoo form along his left arm. It looked like a part of her was on his back, but I couldn't see to be completely sure. I didn't see the kittens but I knew from experience that they could be anywhere, ready to pounce on my feet and ankles.

I didn't want to go back to my bed, alone with all my thoughts. I wanted to be here, with him. With my heart lodged somewhere in my throat, I darted over to the bed, lifted the blanket and climbed in.

The movements didn't wake Roth, and for that, I was relieved, because I felt weird, sneaking into his bed like an all-star creeper. Rolled on my side, facing him, I took the creeper status to a whole new level as I let my gaze roam over his face. My fingers itched to trace the line of his cheek, but I kept my hands folded up under my chin, and after a few minutes, all the whirling thoughts in my head calmed. Being near him, well, it settled me in a way I so desperately needed.

While I listened to his steady and even breaths, my eyes drifted shut. Only a few minutes later, as I started to fall asleep, I heard what sounded like a mini engine humming, coming from the other side of Roth. It took me a second to realize that it was one of those devil kittens, and despite how evil they were, a smile tugged at my lips.

I slept deeply, lulled by the nearby warmth of Roth's body, and I wasn't sure how many hours had passed when I felt an arm snag me around the waist and tug me to the side. The front of me hit a hard chest, and I blinked my eyes open.

Amber eyes stared into mine. "Morning."

His voice was rough with sleep and his breath was minty, as if he'd brushed his teeth before crawling back into bed.

Sleep clung to my thoughts as I dragged my gaze up. His hair was damp.

He must've read my confusion in my face. "I freshened up," he explained. Lifting one hand, he caught a strand of my hair with his fingers and tucked it behind my ear. "You were dead to the world when I woke up. Thought I'd use the time to erase the funk that lingered from last night." His gaze moved over my face as the tips of his fingers trailed a path along the line of my brow. "I have to admit, waking up and finding you in my bed was a pleasant surprise."

My tongue came unstuck. "It was?"

"Yeah." His finger now traced my nose. "When I woke up, I realized I'd never done that before. Not with you. Not with anyone. I always..."

The few times I'd fallen asleep in bed with him, he'd always been gone when I woke up, with the exception of the time I was healing, but he didn't seem to count that and neither did I.

A strange smile played across his lips. Not strange in a bad way, but just one I'd never seen from him before. It oozed boyish charm. "I liked it so much that I'm now spoiled. One morning and I'm spoiled for life. I want you here every morning, with me. Well, maybe in the master bedroom. That bed is more comfortable."

The haze of sleep was easing away, and I found myself grinning at him like an utter doofus. "I thought this bed was nice."

"Because I was in it?"

"Wow." My goofy grin spread. "Good to see your ego is still functioning normally."

Dragging his finger over my brow, he chuckled deeply. The sound faded, as did his grin. "About last night? I'm... I'm sorry about that," he said, struggling with the apology, and for some reason that made me want to giggle. Demons did not apologize easily. The word *sorry* wasn't in their vocab. "I honestly thought you were leaving and I got myself shit-faced so I wouldn't go after you. That's not an excuse. I know, but I really am sah…sorry about that."

"It's okay. You were cute."

"Cute?" His fingers had made their way to my jaw. "I prefer sexy beast."

A giggle finally escaped me. "Sorry, I'm pretty sure that description is reserved for Thumper."

His gaze searched mine as his fingers stopped on my chin, right under the center of my lips. "How are you doing?" When I didn't answer, he smoothed his thumb along my lower lip. "I can put two and two together. You talked to Zayne yesterday afternoon and you're waking up with me today. I know it couldn't have been easy for you."

"It wasn't," I whispered, thinking of the anguish I'd seen in Zayne's expression. Those were a part of the thoughts that haunted me last night.

Light beamed through the crack in the thick curtains beyond the bed, caressing his cheek. "So how are you?"

At first I started to tell him that I was okay, but that would be a lie. Sort of. And I didn't want there to be any more lies between us. "It was hard," I admitted, placing my hand on his chest. He jerked a little, and I liked that—that my touch had that kind of effect. "Probably one of the hardest things I've had to do, because I care about him. I love him and I never wanted to hurt him. Ever."

"I know." His lips brushed my forehead. "Losing you would not be easy, but I think…"

"What?" I let *my* fingers do a bit of exploring. It was strange,

I thought, as I drew a circle around his chest, that touching him like this was kind of empowering. Not in the same way holding my ground against Raver demons or standing up to my clan was, but it was still a heady sensation.

"I can't believe I'm going to say this," he confided with a sigh. "Stony is a good guy, but he's probably going to need his space."

I closed my eyes briefly. "Yeah, I know."

The arm around my waist tightened. "Can we do something?"

My fingers stopped on the first tightly rolled ab. "Um."

"Dirty girl, get your mind out of the gutter. I wasn't talking about that stuff. Yet," he added in a way that made my tummy tighten. "What I meant was, can we start last night over?"

I didn't get it. "How so?"

"I was plastered, but I think you told me you wanted to be with me, and well, I want to hear you say that again."

My heart did a backflip and I tilted my head back, so that our mouths were close. "I want to be here with you." The arm around me tightened even more, sealing me to his chest like he had last night, and once again, I really liked it. "I want to be with you."

Roth pressed his forehead against mine as he rolled slightly onto his back, bringing me with him. I ended up lying half on him, both hands braced on his chest and my legs tangled in his. The arm on my waist was unshakable and the hand curled around the nape of my neck sent a riot of sensations skittering down my spine.

But I wasn't done. Staring into eyes that were as bright and beautiful as any tawny jewel, I said what I had never said before. And I said it with every ounce of my being behind it.

"I love you, Roth." My voice shook with emotion. "I'm in love with you."

Roth shifted again. This time I was on my back and he was above me, his one leg thrust between mine and his hand still cradling my neck. "Say it one more time," he pleaded in a voice barely above a whisper.

"I love you. I love you." And I said it again and again, until I couldn't say it anymore, because he'd silenced me with his mouth.

The kiss was nothing like last night. His lips were gentle on mine, a sweet sweep that was at such odds with his enormous strength, and I felt it in every part of me. He kissed me softly, and then lifted up just enough so that I could see him. Tugging my hand off his shoulder, he clasped his fingers around mine and drew our joined hands to his chest and pressed them together. I could feel his heart beating strongly.

"I covet you like any good demon would." His other hand tightened at the back of my neck. "And my desire for you increases every waking second in a way that should frighten me, but really just excites me. But most of all, I love you," he said, and my entire body jolted at the words. He didn't seem to notice. "I, Astaroth, Crown Prince of Hell, am in love with you, Layla Shaw. Yesterday. Today. Tomorrow. A hundred decades from now, I will still be in love with you, and it will be as fierce today as it will be a decade later."

Hearing his words was like bear-hugging the sun. Warmth poured into me and he drove those words home with a kiss that went beyond the soft, questing one we'd just shared. It was deep and thorough, and I felt like he was claiming me and I was claiming him in return. That finally, after all this time, we'd destroyed that line between us and there was no going back.

"I love you" was said over and over, in between kisses and then in between the moans those kisses eventually wrought from us. Even when we moved beyond the words, it was screamed in every kiss and touch.

Dropping our hands, Roth gripped my hip as he pressed his body to mine. The thin pajama bottoms offered no real barrier between us, not when we were so greedy for each other. I wanted him, so badly that I ached in a way that had to be physical, totally was physical, but it went further, deeper, tattooing my skin, carving out my muscle and etching into my bones. And he had to feel the same, because I could feel how much he wanted this with every roll of his hips and when he slipped his hand under my shirt, dragging the material up and up, I could barely breathe. My heart jackhammered as he rose up on one arm and stared down at me.

I was bare from the waist up, and while this wasn't the first time he'd seen so much of me, a nest of cannibalistic butterflies started flapping their wings in my belly. My experience in these situations was limited, but the stark hunger in his fiery gaze was evident and I knew in the very core of my being that he was thrilled with what he saw.

And he proved it with his words.

"Beautiful," he said, voice thick as he lightly trailed his fingers across my belly. I jerked, and then bit down on my lip. "You are so beautiful, Layla. And if I could pick one thing I could stare at for the rest of eternity, it would be you."

My heart swelled so fast and so big I thought I'd float right up to the ceiling and into the stars. Maybe even to the Heavens themselves.

Roth's fingers drifted up, his caress reverent. "It would always be you."

Then he was kissing me again, and these kisses, these moments were precious, powerful and beautiful in their own way.

Roth's lips skated over my cheek toward my ear, and he whispered words that sent a heady flush across my skin and caused my muscles to curl in a strange, delightful way. When he lifted his head, his gaze was questioning, wanting and a thousand other things.

I nodded.

One side of his lips tipped up, and then he said, "Thank you."

Not a single part of me understood why he was thanking me, but then all thoughts flew out the window, because he kissed the corner of my lips, and then started a line of tiny kisses that trailed from my chin down my throat and then farther still.

My fingers dug into the comforter when he stopped, and then lingered, drawing a stuttered gasp from me. I really didn't get why he was thanking me while he was doing this, because it should truly be the other way around.

His lips skimmed over my ribs. "I think we need to get you a tattoo."

It took me a few minutes for his words to make sense. "A…a tattoo?"

"Yeah." He kissed just above my belly button. "A familiar."

"I can do that?"

Roth lifted his chin and grinned in a way that caused my heart to flop around. "I don't see why not, and I know who can do one for you." His gaze traveled down the length of me, sending a shiver dancing over my skin. "This would be a good spot." He dragged his hand over the side of my ribs. "Or here?" That same hand made its way under the band of my pajama bottoms and curled around my hip. His gaze heated. "I really like the idea of it being here."

"Does it really matter where it's inked on?" I asked. "It's going to move anyway, right?"

"Oh, it matters." He kissed the spot below my navel. "Mostly just matters to me."

I laughed. "Okay, then."

Grinning, he rose once more, climbing over me. His arms were huge and powerful and his hands came down on either side of my head. My breath caught as his lips took control of mine. I wrapped my arms around him, holding him close. His tongue swept over mine, and the taste of him drove me crazy.

Roth went on the move again, sliding down once more. My fingers played in his hair, and I could no longer keep track of where he was heading, because he obliterated any comprehensive thinking skills.

I don't even know how my bottoms came off or where they ended up. It was like magic. Roth was magic. He also had this delightful mischievous tilt to his lip as his hands traveled up the outside of my thighs. There was nothing between my skin and his hands, and I could feel every touch and even the softest caress was like being hit by volts of electricity.

"Shortie?"

I loosened my grip on his hair, letting my hands fall back to the comforter. "Yeah?"

"What about getting a tat here?" He kissed the side of my thigh, right above my knee, on the inside. "It's a very interesting place. I like it."

I bit down on my lower lip. "I'm sure you do."

His eyes flared a bright ocher. "You know what else I've been thinking?"

With him, it was anyone's guess.

"I think I'm going to have to make it official. You know, me being the president of the demon horde Layla fan club."

A laugh burst out of me. "What are you going to do? Make yourself a shirt that says you're the official president?"

"And buttons. I'm totally going to make myself some buttons."

I started to laugh, but his fingers found the thin material— the only thing left on me—and things were most definitely going further than they had before. I was nervous, but I also trusted him. I remembered what he'd whispered in my ear earlier. I knew this would only go so far. Before my nerves could get the better of me, his lips were where his hands were, and I was no longer thinking about anything. There was only feeling—just him and the crazy, beautiful rush of sensations he coaxed out of me. He was a master at it, absolutely brilliant, because I didn't feel like me. I didn't shake and tremble like this and those soft noises were so not coming from me. I was like a piece of cloth being pulled too tight, until suddenly all the tension broke, and I was caught in the whirlwind, thrown so very high, I could kiss the stars.

Roth slowly rose, wiggling an arm under me and pulling me against his chest. When I opened my eyes, he looked like he'd had his mind blown, but that was strange, because he was the one doing all the mind-blowing. I was the one on the receiving end.

"That…" My tongue didn't want to work. "That was amazing."

His smile was part arrogance, like he already knew exactly

how awesome that was, but there was something boyish about the curve of his lips. He stretched out beside me, keeping me close. He lowered his head, kissing me softly, and I was boneless and weak in his arms.

His mouth was hot against my damp brow. "I want an eternity of mornings like this." He dropped a kiss next to my ear. "An eternity."

A chill blew through me as my eyes popped open. The happy glow dulled and the haze scattered. I suddenly realized something very important, something that neither of us had even thought of at this point. Roth would never grow any older. For as long as he walked this earth, he would look as he did today, while I would age and die like any other mortal out there thanks to my Warden blood.

Roth had an eternity.

I didn't.

eight

THE CHILLED, UNSETTLED FEELING FOLLOWED me the rest of the morning and I hated that, because Roth and I were finally on the same page for the first time, and what we had done—what *he* had done—was frankly amazing and beautiful, and yes, I would want an eternity of mornings like that. Now I felt haunted, as if there was a shadow looming over us, turning infinite time into minutes or seconds. Which was stupid, because I recognized that I had a long, long time before I needed to worry about the awkwardness of a hot guy spending time with me when I was well into my golden years.

But I kept picturing Roth looking as fine and fresh as he did this morning while he rolled out of bed and cast a knowing grin in my direction. In my head, I didn't look like I did right now. Instead, I had gray hair, a face that rivaled one of those dogs who had wrinkled skin and a hunched-over back. And instead of doing what we did this morning, we'd spend time playing bingo.

I kind of liked bingo, though.

Anyway, the whole thing went well beyond uncomfortable.

There were more pressing issues we needed to address now, which was why we were gathered in the kitchen with Cayman and another demon I'd never met before but who went by the name Edward. I seriously doubted that was the blond's real name, because the name Edward really didn't strike fear in the heart of anyone.

Cayman was sitting on the counter near the sink, swinging his feet like he was at the playground. I was at the island, having eaten my weight in sausage, and Roth was standing next to me. When we'd walked into the kitchen together, I'd half expected Cayman to whip out a camera and start taking pictures of us. His expression had been downright gleeful. I was doing my best not to look at Roth in that moment, because when I did, I thought about what he did this morning and what we hadn't done, and then I went all red-faced. Things might've progressed further if Roth hadn't sensed the other demon's presence, forcing us to leave the bedroom to investigate.

Edward stood by Cayman and his eyes carried an odd light that was reflected when he tilted his head a certain way. He definitely wasn't an Upper Level demon, and I thought he might be a Fiend.

"So, what's on the menu today, kids?" Cayman asked.

Roth's slow grin sent fire across my cheeks as he cast a long glance in my direction. He opened his mouth, but the look I sent him promised murder if he answered that question the way I thought he might.

He chuckled as he propped his hip against the counter. "I figure we need to hit the city, start searching out areas that we think the Lilin might be holed up in. The Wardens are doing the same, but I doubt they're going to be successful."

"The Lilin will sense them coming a mile away," Edward agreed. "While we sort of blend in with the demon masses, at least until we get a chance to get close."

I folded my arms across my belly, where Bambi was currently residing after making her way there when we left the bedroom. I thought about how the Upper Level demon reacted to me yesterday, then pushed the memory aside. "Do you think the witches that worship Lilith would be harboring the Lilin?"

Cayman shook his head. "I don't think so. They're obsessed with your mother, but they know how risky it would be to give something as evil as the Lilin shelter."

Normally, having Lilith referred to as my mother would send me into an epic tizzy of unheard-of proportions, but now it was just...well, it was just the truth. Lilith was my mom, whether I wanted her to be or not. "But would any demon give it shelter at this point?" I asked.

"Not a smart one." Roth shifted, placing a hand on my lower back. Though I wore a sweater, one of the horribly skintight ones Cayman had picked up from a corner somewhere no doubt, the weight of his hand still seared my skin. "They would have to know that not only will the Wardens be gunning for the Lilin, so will the Boss, and by extension, so will I, and they really don't want to get on my bad side."

"Aren't you one bad mamajama—" Edward leaned back against the counter and his elbow brushed the coffeemaker. I jerked on the stool when the machine suddenly sparked, the smell of burnt ozone filling the kitchen as he glanced over his shoulder. The pot cracked straight down the middle as Edward faced us. "Uh, sorry about that."

Yep. Most definitely a Fiend.

Roth scowled. "You're going to have that replaced by tomorrow morning."

The demon grimaced. "Yes, sir."

Sir? Lowering my gaze to the countertop, I pressed my lips together to stop from grinning.

"None of the Fiends will help the Lilin. I can assure you of that," Edward continued, shaking off his embarrassment, and I wondered if he was some sort of spokesperson for his kind.

There was still so much I didn't know about the demon population, and that made me squirm in my seat. I had tagged so many of them in the past, sentencing them back to Hell, and I figured that the Boss didn't appreciate failure of any kind. Did the Boss punish Fiends like the one in the room with us, whose only crime appeared to be massacring appliances? Guilt churned.

Exhaling softly, I glanced up as I scooped my hair up and started twisting it for no reason other than to have something to do with my hands. "Well, this is a big city. We can't just start roaming around aimlessly."

"Damn," murmured Cayman. He winked. "I was looking forward to that."

I rolled my eyes. "What we need to do is start tracking any suspicious deaths—otherwise healthy people dropping dead. I doubt the Lilin is just going to sit around and do nothing. If it starts pulling souls, the bodies have to pile up."

"Good idea," Edward said.

"That's my girl." Roth placed his fingers under my chin, tipping my head back and to the side. His lips were on mine in a nanosecond, and at first, I stiffened. I wasn't used to being kissed in front of others. I wasn't all that used to being kissed, period. Our relationship was so new, less than twenty-four hours, but his kisses had this ability to melt reservations and concerns. I softened, and the room fell away. He kissed me like there was no one else around us, but we weren't alone.

Someone cleared his throat, and then Cayman groaned, "Really, guys?"

My face was burning as I pulled away, but Roth was unfazed. "What?" he asked.

"While I'm glad you guys have decided to become the twosome of the year, I really don't want to see you sucking face," Cayman commented. I wasn't sure I believed him since he was all Team Roth. "It does things to my indigestion. Bad things."

"I don't mind," Edward said.

My eyes widened. Okay. That was weird and...and gross.

Roth straightened, but dropped his arm around my shoulders. "Cayman, you can keep an eye out on the morgues and hospitals, and Eddie-boy, keep your eyes on the clubs throughout the city. Just don't touch anything."

The Fiend actually looked sheepish as he nodded.

"What are we going to do?" I asked, and when Roth's eyes deepened, I knew what direction he was heading in. Reaching up, I placed my hand on his mouth. "Don't."

He nipped at my fingers and grinned when I pulled my hand away. "There's a couple of places we should check out."

We all started to part ways at that point, and it felt good to be doing something other than sitting around. I headed into the living room to grab a hair tie I'd left on the end table. Picking it up, I turned around to find Cayman standing a foot away.

"You still want to see Grim next week, Layla-Low-Bottom-Butts?" he asked.

I stared at him a moment, letting that nickname sink in, and then I glanced at the doorway. "Yes, but I haven't said anything to Roth yet."

"I wouldn't, because he's not going to be down with it." He kept his voice low while he spoke fast. "Remember, sweet pea. I told you that the Boss isn't entirely pleased with him. He goes down there, they're going to keep him detained. You don't want that."

My stomach hollowed as I stepped closer to Cayman. "Can the Boss just come up and get him if he wants to?"

He tilted his head to the side. "Yes, but it's doubtful right now. Later? Who knows? I can distract Roth next Friday and give you time to get down there, but once you're there, you're going to have to hurry."

"Hurry? In case you've forgotten, I've never been to Hell so I have no idea what the landscape is like," I pointed out, trying not to freak out over the fact that I was going to go to Hell. Literally. "Need a little bit of direction here."

Cayman grinned. "It's easier than you think. Trust me, butterball. You'll know exactly where to go once you get there." Then he winked. "By the way, I'm proud of you. You made the right decision yesterday, choosing the future—choosing Roth."

I opened my mouth, but he was gone before I could say a word. Turning slowly, I looked around the now-empty room. "I hate it when he does that."

"What?"

Jumping at the sound of Roth's voice, I couldn't say I was that surprised to find him standing a foot behind me. "That!

You guys just popping in and out of rooms. It's freaky and unnatural."

"You're just jealous because you can't do that."

I rolled my eyes, but he was kind of right. I was sort of jealous of not having that nifty ability. If I did, I would be popping here, there and everywhere. Bambi chose that moment to switch positions. She slithered around my waist, resting her head along my ribs. I'd also pop her butt on the couch when she got antsy.

"What was Cayman doing in here?" Roth picked up a strand of my hair and started roping the length around his finger.

The idea of lying to Roth, especially after everything, made me feel like I'd just bathed in grime, but I knew if I told him what I planned to do about Sam's soul, he wouldn't let me go down there alone, and maybe not at all. I couldn't allow him to stop me. And this was more than just protecting Roth from an unhappy Boss. Saving Sam's soul was bigger than what either of us wanted.

"He was just being Cayman," I said finally.

Roth tugged on the strand of hair he'd wrapped around his finger, guiding me closer to him. "That's a loaded statement." His eyes met mine, and my heart sped up. Leaning down, he rested his forehead against mine. "Guess what?"

"What?"

"If you behave yourself today, I have a surprise for you later."

My lips curved up. "If I behave myself?"

"Uh-huh." He kissed my brow as he straightened, letting go of my hair. "And by behaving yourself, I mean being as naughty as you can possibly be."

Laughing, I gathered up my hair, twisting it into a quick bun. "I'm not sure I can be that naughty if we're in public, looking for the Lilin."

"There's always time for naughtiness, Shortie."

"I'm not surprised that you believe this."

He shot me a look. "When have any of my beliefs been wrong?"

I arched a brow. "Many, many times."

"I think you have a distorted memory," he returned, and I laughed again, missing this—the playful banter—and I was relieved to see that it hadn't been tarnished by everything it had taken us to get to this point.

"Keep telling yourself that." I smiled when he pouted. "Before any surprises, I want to swing by and see Stacey."

"Can do." He lifted his hand, brushing his knuckles across my cheek, and it was another thing about Roth that had never changed, not even when we were apart. He was definitely a touchy-feely kind of demon. "You want to visit her alone?"

His thoughtfulness didn't really surprise me anymore. Not that it didn't still wow me, because it did, and my heart was doing that swelling thing again, but I couldn't figure out how he didn't see his own goodness. I stretched up and kissed the corner of his lips before settling back down. "I think she'll be happy to see you."

"Of course she will be," he murmured, his gaze lingering on my lips. I shivered even though I wasn't cold. Nope. Not at all. "Everyone is happy to see me."

I shook my head. "You ready?" When he nodded, I smiled up at him. "Are you going to tell me where we're going?"

"I would, but that would ruin the fun." He chuckled as my smile slipped into a frown. "Okay. We aren't going anywhere. Well, anywhere in particular. We are going to roam the streets aimlessly."

"Wow. That's a stellar plan."

He bit down on his lower lip as he grinned. "Actually, it's pretty damn clever."

"That's yet to be seen."

Roth grabbed my hand and started to lead me toward the front door. "Here's the deal. I don't think we're going to have to look too hard for the Lilin. Actually, I don't think *you* are going to have to seek the Lilin out."

"And why's that?"

He looked over his shoulder at me, all humor vanishing from his face. "Because I believe the Lilin is going to come looking for *you*."

nine

NOTHING LIKE HEARING A PSYCHOTIC DEMON that you'd unwillingly helped create would be looking for you to make you feel like you needed to enter the creeper relocation program.

But I hoped Roth was correct, because it would make finding the tool easier.

Since it was the afternoon, we drove into the city and parked the car in one of the parking garages. We didn't have great luck when it came to those particular structures, but hitting the sky was out of the question in the daylight. While the city's human residents were all too aware of the Wardens and Roth was similar enough to them in his true form, if a human looked too closely at him, questions would arise that we weren't prepared to answer.

Roth glanced at me as I opened the door. "You didn't bring a jacket?"

I shook my head.

He closed the driver's door. "A scarf?"

"No."

"What about mittens?"

My lips twitched. "Nope."

He eyed me as I walked around the front of the car. "What about a little beanie for your little head?"

I laughed. "No, *Dad*. I'm fine."

His eyes glittered. "I like it when you call me—"

"Stop."

He tilted his head to the side. "On a serious note, it's cold out there, Shortie."

That much I already knew. Roth was wearing only a long-sleeved shirt and jeans, because like full-blooded Wardens, his internal temperature was somewhere between steaming and boiling. One would think because I was a mixture of both, I would also have a high tolerance for the cold, but I never did.

Until now, I guessed. It couldn't be more than forty degrees. "I'm not cold."

A strange look crossed his features as he watched me intently. "Odd."

There were odder things about me, say, for example, my *feathered* wings. There wasn't a damn thing normal about that, and as Roth and I safely made it out of the parking garage on F Street, I brought them up.

"So..." I drew the word out as I stepped around a herd of young kids in uniforms and soft, white auras being ushered toward a bus idling at the curb. The packed sidewalk was an array of colors and my attention was immediately drawn to those with darker shades, the crimson reds and plums. Most were suits, clutching briefcases. They had sinned, and sinned in a very bad way. My stomach tightened with need, but the urge was nowhere near as intense as it used to be, and that also confounded me.

Roth took my hand, threading his fingers through mine. My heart got all giddy. I remembered a time when I would've yanked my hand away from his so fast his head would've spun. "What?" he asked.

I was distracted by the fact we were legit holding hands, walking down the crowded sidewalk like a...like a real couple, a normal couple. Air hitched in my throat. This was the first time we were holding hands as a couple, and even though we hadn't called each other boyfriend or girlfriend, we were so that.

A goofy, stupid grin tugged at my lips and as my gaze danced over the people rushing to get wherever they were going, I stopped fighting it. I smiled so widely there was a good chance my face would split right up the middle.

In that second, I didn't think about the ugliness with Zayne or the Lilin or my feathered wings or the thousand other troubles waiting to pounce on us. That happiness in the pit of my belly spread rapidly, like a levee breaking, the warmth whooshing through me. My steps suddenly felt lighter, and I wanted to stop in the middle of the sidewalk, grab Roth's face and plant one on him. How many times had I wanted him to do that before? Even when I'd been pushing him away, I'd wanted him. Now he was mine.

"Layla?" Roth squeezed my hand. "What are you smiling about? Not that I'm complaining. That's a freaking beautiful smile, and it makes me—"

I did what I wanted to do.

Stopping in the middle of the sidewalk, I ignored the harsh glances cast in our direction, and no one said a thing to us after receiving one look from Roth. I stretched on the tips of my toes. With my free hand wrapped around the nape of his neck,

I guided his head down. Surprise flickered across his face, and then I closed my eyes, pressing my mouth to his. The kiss was brief, but when I pulled away, his expression made my day.

He stared down at me, his eyes wide and the pupils slightly dilated. His lips were parted and that bolt in his tongue glittered. The tops of his cheekbones were flushed. He looked... He looked gobsmacked.

"What...what was that for?"

My smile really was going to break my face. "Just because... well, there were so many times that I secretly wished you'd done that in the past, and I thought, why can't I?"

His gaze searched my face. "I just want you to know that whenever you feel the need to do that, you do it. I don't care what we're doing, I'm always going to be down for that. Always."

It was my turn to flush, but I focused on the important stuff as we started walking again. Knowing no one would pay attention to what I said, because they heard way stranger stuff on the streets of DC, I forged forward. "So, what do you think about my *feathered* wings?"

He gave a choked laugh. "I like the way you say *feathered*."

I made a face.

"I think they're kind of hot," he added.

I rolled my eyes as we stopped at an intersection. "Of course you do, but that really doesn't tell me much. I mean, that's not normal, right? I know Zayne has seen them before, and so have you, but he said he'd only seen them once, on an Upper. And why now? Why would I look different now after all this time?"

A thoughtful look crossed his face as we waited for the light to turn. "Well, you only started shifting recently. Maybe this was how you were supposed to look."

"Doubtful," I muttered, and as the little green man lit up on the sign, I started forward.

"Yeah, I was just trying to be optimistic." Roth slowed his long-legged pace as he scanned the crowds around us. A horn blew, followed by another, and the scent of roasted meat was strong as we passed a yummy-looking restaurant. "Look, I've seen wings like that before, but it doesn't make sense."

"Why doesn't—?" I cut myself off as I caught a glimpse of brilliant white reflecting off the windowed front of an office building. I stopped, my heart speeding up as I searched for its source.

Roth immediately sensed the change. "What?"

"I see an all-white aura," I explained, walking again as I strained to catch sight of it through the dizzying shades passing us. "It was dazzling, way too bright to be a human."

"A Warden?"

I nodded. It had to be a Warden, unless it was an Alpha. Though I doubted the latter would be roaming the streets. As far as I knew, they looked the way they did all the time, and there was no hiding those wings.

Roth's hand tightened around mine, and a general sense of alarm took root in my stomach. It could be any Warden, but if I'd caught sight of their aura, they could've sensed Roth and me in turn. If it was Nicolai or Dez out there, I thought they'd approach. Maybe not Zayne at this point, and that killed me to even acknowledge.

We walked another block, silent and on alert. Just as we were several feet from an alley, I felt the awareness. The Warden was nearby.

Roth's chin dipped down. "You feel that?"

I nodded, and as we crossed the mouth of the alley, I caught sight of brilliant white again, and my head swung sharply to the right. All the way toward the back of the alley, there was a huge source of pearly goodness. The aura faded and I caught a glimpse of what existed beyond the glow.

Ice shot down my spine as I sucked in a sharp breath. Even from across the distance, I recognized that face. Who wouldn't? The jagged scar that sliced from the corner of his eye to his lips was unmistakable.

It was Elijah.

My father.

In the back of my head, it registered somewhat dimly how misleading that white aura was. He had wanted me dead my whole life, his own daughter. But Wardens had pure souls, no matter what sins stained them.

Slipping my hand free from Roth's, I didn't think as I shot down the alley, racing toward the back where I'd seen him. I didn't know why I was even chasing after him. I hadn't seen him since he'd ordered his son, my half brother, to take me out. When Petr had vanished, Elijah had disappeared, and back then, I'd been under the protection of my clan. Not so much anymore.

But I didn't need their protection now.

Right now none of us needed Elijah skulking around the city. We had enough problems, and if he was here to mess with me, which he had to be, I'd rather deal with him now instead of looking over my shoulder, waiting for him to strike.

"Dammit," I heard Roth growl just before he took off after me.

I was fast when I wanted to be, but as I rounded the back of the alley, my target wasn't there. My head jerked up. Elijah was scaling the fire escape at a rapid clip, the dark trench coat he wore whipping out behind him.

"This could be a trap," Roth reasoned as he caught up to me, staring up toward the rooftop. He wasn't telling me anything I didn't already know. "Layla, we need to think about this."

"We don't need to deal with him haunting us. It's bad enough that his son has been doing so as a wraith." I turned to him. "That's the last thing any of us need to be worried about."

"Shortie…"

I met his stare for a moment and then I spun around. Running to the fire escape, I jumped and caught the rail. My body swung to the side and then back. My feet hit the ladder.

"Okay," Roth called out from behind me. "You're crazy, but that was also crazy hot." He grunted as he landed on the ladder behind me. "Just thought I'd share that with you."

I flew up the ladder, determined. It took only seconds to climb what had to be at least ten stories, and in the back of my mind, I wondered how that was possible. I'd always been faster and stronger than a human, but not like this. Now just wasn't the time to really delve into why.

Reaching the top of the ladder, I propelled myself over the ledge, landing in a crouch. My eyes widened as I took in the scene before me and my stomach dropped a little.

Ah, Roth might've been right.

He landed beside me, cursing under his breath as we both rose. Standing at the other end of the rooftop was Elijah. He wasn't alone. Three Wardens were with him. I recognized them from when his clan had visited the compound.

Wind whipped across the roof, blowing Elijah's jacket out around him as his cold gaze centered on me. An ugly, hateful emotion rose within me, spreading through my veins like battery acid. "Hello, *Dad*."

Surprise etched into his harsh features. It was brief, gone when his lips curved into a sneer, distorting the ragged scar. "Do not call me that."

"Why?" I asked as Roth moved closer to me, but I was focused on this being who was supposed to love me. Wasn't that what mothers and fathers did, like innately? Why were mine the exception to the rule? "You're my father."

One of the other Wardens, a tall, dark-haired man, glanced at Elijah questioningly. Did they not know? A horrible smile pulled at my lips and it was without any warmth. Instead, it was full of scorn and seventeen years of wondering. "Yeah, maybe you remember how you hooked up with Lilith—*the* Lilith—"

"Shut up," he hissed, his hands forming meaty fists.

A low grumble of warning rumbled from Roth as a blast of heat rolled off him, but my smile, it spread. "And the two of you produced little old me. What? You didn't think I knew?"

Two of the Wardens behind him exchanged uncertain looks. "What?" I repeated. "They didn't know?"

"That doesn't matter." His nose began to flatten and his jaw lengthened, extending to make room for the massive fangs that could cut effortlessly through steel and marble.

"It doesn't?" I knew I was pushing him. His fury was a tangible third party on this rooftop. I could practically reach out and touch it, but I was too focused on my own anger to be afraid. After all this time, I was finally able to confront him. It was like a secret fantasy of mine was finally coming true. "You boinked Lilith."

"Boinked?" Roth chuckled under his breath and then said, "God, I love you."

Elijah jumped on that comment. "Love? From a demon? Are you serious?"

"Don't," I warned, feeling the space below my neck start to tingle. "Don't try to act like you know anything about love. You're no better than me, and you're sure as Hell no better than him. He's a thousand times better than you could ever hope to be."

Elijah snorted. "Him? A demon? You are—"

"He's the Crown Prince," I snapped, my hands curling tight. "Not *just* a demon. But even if he was merely a Fiend, he'd still be too good for the likes of you."

"That's my girl," Roth murmured.

"Why are you here?" I demanded, fueled by an anger that burned so deep and so bright, it was like it was my own personal sun. "Wait, let me guess. You want to kill me?"

"I was tracking you. I knew that eventually you'd resurface." His skin started to darken. "And I should've taken care of this when you were nothing but a babe. I should've known the moment that bitch left you with me that you weren't right. You'd be just like the whore—"

"Proceed very carefully with what you're about to say," Roth advised softly. "That's my girl you're about to insult, and I'm not going to be happy about that. At all."

"Whatever." I forced a shrug. Yeah, what Elijah had said stung, but I was so over my daddy issues. "Same stuff. Different day. Try something new next time."

The dark-haired Warden behind Elijah bared his fangs, but Elijah cut him off.

"I cannot say I'm surprised to find you with a demon."

Roth stepped forward, positioning himself between Elijah and me. "I cannot say I'm surprised to find you're just as ugly as your son. Oh, wait. Dead son. My bad."

Elijah's chilled gaze swung in his direction. "Do not speak of my son."

"I won't speak of him, only because he's worse than the scum that lines the streets below," Roth said, his voice eerily calm. "But do you want to know what I did with his spine after I tore it from his body?"

That did it.

Mostly because after I'd taken Petr's soul in self-defense, Roth had removed Petr's spine from his body, and I was guessing Elijah had figured that out.

The Wardens shifted. Clothing ripped as bodies expanded and skin hardened. Wings spread and claws appeared. The trench Elijah wore shredded up the back. He was impressive in his true form. Horns parted his dark hair.

"I'm going to end both of you," he promised.

"Please," laughed Roth.

Then Roth went all kinds of badass. He didn't shift. He didn't need to at this point, because he didn't feel that they were a big enough threat to warrant it.

The dark-haired Warden rushed forward and Roth dropped low, kicking out and catching the Warden at the kneecaps, knocking his legs right out from under him. His heavy weight shook the roof, but he was only down for half a second. Back on his feet, he swung at Roth, but he was fast as lightning. Roth ducked under the Warden's outstretched arm and popped up behind him. He planted his booted foot into the back of the Warden, bringing him to his knees.

Over the Warden's head, Roth looked up and winked at me.

Winked at me in the middle of a fight.

Wow.

The other two Wardens charged Roth, and my heart seized as one nearly reached him. He spun. Red light pulsed from his palm. Like his fingers were made of gasoline, fire licked over his hand and then shot out like a missile, narrowly missing the Warden.

Elijah started toward me.

"Bambi!" I summoned the familiar. "Help Roth."

There was a tickle above my belly button and then from under the hem of my sweater, a twisty, dark shadow floated out and spilled into the space in front of me. The shadow broke into a million marble-size balls, bouncing silently off the rooftop. They shot toward one another, piecing together rapidly.

Bambi raised her diamond-shaped head, her red eyes glimmering in the sunlight. Her mouth opened, revealing fangs the size of my hand. She looked hungry.

Then again, Bambi always looked hungry.

The snake shot across the rooftop, heading right for a lighter-haired Warden. Roth whirled out of the way as Bambi struck, nailing the Warden in the throat. There was a high-pitched yelping sound.

Roth's low laugh sent chills over my skin as he moved toward the third Warden, toying with him, clearly enjoying himself. He was sort of beautiful to watch, the grace in the way he moved, almost like a dancer performing on stage.

"You defile your body with familiars now?" Elijah's voice was laden with disgust.

"Really? Do I need to repeat myself? You hooked up with Lilith!"

Elijah snarled. "And I regret giving you creation with every single breath I take. Just as I'm sure Abbot has regretted saving your life."

Ouch. That— Okay, that cut deeper than I thought, and I flinched, because the wound was so raw. But that pain gave way to something red-hot in me. Muscles in my stomach and legs tightened, and I let the shift come over me.

It was on like Donkey Kong.

Cool air hit my back as my shirt tore at the collar. My wings unfurled, arcing behind me as I felt my skin harden as if it was icing over.

Elijah immediately drew up short, his mouth dropping open. "What the…?"

"Yeah. My wings are *feathered* now. It's weird. I know."

He shook his head as he took a step back from me— literally backed away. Instead of gawking over that, I used it to my advantage. Relying on all the offensive techniques that Zayne had showed me over the years, I harnessed the power in my legs and my core. I spun around, faster than I had ever moved before, and kicked out and up, catching Elijah in the chest.

The blow staggered him, but that was a small victory. Throwing a punch that would make a boxer proud, I cold-cocked Elijah in the jaw, snapping his head back. Pain burst across my hand, but I ignored it as I looked up, meeting Roth's gaze.

"Damn," he said, not taking his eyes off me as his hand snapped out, catching the Warden by the throat. Pride and something far deeper churned in those tawny depths. "Still hot as Hell."

I flashed a quick grin in his direction before I turned back to Elijah just in time to miss the clawed hand that was aiming for my face.

"You cannot be," he grunted, pupils dilated.

I jumped back as he reached for me again, but he caught my wing in his grip. He twisted his hand. I heard an almost delicate crack, and startling pain arced across my wing, slamming into my shoulder and powering down my spine.

Unable to stop it, a cry punched out of me, but that spark of pain ignited a fire in me. I started to bring my knee up, but before I could utter "jerk face," Elijah slammed his palm into my chest.

The blow knocked me off my feet and through the air as if he'd tossed me. I flew back, over the edge of the roof overlooking the alley.

"Layla!" Fear filled Roth's shout.

As I started to topple into nothing but air, instinct came out of cruise control. The pain in my left wing knocked the air out of my lungs, but I pushed through it, grinding my teeth as I caught myself. The movement was like taking a lighted match to my wing, but I darted up several feet above the rooftop.

He'd broken my wing!

Startled, Elijah shouted as he reached into the torn coat and pulled out a dagger, and I knew without even getting close that it was iron—and if you had even the tiniest amount of demon blood, iron could be deadly.

He crouched, and then shot into the air, and that fire in me burned into an inferno. I shot across the rooftop as Elijah raised his hand, swinging the dagger toward me. I dropped to the concrete, and the dagger swung over my head. I grabbed hold of his legs, my claws digging in as I yanked down with all my strength.

Elijah hadn't expected that move, and he went down as I made a pass at him, the tips of my claws missing him by an inch. Spinning around, I swung out my clawed hand. I didn't graze him this time. My claws hit him across the chest, digging in deep, tearing open the hardened skin. Blood spurted and then sprayed. Shock splashed across Elijah's face as he stumbled back, toward the roof's edge, his hands pressing against his chest. It wasn't a fatal blow, but as he stared at me, I saw my opening. His throat was vulnerable and exposed. If I caught him there, he wouldn't recover.

I took a step toward him, my wings twitching as I raised my hand again. My muscles were strung tight with anticipation. I wanted to bring him to his knees, end him. He was *my* father and he'd tried to have me killed more times than I probably even knew of. Killing him would be understandable, justified even, because if I didn't, he was surely going to come after me again and again.

My eyes locked with his blue ones, and all that fury, and all that hurt swirled together into a cyclone of messy, dirty emotions. All those years of feeling like I didn't belong, that I was cast out and unwanted. The shock of knowing that my own flesh and blood wanted me dead slammed into me just as hard as it had when I'd first learned the truth, and I…

I felt sad for him.

I *could've* been the little girl that looked up to him. I *could've* been a good daughter to him. I *could've* had years getting to know him. I *could've* loved him.

But he had made the choice to never have any of that.

In the end, he wasn't worth the lifetime of guilt I'd shoulder.

Lowering my hand, I took a step back from Elijah as I felt

a Warden hit the rooftop, hard enough to crack the cement. Even as I started to speak, a dark blur—a shadow—appeared over the ledge, and then shot across the rooftop.

Before any of us could move or react, Sam was there, standing in between Elijah and me. Not Sam, I realized with a fresh jolt of pain, but the Lilin. It didn't stop to chat as it darted toward Elijah. The last Warden standing shouted, his words garbled by his cracked face and his yell cut short as Roth took him down, knocking him out.

The Lilin was on Elijah in a nanosecond, wrapping its hand around the Warden's throat and dragging him down a foot to its level. At first, I was just stunned into immobility. Seeing what looked like Sam completely incapacitate a Warden was bizarre. My head almost couldn't wrap around the fact that this wasn't scrawny Sam, but a souped-up version of everyone's worse nightmare.

The Lilin's shoulders rose as it inhaled deeply. Horror swamped me as I realized it was feeding on Elijah. His aura blinked like a light going out, and then it was gone. Cold wind blasted into me, throwing around the strands of hair that had come loose across my face as I staggered to the side, already knowing it was too late. The Lilin was too fast, too deadly. It had struck like a cobra, and its venom was the deadliest.

Roth was suddenly behind me, wrapping an arm around my waist, holding me back, but truth be told, I wasn't moving, because I knew—God, I knew—it was done.

Within seconds, the Lilin released Elijah. The Warden's back was unnaturally stiff as he backed into the ledge. I expected him to transform into something horrifying at that point, like Petr had when I stripped his soul away, but that didn't happen.

Elijah's skin pinked as he slipped back into his human form and his wings folded into his back. Fangs and claws receded. The wound in his chest, the wound I'd given him, was even gorier now, and the scar along his face stood out starkly.

There was no wraith.

There was nothing left of Elijah's soul.

Those blue eyes usually filled with such hate were dull and unfocused as Elijah fell backward, over the ledge. Gone.

Whipping around, the Lilin faced us. Immediately, it began to transform, its body contorted as it doubled over before it straightened, throwing its head back. The length of it stretched, and then it expanded, bulking up.

"Oh my God," I whispered as an all-new awfulness hit me.

The Lilin was taking on Elijah's form, just as it had Sam's. It was becoming something totally different, and within mere moments, what looked like Sam was no longer standing in front of us.

Instead, there was an exact replica of Elijah, down to the scar cutting across the side of his face, right to the corner of his lips.

"You're welcome." The Lilin even sounded like Elijah. The only thing missing was his aura. As had been the case with the Sam doppelgänger, there was nothing around the Lilin.

The Lilin bent on powerful legs as it shook out its shoulders. Its skin hardened to granite and massive wings appeared, spreading out from behind it. One side of its lips curled up in a smirk, and then it launched into the air, quickly disappearing over the rise of the other buildings.

Breathing heavily, I tugged on Roth and his arm slipped away from me. I walked toward the edge of the building and peered down, all the way down to the street below. A crowd of people had gathered. Some were backing away, their hands fluttering to their mouths. Someone whipped around and doubled over.

I squeezed my eyes shut as my stomach twisted. The real Elijah had hit the sidewalk below and it was…messy. Throat tight, I turned away and forced a deep breath. "We have to warn the other Wardens."

ten

FLURRIES FELL FROM THE THICK CLOUDS ABOVE
and a fine coating of snow dusted the roofs of the buildings. Dusk was slowly invading the city, and down below,
streetlamps were flickering on, along with the white Christmas lights that had been strung along the trees.

As I stood near the ledge and stared down, watching humans hurry along or stopping to hail a cab, I thought if I could
capture this moment with a camera, it would almost look like
the perfect holiday greeting card.

There was something calming about the fact that millions
of people were going about their lives, completely unaware
of the very real darkness threatening their city. After all this
time, I finally got it—why the Alphas demanded that humans
remain clueless when it came to the existence of demons. It
had to do with more than just the desire for faith in a higher
power. It was also about protection, allowing the humans to
live their lives every day, because if they did know the truth,
the world would be irrevocably changed, damaged beyond
merely the careless way humans treated other humans.

Warmth beat back the cold as Roth came to stand behind me. He wrapped his arm around my waist and rested his chin atop my head. There was no stiffness in his embrace or in my reaction to it. Although this was all new to both of us, this openness about our feelings, there was none of that awkwardness that I imagined most couples faced.

We weren't on the same building as earlier. Now we were near the federal district, waiting for members of my clan. Out of habit, I had texted Zayne a short message, telling him not to trust Elijah, that if they saw him, it wasn't the Warden they knew. Minutes had gone by before he'd responded, proving that he hadn't been asleep, encased in stone, like he should've been at that time. He'd requested a meeting, and so now we were waiting. Nerves formed a tangle in the pit of my stomach. I was going to see Zayne again, and that was going to be tough enough, but worse still, I figured I would also see other clan members. Maybe even Abbot, and I was nothing but a ball of anxious dread.

Roth hadn't been too thrilled about any of this, which explained why Bambi was once again curled around my waist and Cayman was also here, along with Edward. They stood on the corners of the building like two sentries.

Really well-dressed sentries.

Both were in dark trousers and a white shirt, donning polished leather shoes. I had no idea why. Maybe they had left ballroom dancing classes or something. I could totally see Cayman doing that.

"How's your back?" Roth asked after a few moments.

I hadn't mentioned that my back ached from where Elijah had gripped my wing, but Roth was careful to avoid the area and not irritate the dull pulse. "It doesn't hurt that bad, but I think he might've broken something."

The muscles along his arm bunched. "When we get home, I want to check it out if shifting doesn't hurt you too badly."

Home. Home was with Roth. That was so right I didn't even need to question it. We stood in silence for a handful of seconds, and then I blurted out, "I get it."

His hand flattened along my stomach, just above my navel as he lifted his chin. Bambi moved on my skin, stretching out and shifting closer to him. "You get what?" he asked quietly.

"Why the Alphas demand that the humans don't know the truth," I explained, resting my head back against his chest. "I used to think that it was so stupid. How did knowing the truth really hurt anything? They'd know there really was a Heaven and Hell and everything in between. Maybe people would act right then."

"Maybe," he murmured, his arm tightening as he shifted us slightly.

"But that's the thing. People probably would act right, but only because they wouldn't live, not in the moment." The wind picked up, and I smiled a little when I realized that Roth had moved to block it. "They would be petrified. That's why they can't know. Or at least part of the reason."

"Makes sense, I guess. It's hard for me to understand, being that I came into creation knowing, well, everything." He chuckled when I rolled my eyes even though there was no way he could've seen that. "So, what? You want to protect them now?"

I frowned slightly as I stared down at the city. "I've always wanted to protect them."

His chest rose against my back. "You're more than that, Layla. Don't you want a life outside of tagging demons?"

"I don't know about that anymore. You know that." I twisted around and tilted my head back, facing him. He was staring down, his head cocked in the way he did whenever he was trying to understand some kind of human emotion he just couldn't grasp. "And I do want more."

"Like what?" he challenged. "What do you want to do when this is over?"

When what was over? The fight with the Lilin? Reclaiming Sam's soul? The war between the Wardens and demons? I had no idea if or when any of this would be over, but I had to hang on to hope that it would be. That both of us would still be standing, as would all those I cherished. I couldn't allow myself to even briefly consider the idea that there wouldn't be an after.

"I think… I think I'd like to go to college," I told him. "Well, that means I have to finish high school first. That makes sense."

His lips twitched. "That's your big plan?"

I thought back to all those applications I had lining my old bedroom floor back at the compound and I nodded. "Yeah, and I… I want to travel first. I want to see places outside of this city."

"Like where?" he asked, raising his hand and tracing the line of my jaw with his fingers. "I'm still banking on Hawaii."

I grinned. "That would be nice. So, yeah, put that on the list."

"Need other places to make a list, Shortie."

"Okay. I want to see New York City—Dez says it's amazing. And Miami. I want to walk on a beach." Getting into it, I started ticking off places. "I want to stroll the French Quarter in New Orleans, and I want to visit Galveston—"

"Galveston...Texas? Why?"

"Read a book once that took place there. It doesn't matter. I want to see Dallas, like real cowboys and stuff."

He laughed as he tucked a strand of my hair back. "Real cowboys are kind of hard to find."

"We'll find them. I'm positive. And then I want to see the Hollywood sign and maybe even Portland. It rains there a lot, right? Not sure I'd want to stay there long, but I think I'd actually like to see Mount Rushmore— Oh, and Canada. I can keep going," I said. "But I think that's a good start."

His eyes had that hooded quality that brought a flush to my cheeks. "That's a great list."

"What about you?" I asked. "What do you want to do when this is all over?"

"For real?" When I nodded, he lowered his head, dropping a quick kiss on the tip of my nose. "I can't believe you even have to ask that. I plan to be wherever you are."

My lips immediately curved into one of those big, funny-looking smiles as my heart swelled in my chest like an old-school cartoon character's. I was waiting for my eyes to turn into exaggerated hearts that popped out. "That is...that is the perfect answer."

"That's because I am perfect."

"Well, *that* wasn't the perfect answer," I said drily.

Cayman's warning cut off Roth's answering laugh. "They're coming."

We turned to where he gestured. Off in the distance, they looked like great birds parting the clouds. My stomach dropped as they dipped low, coming in for a landing. Zayne was definitely there; he was in the middle of the bunch, and even in his true form, I knew that it was him.

Three other Wardens were with him, and as they neared the rooftop, I recognized them as Nicolai and Dez. A bit of the unease, not all of it, lessened. Dez was from the New York clan and he'd first visited DC with his mate, Jasmine. While he'd been unsure of me at first, he'd quickly seemed to like me. I suppose it was because we were both outsiders, in our way. Nicolai had always had a soft spot for me, and I for him. He wasn't that much older than Zayne when he'd lost his mate and child. Nicolai rarely smiled, but when he did, he could take your breath away.

The fourth member of their crew shocked me.

It had to be Danika.

"Interesting," Roth said, unfolding his arm from around me. He didn't move away, though.

Interesting didn't really sum it up. Wardens didn't allow their females out much, preferring to keep them in gilded cages. It was one of the many things I'd hated about our kind. Granted, I understood that the Warden population was dwindling and females were prime targets for Upper Level demons, but still, the idea of being kept sequestered made me want to punch something.

Just like I knew it drove Danika nuts.

Danika was a lot wilder and crazier than her older sister, Jasmine, and I'd spent the better part of my formative years hating on her for no other reason than the fact that she liked Zayne and would be able to monopolize all his time with a flick of her glossy black hair.

Cayman and Edward didn't move from their perches with the exception of facing the direction the Wardens were coming from. The crew of four landed on the rooftop, their impact cracking like thunder. Then Cayman glanced at Roth, who nodded. Both Cayman and Edward disappeared, as if they were never there, but I could still feel them. They were nearby, monitoring the situation, and if I could feel them, so could the Wardens.

Zayne strode forward, his chin bent low and his wings tucked back. My stomach flopped unsteadily as my gaze swerved to Nicolai and then to Danika. They were blocking her, keeping her behind them.

Something she clearly wasn't too thrilled about.

Charging forward, she brushed past Zayne, who cast his gaze to the sky, a muscle throbbing along his jaw. She shifted into human form as she headed straight for where Roth and I stood, her gray skin giving way to flawless alabaster. Dez muttered something under his breath while Nicolai followed after her, a look of concern pulling at the corners of his lips.

Without looking back at the males, she threw her hand up in their direction and all she said was, "Don't even try to stop me."

Nicolai skidded to a stop, his brows raised.

I stiffened, as did Roth.

Absolutely fearless, Danika stalked right up to us and before I could blink an eye, she'd thrown her arms around me and squeezed. A fruity scent, like apples, surrounded me as Bambi slithered onto my back, away from her. Danika was as strong as a linebacker, and I swallowed a squeak as I was pressed against her hard chest. The dull ache flared into a sharp throbbing sensation on either side of my spine, reinforcing my paranoid belief that Elijah might have broken one of my wings—one of my *feathered* wings.

"Careful," Roth advised, only loud enough for us to hear. "She's been hurt."

"Oh God! I'm sorry." Danika immediately released me, and I would've stumbled back if Roth hadn't been there to steady me. "What happened? What's—"

"I'm all right," I assured her, caught off guard by her welcome. I still wasn't used to our new friendship.

She glanced at Roth warily and it was obvious she didn't 100 percent trust him. He smiled back at her, tight-lipped and daring. "I've been so worried," she continued, taking a small step back as she ran her hands along her denim-clad hips.

"When Zayne said you reached out because something happened and they were coming to meet you, I had to come. I needed to say I'm sorry."

"Danika," Nicolai called gently.

"Sorry for what?" I asked, looking toward the other Wardens. Zayne was now eyeballing Roth like he wanted to toss him off the roof. Dez didn't look entirely surprised, but Nicolai—well, he looked like he wanted to scoop her up and fly off, which was... That was odd.

"For what they did to you," she said, her cheeks flushing pink. "This clan. It wasn't right, and I wanted to kick Abbot in the balls."

"Apologies are given out far too often to mean anything, but I like you," murmured Roth. "I really do."

Her gaze darted from him to me, and she then took another step back while Nicolai moved in closer. "Anyway, it was wrong. You would never purposely hurt Zayne or anyone else."

Well, the thing was, I had hurt Zayne, even if not physically, and there was no mistaking that. I had to believe that she knew. When I glanced at him again, he still hadn't looked in my direction. Feeling icky about that, I refocused. "Thank you, Danika, I…um, I appreciate that." I turned to Nicolai and Dez. "And I owe you guys everything, too. Thank you for finding Roth and helping me get out of that warehouse. You all helped save my life."

And that was true.

Because of them, I was standing today. Instead of going along with Abbot, they had found Roth and stood against their own clan at great personal risk to save me.

"It's good to see that you're recovered," Dez said, and I smiled.

"I second that. I've known you most of your life, little one, and I never once believed you were responsible for what was happening at the compound or outside of it," Nicolai added, and I got warm and fuzzy on the inside. "You might be glad to know that the place is hardly trouble-free with you gone. We still haven't managed to exorcise Petr's wraith. Whenever we try, he senses it and leaves the house."

"He's proving to be as much of a jackass as he was in real life," Dez commented, proving that Elijah's son, my half brother, had not been well liked. He paused. "Jasmine says hi, by the way."

"Tell her hi from me," I replied lamely, and like an idiot, I raised my hand and wiggled my fingers.

Dez grinned as he looked away, something he often did around me. I sort of wanted to jab myself in the eyes with my jazz fingers.

"What happened?" Zayne finally spoke, and when he did, my gaze swung to him. He was staring at Roth, and that made my stomach twist painfully. "The text said there was an incident with Elijah and not to trust him?"

Nicolai crossed his arms along his chest as he tucked his wings back. Remaining in his Warden form, like the other two, he was an impressive sight. "We have never trusted Elijah." His eyes were focused on me. "His beliefs and actions have always been a source of discontent among us."

"Well." Roth drew the word out. "Elijah isn't going to be a source of much of anything anymore."

All the Wardens' gazes shot to him, and his tight-lipped grin spread. "Details would be nice," Zayne demanded, the cool breeze tossing fair strands around his dark horns.

I waded in before the conversation went downhill. "Elijah is…he's no more," I explained, and then rushed on when I heard Dez's sharp curse. "We didn't kill him."

"Not that we didn't try," Roth amended, and when I shot him a look, he shrugged. "Why lie, Shortie? We were out searching for the Lilin—"

"We are handling that," Zayne cut in, his chin rising.

"Sure you are," Roth replied, and although that was a taunt, I knew he was capable of far more when it came to being an asshole to Zayne. This was watered down. "And how's that going for you all?"

Zayne's jaw worked as if he were going to grind down every one of his teeth. When there was no immediate response, Roth threw out, "Any leads? Nope. Didn't think so."

I shifted my weight from foot to foot while Dez narrowed his eyes and Danika started staring at the floor of the rooftop.

"Anyway, as I was saying, we were out searching for the Lilin when Layla saw Elijah. He and three other clan members were tracking us from the rooftops. We confronted them and they attacked."

"He still wants me dead," I explained. "Nothing new there."

Zayne glanced in my direction, but didn't make eye contact. "So what happened?"

"Well, Bambi ate one of the Wardens. So kind of not sorry about that," Roth went on, and Bambi flicked her tail along my hip, as if she was happy at the shout-out. I squeezed my eyes shut briefly. "I sort of put another out of commission. Permanently. Self-defense. I swear."

"I'm sure of that," Nicolai murmured as he moved to stand slightly in front of Danika.

She didn't appear all that bothered. "If they were from his clan, they won't be missed."

"Danika," Dez admonished.

"What?" She threw her hands up. "It's the truth. They're all jackasses. We all know that."

Nicolai's lips twitched. "What happened to the third Warden?"

"He was taking a nap on the rooftop when we left him. Not sure if he's woken up or some demon has come along and done bad, bad things to him." Roth shrugged again. "Don't know. Don't care."

"And Elijah?" Zayne asked, his voice tight.

I drew in a deep breath as I reached up, pushing the loose hair back from my face. "I was fighting him—"

"You were fighting Elijah?" Nicolai's brows flew up.

"Uh. Yeah?"

Danika smiled broadly. "Awesome."

I shook my head. "The Lilin showed up and got between

us. It took Elijah's soul—it consumed it. There was no wraith. Nothing left, and then the Lilin changed its appearance."

"It looks like Elijah now," Roth tacked on. "That's why Layla thought it would be a smart idea to warn you. The other Warden that was with him, if that Warden is still alive, was out cold when the Lilin took Elijah's soul. He would have no idea that isn't the real Elijah if the Lilin goes back to the clan."

"Damn," muttered Dez. "I'm not sure if we know where they are holed up here to warn them. Perhaps Geoff knows."

Nicolai's expression turned thoughtful. "If not, I have a feeling Abbot might have an idea."

I cringed inwardly at the mention of Abbot's name, but forged on. "Like I said, we wanted to warn you all, just in case it tries to go to the compound." The next part was the worst. "Based on how the Lilin was able to pull off a Sam impersonation so convincingly, I think the Lilin gets the person's memories when it consumes the soul."

"That makes sense," Danika said, glancing back at the males. "The soul is the essence, the very core of our beings. It would hold everything."

Nicolai exhaled roughly. "If that's the case, then the Lilin would know a lot."

"Too much," Zayne stated, and started to turn, his deep gray wings unfurling. "We need to talk to my father and the others."

Dez and Nicolai agreed with the statement. Danika lingered, glancing between Roth and me. "Don't be a stranger," she said, voice low. "Okay? We all need to work together if we're going to stop that thing."

I nodded, feeling weird as I watched them. It was hard to think of a time when Zayne was leaving somewhere, and I wasn't going with him. As the Wardens turned, I stepped forward. Although deep down I knew I should just let them go—let *him* go—I couldn't stop myself. There were too many years between us to simply pretend we were strangers.

"Zayne?" I called out.

He was at the ledge when I spoke his name, and I thought I saw his shoulders bunch, but he knelt, and then launched himself into the sky without looking back.

Without acknowledging me.

eleven

NIGHT HAD FALLEN BY THE TIME WE MADE IT to the Palisades to meet up with Cayman.

The club under Roth's apartment building was packed with demons, as well as humans with dark, murky auras surrounding them. There was a bit of churning in my stomach, but nothing substantial. Sultry music thrummed as the succubi swayed their diamond-covered hips on the stage. They shimmered and twinkled like the Christmas lights strung across the ceiling.

The Christmas lights were ironic, all things considered.

Roth's hand was firmly wrapped around mine as he led me around the stage. As we passed the darkened corners, I strained to see what was going on in there, but all I could make out was another card game between a female demon and a human who wasn't looking too hot, if the yellowish tint to his skin was any indication.

One of the dancers in the cage reached out to me, and then giggled wildly when Roth shot her a warning scowl. His hand tightened around mine. "I'm not going to wander off on you,"

I said to him. Last time we'd been there, he'd told me not to dance with anyone, and, well, I ended up dancing with a succubus and an incubus. Sometimes I needed an adult.

His laugh traveled over the music. "I'm really not taking any chances right now."

"Right now?"

Letting go of my hand, he draped his arm over my shoulders and tucked me against his side as we made our way around the tables. He lowered his head, brushing his lips against my cheek, and then he said into my ear, "Have I told you how much I love those pants?"

"Huh?" Glancing down, I bit back a groan. They were skintight, and I'd practically had to lie down this morning to zip them up. "Your and Cayman's taste in clothing sucks."

He chuckled. "I cannot stop staring at your—"

"Eyes?" I suggested helpfully.

"Mmm." He kissed my earlobe as we finally passed the stage.

"How about my nose?"

"Not quite," he replied.

I grinned. "You must be checking out my kneecaps then."

"Closer." He paused as we neared the bar. "Later, I can give you a hands-on explanation of what I've been staring at all day."

My cheeks flushed. "You're so helpful."

"What can I say? You bring out my altruistic side."

Cayman stepped out from behind the bar before I could respond to that last statement, tossing the white rag on the counter. "Let's hit the office."

I'd never seen the office before, so I was curious. Cayman led us through a door just outside the bar that read

EMPLOYEES ONLY, but someone had scratched out all the letters except three, leaving LOL behind.

Nice.

The hallway was narrow, lit by actual torches shoved into wall sconces. "Interesting decorating choice," I said.

Cayman grinned as Roth closed the door behind us, cutting off the hum of music. "My sugar bear, you know we like all flair."

Roth snorted.

The office was the third door down and the room wasn't at all like I expected; and to be honest, I wasn't even sure what I expected, but definitely not this. The space was decked out in pale colors—robin's egg blue walls, white desk and empty bookshelf. A fuzzy pink chair was sitting in front of the desk, next to a leopard print recliner. A gray leather couch was against the wall. Above it was a giant framed photo of One Direction.

And it was signed by all the members, even the one who'd left.

My mouth dropped open.

"I did not decorate this office," Roth explained, seeing the look on my face.

Cayman dropped into a rather normal-looking chair behind the desk and kicked his feet up. "He wanted black. Black walls. Black furniture. Blah. Blah. I like a little color every now and then."

Keeping my opinion to myself, I shuffled over to the couch and plopped down.

Before we hit the club, I'd sent Stacey a text, explaining what happened while Roth filled Cayman in. In return she sent a lot of exclamation points and a slew of frownie faces over what had happened with Elijah. Though she knew there was absolutely no love lost between him and me, she also knew that seeing Elijah die hadn't been easy.

And knowing that whatever part of him remained outside of the Lilin was in Hell also didn't sit well. I hated the dude, but an eternity in Hell, among creatures he'd helped put there, couldn't be a walk in a park.

Worse yet, now that I saw what had happened with Elijah, I knew what had gone down with Sam, and I felt sick to my core. Somewhere out there was Sam's body, cold and forgotten, and I already knew where whatever was left of his soul was.

I didn't want to think about any of that, but I couldn't stop myself. My thoughts would move to one thing, and then bounce back to Sam, to what had happened to him.

After Roth finished up with Cayman, I jumped up from the couch. "Can we go up to your loft instead of going back to the house?"

"If that's what you want," he said, pushing off from where he'd been leaning against the desk. "I doubt the Wardens will come looking for us now. It will be safe."

Relieved to hear that, I knew I'd be happy to see the loft again. I was feeling a little nostalgic, and I actually preferred it over the massive home in Maryland. Sure, the McMansion had nice features and all, but it was too big and felt cold, formal.

Cayman tweaked my nose as he walked past, heading out the office door. "I'll send some greasy goodness up."

My stomach grumbled, reminding me that I hadn't eaten since that morning. We had to take the stairs since the elevators only went down, like down *there*, and by the time I'd hoofed it all the way to the top floor, I kind of wished I had climbed onto Roth's back.

The little teacup hounds weren't guarding the door. "Where are your friends?"

"It's feeding time," he said. "You don't need to know more than that."

Yikes.

When Roth opened his loft, warm air greeted us. He stepped in, flipping on the lights, and I walked into the middle of the room, looking around.

"Everything looks like it used to," I said, eyeing the massive king-size bed. Black sheets were smoothed and tucked in, and as I looked toward the door that led up to the rooftop, I saw that not a single speck of dust tarnished the piano. The morbid paintings of fire and dark shadows were still precisely hung.

Roth moved over to the bookshelf full of ancient, boring-looking tomes and kicked off his shoes. "No one would change it."

"Someone has been keeping it clean, though."

"Cayman."

That made sense, I supposed.

"Did you expect it to look different?" he asked, tugging his shirt off his head.

My mouth dried like it had the first time I stood in his loft and watched him do that. His body was a chiseled piece of art. "I... I guess I did."

His lashes lowered and his smile was smug, as if he knew I'd been more than momentarily distracted by him. "We have been gone from here for what feels like forever. Hasn't been that long, though."

Roth was right.

But so much had changed since then. *I* had changed, so it was weird to see something untouched from...from before.

He brushed his hand over his sternum, down to the belt on his jeans, near the colorful dragon tattoo, and something about the movement hollowed out my stomach. I drew in a stuttered breath. His lashes lifted and heated amber eyes met mine.

The heady tension was there, pulling and tugging us toward one another. It had always been there between us, and it wasn't weakening.

Three shadows drifted off his body, slowly floating to the floor. They solidified into the form of the kittens. Two of them immediately darted under the bed. The third—Thor— trotted over to me, rubbed up against my leg, purring like a mini engine, and then also disappeared under the bed without drawing my blood, which was an improvement.

"I wonder what they do under there."

Roth raised one broad shoulder. "I actually don't want to know."

"That's probably a wise choice." I moved to the bed and sat on the corner, tugging off my boots. "I'm glad we're here. I've missed this place."

He smiled slightly as I pulled my feet off the floor, not trusting those damn kittens even if they were playing nice with me right now. "It does have its charm."

I started to respond, but Roth took a moment to stretch and there was just something about seeing all that muscle and skin working together fluidly that made me lose complete track of my thoughts.

"What something to drink?" he asked.

Mute, I shook my head.

As he lowered his arms, he prowled over to the black mini fridge and pulled out a bottle of water. Screwing off the cap, he took a healthy drink before placing the bottle down. Then he faced me.

Roth watched me, not like he expected me to break down at any given moment, but simply like he was concerned. He didn't have to ask as he walked over to me.

"I... I keep thinking that was how...how Sam died," I admitted. "I'll think of something else and then he's back in my mind."

Roth knelt before me. "Layla—"

"You saw what the Lilin did. He took my... He took Elijah's soul and then *swallowed* it. The soul was consumed and it looked like him afterward." Lifting my gaze, I met Roth's. "That was how Sam died and that's why the Lilin was able to look like him. It had to have been so painful." I squeezed my eyes shut briefly. "But quick, right? It looked like it happened so quick with Elijah."

He placed his hands on my knees, rubbing gently. "It was quick."

Shoulders dropping, I shook my head slightly. "I... I'm not really upset about Elijah and he was my father. What does that say about me?"

His expression hardened. "That says nothing about you. That asshole donated sperm. That's the truth. That is all. He was not your father. You don't owe him a single moment of sadness. You owe him nothing."

What he said was true, but... "It's still hard not to feel guilty."

He didn't respond while he studied me closely. "You...you are so human sometimes, Layla, and yet, there is not a drop of human blood in you."

"Socialization?" I offered, and Roth laughed under his

breath. "I'm serious, though. Stacey and…and Sam's influence on me, I think. They kept me human, and I like that. I like that I feel human."

"I love that about you." His response was quick, surprising me.

"Really?"

He nodded solemnly, and I smiled a little. "You don't owe Elijah anything," he reinforced. "Please tell me you understand that."

"I do." But it was harder to accept it.

His gaze returned to searching. "You're not planning anything, are you?"

I stilled. "Like what?"

"To get Sam's soul?" he asked, his eyes latched onto mine. "Don't try to deny it—I know that's what you want. I will go and—"

"No. You cannot go down there. I know that if you do, they'll keep you there," I interrupted. "You can't."

His eyes narrowed. "Someone has been talking to Cayman."

I didn't deny that. "I don't want you to put yourself at risk."

"Not even for Sam?" he challenged.

Knowing what I planned to do made it hard to say the next word. "No."

"And I don't want you to risk it for him," he replied. "I don't care if that sounds cruel. You don't want me to take the chance. I feel the same about you."

Saying what I did next was even harder than that one word, because I was going to lie and I didn't want any lies between us, but I had to do something for Sam. There was no way around it and I knew if I told Roth, he would find a way to stop me or he would go with me. Neither of those two things could happen.

"How could I get Sam's soul?" I asked. "I wouldn't even know where to begin."

Roth didn't reply as he stared at me, and I knew that he had the answers. If Cayman did, he had to, but if Cayman also knew Grim wasn't in Hell right now, then there was a big chance that Roth was aware of that, too. And I also knew there was a possibility that Roth planned on going to Grim despite the risks.

I would have to get there before he did.

"Do you think you can shift real quick, before Cayman gets here with the food? I want to check out your wings."

Denying Roth this was just going to delay the inevitable and I was thankful for the change in conversation. I shrugged out of my sweater. There were two small tears in the back from where my wings had ripped through the material earlier, but the tank top underneath felt intact.

Before I changed forms, I tried what Roth had done with the kittens. I skimmed my fingers over the area Bambi rested on and low and behold, she came right off my skin. Neat.

Bambi made her way to Roth first, nudging his thigh with her nose. He reached down, patting her head. Appeased by that, she slithered over to the low-backed chair near the piano. Curling up, she rested her head on the arm and appeared to stare out the window.

Shifting wasn't hard anymore. I really didn't even have to concentrate or even stand up. I wanted it to happen and it did. My back tingled and then my wings started coming out, the left wing aching, and when I glanced back at it, it drooped slightly, like baby Izzy's wings did.

"I think it's broken," I told him.

Roth walked over to the bed and sat down, twisting toward me. He checked out the wing. "Does it hurt?"

"It aches," I admitted. "Not too bad."

His gaze moved to my face and then back to my wing. "It could've been broken, but it looks like it's already healing." His fingers brushed along the edge of the feathers, not near the aching part. While his touch was gentle, it still sent a shudder through me. He immediately pulled his hand back. "Did I hurt you?"

"No. They're just supersensitive."

He arched a brow as he opened his mouth and then closed it. I grinned and said, "I think your mind just went into the gutter."

"Shortie, my mind exists there." He winked at my laugh, and then studied my wing for a few more moments. "I think if you can give it a rest for a couple hours, a day tops, you'll be completely fine."

I glanced back at the sad, gimpy wing. "Do you think the feathers will fall off?"

"What?"

My cheeks burned. "Maybe I'm going through some kind of metamorphosis and I'm going to shed these feathers."

He looked like he wanted to laugh, but wisely kissed my bare shoulder instead. Standing from the bed, he walked over to where he'd left his water. "You really hate those things, don't you?"

"I don't hate them. Not exactly." I moved my right wing closer to me and gingerly ran my fingers over the feathers. "I just don't understand them. So some Upper Level demons have them. I get them, but I'm not an Upper Level demon."

Roth took a drink, and then placed the bottle down. "You know you feel like an Upper Level demon now, to other Wardens and demons, which could be because you're maturing. Maybe the feathers are another sign of that maturity. You're not like the rest of us—or any demon really. You're a blend, and that makes your growth patterns tough to predict." He shrugged a shoulder. "That's the best guess I can come up with, anyway, but I'm a little out of my element here. Most of us were created almost fully formed and the growth that takes others decades to achieve, we finish in a day."

"Aren't you just special," I muttered under my breath.

He grinned. "The feathers and the way you look now when you shift? Yeah, I don't understand that myself. I get that my response isn't helpful, but you're the first who carries both Warden and demon blood—and not just any demon's blood, but Lilith's. This could just be a stage of you finally coming into who you truly are."

At that moment I remembered I hadn't told him about the other demon in the coffee shop. "When I went to talk to Zayne about…well, you know what, there was an Upper Level demon who came into the shop after he left. You know how demons don't normally sense me, right? This one did."

"Upper Level demons are different, Shortie. Some of them probably could sense what you are."

Huh.

I lifted my gaze to his. "But this demon…it ran from me, Roth."

Both brows lifted.

"It legit ran from me and it looked scared," I continued, unsettled by the memory. "I've never known an Upper Level demon to run from anything, not even the Wardens."

"They don't." His features tensed. "The only thing an Upper Level would run from would be the Boss, me, or…"

My heart turned over heavily. "Or what?"

Roth's frown did nothing to deter from his beauty, but it made my stomach drop nonetheless. "They'd run from one of the originals."

"Originals?"

He leaned against the wall, eyeing me with lowered lashes. "The originals, Shortie, the ones that are like the Boss. The ones that fell."

"That fell…?" I whispered to myself, and then it hit me. "You mean, the angels that fell when they were first sent here to help mankind?" When he nodded, my eyes widened. "They have black raven wings?"

His lips did that twitching thing again. "Yeah. So does the Boss."

Pressure settled on my shoulders. "But that…"

"That doesn't make sense, I know. That's why I didn't bring it up. You're not one of the original ones to fall. Obviously," he said, dragging the palm of his hand over his chest. "That's why I think it's some kind of stage. You just started shifting, Shortie. You don't know all that you're fully capable of."

I sighed. If this truly was just a phase, then what would be next? Horns along my spine, like some kind of dinosaur. Or maybe scales like Thumper's. "So why do you think the demon ran?"

"You smell like me."

"Uh… Come again?"

The crooked grin reappeared. "My scent is all over you. Other demons would be able to pick it up."

I resisted the urge to smell myself.

"It's unique to demons," he explained. "Our scents, that is. Sort of like a fingerprint. Most demons with a working brain cell would pick up on my scent and head in the opposite direction."

I was still trying not to smell myself when I remembered that Zayne had once said he could smell Roth on me. Suddenly, what I always smelled around him made sense. "You smell like something sweet and...musky."

The grin faded and a long moment passed as he eyed me intensely. "You smell like sunlight."

My breath halted in my throat. I had no idea what sunlight smelled like, but I imagined it was something good and I also thought that was sweet of him to say.

Unexpectedly self-conscious, I reached over, toying with the edge of my right wing. "I feel like a...peacock."

"Back to birds again, I see." His expression softened. "Many believe peacocks are beautiful."

"How about a cockatoo?"

Roth's eyes lightened. "I'm sure there are some that find them beautiful, also."

"A pigeon?"

He chuckled. "Layla, nothing about you reminds me of a pigeon."

"That's good to know."

There was a pause. "Have you really looked at yourself since this...this change, while you're shifted? Except the first time?"

Lowering my gaze, I shook my head.

"You should do that sometime soon. Maybe you'll see what I see. Maybe you'll see what everyone else sees," he said quietly. "Because you're beautiful, Layla, and while I may say that one word to you a lot, I don't simply toss it around. And

I've seen many, many beautiful things. People as beautiful as demons are atrocious. You, by far, shine brighter than any of them. It's more than what is on the outside. It comes from within you. I've seen a lot of things and nothing, *nothing* comes close to you."

Oh gosh, as I lifted my gaze, I had my heart and all the stars in the sky in my eyes. That was possibly the loveliest thing anyone had ever said to me, and I knew, in every cell that made up my being, that he believed in those words. They were true to him. Those words were his reality.

Cayman arrived with the food before I could formulate a half-decent response and Roth flipped on the TV. I shifted back, and then we delved into a platter of hamburgers, chicken tenders and fries. He dipped everything in ranch dressing, even his burger, something I hadn't noticed before.

Afterward I headed to the bathroom to wash my hands and face, figuring I needed to after I basically shoved my face in the plate of the food. When I returned, only the light from the television illuminated the room. The plate was gone and Roth was stretched out on the bed, arms behind his head. His stomach was impossibly flat while I knew I looked like I was carrying a food baby.

Sometimes, and this was one of those moments, I felt completely in over my head when it came to Roth.

Walking over to him, I climbed onto the bed and lay down on my side, facing him. My heart was racing as if I'd run from the bathroom to the bed a dozen or so times.

Roth turned his head and looked at me.

I wiggled closer.

He watched me.

I squirmed even closer, until the front of my body was

pressed against the side of his. Without looking up at him, I rested my head on his chest. A moment passed and he lowered his arms.

"The evening didn't pan out like I'd wanted," he said.

That's when I remembered his surprise. "That's okay."

"I wanted to take you out on a date," he went on, almost as if he hadn't heard me. "Something normal. Dinner. Maybe a movie."

Lifting my head, I gazed up at him, startled.

His eyes met mine. "I know that sounds crazy with everything going on, but that's what…that's what humans do. They go out. Eat food. Watch a movie neither of them is really paying attention to."

"They do."

He shifted onto his side and scooted down so he was eye level with me. "I think they spend the whole dinner and movie thinking about the other person, about what's going to happen when it's time to leave. Will she invite him in? Will he invite her? Will there be a kiss? More?"

My toes curled. "Is that how you would spend the time?"

"Yes. A hundred percent yes," he said. "I wanted to give you that date, though. I wanted to give you that night. That was my surprise."

Moved through and through, I stretched over and kissed him lightly on the lips. "I want that night with you, but I don't need it. What I need is this—these seconds and minutes with you. That's what I'll always need."

His hand settled on my arm. "You deserve more than that."

Because he said that, *he* deserved another kiss. And because he said that, I fell more in love, even when I didn't know that was possible. "We had dinner tonight and the TV is on now.

That's as good as a movie. And you've taken my mind off the bad things and you've told me I'm beautiful. You've given me the night you wanted."

He stared at me for a moment, and then his lips curved up at the corners. His smile raced across his face, softening the harsh lines. Several moments passed before he spoke. "Do you know why sometimes I have to move away from you?" he asked, skimming his fingers along my arm.

The statement caught me off guard. "No."

Roth tracked the movement of his hand with his gaze. "Whenever I'm around you, I always want to be touching you."

Muscles low in my stomach tightened in response to his admission.

"I'm not even sure if it's a want or more of a need to do so," he continued, and his thick lashes lowered, shielding his eyes. His fingers moved along my stomach to my hip. "It's always been that way, from the first time I saw you. Even then I wanted to touch you. I think it's because…there is nothing like you where I'm from. Your inherent goodness," he said, lifting his gaze to mine. "I can feel it. I don't know, maybe I just like the way your skin feels under my hands. Who knows? I might have a boundaries problem."

I grinned. "Maybe just a little, but I don't mind."

We lay in silence for a few moments and my thoughts began to wander beyond tonight, beyond all our most pressing problems, and into a very unknown future. "I was thinking."

"Oh no."

I laughed lightly, and then whatever humor I was feeling vanished. "What are we going to do?" I whispered.

Roth stiffened. "That's a broad question, Shortie."

"I know." Snuggling close, I let the warmth of his body steal inside of me. "But I'm thinking about a decade from now."

"Hmm. A decade. I like the sound of that."

"I was thinking about two decades from now. Three. When I'm in my forties and look forty, and you look like you do right now," I explained, staring into the darkness. "Isn't that going to be weird?"

"No."

There wasn't a moment of hesitation on his end, but I laughed. "Oh come on, at some point, you're going to look like my son. The Warden blood in me means I age, Roth. I might look younger than I am when I'm older, but I will age and I will—"

"Don't say it." His voice was clipped. "Don't finish that sentence."

I swallowed as I lifted my head, meeting his bright gaze. "But it is true. How will we be together when I'm ninety and you look eighteen? How—?"

"I don't know how we'll make it work, but we will make it work. Somehow. And who knows if you will continue to age? I get that you've aged so far, but maybe that will stop. Layla, you're part demon. Demons don't age. Maybe the Warden blood has watered down some aspects, but look what's happened when you've shifted recently. You're changing and you don't—we don't—know all of what that means."

"You make it sound so easy," I said after a moment. "Like me looking like your grandmother one day isn't a big deal."

"It's not." He cupped my cheek. "I don't think you understand what it means when a demon falls in love, Layla. It doesn't go away. It doesn't fade, even if we want it to. We love until death. That's not just something we say. We love and we love once and it's forever. No matter what. And that's a bit twisted if you think about it, but luckily you feel the same way, so this isn't awkward. You feel me?"

Paimon, the Upper Level demon who'd loved Lilith and who'd kick-started all of this when he tried to free her, had said something similar, but coming from Roth, it was like the first taste of chocolate. It didn't wash away all my concerns, but it made me feel better about them, gave me hope that we could face them together, even if I needed a walker when we were facing the problem.

"God, Roth, sometimes…sometimes you're just perfect."

I expected a snarky response, like he would normally give me, but his hand traveled up to my cheek, and then slid around the nape of my neck. He guided me so I was nestled against him, my head tucked under his chin and one of his legs curled around mine. "Can I tell you something?"

"Of course."

Roth's thumb moved idly along the base of my scalp. "It's moments like these that I need, too."

twelve

STANDING IN FRONT OF THE CHAIR, I FELT LIKE I'd drunk a case of highly caffeinated drinks. Nervous energy consumed me, and I shifted from one foot to the other, not unlike I'd seen Thumper do at Stacey's house.

"Can this wait?" I asked, wiping my damp palms along my hips. "I mean, I really think this can wait."

Grinning like a cat that just cornered a herd of mice, Roth knew better than to get too close to me at the moment, because there was a good chance I might punch him. "Now is as good a time as any, Shortie."

I wrinkled my nose as I folded my arms across my chest and glanced over to where Cayman was fiddling with a massive contraption that looked like a power tool, but I knew it wasn't. "Can he really do this?"

Lifting his gaze to me, Cayman smiled. "I can do just about everything, teacup."

"Not everything," Roth reminded him.

Cayman shrugged, and then he hit something on the tool he held and a droning hum filled the office in the back of the club. My eyes widened as my muscles stiffened. "Is it…supposed to be that loud?"

Cayman laughed.

"Shortie, you've faced down Nightcrawlers and Raver demons, you cannot be that scared of getting a tattoo."

I whipped around toward Roth. "You're not the one getting the tattoo, so maybe you should just shut up."

Behind me, Cayman snorted, and I whirled toward him, shooting him my best death glare. "You, too. Shut it."

He shut it.

"I have five tats, Shortie, I know what it feels like," Roth cajoled, his hands raised at his sides. "It'll sting, but you're strong. You'll deal."

I didn't want to deal.

I also didn't want to be acting like such a baby, but I couldn't look forward to sitting down and allowing someone to dig ink into my body. Why had I thought this was a good idea?

Cayman rose. "Are we going to do this or not? Because I'm sure all of us have stuff to do. Like you all have a Lilin to find and I have deals to broker."

"It's up to you, Layla," Roth said. "If you don't want to do this, we don't have to."

A huge part of me wanted to jump on the out he offered, but getting a familiar tattooed on my skin was the smart thing to do. It would make me stronger and I'd have my own built-in backup system if things got out of hand. So I needed to woman up. "I want to do this."

Roth smiled at me while Cayman came around the desk. "Then hop up on the chair," the demon ordered. "And we'll get this show on the road."

I sat as instructed and nearly squealed when Cayman hit

something on the side and unexpectedly set the chair to a re-clining position. I gripped the arms of the chair, glaring at him. "A warning would've been nice."

"And what fun would that have been?" he replied. "You know what you're getting?"

Glancing at Roth, I nodded slowly. We'd talked about it last night, and it had been harder than I imagined when it came to picking a familiar. Most of my ideas were lame. At one point, I'd suggested a llama, which was about when Roth had announced that it was time for bed since my brain clearly needed to recharge.

"A fox," I told Cayman. "Because they are fast and clever."

"Like me," added Roth.

I rolled my eyes. "Not because it's like Roth."

"A fox? Interesting," murmured Cayman as he waved his left hand. A low stool appeared out of thin air, and I thought that was rather nifty. "I'm going to need some space to do that. Pull up your shirt."

Roth's head swung in his direction. "You might want to rethink that request."

Cayman snorted as he looked up through a lock of hair. "Please. As pretty as our little strudel cake is, she doesn't do it for me. You taking off your shirt, however, floats my boat and anchor."

I pursed my lips as Roth muttered, "Whatever."

Taking a deep breath, I pulled my shirt up so my stomach was exposed. "I have a feeling this is going to hurt."

"You'll be fine." Roth moved behind the chair, placing his hands on my shoulders. "You got this."

Cayman handled the instrument like he knew what he was doing as he started to lean over me. I tensed and he shook his head. "You're lucky, butter butts. This is going to go a lot faster and easier than it does for the humans."

"Why?"

He glanced up at me. "Because of magic." He said it like I didn't have two brain cells to rub together. "And because you will heal a hell of a lot faster than a human will. You won't even need to cover the tat."

"Okay." I was going to have to believe him.

"What are you going to call your fox?" Cayman asked.

I was so tense there was a good chance parts of my body would start breaking. "Robin."

His brows rose. "Why Robin?"

"My favorite Disney movie is the one where a fox is Robin Hood," I explained. "So Robin."

"That's my girl," Roth said from behind me. "Through and through."

Cayman glanced up at Roth, and then he placed his hand along my ribs. I jumped a little at the contact, and then, because I couldn't look away even though I should, I watched him bring the tattoo gun to my skin.

"Holy shit!" I shrieked, increasing my death grip on the arms of the chair. Sharp stinging pain, like I'd rolled around in a hornet's nest, lit up my entire stomach. "Just a little bit of pain? Are you kidding me?"

"It'll get better," Roth said, rubbing my shoulders.

Without even looking at him, I could hear the smile in his voice, and I wanted to punch him in the face. My stomach burned as Cayman did the tattoo, and only after about an eternity did the pain lessen, and I think that was because my stomach just went numb. But I sat there and I took it like a good little half demon, half Warden, and I fought the urge to shift in order to protect myself.

Roth did his best to distract me by preparing me for what it would be like to have my own familiar and not just one we sort of shared joint custody of.

Robin, my foxy-fox familiar, would probably sleep for the first day or so and not move around a lot, and he wouldn't come off my skin during that time. Roth explained that Robin would bond with me not just physically, but emotionally and mentally. As Robin rested, the familiar would tap into my memories. It would *learn* me, and yeah, that was kind of freaky, but like with Bambi and Roth, Robin would be able to proactively sense whenever I was in trouble or needed him to take form.

I just hoped he didn't appear as a giant, mutant fox, because that would also be extremely creepy.

I had no idea how much time passed, but finally Cayman rocked back, turning off the tattoo gun. "Done," he said, stretching his arms above his back.

Glancing down at my sore stomach, all I could do was stare. There was a huge-ass tattoo there, stretching from under my right rib cage to my navel. Maybe that wasn't big to some, but to me, it was ginormous.

And it was beautiful.

Since I hadn't been paying attention to what Cayman had been doing when he stopped and started, what I saw was a complete surprise to me. The reddish-brown coat of the fox was so realistic that I almost expected to be able to feel the fur if I reached down to touch it. The fox's tail was bushy and streaked with white. It was curled up, its hind legs tucked close to its body and its long snout resting on its front legs. Cayman's detail was extraordinary, down to the thick lashes, the white tufts of fur around the closed eyes and the black whiskers.

And what was also truly amazing was how quickly the redness was fading around the edges of the tattoo. Cayman hadn't been joking when he said I was lucky. Within an hour or so, I knew the skin would be completely healed.

Without warning, one of the fox's whiskers twitched and I jumped in the chair. Grinning, I looked up at Roth. "His whisker moved!"

His smile reached his eyes, lightening the color. "That's fast. I have a feeling this one is going to be active."

"I hope he and Bambi get along." It was kind of like introducing the big sister to the little brother, and hoping she didn't pitch the interloper in front of a speeding truck.

"They will," he said, curling his hand around the nape of my neck. "You did good, Shortie. You deserve a reward."

I arched a brow, knowing I hadn't really done that good. Frankly, I'd acted like a giant baby. "A reward?"

Roth nodded and then leaned down, kissing me, and not just a quick peck on the lips, either. All my senses refocused solely on him. I didn't even feel the dull ache along my stomach. His hand slipped to my chin, holding me in place as he deepened the kiss and I got to check out that bolt in his tongue.

Oh, that kiss… It made me think of other things—things that weren't entirely appropriate when it came to where we were and the fact that the day yawned wide-open in front of us. Last night, after we talked about the familiar, we'd been too drained to do anything but sleep, and now I was wishing we had used that private time more wisely. We needed to get a move on it, as there was really important stuff that needed to get done, but my body flushed and I reached up, wrapping my hand around the back of his head, threading my fingers through his messy hair.

"Don't mind me," Cayman said. "I'm not here. Nope. I'm not the awkward third party, having to witness you two eat each other's face."

Lifting his head, Roth cast a dark look in Cayman's direction while I just sat there, enjoying the aftereffects of the kiss. "You know, you could've simply left."

"Don't bring logic into this conversation," he said, standing. When I looked at him, I saw that the tattoo gun was gone. He winked at me as I tugged my shirt down. "Like Roth said, don't be surprised if your familiar doesn't move around much at first. He's basically sleeping, but when he's ready and he senses you're in any kind of danger, he's probably going to come off."

I nodded and then scooted off the chair, standing. I didn't feel exactly different now that I had my own familiar, but I was a bit excited to see Robin in the flesh for the first time.

Now it was time to hit the streets. There was a good chance that since the Lilin had shown up yesterday, it would again today, but we would be prepared this time. We had to be.

Cayman backed up to the desk and leaned against it, crossing his arms. "Before you guys leave, can you do me a favor, Roth?"

"Depends," he drawled.

"You have a book upstairs—the one about lesser demons. Can I borrow that?"

Roth raised a brow. "Yeah. When have you ever asked before?"

"I'm turning over a new leaf."

Amber eyes narrowed on Cayman. "You can borrow it."

"Can you grab it for me?"

Roth stared at him.

"I'm *le* tired," Cayman said, mimicking a French accent I'd heard on a YouTube video once. "Plus, I don't want to pop in later and get it if you and Layla are in there, engaged in shenanigans, because then you'd have to hurt me if I saw her lady bits and—"

"Okay," Roth cut him off, scrubbing his fingers through his hair, irritated. "Just stop talking."

Cayman smiled.

Muttering under his breath, Roth walked toward the door, and then disappeared. I blinked, hating when they did that. Resisting the urge to pat my now-tattooed belly, I kept my hands at my sides. "That was a strange request."

"I really don't want the book. Reading is so boring," he replied, pushing off the table.

I frowned. "Then why—"

"We don't have a lot of time. I went into the loft this morning and shoved that book behind a bunch of other dusty books that looked boring as Hell, but he'll be down here in a few moments," he explained. "I got word last night that Grim returned early to Hell. He's there."

At first, all I could do was stare at Cayman. Grim—*the* Grim Reaper—was back in Hell, the only being that could release Sam's soul. Excitement and dread exploded like a rocket inside me. I could finally do something for Sam, but I also knew this wasn't going to be easy.

"If you're ready to go down there, I'd suggest you do it soon in case Grim changes his plans," he went on. "And I hear he's in a good mood. So now would be a great time to beg and plead. Because that's all you really have to offer him, right? Your begging?"

I blinked. "That's all I can think of. He's the Grim, and if he spends part of his time in Heaven, he can't really be all evil."

"So you're hoping you can appeal to his innate sense of goodness and justice?" he asked, and when I nodded, he laughed. "Oh, Loopy Layla, you are so cute."

Folding my arms, I exhaled loudly. "What else do I have to offer him? If you have a suggestion, it would be helpful."

"I don't." He flicked a blond lock out of his face as he shrugged. "Truth is, I don't even know what Grim could want in return or if he'd want anything at all. You'll just have to find out. Are you still wanting to do this?"

In the back of my head, I fully recognized what a horrible idea this was turning out to be. Who was I to waltz into Hell and demand that what was virtually the angel of death do something, but what other choice did I have? I couldn't risk Roth doing it, knowing that if he went into Hell right now, he might not come back out, and I couldn't leave Sam in there. I couldn't be complacent and I had to try something.

"I'm in," I said, and my nerves stretched tight.

He inclined his head and the typical playfulness was gone from his expression. "When?"

My heart was pounding as I glanced at the door. Being in Hell was going to be as dangerous as walking across the beltway during rush hour. So many things could go wrong, and if I left right now, Roth popping out of this room could possibly be the last time I saw him. The texts I had with Stacey could be our last correspondence ever, and when I saw Zayne yesterday, that could be the last time. Having another couple of hours or days wasn't going to fix anything with Zayne, but it would give me time to see Stacey and it would give me time with Roth to...

To squeeze a forever into a few short hours.

To experience everything we hadn't yet explored before we lost the chance.

"Can I have tonight?" I asked.

Cayman eyed me and then nodded. "Meet me in the lobby in the morning. Make the most of today. Anything is possible tomorrow."

thirteen

THAT EVENING, I STOOD IN THE BATHROOM OF Roth's loft and stared at my reflection. My face was flushed, eyes way too big, as usual, and nothing really looked that different about me. But I felt different. Older somehow, and I wasn't sure what had sparked that.

Outside of the bathroom, I could hear Roth moving around and the soft hum of the TV was comforting. I glanced at the door, and my heart turned into a sledgehammer. It wasn't until the moment Cayman told me that Grim was back in Hell that it really slammed into me that I was going to go traipsing into Hell to talk to the Grim Reaper. Cayman didn't need to warn me that it would be dangerous. I knew it would be. Anything could go wrong, and tonight could be my last night with Roth.

I wanted—no, needed—to be close to him tonight.

If something went wrong tomorrow, I wanted to experience as much as I could before then. I wanted to experience Roth. It wasn't a decision I took lightly. I'd been obsessing over it all day while we roamed the streets, coming up empty-handed. What I wanted from tonight was a big deal. While Roth and I had done *things*, we hadn't done that one *thing*, and I assumed the nervousness I felt was normal. Roth had way more experience than me when it came to this, but as my gaze shifted back to the mirror, I knew I was ready. I just hoped I... I didn't embarrass myself. That he didn't think I was naive or had no idea what I was doing, because I seriously had no idea what I was doing in this arena.

My gaze dipped to the straps on my camisole and my skin heated in a flash. When I entered the bathroom, I'd been fully clothed. Of course. But now my jeans and the sweater I wore were folded on the rim of the bathtub, and shoved in between them was my bra. The material of the cami was thin, so much so that I didn't need to look down to know exactly what could and could not be seen. And I didn't need the tiny chill bumps racing up and down my legs to remind me that while my undies weren't exactly skimpy, they sure as heck didn't cover all that much. I'd never roamed undressed like this, and I had no idea what my butt looked like in these un-dies and I really didn't want to know.

I wiggled my toes on the cool tile floor.

"I can do this," I whispered at my reflection. "I am a badass hybrid...not a donkey...creature. With *feathered* wings. That are pretty and weird. I can do this."

My pep talk wasn't helping.

I just needed to open the door and walk my confident booty out into the bedroom, grab Roth by the shoulders, toss him onto the bed total She-Ra style, and get down to business.

I frowned.

Well, none of that sounded exactly romantic, and really, I just needed to walk out of this room without looking like a total idiot. Forget everything else. Tugging my hair over my shoulders, I took a deep breath, threw up a little in my mouth, and then turned to the door, yanking it nearly off its hinges as I hauled it open.

I took two steps and then stopped.

Roth was standing in front of the bed, staring at the TV with his arm extended, remote in his hand. He glanced in my direction and froze.

My heart was lodged in my throat, and I couldn't get a single word out as he turned to me, the remote slipping out of his fingers, falling to the floor. It cracked like thunder, but neither of us reacted to the sound.

His gaze started at the top of my head and glided all the way down to the tips of my curled toes, and then slowly made the trek back up to my eyes. The intensity in his gaze created a flutter low in my belly. When he spoke, his voice was rough, sending a series of chills up and down my spine. "I don't know what made you change your sleeping attire, but I just want to let you know that I am a hundred and fifty-five percent behind it."

All I could think was that he liked what he saw and that was a good sign.

"Actually, if you want to dress like that whenever we're alone—to eat dinner, watch the TV, read a book or whatever, I also support that."

Another great sign.

His heated gaze dipped once more and he made this sound in the back of his throat, eliciting another round of shivers. "Damn, Layla, I…"

He seemed to run out of words, and that made me feel a little better standing there, my hands trembling. He was obviously affected, and that affected me, causing weight to settle in certain areas of my body.

My legs carried me toward him and they felt strangely weak. The closer I got to him, the more tension poured off him. He stiffened, his pupils dilating slightly, and I could barely get air into my lungs as I placed my hands on his chest. The heat of his skin burned through his shirt, and I felt his chest rise with a deep breath. I stretched up, pressing the length of my body against his.

I didn't have to ask.

Roth met me halfway, lowering his mouth to mine, and although I was the one to initiate the kiss, he was the one who startled me with the passion behind it. I'd set out to seduce him, which was laughable if I really thought about it, but I wasn't really thinking. The moment his lips touched mine, I was consumed with how he tasted and felt, how my heart was jackhammering when he circled an arm around my waist and lifted me up so that my feet were atop his bare ones. His other hand closed around the nape of my neck, and we were kissing, really kissing, and I could feel the bolt in his tongue. There wasn't an inch of space between our bodies. I folded my arms around his neck, my fingers sliding through the soft locks of hair.

He suddenly lifted his mouth from mine. Each breath he took as he stared down at me was ragged, and I felt it in every part of me. "I can't believe I'm going to say this, but we...we need to slow it down."

My lips felt swollen and my skin was buzzing, but my heart was about to come out of my chest. "I... I don't want to slow down."

His eyes flared a bright, tawny color as his arm tightened around me. "Layla—"

"I don't want to stop." My skin felt way too tight as I rushed on. "I don't want to slow down. I want to go fast." The moment those words were out of my mouth, I wanted to smack myself. "I mean, I want—"

"I get what you're saying," he said thickly. "Damn, do I ever."

Swallowing hard, I started for his mouth again, but the hand at the back of my neck stilled me. Confused, I felt the tendrils of embarrassment start to build. "I don't...understand. You don't want this?"

"Is that a serious question?"

"Yeah."

With his arm, he lifted me up just a few more inches, until our bodies were pieced together in all the ways that counted. "What do you think the answer to that question is?"

Heat burst through my veins, not out of embarrassment, but because I could feel every part of him. "I... I think you do."

"There's nothing else I want more than that in this moment. Layla, I want you. I want you so badly that every time I'm alone with you—Hell, whenever I'm in the near vicinity of you—it takes every ounce of restraint I have not to have you. Make no mistake, the very thought of being with you undoes me," he said, his voice gruff, and I shivered at the intensity behind his words. "But I only want to go there if you're ready. There's no middle ground. There're no maybes, and I'll wait for however long that takes."

Absolute wonder filled me—floored me. It was such an un-demon-like response, yet again, and actually so unlike most guys of any species.

Deep down, I knew a tiny part of me hadn't been entirely ready up until this very moment, that I was doing this because of the potential of never seeing him again after tomorrow. I was rushing toward it, because I was afraid we wouldn't get the chance again, and that was really the wrong reason to want to take our relationship to the next level. But this—what he'd just said to me—erased all my doubts. Not the inherent nervousness that came with such a major thing, but it vanquished any lingering concerns I had.

I was ready.

I was ready because he was willing to slow it down. He was willing to wait. He was willing to let me set the pace.

My hand didn't tremble as I placed it against his cheek, and my gaze was steady when I met his. "I'm ready, Roth."

His eyes slammed shut. "Layla." He said my name harshly. "I'm not a saint. You know this. I want to—"

"I don't want you to be a saint. I want you to be you," I told him, moving my thumb along his lower lip. "I love you and I want this."

He didn't seem to breathe as the seconds stretched out between us. "Are you sure?"

"Yes." Then I nodded for extra emphasis, just in case he was confused.

A long moment passed before Roth showed any reaction to what I said, and then he smiled. Not the big, breathtaking one, but a smaller, more intimate one that wrapped around my heart. And then he kissed me.

The initial touch of our mouths was different from the earlier kiss. It was feather soft, heartbreakingly tender—a kiss of reverence. I didn't even know you could be kissed like that. But the contact...it evolved with the second pass of his lips, and mine parted, welcoming him, and that kiss was far more than something physical.

In that kiss, I could feel our love for one another, our acceptance of each other. It was like taking all our hopes and dreams and rolling them up into one kiss, and it packed so much powerful emotion, that it was a punch to the very core of both of us. It was just a kiss and it was nearly too much and it still wasn't enough, and it was just beautiful.

Roth lifted his head again, but this time it wasn't to stop us. Our gazes locked, and a wealth of emotion showed in his tawny eyes as he stared down at me. "You make me…" He swallowed again. "You make me wish I had a soul so that I could be worthy of you."

I drew in a sharp breath. "You are worthy of me."

Roth held my gaze and then his lips were on mine again. We were moving and when the back of my legs hit the bed, he guided me until I was lying down the middle of it. My hands fluttered to the comforter as I watched him standing above me.

His smile was soft as he reached down and tugged his shirt off, tossing it somewhere behind me, and my stomach hollowed as his lean muscles moved with fluid grace. The kittens were off him, most likely hidden somewhere in the room. Bambi's tail was visible along the stretch of taut skin and the dragon was where he always was.

He went to the nightstand and grabbed a small package, tossing it on the bed. "I don't know if we can produce a child—if I can or you can. So I think we just need to be careful."

My face was on fire. "Good call."

Inclining his head to the side, he grinned. "Yeah. Maybe one day, we'll test that out."

I think my heart might've stopped, because making a baby wasn't something I'd even briefly considered. Growing up, I'd assumed that it was never in the cards because of what I was and wasn't. I'd been taught that I didn't have the attributes for childbearing, and whether that meant it was genetically impossible for me or just not the Wardens' preference, I didn't know. But the idea of doing so one day in the future was strange, elating and scary.

Moving toward the bed, he placed his knees on either side of my legs as he crawled above me. Air constricted in my lungs as he caged me in. Our eyes met, and I swore Roth stopped breathing for a moment. Then he slowly lowered himself down, and the weight of him was shattering.

He stared down at me, the tips of his fingers trailing over the curve of my cheek. "I want this to be perfect for you."

My heart swelled. "It will be, because it's with you."

One side of his lips kicked up. "I feel like I've—" A choked laugh cut him off. "Like I've never done this before."

"Well, that makes two of us." I smiled. "So this could be really good or—"

"It's going to be more than really good," he said, dragging his thumb along my lower lip, mimicking my earlier caress. "Yeah, it's going to be more."

I shivered as he lowered his head, stopping just short of kissing me. "If for whatever reason, you want me to stop at any point in this, tell me. Okay? Promise me."

"I promise," I whispered, wrapping my arm around his neck.

Something soft and amazing flashed across his features, and then we were kissing, and we kissed for what felt like forever. Each kiss had a drugging sort of effect, loosening the rigidness in my muscles. And each kiss was like an eraser, removing everything outside this little world we were creating. I lost myself in him, and he lost himself in me. Time slowed and rushed by, and we were hot and flushed as the kisses increased, twisting against each other.

When Roth lifted his head once more, he didn't speak or move for a long moment, and my chest squeezed as I dragged my fingers through his hair. He dipped his head, kissing my cheek. "Remember your promise."

I remembered, but I wasn't going to stop him and I wasn't going to deny what both of us wanted. He seemed to realize that because as he settled over me again, not quite touching me, he closed his eyes, expression strained. Electricity snapped between us, tugging at us as a raw feeling pulsed. I turned my head, seeking his mouth, and when I found it, I poured everything I felt for him into the kiss. My hands slipped over the thick cords of his neck, traveled the muscles where they bunched in his shoulders, down his lean sides, and then around to his abs, going lower—over each taut ridge, and lower still. He drew in a sharp breath as I reached the button on his jeans.

He caught my hand, tugging it away and pressing it down into the mattress. My heart jumped as heat rolled off his body. His skin seemed too thin and there were shadows lingering just behind the layer of flesh as he drew his hand down to the hem of my camisole.

I really wasn't thinking as I lifted my shoulders and the cami ended up somewhere with his shirt, or when I lifted my hips and the last bit of clothing was gone. I wasn't thinking when his body bowed and he kissed the space just below my new tattoo. And there were no thoughts when, with trembling hands, he began to explore me. My heart was tripping over itself and the fire in my stomach had turned into a wave of molten lava coursing through my veins.

Then his clothes came off, and he was possibly the most beautiful thing I'd ever seen, and when his lips met mine, I was nearly overcome by the strength of the emotions flowing between us. And everything—everything he began to do was downright delicious. We were pressing against one another, straining until I was floating in heavy sensations. My skin came alive wherever we touched, and our hands were everywhere—I was lost in him as his lips blazed a fiery path down my throat and lower, much lower, like he'd done before, and like before, I flew apart with each precise, measured touch, and he pieced me back together with deep, slow kisses.

When he rose above me once more, his fingers were at my hips and he shook as he rested his forehead against mine. Our skin was damp, our bodies flushed. "I need... I need a minute," he said in a rough, low voice.

I looked at him, really looked at him, and saw that he was close to losing control of his human form. His skin had darkened and smoothed to granite. When I saw his eyes, they were golden, but the pupils had stretched vertically.

Emboldened by the effect I had on him, I touched him, remembering the comment he'd made so long ago about being pierced in other areas, and he so had not been joking about that. He made this sound that curled my toes. His eyes closed as his chest rose deeply and when they reopened, his pupils were back to normal.

His hands were back on me and he slowed everything down, until both of us were clamoring at one another, unable to wait, and then it happened.

I wasn't entirely sure what to expect since it wasn't something I'd gotten details on before, not even from Stacey. There was a spark of pain that stole my breath, but Roth…he smoothed over that pain and turned it into something utterly amazing, exquisitely beautiful. It felt like being on a roller coaster, about to plummet hundreds of feet down, and when I did, Roth was there.

And I'd never experienced anything like this before. It was perfect and powerful, and as Roth whispered those three words over and over, our bodies moved against each other. In this moment, Roth wasn't the Crown Prince and I wasn't, well, whatever I was. We were just two people in love, and that was everything.

Minutes might have passed, maybe even hours; I couldn't be sure, but eventually our hearts slowed and we were lying tangled together in the middle of the bed, his arms around me, holding me close.

"You okay?" he asked, sounding like he hadn't spoken in ages.

It took me a moment to get my tongue to work. "I feel… perfect."

His lips brushed mine. "I didn't hurt you?"

I shook my head as my eyes drifted shut. "No. You were…"

"Amazing? Divine? Mind-blowing—"

Laughing softly, I snuggled in against him. "Yes. To all of those things."

His embrace tightened and neither of us spoke for a long moment as he smoothed his hand up and down the center of my back, lulling me into a pleasant, blissed-out haze. "Thank you," he said.

"What are you thanking me for?" I whispered.

Roth kissed my brow. "For everything you have given me."

fourteen

I DOZED OFF IN ROTH'S ARMS, BUT WHEN I stretched out my arms some unknown time later, I found the bed was empty. Blinking open my eyes, I was met with darkness. It was still night, and as I wiggled my toes, I refused to allow thoughts of the morning to creep into my languid happiness.

Rolling over, I waited until my eyes adjusted to the dark. I thought he might be in the bathroom, but as my gaze flitted across the room, I saw him by the piano. My heart sped up, my mind immediately veering to what we'd done, what we'd shared.

The sheets were pooled around my hips and I was too lazy to fix them. Instead, I loosely folded my arms across my chest.

He was sitting on the bench, facing me, with his arms draped over his bent knees. I couldn't make out most of him as I snuggled onto my side. "What are you doing?"

Roth stood and glided out of the shadows. His expression was relaxed and open, but he didn't look normal. Roth could never look just normal, but as he stood there, he looked as close as he'd ever be. "I'm probably going to sound like a creep, but I was watching you."

"That is a hallmark of a creeper."

One side of his lips curled up and a dimple appeared in his right cheek. "I can't help myself. You're just too beautiful to look away from. It's true. I'm a demon. I don't lie."

I stared at him.

His grin spread. "I got up to get something to drink," he admitted. "And I glanced back at you. I don't even know why. I just did and then I *stopped*." His smile faded a bit. "Maybe I can't believe that you're really here. That *we're* here." He raised a shoulder and smooth skin stretched over taut muscles. "And then I sat down and I started thinking about...about everything with the Lilin, and now I've been entertaining the idea of gathering you up while you slept and basically kidnapping you. Hawaii still seems like a good place. Screw whatever happens with the Lilin and all of that. We could survive. I'd make sure of that."

Reaching down, my fingers curled around the edge of the comforter. "Roth..."

He sighed as he raised a hand, scrubbing his fingers through his messy dark hair. "I know. You can't walk away from any of this. None of us can." He dropped his arm. "So that was what I was thinking about while I was staring at you." Those amber eyes flashed with mischief, and I relaxed. I wasn't ready for the world outside to intrude. "Did I tell you that you're beautiful?"

"Yes." Lifting my hand to the poof that was currently my hair, I laughed as I pressed my cheek against the pillow. "But I don't know how you could think so. I'm a mess."

He tipped his head to the side and pivoted around, heading toward the bathroom. After a few seconds, he returned with a hairbrush in hand. With his jeans unbuttoned, they hung indecently low. I could definitely see where Thumper's tail was heading.

Not that I hadn't really seen that earlier.

Cheeks flaming, I pressed my entire face into the pillow, hiding what had to be the goofiest smile known to man. Despite all the craziness we were facing and the uncertainty of what the next hour or tomorrow could drop on us, my little piece of the world felt bright and warm.

What Roth and I had shared, what we had done, was beyond beautiful and wasn't something I could simplify with words. For it to have been that way between us, we had to be in love with each other—madly, deeply in love.

I was the corniest cornball in a cornfield full of popcorn.

Roth touched my shoulder. "Sit up."

"Meh," I murmured into the pillow.

He chuckled. "Sit up. Please."

Demons rarely said please. I was beginning to think it was a word not in their core vocabulary, so I sat up, tugging the comforter to my chest. Roth slipped in behind me. One leg was bent against my side, the other dangled off the edge of the bed.

I looked back at him, but before I could speak, he lowered his mouth to mine and kissed me. The touch of cool metal against my tongue was all too brief. He pulled away and gently turned my chin so I was facing away from him.

"Let me see what I can do with this," he said, gathering up my hair. "You're right. This is a mess. You look like you could've been in an '80s music video. What did you do to it?"

"I didn't do anything. That—" I pointed at my head "—is all your doing."

He started to ease the brush through my hair. "Blame the demon. I see how you are."

As Roth worked his way through the tangles, it really hit me that the Crown Prince of Hell was actually brushing my hair. That was beyond bizarre but also incredibly sweet. My warm and fuzzy glow from earlier was turning into emotional weepiness. Tears pricked at my eyes.

I needed a mood stabilizer.

Roth was extraordinarily patient when it came to working out the knots, more so than me. At this point, I was usually cussing and yanking the brush through my hair. He hummed under his breath as he worked, and I immediately recognized the tune.

"Is 'Paradise City' your favorite song?" I asked.

"The song just kind of got stuck in my head," he said. "For a couple of years, all we could get down below was the classic rock station, and the 'grass is green' line always stuck out to me."

I grinned as I pictured Hell getting Sirius radio. "Why?"

There was a beat of silence. "The grass is never green down below, Shortie."

My lips slipped down at the corners. "It's not? What color is it?"

"Gray," he answered. "Everything is pretty much gray. Except for the blood. And there's a lot of blood."

A shudder worked its way down my spine. "Sounds lovely."

"It's a weird place. Like I said before, it mimics topside but does a shitty job at it. Everything is shiny at first, almost… pretty. Every single time I go down there, it's like that—it's like that for everyone, but it doesn't take long for things to start to go downhill. It fades. Buildings crumble, the sky looks like it's polluted with dirt, and the grass...yeah, it's gray." He eased the brush through my hair, stopping at another tangle. "Everything is twisted and tarnished down there. Things are real up here. Down below they are sad replicas that fall apart."

I remembered when Roth had admitted before that this was one of the reasons he enjoyed coming topside. My heart turned over heavily. "Will...will you have to go back?"

He didn't answer immediately, causing knots to form in my belly. "I don't know, Shortie. If the Boss calls me back, I can only disobey for so long."

Closing my eyes against the ache in my chest, I knew this was something we were going to eventually have to face. "Has the Boss called you back yet?"

"No." He paused, pressing a kiss against my bare shoulder. "The Boss kind of lets most of us come and go as we please, unless we are needed for something. As long as I stay on the Boss's good side, I should be good."

That wasn't reassuring. "But I thought the Boss was displeased with you."

"The Boss is always displeased," he replied. "There's a big difference between him being displeased and me being on the Boss's bad side."

I took that statement to heart, but I couldn't imagine Roth staying on the Boss's good side forever.

"Don't worry about it," he said, returning to my hair. I could feel him separate the now-untangled strands into three sections. "Right now, that's not the biggest of our problems."

I snorted. "True. But I can't help but worry that one day, you're going to...that you're going to just disappear."

"I want you to listen when I say this." He rested his chin on my shoulder, and when I turned my head toward his, he was peering up at me through thick lashes. "Nothing in this world or down below is going to keep me from you. Nothing, Layla. That's a promise I will never break."

A deep, powerful emotion stirred inside me. "I will make you the same promise."

Those thick lashes swept down, shielding his eyes. "You will?"

"Yes." And I meant my next words. "I'm not going to let anything keep you from me and that includes your Boss."

Roth chuckled as he lifted his head, pausing to press a kiss against the side of my neck. "I like it when you get all feisty." He returned to my hair, moving it back into the three sections. Several moments passed. "When I was in the pits, I really didn't think I was going to get out of there. I figured the Boss would either not care enough to pull my happy ass out of it or would forget."

I bit down on my lip as he spoke. Roth had never talked about his time in the pits without being sarcastic about it.

"I honestly have no idea how long I was in there. Time moves differently down below," he continued, twisting the sections of hair around each other. "It wasn't pleasant." A dry laugh cracked out of him. "Actually, it freaking sucked, but you got me through it."

It took a moment for his words to sink in. "How?"

"Easy. I thought about you. You were all I thought about." His voice was quiet as my heart squeezed painfully. "I focused on the time we spent together, and as crazy as it sounds, I thought about you being topside with Zayne."

I winced. How was that helpful?

Seconds later he answered my unspoken question. "Knowing that you'd be safe and would eventually be happy made it somewhat more bearable. And I know—I know—that Zayne would've laid down his life to protect you. Probably still would. You'd be okay. So knowing that helped when it got...well, when it got hard."

A lump formed in the back of my throat. "I wish I could take away the time you've spent in the pits."

His knuckles brushed along the center of my back as he continued with the braid he was making. "You already have."

The lump tripled. "And I wish you never had to sacrifice yourself."

"I wouldn't change a thing."

"I know," I whispered, closing my eyes again. It took me a moment to find the right words. "You know that I care about Zayne deeply. That's never going to change. Even though right now he'd probably rather punt-kick me into traffic than talk to me, I'm always going to love him."

Pausing, I drew in a deep breath. "I told you this before. I love Zayne, but I'm not *in* love with him, and I don't know if that would've ever changed. Could I have been with him?" I raised a shoulder. "Yeah, I could've been, but it would never be like this—like it is between you and me. I don't know how long I would've stayed happy with Zayne if he and I got together and you never came back. Or if he would've remained happy with it himself, but at some point, what I felt for him wouldn't have been enough. That's unfair to him. So I'm glad that knowing I had someone helped you get through that, and to be honest, that blows my mind, but I want you to know that it would've...it would've never been enough for me."

Roth reached around me, placing his hand above my heart.

He flattened his palm, and I lifted my arm, folding my hand over his. His breath was warm against my shoulder when he spoke. "I know."

Drawing back, he flipped the braid over my shoulder. "All done."

I reached up and smoothed my fingers over the thick braid. "You're really good at this. Better than me. Did you practice on your demon friends?"

"Only on all my dolls."

I laughed as Roth tossed the brush aside. It bounced off the foot of the bed and hit the floor. A second later, Fury dashed out from under the bed and pounced on the brush. Its black-and-white hair was raised and its ears were pinned back. The kitten grabbed hold of the handle of the brush, and then dragged it under the bed. I had no idea what it planned to do with it under there.

Twisting at the waist, I faced Roth. Our eyes met. He grinned. The next breath I took was shaky. "I love you. Just wanted to throw that out there."

"I desire you." Lowering his head, his lips skated up the side of my neck, to the sensitive spot below my ear. "I want you. I need you." He nipped the fleshy part of my lobe, causing me to gasp. "And I love you."

The next thing I knew I was on my back and Roth was settling over me, and those little nips were traveling down my neck and lower, and it wasn't too long before all the work he'd done on my hair went to complete waste in the most glorious of ways.

I was staring at my reflection again.

My eyes still seemed too big and my face was flushed, but

this time I wasn't half-naked. Which, honest to God, seemed like a major feat considering—well, once we crossed into that new level of our relationship, Roth really was...

My face burned even brighter and I lowered my gaze as I tugged on the collar of my sweater. Okay. I needed to focus. Last night and in the middle of the night and this morning were amazing, but today was going to be insane. I would be going into Hell. Nervousness didn't even touch what I was feeling, and I still had no idea how I was going to distract Roth so he wouldn't know what I was planning. He thought we were heading out to look for the Lilin. He'd mentioned swinging by another demon-run club in the city. While I was kind of excited to see that, it was not going to happen today.

And I also didn't know what I was going to do when I got back—if I got back—because Roth was going be so mad.

Bambi shifted on my back, flicking her tail along the left side of my ribs, coming close to nudging Robin. As soon as I'd gotten up this morning, she'd plastered herself onto me, which hadn't been a part of the plan, but it wasn't like I could pitch a fit about her being on me. Roth would know something was up, which sucked, because the last thing I wanted to do was put Bambi in a precarious position.

She was practically our kid.

Twisting my hair up, I shoved a million bobby pins in, and then left the bathroom. Roth was lounging against the wall, his long legs crossed at the ankles, hands shoved into the pockets of his jeans. I saw him and I might've forgotten what I was doing.

Roth was striking.

With his black hair falling into amber eyes and the shirt clinging to all the right areas, he was breathtaking, but it was that smile, the one that showed off his dimples and transformed his entire being when he looked at me that—that owned me. And he was smiling at me like that now.

"I like your pants," he said.

I glanced down. They were black. Leather. I sighed. "I'm never allowing Cayman to go shopping for me again."

He chuckled as he pushed off the wall. "I hope he shops for you from now on." Walking past me, toward the door, he slid his hand over my leather-clad legs. "Or at least keep these."

I rolled my eyes as I turned around.

"Mmm." His gaze traveled over me. "Please keep them."

Laughing, I planted my hands on his back and shoved him toward the door. "Only because you asked nicely."

"And because your ass looks sumptuous in them?"

"Geez," I choked out, shaking my head as he closed the door behind us.

Out in the hallway, he draped his arm over my shoulders and hauled me close to his side. We started down the hall. "I think that's a valid reason."

"I'm sure you do."

His hand moved up and down my upper arm as we hit the stairwell and began the long, *long* journey down to the lobby. "How your ass looks is a very important thing when shopping for pants, Shortie."

I pressed my lips together to keep from laughing. "I'm sure there are things that are even more important."

He scoffed. "Like what?"

"Oh, I don't know. How about comfort?"

"Boring."

"What about usefulness?"

He sent me a look. "There is nothing more useful than

leather pants. They'll protect your ass while making it look fine."

We were nearing the first floor. "You have an answer for everything, don't you?"

"Yes."

"It's annoying," I muttered, glancing at the gray, cement door, and my pulse kicked up.

"You still love me," he replied.

"True." I squared my shoulders as Roth opened the door.

We stepped out into the grandiose lobby with his arm still hanging over my shoulders. Like the first time I'd seen the lobby, it was awe-inspiring. I didn't get to see it a lot, because we always came in through the parking garage or the basement club entrance and then we stuck to the stairwell.

An enormous chandelier hung in the center of the lobby, casting bright light into every corner, but it was the mural painted on the ceiling that really drew the eye. Angels. Lots of angels hovering above, engaged in a hard-core battle, fighting one another with fiery swords. Some were falling through sudsy white clouds. Others were raising their blades. The detail was extraordinary, down to the red-orange flames and the grimaces of pain. Even the virtuous glint in their eyes was there.

I quickly looked away from the painting, unsettled by it when before I'd just been amused.

Vintage leather couches were everywhere, and they weren't empty. People of all ages were scattered about, sitting alone or in groups, talking and laughing. Some were chatting on phones. The scent of coffee was thick in the air. To a human, they'd all look normal, but their eyes gave off weird glints.

They weren't exactly people, not in the technical sense.

A few gave me a weird look. Others downright ignored

me. One, a young woman dressed in some kind of bustier I could easily see Cayman purchasing, stood from a recliner, her wide eyes glittering as she hurried across the lobby, disappearing down a hallway.

I had no idea if that had to do with me or with Roth's presence. I really didn't get the demon dynamics when it came to Roth, but none of the demons milling about in the lobby came near us.

As I started to turn to Roth, Cayman appeared in the middle of the lobby, under the chandelier. Stiffening, I watched him swagger toward us, his floral pink and teal Hawaiian shirt possibly the gaudiest thing I'd ever seen.

"Okay. I officially change my opinion on Cayman shopping for you," Roth said.

I snickered.

Cayman ignored the comments. "It's a great morning, isn't it?" he said brightly, stepping to the side of Roth. "The sun is out, but they're calling for snow tonight. Lots of snow. So much snow—"

The crack jolted me.

He had moved so fast, I didn't realize what he'd done until Roth's legs folded and collapsed. Heart leaping into my throat, I tried to grab Roth, but he was too heavy and I ended up going down on my knees.

Cayman had snapped Roth's neck.

fifteen

HORROR FILLED ME AS ROTH'S HEAD FELL TO the side at an awkward angle. "Oh my God!" I shouted, looking up at Cayman. "What did you do? What did you—?"

"We needed to distract him." He gestured at the floor. "He's distracted. And you have no idea how long I've wanted to do that. Let me have my moment."

My mouth dropped open.

A demon walking across the lobby carrying coffee in white to-go cups pivoted on her pointy black heel. "I don't want any part of this," she said, hurrying away.

My hands shook as I glanced down at a still Roth. I couldn't breathe, and as I stood, my skin started to harden, the skin on either side of my spine tingled.

"Whoa." Cayman threw up his hands. "Simmer down, crouching demon, hidden Warden. He's fine. Look, if he was seriously in danger, Bambi would be off you in two seconds. He's going to wake up in a couple of minutes, beat the crap out of me, realize you're gone, and when I snap his neck again to stop him from going after you, we're going to rinse and repeat, so please—please don't take forever."

My heart hadn't slowed down. "If he's hurt—"

"He's not," a demon from the couch said, his face ashen as he stared at Roth. "You can't kill the Prince that way and when he wakes up—"

"Yeah, he's going to be pissed." Cayman sighed.

"I didn't even get to say goodbye to him, Cayman." I sucked in a shallow breath. "What if I—?"

"Don't finish that sentence. You will be back. Layla, you need to get a move on it. Don't let the butt-whupping I'm going to receive be all in vain. You need to go." He pointed behind me, and I looked back toward the gold-painted elevators.

I needed to go.

Heart pounding, I knelt and brushed my lips along Roth's cheek as I smoothed my hand over his head, brushing his hair back from his face. I didn't want to leave him. I wanted to sit there until his eyes opened, but I couldn't.

"I love you," I whispered, voice choked as I curled my right hand into a fist.

Standing, I turned to Cayman and cocked back my arm, punching him right in the stomach as hard as I could. Several demons gasped.

"*Omph,*" he grunted, doubling over and clasping his stomach. "Sweet Moses in molasses."

Feeling a wee bit better about the situation, I forced myself to pivot around and walk toward the elevator. I didn't look back, because if I did, I wasn't sure I would keep walking. I liked to think that I would've, that I would've recognized that this situation was bigger than me and Roth, but I wasn't sure if I was that good a person, that selfless.

The gold elevators waited for me and I smacked the one round button on the panel a little harder than necessary. With a soft, almost-human-sounding groan, the doors slid open. I stepped inside, turning around to face the hall.

Cayman appeared in front of the elevators, rubbing his stomach. "Be careful, Layla. Remember, nothing in Hell is what it seems."

Before I could respond, the doors sealed shut and the elevator jerked into movement. I stepped back, swallowing hard as it started a slow descent down. There was no music, no inside panels on the elevator, and the door seemed to be made of some kind of weird material. I brushed my fingers along the inside of the door and then jerked my hand back with a startled gasp.

It felt like...like *skin*.

My stomach cramped, and I thought I might hurl as it rippled.

A strange orangey glow reflected off the walls of the elevator. Lifting my gaze to the ceiling, I smacked my hand over my mouth.

There wasn't really a ceiling above me.

A roof of flames rolled, burning bright, licking along the edges of the walls. My eyes widened as I expected it to engulf the entire elevator, but the flames didn't spread. The elevator jolted and that slow descent sped up.

I was knocked back against the wall. Throwing my hands out, I gripped the rail as the elevator suddenly dropped at a rapid clip. Heart thumping, my knuckles ached from how tightly I was gripping the piece of metal. The elevator felt like it was going to split apart.

Without warning, it jerked to a stop, throwing me off balance. My knees cracked off the floor, the pain dull compared to the sudden dizziness seizing me. It took several moments for the wooziness to subside, and I realized then, the elevator had stopped moving.

Pushing myself up, I'd just straightened when the elevator doors parted softly. My mouth dropped open as I got my first glimpse of…Hell?

Not at all.

What lay beyond the open elevator doors was white walls—a white floor, a white ceiling. Shiny white. Pristine. My feet carried me out of the elevator, into a wide and vast circular lobby with hundreds if not thousands of hallways. There was music playing. Horrible, jaunty lobby music; the kind that would drive you crazy if you had to listen to it for longer than five minutes. I couldn't believe what I was seeing. Hell had a lobby.

Nothing was guarding the lobby. No demons waited to pounce on me, and that surprised me. Then again, Cayman had warned me that nothing in Hell was what it seemed. Maybe I just couldn't see the demons. As I wheeled around, searching for hidden dangers, I realized there were gold placards on the walls near each hallway, displaying the names of…

"Holy crap," I whispered.

Names of all the demons were clearly etched into the gold placards. Some I didn't recognize. Others made my stomach twist and then drop. *ABADDON. VINE. MOLOCH. BAEL.* The names went on and on. Straight across from the elevator was the hallway labeled THE BOSS and beside it was one that caught my breath.

ASTAROTH.

I almost started toward it, because something inside of me wanted to see how Roth really lived when he was down here, but I stopped myself. I didn't have time for this.

Across from those names was THE PITS. And there, three down from that, was the name I'd been looking for: GRIM.

Taking a deep, fortifying breath, I walked briskly toward the hall bearing Grim's name and then down the long, brightly lit, relatively cool tunnel. There were no windows. No scents to speak of. The air was stagnant but clean, and still, the hairs all over my body began to rise.

I reached a double set of windowless doors and before I could do anything, they opened silently, revealing a world I'd never seen before as a blast of oppressive heat smacked into me.

Stopping an inch from the exit, I bit down on my lip. This...this was what I'd expected. In a way. The sky beyond the hall was a burnt red. There were no clouds. No sun or moon. Just a deep, orangey red that seemed to have no source. The scent of sulfur and something I couldn't quite make out turned my stomach.

A road made of some kind of stone separated tall, ash-colored buildings. They rose like skyscrapers, reaching into that strange sky, their windows dark with no sign of life inside them. My gaze tracked over the formidable, intimidating buildings to the massive structure at the end of the road, several city blocks away. It was the largest of all the buildings, but designed like something straight out of the Middle Ages. Twin steeples rose from either side of the pitch roof, and it gave the impression that it was more of a fortress than a home. Sort of like the compound I'd grown up in.

I swallowed hard, knowing that was where I was going to have to go, because of course, it wasn't like Grim could live in a cute house with a picket fence or something. Oh no, it had to be the *Lord of the Rings*-type castle all the way down there.

Knowing I didn't have a lot of time and that time in general worked vastly different down here, I pulled up my big-girl undies and stepped out of the hallway.

It happened immediately.

Without any warning, a shiver rippled across my skin and I felt Bambi and Robin leave my body. Panicked, I tried to stop them, because I wasn't sure if Robin was ready for that, but there was no calling them back.

Two shadows drifted out from underneath my shirt, forming two irregular shaped circles. They trembled, and then dropped to the stone roadway, spilling into a million tiny balls that shot together. The inky black balls rose into the air, but they didn't drop to the ground like they normally would.

The dots spun and spun until a thick shadow formed. Before me, as my mouth hung open, legs formed, along with torsos and arms and *heads*. For a second, they were two people-shaped pools of black oil, and then, within a heartbeat, the murkiness gave way to detail.

A boy and a girl stood in front of me.

My jaw was starting to ache from how long I was gaping, but I couldn't snap my mouth shut. They weren't little boys and girls. Actually, they looked slightly older than me, but they were definitely of the male and female humanoid variety.

The guy was tall and slender, with auburn hair that fell into crimson-colored eyes. Shirtless, he was all wiry grace. A fine dusting of reddish hair covered his bare skin. Standing next to him was a woman with hair a deep red, nearly matching her eyes. Dressed in a black tank top and jeans, she almost looked normal. *Almost.* Patches of her skin weren't exactly…skin. More like tiny scales breaking through, all so very…snake-like.

Oh my God.

The woman grinned brightly. "Hey, girl, hey."

"Hey," I said slowly, glancing between the two. "Um…"

Raising his chin in a greeting, the guy's nose twitched and then…then his ears did the same. "Hi."

Oh my God.

"I so knew you were up to shenanigans, and I was right!" Turning to the guy, the girl raised her hand, flipping him off. "Told you so. Told you that she was going to come here. So you should be glad I'm here, so you don't get eaten by dragons. And yes, there are dragons here. And not as nice as Thumper, either."

"You're just so smart," he replied drily.

"Damn tootin'." She spun toward me. "He's not very helpful right now, since he's like new to all of this. I needed to come along."

"You… You are…" I almost couldn't bring myself to say it. "You're Bambi."

Hopping, she clapped her hands together. "And you're Layla. And he's Dumbass."

Dumbass sighed. "I'm Robin. You know, your real familiar. Not the parasite who needs to go back to Daddy."

Bambi snorted. "How about you go back to yourself. Huh? How about that?"

That didn't even make sense, but the fact that I was staring at Bambi and Robin and they looked like humans didn't make sense, either. "So you two... This is what you really look like?"

She nodded. "Yep. When we can, which tragically isn't very often. But we can talk to one another even in our animal forms. Sort of telepathically." She pouted. "Robin here is a bore. He's really just slept this whole time."

He scowled in her direction. "Because I needed to get charged up."

"Whatever," she quipped. "I miss my boys. Nitro and Fury and Thor. They're fun. Thumper is like you. Another bore who just sleeps all the time, and when he doesn't, he's a grumpy tool."

I blinked slowly as Bambi raised her arms above her head, stretching. Her top rose, flashing a taut stomach, and it suddenly hit me that Roth had a chick on him. Roth seriously had a chick all over him, all the time! On lots of parts of his body. And I had a dude on my stomach!

Roth and Cayman had failed to mention this little detail to me.

An ugly, insidious feeling crept into me and I couldn't stop myself from saying, "You are on Roth."

"Um, yeah. And sometimes I'm on you. Duh." She frowned. "Did you hurt your head or something?"

Okay. I squeezed my eyes shut briefly. The jealousy was ridiculous. I couldn't be jealous over Bambi, who might be a hot girl but also was a snake most of the time—a legit, giant snake that ate gross things.

Besides, I had a dude on me— "Oh my God," I groaned, looking at Robin. "You were on me last night. You were on me—"

"The moment you all started losing clothes, I totally

checked out." He raised his hands, wrinkling his nose. "Did not want to see any of that. Didn't feel any of that."

"I…" There were no words.

"Look," Bambi said, "for most of the time we're on you, we aren't paying attention to what you're doing. Well, not true. When you were with Zayne, I was so paying attention."

I pinched the bridge of my nose. "So the kittens? They…"

"They are hot. Oh my golly God, they're triplets," Bambi said, smacking my arm with enough force to stagger me. "Triplets, Layla. There are actually three of them."

"I got that." I rubbed my stinging arm. "Thanks."

Robin folded his arms as he cast his gaze to the orangey sky. "I have a feeling we should not be here."

"This is unspeakably weird," I muttered, trying to grasp the fact that I was talking to the familiars.

Bambi flipped that crimson hair over her shoulder. "I think it's fantastically delightful." Prancing forward, she stuck out her tongue in Robin's direction. Even in her human form, the tongue was still forked. "But you know what's *not* delightful? Your taste in men. I was really hoping you'd hook up with Zayne. He looked yummy."

"You've already eaten one Warden—"

"Honey, that's not the kind of eating I'm thinking of when I clap eyes on that big, blond ball of sweet, sweet loving."

My eyes widened as Robin rolled his. "I'm…uh, sorry to disappoint you?"

Bambi continued as if I hadn't spoken. "I liked it when he would pet me and I think you liked it, too," she said, and my face went up in flames, because I knew exactly the moment she was referring to. "But I wonder how he'd feel if he knew what part of me he was actually feeling up. It wasn't my neck."

"That's disgusting," Robin said.

She snickered. "It was *amazing*."

Okay. I knew I needed to focus on the important stuff, but I was still stuck on the fact they were here. "How is this possible?" I asked.

Bambi opened her mouth, but it was a male's voice from behind me that answered. "Ah, spoken like a true newcomer. Allow me to enlighten you, young innocent. Whenever familiars are in Hell, they automatically take this form. Obviously, no one thought to tell you, because they believed it would be a nonissue."

Spinning around, I fought the urge to back up. Instinct demanded that I move far, far away from the tall man who stood in front of the doors leading to the hallway. *Tall* really didn't do him justice. He had to be near seven feet in height. A ruggedly handsome man, if dark beards and hard, glacial eyes were your kind of thing.

"They can also take this form topside," he continued.

Bambi giggled from behind me. "Astaroth lets me do that. Not often. But when he does, it's always fun. I wish he would do it more often."

The man arched a brow. "Probably not the wisest of decisions. You see," he added, directing his attention to me again, "the familiars have very little impulse control and they do not operate by any human moral compass."

"Damn skippy we don't," Bambi agreed.

"You and I need to talk," the man told me, raising his hand. He snapped his fingers, and I felt more than saw that the familiars were gone. "Don't worry. They're fine. Well, they will be provided they stay away from the pits and any demon who may be a bit angry with the Prince, but I'm sure those two will cause more trouble than any trouble that can find them. Rest assured they will be returned to you once you leave."

My eyes widened as my heart rate kicked up. I saw no aura around the man, but if I had, I imagined it would be dark and vast. Power radiated out from him, the supreme kind. He hadn't made one move toward me, but I knew within a second, he could end me.

He could end us all.

"I knew you would come," he continued, his lips curving up slightly behind the beard. "I even hastened my arrival from the pearly gates in anticipation of this moment. But have you nothing to say, child? After all, you wanted to see me. And here I am."

This was Grim—the Grim Reaper.

sixteen

HOLY CANOLA OIL IN MY FACE, I WAS DOING MY best not to spaz out, but *this* was the Grim Reaper, and he had been *expecting* me. Of course he had been, because he was who he was, and he probably saw *everything*.

Which was awkward to think about.

A tremor of unease coursed through me as a million questions sprang forth, ones I knew better than to ask him. But I wanted to. I wanted to know if he really was the angel of death. If he could take me to Sam now? If he knew Lilith? If he saw where Elijah had gone, after the Lilin had killed him? And what about all those other poor people? The questions kept bursting free, and it took everything in me to remain silent.

Grim smiled behind the trimmed beard. "The Prince is going to be very upset with you when you return."

"Yeah." There was no denying that. I just hoped I *would* return.

His smile spread but did not reach his eyes or soften his face. Frankly, it made him more creepy. "Especially considering I've blocked any entrance into Hell. He cannot come for you. I did not want to be interrupted—we need our time together, and yes, I have that kind of power and then some."

My heart turned over heavily as my mouth dried. *Our time together* gave me the heebie-jeebies. I couldn't go back, though. "I had to come. I had to—"

"I know why you're here, but I don't want to talk about that." He started to walk past me, toward the fortress. "Not yet."

I turned to follow him. "But—"

"If you were wise, you would not question me. Please tell me you are wise."

Chagrined, I held back what I really wanted to say. "I like to think I am."

"Then you will walk with me," he replied with mock courtesy, tossing the words over his shoulder. "And you will talk with me about what I want to talk about."

I had no idea what Grim could want to talk about with me that didn't have to do with Sam, but I hurried to catch up with him.

"That's a smart girl," he murmured as he walked down the center of the empty road, his hands shoved into the pockets of his trousers. The buildings surrounding us were quiet. "Pity, though, that you're not very observant."

Pressing my lips together to keep myself from saying something I was sure to regret, I focused on the stones in the road. They too had a reddish tone to them.

"For example, what do you think you know about your mother?" Grim asked, startling me. "Yes, Lilith. That's what I want to talk about. Did you know, child, that Lilith is not a demon? Well, not exactly?"

For a moment, I couldn't speak. "She is a demon. Everyone says—"

"Everyone can say whatever they'd like to say, but that does not mean they are correct, and the truth is sometimes lost in translation when the facts are not understood," he replied, the corners of his lips tipping up. "And the truth is, the facts are, that Lilith is not merely a demon."

We passed a hut-type building, smushed between the taller, fiercer skyscrapers. Out of the corner of my eye, I thought I saw movement in the hovel's window, but when I looked, I saw nothing. "I... I don't understand."

"I have a feeling you understand very little." He delivered the insult quite smoothly. "You know Lilith's background, correct? She was kicked out of Eden because she was, well, demanding. From there, she coupled with demons, and out of that she created a whole new breed of them—but none of that happened immediately. Oh no. You see, Lilith's plight had gained her the sympathy of a very powerful being. She became...friends with the unlikely ally, and when Eden fell apart and all its former inhabitants were stripped of their immortality due to sin, so was Lilith. And her new friend, well, that being did not feel it was right that Lilith would be...punished yet again."

"I think I can guess who that being was," I said, hoping he didn't knock me into the next century for taking a stab at it. "The Boss?"

"Correct. At the time, they were two peas in a rather disturbed pod. The Boss hadn't created any demons before meeting Lilith and had no idea how it was done, but the Boss refused to allow Lilith to die a mortal death. Who knows if the Boss had a real fondness for Lilith or simply did this as a way of…of giving the big guy in the sky the middle finger once more. The why of it all doesn't really matter in the end.

"The Boss discovered that the blood of an original angel that had fallen, if ingested, granted immortality among other things. That blood was given to Lilith and her immortality was restored." He paused while I processed that new knowledge. "I'm sure the Boss regrets that gift now, but hindsight is useless."

He smiled broadly as we approached a narrow bridge built with the same stone we walked upon. The scent of sulfur and metal grew stronger.

"So Lilith…she really isn't a demon then. She was, well, whatever the first people were, then made mortal, and then given the blood of a fallen angel." My frown grew. "Yeah, that… What in the world is she then?"

One shoulder rose as he glanced down at me. "What in the world are you?"

A cold chill snaked down my spine despite the stifling, acidic air. "I guess I don't really know."

"It's interesting how nature always takes care of its own, developing a checks and balance system, its own Law of Balance. Despite having her immortality restored to her, Lilith had one weakness, basically an off switch. If she were to deliver a child naturally, if anything happened to that child, it would end her. By giving life to you, she ultimately set into motion the only true weapon that could kill her. Nature. That's the true bitch."

My eyes widened. Then that meant…when I died, so would Lilith? *I* was her off switch. Wow.

"To be honest, I never understood why she decided to take the risk of creating you. No offense."

"None taken," I muttered. "Maybe she didn't know about the...off switch?"

"Oh, I'm sure she knew. Her arrogance rivals that of the Boss," he replied, and I stiffened, half expecting the Boss to appear in front of us to make us pay for his insult. "She thought that her child would be just like her—traitorous, obsessed with power and control. And it was a devious plan. Fornicating with a Warden, leaving the child to be raised among the enemy in order to ultimately usurp the Wardens and possibly even the Boss. Lilith wanted the *world* since she felt it all had been taken from her when she was exiled from Eden. It did not matter that she had been granted immortality anew and could have found some sense of peace. She wanted revenge against all of mankind—always did and always will. Birthing you was a devious plan, but ultimately a failed endeavor—for you are not like her. Not in that way."

"No," I whispered, stepping onto the bridge. I didn't know how I felt to have it confirmed that to Lilith—my mother—I was nothing more than a tool, a weapon in a never-ending war. Anger and disappointment roiled together, and I forced out a rough laugh. What I had meant to Lilith couldn't matter now. It hadn't mattered before. "I'm not like her."

"But you are also not like the Wardens, or so you think." He chuckled softly, stopping to gaze over the stone wall of the bridge, down to the river below. And what a river it was.

A deep red, the river bubbled and foamed with sludge, and I had a feeling that was where the nasty scent was coming from. I didn't want to know what the river actually consisted of, but it looked chunky, so I doubted it was water.

"I'm going to tell you a little story, one that you should pay very close attention to."

I wasn't sure I could handle another story, but I forced my-self to focus.

Removing his hands from his pockets, he lightly placed them on the wall. "When the angels were sent to enlighten man, they failed in the most glorious way. They succumbed to evil and temptation, became gluttonous with food and drink. They *fornicated*." Pausing to grin, he glanced at me. "And there were many failures, Layla. So many that the big guy in the sky knew he had a major problem on his hands. These angels were powerful, created after his own virtues, and they were corrupt. They could undo everything he created, so they were to be dealt with, punished by the Alphas."

Lost in a part of history that had never been willingly shared or spoken of, I was silent as I listened. I was also try-ing not to breathe too deeply, because the stench was close to knocking me out.

"Some of those that fell, the original angels sent to man, escaped punishment by descending into Hell. The Boss wel-comed them with open arms. They are your fallen, the origi-nals that other demons fear. There are those that refer to them as demons, but they are not and have never been created by the Boss or spawned by another demon. It would be wise to remember where they came from," he explained, tilting his chin up. His shoulders tensed under the plain white shirt he wore. "Then there were those who fell who took their pun-ishment, those pious creatures who realized that they were at fault and whose love for their creator was greater than their desire for freedom. And they were punished. Do you know how, Layla?"

My name drifted off his lips like an arctic blast and I shiv-ered. "No."

He twisted toward me, leaning against the wall with a confidence in the craftsmanship I did not share. "They were turned to stone."

I gasped as understanding floored me.

"You see my meaning." His eyes glittered coldly. "Those who fell and accepted their punishment were turned to stone—and were given horrifying, bestial appearances not just to remind mankind that evil existed, but to serve as a tangible lesson to those who should be above temptation that they too can fall from grace."

"Whoa." My head spun. The Wardens originally were angels that had fallen? Suddenly what Roth tauntingly called them—heavenly rejects—made sense. He'd known, but had always said it hadn't been his story to tell.

"For many centuries, those penitent fallen remained entombed—until the Alphas woke them to combat the rapidly expanding demon population and the Lilin who were created so many centuries ago," Grim went on, turning his gaze back to the river. "They didn't wake all of them, Layla. Some still slumber. Even your clan wouldn't know that, but those whose sins were most offensive are those still trapped in their punishment."

"God," I breathed, thinking of all the gargoyles adorning the buildings just in DC alone. This whole time I'd believed man had simply carved them.

"Those who were awakened became the first Wardens, but their punishment had changed them. That is why they have two forms, and it is also why, in their true form, they resemble the very creatures they are charged with dispatching. Ironic, isn't it?" He smiled again. "I am sure your clan hasn't forgotten their true history, but they would love to, wouldn't they? The only beings more arrogant than the Alphas would be the Wardens."

There was another thing I couldn't deny. "This is all fascinating, but—"

"Why am I telling you this, the history of your mother and the race that raised you as their own? You want something from me, but I want you to understand what you are." He pushed away from the wall, facing me from a mere foot away. "You stand before me, cowering like a helpless girl."

The hairs were standing along the back of my neck again. "That's because you are...you are the Grim—"

"I know what I am. At least I can say that. You can't."

"Yeah, I get that, but—"

His hand snapped out, wrapping around my throat. I'd taken my last breath before I knew it. Panic flooded me as I reached up, gripping the massive hand. I willed my body to shift, but Grim smiled as he lifted me clear off my feet.

"You can't shift. Not here. Cayman did not tell you that? Foolish demon, he tends to leave out important information. You're not from this realm, child, therefore you cannot take your true form here," he said, lifting me even higher. "I could snap your neck in a second and do you know what would happen?"

I would die.

Wasn't like I could say that since I was busy trying to conserve whatever oxygen was left in my lungs, which wasn't much. My chest was burning, my heart pounding fiercely.

"It would hurt. It would knock you out, but no, you would not die," he continued, as if he could read my thoughts. "Frankly, the only thing that will kill you is an iron dagger to the heart or if someone cuts off your head." His words were breaking through the burning haze, but they made little sense. "Fire? Nope. Falling from a hundred stories? It cannot kill you. Gutted? No. Once you understand that, you will be stronger and fiercer than any Warden to walk topside, and even Upper Level demons will flee your presence."

Suddenly he released his hold on me. I hit the bridge, staggering into the stone wall. It crumbled like ash under my weight, falling into the teeming water below. I teetered on the edge, arms flailing.

He caught me by the arm, hauling me away from the edge and against his chest. The full body contact was like cuddling up to a snowman—a psychotic snowman. My skin chilled, and as I exhaled roughly, then dragged in air in huge gulps, a misty cloud formed in front of my lips.

"Now do you see what I've been trying to show you, the purpose of all my stories? You are not a demon. You have never been a demon, you silly girl."

seventeen

YOU'RE NOT A DEMON.

I stopped struggling for air as I stared into his cold eyes. What he'd told me about Lilith and the Wardens had rocked me, but now I was struck stupid by pure disbelief. "That doesn't make sense," I gasped out.

"Why? Because your clan believes you to be one? Because the Prince has never said differently? That's what he's been told by the Boss, because if the Upper Level demons knew what the Boss had done for Lilith all those years ago, they would not be happy. No demon likes the idea that the Boss has played favorites and still does. The Prince had no reason to believe differently. To all of them, you feel like a demon, only because you feel like an original fallen angel." His grip was tight, bordering on cruel. "If you paid attention to my story, you can follow where I'm going with this."

Parts of my body were frozen from contact with him, so I really wasn't following jack right now.

Grim lowered his head, and I stiffened as his mouth stopped a mere inch from mine. "You were part Warden and part whatever the Hell Lilith is when you were born, which makes you something entirely different. The Warden blood in you weakened whatever Lilith passed on. You were as mortal as any of them, not nearly as powerful, with your only gift a deadly kiss, but those damn witches…" He laughed, and his icy breath coasted over my lips, causing me to shudder. "Those who worship your mother. They gave you something to drink, did they not, following your stabbing and the Prince's heroic rescue? Whisking you out of my grasp quite efficiently. Didn't they?"

"Yes," I gritted out. "We didn't know what it was. Roth didn't know—"

"But can you guess what it is now? Prove you've been paying attention to my little history lesson?"

Blood thundered in my head, and I knew where he was going with this, but I couldn't believe it—the idea that I'd been given blood from one of the original fallen angels. First off, that was freaking gross. Secondly, I… "Why would they do that? How did they have it?"

"That's for them to answer." His lashes lowered, shielding his eyes. "But what they did—it zeroed out whatever Warden blood you had in you. Now…you are something else entirely."

I thought about how Zayne and Danika had said that I felt like an Upper Level demon, but that was before the witches had given me that…that brew. But it all started to connect together. Roth was partly right. I was still transforming, and since I wasn't what anyone expected me to be, what the Wardens were sensing could've been whatever I was maturing into. Plus a demon had run from me since I'd drunk that stuff, and I did look different.

"Oh my God," I whispered, forgetting who was holding me. "That's why I have *feathers* in my wings."

His mouth twitched. "Among other things."

"I'm… I'm immortal?"

He let go of me and stepped back, but I was so floored that I barely registered the warmth slowly creeping back into me. "As immortal as anything that can only be killed those two ways I mentioned before. The moment you consumed the blood of the originals, you became what the Alphas would call an abomination. But what they fail to appreciate is that you alone can ultimately stop what is coming."

Stunned by everything he'd said, I raised a shaky hand, pushing the hair that had come loose back from my face. I'd come here to retrieve Sam's soul and ended up discovering that everything I thought I'd known about my life, my identity, had been wrong—again. Part of me didn't know what to think about that. The other part was bubbling with sweet awareness. Incredibly selfish, sure. But there would be no walkers in my future while Roth remained ageless.

"You are like Lilith—utterly unique. Something that should not exist but does. So, too, is the Lilin. It should not exist, but you…you can stop it."

My gaze tracked to him as I lowered my hand. "I will stop it."

"Really?" He inclined his head. "Because all you've done since the Lilin revealed itself is mourn your friend, pout, indulge in relationship drama I would normally only expect from a pitiful human teenager and surrender your chastity."

I jerked back, a rigidness taking over my muscles. "What?"

"I think I spoke clearly." He stalked toward me, and this time, I didn't back up, though my throat still ached from the last time I held my ground. "You need to stop the Lilin, but the only thing you've really accomplished is the loss of your virginity. Still, I suppose congratulations are in order. It is a milestone, after all. Please pass my good tidings to the Prince."

Embarrassed and furious, I felt my mouth drop open. "That's not true!"

"It's not?" Grim tipped his head back and laughed darkly. "Tell me, what else have you managed?"

I opened my mouth, ready to fire off everything that I'd— that *we'd* been working on—but the only things he'd really failed to mention were our botched attempts at locating the Lilin, the end of Elijah, and my new tattoo, who was now off doing God knows what with Bambi—who, by the way, shouldn't even be here.

Verbally backed into a corner, I said the first thing that shot to the tip of my tongue. "I didn't ask for any of this!"

The moment those words left my mouth, I knew they were a mistake. Besides the fact it didn't do much for the conversation, it was possibly the most incredibly childish thing I'd ever said.

And that was saying something.

Grim smirked. "No one ever asks for what life deals them. You are hardly special."

My gaze lowered to his boots, and then I squeezed my eyes shut. God, he was right. No matter what I had going on in my life, I hadn't done enough to stop the evil I'd inadvertently helped create when Paimon had performed the ritual in his attempt to free Lilith—and more innocent people would die as a result. I wasn't sure what more I could've done, but obviously there was something.

Taking a deep breath, I lifted my eyes to his. "You're right. I haven't been doing enough, but I will do anything to stop the Lilin."

His eyes glinted strangely, as if they held their own light source. "Anything?"

"Anything," I repeated, though the words did not change why I was here. "But I'm not going to forget about Sam. His soul is here and it doesn't belong here."

He moved again, lightning quick, but I jumped back as I threw up my arm, blocking his attempt at another throat grab. Pain pulsed down my arm, and there'd probably be a bruise there later, but better there than around my neck.

Grim drew back, and I thought I saw approval flaring in his eyes. "Perhaps you still do not understand what is at risk here."

Then, without any warning, he gripped my wrist, and we were no longer on the bridge; we were in some kind of building and a wall of flames loomed in front of us. Heat rolled off the burning wall as crackling flames touched the floor and ceiling, but somehow, like the fire in the elevator, they didn't spread.

Thrown off by the sudden change, I stumbled back and into Grim. Jerking away, I didn't make it very far before a strong arm clamped down, around my waist, drawing me back. Air punched out of my lungs.

"I think there's someone you need to meet," he said, voice low in my ear.

The flames pulsed, and then dropped from the ceiling, disappearing into the floor and revealing what existed beyond. It was a room—a bedroom of sorts, with a great, ornate bed and rich furs covering the bare stone floor. There was a small table and two chairs, even a TV, and a hysterical laugh bubbled up inside me as I remembered what Roth had said about the reception down here. From the ceiling there was a thick steel bolt connected to a chain that ran down the wall, and

I tracked the length of the chain to the neck of the woman who stood to the right, her slim hip propped against the wall.

My breath caught.

She wore all white, a gossamer gown that showed everything from the collar to the hem, and all the shadowy places in between. This woman, with her hair so blond it was almost white and eyes that were a pale shade of gray, was startlingly beautiful, unusually so with eyes tipped at the corners and a lush, red mouth.

And that red mouth curved up in a smug smile.

Then she spoke in a voice that was ancient and heavy as the furs lining the floor. "Well, it's about time."

"Lilith," I breathed.

eighteen

FOR THE FIRST TIME IN MY LIFE, I WAS STANDING in front of Lilith—my mother—and she was a living, breathing creature. I don't know why that shocked me the most, but she'd always been more myth than real in my mind.

There was something inside me that was repelled by the chain around her slender neck. It was a weird feeling, one of familial bonding. After all, no matter what, she was my mother, and she was chained. I didn't like it. I didn't even like the feeling, and I didn't know what to make of any of that.

"*Mother* would've been a more appropriate greeting," she said, and that voice was like a thousand Bambis, slithering under my skin. "But then again, I should not expect such courtesy from you."

I blinked at the thinly veiled insult.

Well then…

Lilith didn't so much as walk toward the center of the room as she drifted. I wasn't sure her feet touched the stone at all. "Why is she here? I do not believe it is to free me, not with you here."

"You know you will never be freed," Grim replied acidly. "No matter what the Lilin thinks, your time down here is hardly finite."

A change swept over her face, softening the ethereal beauty. "My son? Do you bring word of him?"

The breathlessness of her voice was a kick to the chest that woke me up. "Your son? You mean, that insane thing running around topside, wreaking havoc?"

Her pale eyes narrowed on me. "That is your brother you're talking about. Have some respect."

"My brother?" I snorted. "Yeah. No."

She shook her head and the long waves danced around her face. "You cannot deny what is. He is a part of you. You are a part of me. The three of us are connected."

I stiffened. "I'm not a part of you or him."

Lilith raised her chin. "You always were such a disappointment to me," she said, and I flinched, unable to help myself. "I had such great hope for you. You were to be the one to not only free me, but to rise with me. We would've changed the world, but this?" She paused, raising her hands. "This is what I have to show for it. You do not respect me. You do not honor me."

"Wow," I murmured, drawing in a shaky breath. "Just wow. Have you ever cared for anyone—loved them?"

"Love?" She wrinkled her nose distastefully.

"Paimon loved you," I replied.

She rolled her eyes. "That fool. He failed at releasing me and he is the reason they all watch too closely now. There is no such thing as love, and please, do not expose a whole new level of idiocy by arguing with me. I'll ask again." She cast her gaze to Grim, who was still holding me from behind. "Why is she here?"

"I'll ask the questions." Grim's hold on my waist didn't loosen, as if he expected me to race forward and tear the chain from the ceiling. Needless worry. That wasn't going to happen. "Will you call back the Lilin? You know you can. Even from this cell, you can stop this."

"Why can't you make her?" I asked.

Grim all but growled. "It is not that simple."

Lilith's gaze flickered between us, and then she tossed her head back, letting out a throaty laugh. "Is that a serious question? You ask me to stop my son?" Lowering her head, her gaze flashed like steel. "If I cannot have my way, then I cannot wait for the destruction he will heap upon mankind. He will bring about the one thing that I could never accomplish—the end."

"Why?" I demanded. "Why would you want that? No one wins in that scenario. Not even you."

"Why?" Disbelief flooded her face. "Have you no idea what I've suffered? First thanks to the one who created me and then at the hands of man? Have you no clue what I've lost? My freedom stripped from me time and time again! My choices thrown away! I was cast from Eden, left to fend for myself in a dark world full of horror! You have no idea what I've experienced. Do not dare to ask why."

"You have suffered," Grim said quietly. "And so have the many souls I've claimed because of your hand."

She laughed bitterly. "And I do not regret a single thing." She glanced down at me. "Well, maybe just a few things."

I jolted and blurted out the first thing that came to mind. "I'm your daughter."

Her face tensed. "Then honor me."

"I can't," I whispered, choked. "Not if honoring you means millions of people will die."

"Then we are done here."

"So we are," murmured Grim.

The wall of flames returned with a thunderous pop, and then we were no longer there. We were back at the bridge, and Grim released me. I stumbled away from him, to the wall.

I stared down at the water for several moments, feeling nauseous and…and heartsick. There was a wound there, one I'd spent the better part of my life ignoring or pretending wasn't a big deal, but it was and it did hurt. No matter what Lilith was, she was my mother, and neither she nor my father had ever cared for me. "Why did you bring me to her? Other than to prove she doesn't and never has cared about me?"

"It might have seemed cruel, but you needed to see what she truly is, because it shows you what the Lilin truly is. Nothing will change either of them. No amount of rationale or negotiation. The Lilin must be stopped."

"I know. I didn't need to meet her to understand that." Weary from everything Grim had told me and from meeting the mother for whom I'd been such a disappointment, I faced him. I was done with this. "I want Sam's soul. You can release it, so it can go where it's supposed to, and I will stop the Lilin. But I want his soul released."

Grim stared at me, his expression apathetic. "I cannot do that."

Prepared for that response, I clasped my hands together to keep from swinging and discovering how easy it would be for Grim to take me out despite my newly discovered immortality. "Please. He doesn't deserve this. *Please*. I'll do anything you want me to do."

"You should never offer such a bargain to anyone." His gaze held no cruelty, but I shivered nonetheless. "Especially not me, because I may request from you something you are not willing to give."

The shiver hit me again. "I have to do this for him. You don't understand. Sam was a good person—a truly good person. His soul was nearly pure. He doesn't deserve an eternity of being tormented."

"I do not disagree, but there is nothing I can do."

My hands started to shake and I separated them. "No. I know you can. You control the souls that have passed. You're the—"

"I know what I am, girl, as I told you before," he snapped, the passivity in his expression bleeding into irritation. "And I know I cannot release what I do not have."

Frustration poured out of my voice. "Then who has his soul? Who do I need to beg? Because I will."

"You do not understand." Grim shook his head, almost sadly. "His soul is no more. Can you comprehend that? Despite what Lilith said, what you are and what a Lilin is are two very different things."

"What?" I whispered, my heart suddenly beating too fast. I understood what he was saying, but I wanted to be wrong. I needed to be wrong. My lower lip trembled. "Where is his soul?"

"The Lilin *consumed* it, girl. You know that. How else could it take on his form or any other? When the Lilin consumes a soul, it is not the same as stripping it. That is why any Lilin, even only one, is so incredibly dangerous."

Horror swamped me. No. No. No. I didn't know this. There wasn't a Lilin-handling manual that explains these things. I'd assumed that there would still be some part of Sam's essence that would've been sent to Hell. I had assumed that the Lilin's ability was like mine. I hadn't allowed the idea of anything else to cross my mind.

"Are you…?" I could barely get the words out from around the ball of bitter emotion forming. "Are you telling me there is nothing that you can do?"

"There is no soul for me to release," he answered quietly.

"Oh God." I closed my eyes, turning away as raw pain and disappointment took my breath away.

It wasn't fair. Not at all. Sam had never hurt a single person and now he just… Ceased to exist? Some would argue that was better than an eternity of torment, but to me, it was worse. That everything Sam had ever been, all that he had ever done, simply did not matter. He was gone, nothing left of him in this world or any other, and that was so wrong.

And what in the world was I going to tell Stacey? This— this would destroy her, but how could I lie, knowing what I knew? But I'd rather shoulder that burden than have her carry that knowledge.

"I didn't say there was nothing that could be done."

My eyes shot open and I spun toward him. "What?"

"The Lilin consumed the soul, and that soul is in him, along with any other souls he's consumed. All is not lost."

For a second, I didn't dare breathe, and then I lost it. "How about starting the conversation off with that instead of letting me think he was simply just gone!"

"How about you watch your tone," he replied tartly.

Every ounce of my being wanted to rage against him, but

I forced myself to calm down, because he held all the knowledge. "I'm sorry," I pushed out. "It's just that Sam is important to me."

Grim arched a brow. "I can see that." Folding his arms across his chest, he eyed me with stark intensity. "You and I want the same thing. You want to free Sam's soul and I want the Lilin stopped. I believe this is what humans would term two birds, one stone. Kill the Lilin. Sam and every other soul he's consumed will be freed."

"Done." Not a second of hesitation.

"Be warned that it will not be so easy. Souls don't last indefinitely, trapped like that. I've never heard of one making it past a handful of months," he said. "Time is of the essence."

Sam had been gone for a while. "Is it too late for him?"

"No," he answered, and I took his word for it, because he was who he was. "But you do not have long. For a variety of reasons."

I nodded, not only grasping onto the hope that I could still help Sam find the peace he deserved but fully understanding that the moment I got topside, I needed to find the Lilin.

"Do not fail in this. It is not just your friend's soul at risk," he added, and a blast of icy wind beat back the oppressive heat. "If the Lilin continues unchecked, the Alphas will step in. They will eradicate all the demons and Wardens topside, and if that happens, Hell will have to retaliate. There is no way Hell could stand aside and allow it. The Boss will release the four horsemen."

I swallowed hard. "I guess you're not talking about the Kentucky Derby kind of horsemen?"

"No." He didn't sound amused. "They will ride, and they will bring about the apocalypse. Billions will die, Layla, and the earth will be laid to waste. Only Lilith and the Lilin could truly want that. Not I. Not the Boss or the Big One in the Sky. None of us want that, because *all* of us will go to war."

"No pressure or anything," I murmured, sighing. "I'm just stopping the apocalypse."

His lips twitched into a grin, but it was gone so quickly I might've imagined it. "Unlike your mother, I have faith in you, Layla. But remember one thing. Everyone pays a price in blood in the end."

nineteen

BAMBI AND ROBIN WERE RETURNED TO ME right before I stepped back into the significantly cooler hallway. The moment they'd appeared, they'd started bickering with one another. About what, I wasn't sure, because I was consumed with everything Grim had told and showed me.

Overwhelmed, I didn't feel the familiars resume their animal forms and attach themselves to me, or really remember much of the walk back to the elevator or the trip topside. My thoughts were still swirling around in a vicious circle when the elevator doors slid open once more.

Gleaming amber eyes met mine, and before I could say a word, or tell him how relieved I was to see him, Roth was in front of me. Barely restrained fury tightened the lines of his face as he stormed into the elevator.

"Have you been hurt?" he demanded.

"What? No."

"Injured in any way that I cannot see?"

When I shook my head, some of the tension, if only a teeny amount, faded from him. I started to raise my hands. "I—"

My words ended in a squeal as he lifted me off my feet. Within a second, I was swinging through the air. I grunted as my midsection hit his shoulder. Out of instinct, I grasped the leather belt around his hips. He pivoted around and the elevator whirled as he stepped out in the lobby.

"Roth—"

"Don't," he growled.

My grip tightened as he stalked forward. "Put me down!"

"Not going to happen."

He turned toward the hall leading to the stairwell and I lifted my head. The lobby was empty with the exception of Cayman. He was by the couches and chairs, and his usually handsome face was marred with a variety of purplish and red bruises.

I had no idea demons could even be bruised.

Cayman grinned, but it looked painful.

Smacking Roth's lower back, I tried to get his attention. "Put me down. Now." When he didn't respond, I started to kick my legs, but his free arm clamped down around the back of my knees. "Roth!"

"Don't," he said again as the door to the stairwell flew open, banging off the cement walls. I winced as the sound echoed. "Just don't say another word until we get upstairs."

My mouth dropped open. "Don't tell me not to talk!"

He chuckled darkly, without any humor. "That's what I just did, Shortie."

Telling myself I'd known he was going to be upset, that the anger had to be a result of him being so concerned over my well-being, I struggled to remain levelheaded. I really just wanted to kick him. "I know you're angry—"

The arm around my legs tightened. "You have no idea how angry I am. None whatsoever."

Squeezing my eyes shut, I counted to ten. I made it to five. "Okay. I understand. But you don't need to carry me up the stairs."

Instead of responding, he put a little bounce in his step, jarring me as he took the stairs two at a time. When we reached the fourth or fifth floor landing, I'd had it. I got that he was angry, but this was ridiculous.

Tapping into the strength I knew I had, I raised my hands and gripped his shoulders as I swung my weight back at the same time. The move caught Roth off guard and his arm loosened enough for me to break the hold.

I slid down the front of his body and the contact sent a flash of heat through my veins. Ignoring it, I backed up, immediately putting a distance between us, which probably was one of the smartest things I'd done so far.

Roth *was* furious.

Anger poured out of every cell of his tightly coiled body and flashed behind his golden eyes. His skin was thinner, exposing the darker tone that existed beyond the flesh. My eyes widened. Not out of fear, because I would never be scared of him, but because there was more than just anger I saw in his features—there was stark anxiety. Yes, he looked fierce, but he also looked like he'd expected not to see me again.

"Roth," I said softly, and his eyes squeezed shut in a grimace at the sound of his name. "I know you're upset. I'm sorry, but I had to go down there and I knew it wasn't safe for—"

"Yes, let's talk about safety!" His voice thundered through the stairwell. "Do you even know how much you risked by

going down there? How incredibly lucky you are to be standing here, unscathed?"

"Yes, but—"

"There isn't a *but* in this, Layla. There are any number of
extremely disturbed and twisted things that could have happened to you. And for what?"

"For what? You knew I had to help Sam. That I couldn't—"

"I could've helped you if you had allowed me!" His eyes
flashed an intense amber. "I know what can happen down
there, and I don't care what Cayman said to you, there was
no way you could've been prepared. Any number of demons
could've taken you, and they would've done things that would
make you beg for death."

I shuddered at the thought, but forced my voice to remain
soothing. "Nothing happened to me, Roth. I'm okay—"

"I didn't know that, now, did I? I woke up after that asshole
snapped my neck and you were gone, Layla, into Hell, and I
couldn't go after you. I tried, but the damn elevator wouldn't
come up. I knew the entrance had been blocked, and you have
no idea what that made me think. I didn't know if you were
okay. I spent a day and a half fearing the worst!" he yelled,
and my stomach dropped, because I'd forgotten time moved
differently downstairs. What felt like an hour tops to me had
been hours and hours of uncertainty for him.

I swallowed. "Roth, I'm sorry. I really am. I didn't want
you to worry."

"If you didn't want me to worry, you never would've con-
spired against me. I offered you my aid and you stripped that
choice from me." His jaw was set in a hard line. "And I was
left utterly powerless when it came to helping you. Dammit,
Layla, I want to throttle you."

"Well, that's not really helping me."

His eyes narrowed, and I realized my lame attempt at humor had pretty much swan-dived down the stairs. "Do you think this is a joke?"

"No," I muttered, starting to lose my patience.

He stepped forward, a muscle throbbing along his jaw. "You risked too much, Layla. You—"

"I wasn't going to risk you!" I shouted, my control stretching and then snapping. I stepped forward, planting my hands on his chest and shoving hard. He stumbled back only half a step. "Do you understand that? I had to go down there to help Sam, but I was not going to risk you and I wouldn't go back and change that if I could. Sorry! You can be mad all you want."

"I'm pissed off because I love you, Layla, and the idea of losing you fucking terrifies me!"

"And I wasn't going to chance losing you! Because I love you, you annoying, self-important and overcontrolling—"

Roth shot forward, clasping my wrists in his. Pressing me back against the wall, he pinned my hands above my head. Our bodies were flushed, and my heart pounded erratically as he dipped his head.

Roth's mouth was on mine, and it was a raw kiss, one that brooked no room for denial. Not that I could ever want to deny him. The kiss was almost too powerful, too primitive. It ripped open the ball of dread that rested low in my belly, because it was the kind of kiss wrought from the fear of losing someone, and that made our situation all the more real.

It made what I had done all the more painful.

I kissed him back, just as hungrily and just as demanding.

He gave. I took. And as we clutched at each other, I knew that there was more love in his words than there had been anger.

After what felt like forever, he lifted his mouth from mine. Resting our foreheads together, he kept his hands over my wrists. He was breathing heavily, and I could feel his heart racing against my chest.

"I can't lose you," he said in a hoarse mutter, his voice twisting up my insides. "I can't."

"You won't," I whispered back, but those two words rang empty to me, even after what Grim had told me. "Are you still mad at me?"

His breath was warm on my lips. "I still want to strangle you." He paused. "But in the most loving way possible."

I pressed my lips together. "Okay then."

Roth's lips brushed over my brow, and then he was stepping back, his hands trailing off my wrists and down my arms. His movements were stiff as he turned to the stairs, and while I could tell most of the anger had faded away, it wasn't completely gone.

He started up the stairs, and after taking a couple deep breaths, I followed him. We didn't talk on the way up to his loft or when we stepped inside. He slammed the door shut behind us. "Bambi. Off."

The familiar left my skin immediately, and instead of floating toward him, the shadow darted under the bed.

"I think you hurt her feelings," I said, facing him. "And you failed to mention to me that the familiars are actually people. That's a pretty big thing to forget, you know, that you have a grown woman crawling around on your skin."

He stopped, both brows raised. "Are you jealous? Because you have a guy on you right now."

I shuddered. "Thanks for reminding me of that."

He stared at me. "Seriously? You're not jealous, are you?"

Sighing, I walked over to the bench in front of the piano and plopped down. "At first, yeah, I was. But then I realized how stupid that was. And besides, she apparently has the hots for Zayne."

"Why doesn't that surprise me? Bambi's always had bad taste."

My lips pursed. "You could've told me."

Roth shot me a dark look as he crossed the room. "To be honest, it hadn't crossed my mind. Silly me for thinking there'd be no chance of you taking a stroll through Hell."

I resisted the urge to roll my eyes. "Bambi made it sound like you let her take that form while she's topside."

"Sometimes." He folded his arms across his chest. "Not often enough that it's something I think about."

"Still, it would've been handy to know. Imagine my surprise when they just popped right off me." I reached down, to where Robin was curled along my hip. "I don't think they like each other. All they did was argue." I glanced at the bed. "I really do think she's hiding."

"Of course she is," he replied, eyeing the bed with a mixture of fondness and irritation. "She knew you were going down there, or at least suspected it. She should've stopped you."

I rested my hands on my knees, meeting his hard gaze. "When I said I was sorry, I meant it. I didn't know Cayman was going to distract you in that manner. I punched him, if that makes you feel any better."

He arched a brow, looking unappeased.

I went on. "But I had to try to help Sam. I had to."

Roth was silent for a long moment and then he exhaled loudly. "You saw Grim? Did you get what you were looking for?"

"I got a whole lot of what I wasn't looking for," I said, sliding my palms along my knees. "He told me what the Wardens were before—who they were."

"Heavenly rejects," he said, his face impassive. "It was never my story to tell. I wasn't even sure you'd believe me if I did."

"In the beginning? Probably not," I admitted, and then forged on. "He told me that some of them were never awakened, that they are still encased in stone. I never knew that. Did you?"

Roth shook his head. "I had heard rumors, but some gargoyles are just stone carvings and nothing more."

"He also told me about Lilith. That she was never a demon."

His brows furrowed. "I think he was messing with you, Layla. Lilith is a demon."

I shook my head tiredly, and then explained everything that Grim had told me about Lilith. I saw the moment when Roth believed me, when I told him how the Boss had covered it up. "So, I feel like a demon. So did Lilith, but only because no one knew what we really were, and I guess with the Boss telling everyone that she was one, no one thought to question it. People see what they want to see. Even demons, I guess."

Roth had moved closer to me as I told him what Grim said, but now he knelt in front of me. "You're not a demon."

"No. Not according to Grim, and it makes sense. You know, how the demons could never sense me in the beginning, not until recently—not until the witches gave me what they did." Understanding flared deep in his eyes, and seeing that made it easier to tell him what else I'd learned. "They gave me the blood of one of the original fallen angels. The same thing they'd given Lilith. That's why I look different now when I shift. I guess it overcame whatever Warden blood I had in me. And ever since then, I don't have the same urges to…to feed. It's still there, but it's nothing like before. I don't need anything to ease it. I can ignore it. Anyway, good news is, I'm kind of immortal, so you don't need to worry about me looking like your grandmother one day."

He stared up at me in silence for a long moment and finally, when I started to worry, he said, "I fail to see where there is any bad news involved in what you've just told me."

I almost smiled. "Well, I'm kind of a bigger freak than you thought I was in the beginning."

"I don't care if you grow a third boob when you shift or if you are part Hellion," he said fervently. "Or if three days a month you end up needing to consume the flesh of the dead."

Um. That was hard-core.

"I'm going to love you all the same." He placed his hands over mine. "But knowing that I'm not going to have to make some crazy deal in the future to prevent you from dying of old age on me is the icing on my cake, babe."

I couldn't even stop the smile from tugging at my lips. "You're ridiculous, you know that? You really would make a deal?"

His gaze was steady. "I would do anything for you."

"Ditto." I watched him lift my hands to his mouth and pressed his lips to the knuckles of each one. "I didn't get Sam's soul."

"I'm sorry," he said, and although his words were spoken low, I knew they were true. And I also knew that the only thing he truly cared about in this moment was that I was sitting in front of him, unhurt.

I curled my fingers around him. "The Lilin still has Sam's soul. Any soul that it consumes, it keeps. Killing the Lilin releases the souls, but Grim said he didn't know if his soul would last much longer inside the Lilin."

Roth smiled, showing off one deep dimple. "Well, then that's also not bad news. We plan on killing the Lilin anyway. That takes care of both problems."

I didn't like to think about whether or not Sam was aware of what was going on while he was trapped inside the Lilin. "That's been our plan, but how? I imagine the Lilin won't be easy to kill."

"It won't be." Letting go of my hands, he rose and walked over to his dresser. Opening the top drawer, he carefully pulled out something wrapped in thick leather. He carried it to the top of the piano, where he placed it down and pulled the material back. "But we'll do it the same way we'd kill any demon—with an iron stake."

Unable to suppress the shudder upon seeing three iron stakes laid out so innocuously, I glanced up at Roth as something occurred to me. "If I'm not a demon, then how did iron injure me before?"

"Because, as far as I know, it's fatal to the originals, too. While they're not demons, they are still cursed in many of the same ways demons are. After all, they sinned in ways that were believed to be unforgivable." He smiled slightly as he looked at me. "You've known about my little collection. This is all that I have left."

Roth didn't handle the weapons, because they would sear his flesh. The binding at the thicker end of the stake only protected him for so long. It wasn't that way for me before since I could handle them, which I had always thought was due to my Warden blood, but now I wasn't sure.

I reached out, quickly brushing my fingers along the cool metal before Roth could stop me. He uttered a harsh curse as he gripped my hand, yanking it back. "It didn't burn," I told him. "Same as before. I guess I'm special."

He narrowed his eyes. "That's one way of putting it."

I made a face, and he chuckled as he folded the leather cloth back over the stakes. Warm, I pushed the sleeves of my sweater up. "We need to stop the Lilin. I know we've been saying that, but—"

"What is this?" He took hold of my fingers, lifting my arm up in the air. At first I didn't get what he was looking at, but as he turned my arm over, I saw the bruises, shaped like three fingers had pressed in. His eyes flashed from my arm to my face, his features tensing. "Did I do this?"

"What?" I shook my head. "No."

Unease bubbled forth as his pupils stretched vertically. "Who did this?"

"Um…"

He tilted his head to the side. "To bruise your skin, someone would've had to have gripped your arm with enough force that if you were human, it would've snapped your bone."

"My arm is fine."

"That doesn't answer my question."

"I don't think I need to answer your question, because you'll flip out."

Roth's lips thinned. "I'm totally calm. I would just like to know who marred your skin so that I can put a name and face to the creature I'm going to kill very slowly."

"I think we might have different definitions of calm," I said wryly.

"I've never been calmer in my life." When I shot him a disbelieving look, his chest rose with a deep breath. "It was Grim, wasn't it? Touchy, impatient bastard."

I didn't answer. Not really. "I have a feeling you can't kill him."

"I can try." His voice was dead serious.

"What good would trying do? We have enough problems without adding to them, and you going after Grim would be a major headache we don't need right now."

Roth lowered his chin as he closed his eyes. "It is in the very fabric of my being to seek revenge against those who hurt my own."

One could never forget what Roth was. I should be concerned or maybe even angry that he'd be willing to seek revenge, but there was a part of me that was secretly thrilled by the level of his protectiveness. Because the truth was, if the situation had been flipped, I'd want to murder whoever hurt him.

"I'll let it go," he continued, raising my arm to his mouth. He pressed a light kiss against the bruise, and my chest got all mushy. "For now."

I groaned as he let go of my arm.

"Hey, that's better than me barging into Hell right now, isn't it?"

"Yeah, when you put it that way, sure."

He walked to the bed and sat down. "Grim said some other things," I said, casting my gaze to the bruises. I tugged my sleeve down. "Things he was a hundred percent correct on."

"Like how I'm going to break every finger on his hand?" He patted the bed.

"No," I sighed as Bambi peeked out from under the bed. She rose gracefully, nudging Roth's leg with her snout. "He pretty much called us out for not really doing anything about the Lilin."

Bambi placed her head on Roth's knee and he absently petted her. Immediately, I thought of what she had said about Zayne and where he had actually stroked her, and I had to tell myself not to walk over there and move Roth's hand to the tip of her snout, because I figured that couldn't be an inappropriate place on her body.

God, I needed to stop thinking about that.

"We're hardly sitting idly by," he said, smiling down at Bambi. "Finding the Lilin is not easy. It's not like he's aligning himself with anyone."

"What about the club you mentioned?"

"Oh, the one I planned on investigating before you snuck off to Hell?"

"That's the one," I said sheepishly.

Roth patted his chest and without him having to say a word, Bambi melded to his skin, disappearing under the hem of his shirt. "We can still check that out, but, Layla, I know how Grim can get under your skin. Could we always do more to fight evil? Yes. Should we stop living our lives in the process? No. We're doing what we can do—more than we have to do."

I started to respond, but there was a knock on the door. Roth's eyes narrowed once more. "Come in if you have the balls."

My brows flew up, but then the door opened to reveal

Cayman, and I sort of understood the greeting as the demon stepped into room.

The normal humor and arrogance was gone from his expression, and there was a sick pinch to his appearance that hadn't been there when I'd seen him in the lobby. I knew immediately it had nothing to do with the tension between him and Roth, but Cayman's gaze was trained on him.

"What?" Roth began to stand, apparently also sensing trouble.

"I'm sorry," Cayman said, his shoulders stiff. "The witches are here. They've come for what I had to promise."

twenty

I SQUEEZED MY EYES SHUT, SWALLOWING A groan.

This was the last thing we needed to be dealing with right now, but the witches had saved my life. They were also responsible for my current state. I wasn't sure if I should be upset with them for giving me something as powerful as the blood of a fallen angel. How could I be? God, it was gross just thinking about the fact that I'd consumed anyone's blood, but they'd given me the closest thing to immortality, something I hadn't really had the chance to fully wrap my head around yet.

Roth and I had no idea what the witches could want in exchange for their help the night Maddox had stabbed me, but by the look on Cayman's face and the dejected way he walked down the hallway leading to the club, it was a cause for grave concern.

I already knew this was going to be bad.

Roth planted both hands on the door, swinging it open as he stalked into the main floor of the club. It was silent, a wholly different atmosphere from what I was accustomed to.

None of the dazzling lights were on, and the space looked almost ordinary in the bright glare of the overhead ones. No dancers graced the horseshoe-shaped stage and the shadowy corners of the club were absent of demons and card games.

The witches sat at one of the high, round-top tables just beyond the stage. There were two of them: the older man who'd received us when we'd gone into the restaurant to meet their crone and learn more about the Lilin, and a younger woman who couldn't have been much older than me. Both were dressed normally, which was such a stupid thing for me to be surprised about, because it wasn't like most male witches ran around wearing a black warlock cloak or females a white, billowy dress. They shared similar characteristics—brown hair and eyes, small nose and mouths, and I wondered if they were related. Father and daughter.

The crone I remembered from our last meeting, the one who'd seemed to call the shots, wasn't with them—but I wasn't surprised, because I doubted that woman could travel much. She was so old that when I first met her, I'd expected her to fall over dead at any given moment and explode in a cloud of dust.

Witches were a very strange breed. They were human, mostly, but somewhere in their bloodline was demonic blood and that was where they got their abilities. But even though they had demonic ancestors, they didn't claim the connection. Witches didn't trust the demons and they didn't trust the Wardens, either. To me, they were neither good nor evil, and typically they stayed far, far away from the drama.

The coven the two sitting before us belonged to worshipped Lilith, and I immediately wanted to launch into a lecture about what a horrible idea that was.

"What's up?" Roth announced as he swaggered right up to

their table, completely fearless while I had the common sense to linger a few steps back. We didn't know what the witches were fully capable of.

The man eyed Roth warily before flipping his gaze to where I stood beside Cayman. "I see that you are well."

"Thanks to you all," I replied while Roth's eyes narrowed. I forced myself to take a step forward, hoping to keep everyone cool. "I'm sorry, but your name?"

He raised his chin slightly. "I'm Paul."

"Paul?" repeated Roth. "Funny, somehow I thought you'd be a Eugene or an Omar."

I turned to Roth slowly.

Paul ignored the comment. "And this is Serifina."

"That's a pretty name," I said, and the girl smiled at me. "I know what your coven gave me when I was hurt." When Paul was silent on that, I had to ask my next question. "How did you have the blood of a fallen angel?"

"Does that matter?" he queried.

"I guess not, but I'm…well, I'm nosy." I shrugged. "It's not something that I imagine people, even witches, just have lying around in abundance."

"It's not. And I can tell you it was not easy to obtain nor did we part with it without great consideration," Paul explained.

Boredom pulled at Roth's expression as he leaned back against the stage. "That's…interesting."

Paul's smile was tight. "All of us have heard of the Prince's arrogance. How reassuring to see that this rumor is correct."

I stiffened as Roth's lips tipped up on one corner, and when he spoke, his voice was as thick as molasses. "Did you also hear the rumor of how I strung a witch up by his teeth once? Because that was also true."

Paul paled, and then his cheeks flushed red while my eyes widened.

"This is going to go downhill quick," Serifina said, her voice soft as her gaze darted between Roth and me. "We do not want that. We've come for what we were promised and that is all."

"And what were you promised?" Roth demanded. "Let's get this over with."

Paul glanced back at Cayman with abject horror etched into his aging features. "You did not tell him?"

Oh no. This did not sound good.

"I haven't asked. It hasn't been a priority of mine," Roth replied, and dismissiveness dripped from his tone.

Paul exhaled roughly. "You will honor the promise."

"Did I say that I would not?"

Serifina was aghast, shaken. "But you don't even know what was asked for in return." She looked at Cayman and seemed to pale even further, to the point I feared she might pass out and topple from the chair.

"My patience is wearing thin," Roth warned.

Paul cleared his throat and appeared to man up. Part of me wanted to stop him from speaking, because the feeling that whatever he was going to say was going to be disastrous was all consuming. "In exchange for saving her life," he said, "we asked for your familiar in return."

I sucked in a sharp, stinging breath as his words bounced around in my head. No. They couldn't have meant what I thought they did.

Roth slowly unfolded his arms. "Excuse me?"

"In exchange for saving h-her, we asked for your familiar,"

Paul answered, his nervousness seeping into the room. "That was the d-deal we made."

Dumbfounded, I turned to Cayman and he was staring at Roth's back. "I told you that you would not like what they wanted in return, but you said give—"

"I told you to give them anything," Roth cut in, voice harsh. "I know what I said."

Cayman flinched, and then lowered his gaze.

"Wait," I said, shaking my head. "You guys can't be serious. Why would you want one of his familiars?"

Serifina carefully slipped off her chair and stood by the table, obviously having more courage than Paul. "Familiars are very powerful beings, especially when they bond with a person. They are like a siphon, or a conduit. When the Prince's familiars bond with someone else, after a period of time, the new—"

"The new person they bond with would develop some of those abilities of the original host," Roth interrupted. "You want my talents."

She swallowed thickly. "That's not the main reason."

"That's enough for me to hear." He stepped forward, and the girl shrank back, but he didn't move any closer. I knew Roth was furious, but I also knew that he would not harm her. "You're demanding a lot."

"A deal is a deal," Paul said quietly. "And I have the distinct feeling there is no price you wouldn't pay for the life we saved. Which is why we do not want just any familiar. We were quite specific in our deal."

Cayman closed his eyes. "They were. Very specific."

Roth sneered in the direction of the witches as my thoughts raced to discover a way out of this. "Which one?"

Neither witch looked like they wanted to speak the name, but Paul finally manned up and stepped forward. "We made the deal for the snake."

"No!" The word burst out of my mouth before I could stop myself. I turned wild eyes on Roth. "Not Bambi. No way."

Roth didn't say anything as he stared at the witches, his shoulders impossibly tensed.

"Why can't it be a different one?" I demanded. Giving up Thumper or the kittens would be hard, but letting go of Bambi would be the worst. "Why her?"

"Because she is the most powerful," Paul replied simply. "She has bonded not only with the Prince but with you. No other familiar has proven that. She has more of a chance of bonding with one of our own."

I spun toward Roth. "No. You don't have to do this. Screw it. They can't hurt me or you." Well, I assumed that they couldn't, but whatever. "We do not have to do this."

Paul turned an incredulous stare on me. "You'd have him break his word?"

"I'd have you shut the Hell up," I snapped, my hands closing into fists. Guilt churned in the pit of my stomach. This was happening because of me. I hadn't purposely gotten myself stabbed, but getting involved with Zayne without truly questioning why I'd been able to kiss him had led to the incident of him kissing me. Which led to everything else that had happened afterward.

"She's right." Cayman rubbed the heel of his hand along his bruised jaw. "Roth, she's right. You know there's a way out of this. I would not...hold it against you. I know how much Bambi means to you, and I knew that when I brokered the deal."

Roth wheeled around to face Cayman. "You brokered the deal believing that I would not honor it?"

Cayman nodded.

Disbelief flickered across Roth's face. "You know what will happen if I do not honor this deal."

Cayman nodded once more.

Roth cursed as he reached up and thrust his fingers through his hair before stalking toward the other demon. I braced myself for a brawl of epic proportions, but Roth clamped his hand around the back of Cayman's head. "You stupid son of a bitch," he said, but it wasn't out of anger. My heart wrenched in my chest. Pain filled Roth's tone. "You would die? You know that's what would happen. If you broker a deal and it's not upheld, you die."

Oh God.

"You would do anything to save her," Cayman whispered, meeting Roth's gaze. "And I would do anything to serve your best interests, even if that means my death. I never expected you to give up Bambi, but that's what it took for them to save Layla. So that's what I promised."

My heart might've stopped as the words sank in. Cayman had made the deal knowing that Roth might not surrender Bambi. He made it to save me, because that was what Roth wanted.

The loyalty Cayman felt for Roth was heartbreaking.

I turned to the witches. "You guys can call off the deal, can't you?"

Serifina shook her head. "The crone wants the female familiar."

"And the crone gets what she wants," Paul finished.

Tears pricked the back of my eyes, and I felt Robin shift

along my side, obviously sensing my whirling emotions. This was not right, not fair at all.

Still holding the back of Cayman's head, Roth closed his eyes briefly, and then let go, pivoting to face the witches. The hard set of his jaw would've sent many a wise man scurrying away.

"She will not be harmed," Serifina insisted, attempting to appease us. "She will be treated like a queen."

Hearing that didn't help, because we didn't know them, and Bambi—it wasn't like she belonged to us. There was so much Bambi had done for us—for me, and now we were supposed to just hand her over to strangers? She was a *part* of us and they were asking that we give her up—that Roth get rid of her.

I walked over to Roth, unsure of what to say. Our eyes met for a moment, and the hard glint was gone just long enough for me to see the true extent of the turmoil he was feeling. I placed my hand on his arm, and he nodded.

"Bambi," he said, his gaze still holding mine. "Off."

I didn't want to see it, but like all the times before, Bambi came off his skin and spilled into the space beside him, rapidly piecing together. Bambi rose, twisting her neck toward the witches before nudging Roth in the hip.

She had to know. I knew that, because that was how the bonding worked, and my chest ached as she stretched over, poking my arm with her snout. Tears blurred my vision as I reached out, running my hand on the soft scales between her eyes.

"There has to be some other way," I said hoarsely.

"There's not," he said, his voice low. "Cayman is not at fault. He did what he was supposed to do."

"I know."

"And I will not do that to him," he continued. "When demons die, it's not like humans. It involves the pits."

That wouldn't be fair either, and even though Roth and Cayman had gone at each other yesterday over me going to Hell, those two were friends. Frankly, I was pretty sure Cayman was Roth's only friend outside of me, and Roth had to choose between two bad options. Give up Bambi to a coven of witches or sentence his friend to death.

Bambi turned to Roth and rose up to her full height. She rested her head on his shoulder, and when she lifted it, Roth pressed a kiss between her eyes. "Which one of you is she supposed to go to? I doubt that you plan on walking out with her in this form."

"No." Serifina smoothed her hands over the dark trousers she wore. "That's why I'm here."

"Is it?" Roth asked, and then he raised his eyes to her. When she nodded, he smiled cruelly. "If you so much as cause her a drop of pain, I will know. And I do not care what consequences I will face, I will hunt not only you down, but your entire coven."

"No harm will come to her," she promised.

Roth looked down at Bambi, and he tried to smile, but he failed. "Go."

But the familiar hesitated, and Roth had to tell her to go again. A very real pain ripped through me as I reached up, brushing the back of my hand across the wetness gathering on my cheek. Finally, after what felt like my heart being cut out of my chest and tossed on the floor, Bambi slithered away from us, her head down.

Roth stepped forward, as if he was going to go after her, but stopped himself. Walking up behind him, I wrapped my arms around his waist. His hands settled on my arms, but instead of pulling them away, he held on to them.

Pushing up the sleeve of her thick sweater, exposing her arm, Serifina waited with trepidation clearly oozing out of her. About a foot in front of her, Bambi came apart, forming a thick shadow that settled onto her arm.

Serifina jolted as Bambi melded onto her skin, clenching her jaw as Bambi disappeared under the sweater. The girl jerked and then twisted, doubling over at the waist. A second later she straightened, her back bowing as Bambi appeared, circling around her neck.

Paul cursed, gripping Serifina by the arms. Bambi let up, though, and I figured it was her little warning that she wasn't very cool with this. The snake disappeared back under the sweater, and by the sudden way her face flushed, I doubted Bambi was currently making herself at home in a very comfortable place.

It was done.

Neither of us could have predicted this. I got why Cayman hadn't said anything up to this point, because I believed knowing that this was coming would've been a harsher blow. Or maybe not. Loss was bitter whether it was expected or unanticipated.

And this was a loss.

"Get. Out. Of. Here," Roth growled, eyes flashing an intense crimson.

There was a moment of hesitation. Paul and Serifina moved more quickly than they probably ever had. They pivoted around, and I watched them go, wanting to grab her brown hair and pull her to the floor, demanding that they give Bambi back to us.

But I couldn't.

A demon did not go back on his promises.

Serifina halted at the doors and turned back to where we stood. Paul dipped his head, speaking too low for us to hear. Serifina drew a breath and looked at each of us in turn. "We understand how serious the issue with the Lilin is. Please do not think that we don't. It's why we need the familiar."

"Because Bambi will help you survive the apocalypse?" I laughed hoarsely. "She's amazing, but even she can't do that."

Pain pinched her face. "That's not what we think, but she will make us stronger. You know that. And she will protect us from all sides, including his." Her gaze darted to Roth briefly. "He will make sure no harm comes to us, not when we have her."

Dammit. She was so right and yet it felt so wrong. "So, she's a hostage instead of a queen?" I fired back.

"Let's go," Paul urged. "There's no use in reasoning with them."

"Yes, go." Roth stepped forward, chin tipped down. "Go before I regret my actions."

Serifina appeared torn, but she held her ground. I had to admire her for that, because Roth looked murderous, and I was sure I didn't look that different. "The Lilin has not gone far," she said, stepping away from Paul when he whirled toward her. "There is a darkness gathering in the city, one that we've never seen before, but we can feel it."

A chill skated down my spine as she continued. "We do not know what it is, but what else could be the cause? Something unnatural is occurring there."

"The city is a pretty big place," I said. "That doesn't really narrow it down for us."

She looked at Paul pointedly. "Tell them." When he hesitated, she raised her voice. "If they don't stop the Lilin, there will be very few places any of us can hide. Tell them."

Disgruntled and red-faced, Paul drew his shoulders up. "We've been keeping a close eye on the Church of God's Children for a while now."

Oh man, I'd all but forgotten about them, which was insane, but a lot had been going on. The Church didn't belong to any mainstream sects and they were some of the worst kind of human beings I'd ever had the displeasure of meeting. Not only did they hate demons, they loathed Wardens.

And they really disliked me.

I tried not to think of the day two of them had followed us into the parking garage, or how I'd lost my cool, doing something really horrible that involved a bible and a man's face. My actions had led to one of their deaths, and although they were really terrible, knowing I'd caused the death of a human was hard to swallow.

"Their fanatical beliefs make them just as dangerous as any demon," Paul continued. "They've been active up until this past Wednesday. Not a single member has been seen or heard from since then." He paused, lips thinning. "We infiltrated them long ago, but our brother has also not been in contact with us."

"We are not foolish enough to check it out," Serifina said. "We are too vulnerable to put ourselves in harm's way, but assuming our suspicions are true, if you find the Church, you may find the darkness—and the Lilin."

twenty-one

THE WHEREABOUTS OF THE CHURCH OF GOD'S Children was no secret. Its address was plastered all over the many flyers I'd ripped down from storefronts and telephone poles. It was near Adams Morgan, which I'd always thought was a strange location for the church since that neighborhood was pretty lively and known for its nightlife. It was becoming more and more of an entertainment district, so the building used as a church truly did stick out like a sore thumb.

But we didn't rush off to Adams Morgan.

The three of us remained in the empty club after the witches left, taking Bambi with them. Roth was the embodiment of barely leashed anger as he stood in the center of the dance floor, his hand opening and closing repeatedly at his side.

He was the first one to speak. "I think we need to be smart about this instead of bum rushing the Church. If the Lilin really is there, I doubt it's sitting and singing hymns with those people."

I glanced at Cayman, who still looked stricken by what had

just happened, and then I refocused. Why in the world would the Lilin be with them? And vice versa?

"As much as I hate to suggest this, we need to call the Wardens," Roth continued as he walked to where the witches had sat, picked up one of the chairs and carefully, meticulously, placed it under the table. "Yeah, their perfect pearly souls would be at risk, but they could act as backup."

"Roth..." I stepped forward.

He ignored me, fixing the other chair. "We have the necessary weapons to take out the Lilin. So do the Wardens. Let's do this."

"Roth," I repeated, this time stronger and louder. His dilated eyes locked onto mine. The glint in them was downright murderous. "Let's stop for a second."

"How about we not?" he replied calmly—too calmly.

The ache in my chest tripled. "What just happened...we have to acknowledge that."

His lips were pressed into a thin, formidable line. "Do we? Because dwelling on it seems pretty pointless. What does it change?"

"It doesn't change anything," I said, as Cayman turned sideways, thrusting his hand through his fair hair. "But we can't pretend it didn't happen. Bambi—"

"I think it's best that I pretend exactly that." Shadows had begun to form under his skin as his features sharpened, forming harsh angles. "Because I am *this* close to ripping that coven apart, and if I do that, it's going back on the deal Cayman made."

Cayman hung his head as he placed his hands on his lean hips. "I had hoped that they would not come to collect."

Roth didn't respond to that, and I didn't know what to say

to make this better. He had lost a loved one. It didn't matter that the loved one was a familiar who mostly took the form of a giant snake. Those two were bonded on a level that even I couldn't fully comprehend, and I had bonded with Bambi. I placed my hand over my side, where Robin rested. I was already bonding with the fox.

"I'm sorry," I said.

His shoulders tensed. "Why are you apologizing? You didn't take her."

"If anyone should apologize, it is me. I brokered the deal," Cayman interjected morosely. "I knew—"

"You were doing your job," Roth snapped, his anger surfacing. "I told you I'd give anything, therefore you made the deal. There is nothing you should be sorry for."

I closed my eyes, forcing myself not to say what I wanted to. Guilt beat at me, but I knew he didn't need to hear that from me right now. As much as I wanted to rage about losing Bambi, this wasn't about me, and whatever I felt was nothing compared to what Roth had to be feeling.

Tucking my hair back behind my ears, I pulled my tattered emotions together, shoved them down and focused. "Okay. I can reach out to Zayne."

Roth nodded and we headed back to his loft so I could grab my phone. Cayman didn't follow, and I felt just as bad for him as I did for Roth. Walking into his room and knowing I would never see Bambi slither her way over to the piano again kicked the breath out of my chest as I walked to my bag, by his desk.

"She'll be okay," Roth said quietly as I drew my phone out. I turned around and found him staring at the piano. "I know she will be. Bambi won't allow herself to be mistreated."

I bit down on my lip. The back of my throat burned.

Sighing, he looked up at me and the anger was still there, brimming just below the surface, but so was the shattered disappointment. "I really hope those witches were right, because I have a lot of pent-up aggression I need to get out of my system."

"I..." I trailed off helplessly, clutching the phone.

His thick lashes lowered. "It'll be okay."

Walking over to him, I placed my free hand on his shoulder, and then stretched up, kissing his cheek. He stiffened for a moment, and then he folded his arms around me, burying his face in the crook of my neck for only the briefest of moments before he pulled away, rubbing his palm along his chest. "Text Zayne."

And that's what I did.

Roth and I waited for the Wardens on the rooftop of a bank near the Adams Morgan area after the sun had set.

Nervous energy made it hard to stand still, and Robin was picking up on it, racing across my stomach like it was his own personal drag strip. Luckily, only about ten minutes passed before movement in the sky drew our attention.

From a distance, they looked like birds of prey at first, as if they'd swoop down and snatch people from the group. But as they drew closer, there was no mistaking what they were. Even those down on the streets below would be able to pick out the differences.

I could also tell that a whole crap ton of Wardens were coming.

"Damn," I muttered, stiffening.

Roth was beside me in under a second. I shouldn't have been surprised. Obviously what was about to go down was a big deal, and I'd known that eventually I was going to have to face more than just Zayne, Dez and Nicolai.

But a part of me wasn't ready.

Nope.

"This is going to be awkward," I said, brushing my hair back out of my face.

"No." Roth placed his hand on my lower back. "But it may be bloody."

I shot him a look. "Behave."

"I cannot promise that whatsoever."

"These are not the ones you need to take out your aggression on."

He smirked. "Let me be the judge of that."

This was so not going to go well, but it was too late to change our plans. The pearly white glows faded and Zayne landed first. In his true form, he was massive. His skin a dark gray, his horns curved back, parting his blond hair. Not ugly or frightening, to me at least, but his gaze was an arctic blast as it drifted over us, a painful reminder of how much had changed.

I wanted to hide from that gaze and everything it dredged up, but I found my lady balls and held them close. I'd put myself in this situation with him and I had to deal with the consequences.

Dez and Nicolai were next, followed by two more clan members, but it was the final arrival that caused dread to explode like buckshot in my stomach and punched a harsh curse out of Roth.

Abbot was here.

The roof shook when he landed behind the clansmen and straightened, a good half a foot taller than the rest. With his hair as golden as his son's, brushing broad shoulders, he'd always reminded me of a great lion.

In a way, Abbot was king.

For years, I'd trembled at the mere sight of him in his human and Warden forms, as he had been the greatest authority I'd known. And for years, I'd struggled to obtain the smallest sliver of pride from him. I'd basically operated on the theory that any attention was good attention, like a puppy. Now? Unfettered rage was what shook me and I sure as Hell didn't care if he was proud of that or not.

Abbot had believed the worst of me with little or no evidence backing it up. It was no wonder why I'd had such loser self-esteem and had also thought the worst. While he hadn't been the one who shoved a freaking dagger into my stomach, he had me *caged* like an animal, and then chained like one.

That was kind of hard to let go of.

"What is he doing here?" Roth queried, and although the question sounded like he was asking about the weather, I knew he wasn't nearly that calm.

Abbot walked to the front, his clan—even his son—sticking close to his side. His gaze drifted over Roth, and he barely managed to keep the contempt off his face, but then he was looking at me, and all the hard lines of his granite face softened. "Layla, I—"

"Don't." The one word that burst out surprised me. "Don't apologize. A handful of words don't make up for what you did."

He drew himself up to his full height. "I know nothing I say will ever erase any of what happened, but I... I regret the role I played in it all."

The role he played? To me, he'd been the freaking captain leading the Kill Layla parade down Main Street.

Abbot wasn't done. "You were mine to raise and protect. I failed you."

"Yes, you did," Roth replied. "I won't, but here's the thing, and this message goes out to everyone. She doesn't need protection. Not anymore."

I got all warm and fuzzy upon hearing that, but the smug feeling quickly evaporated when my gaze caught Zayne's and he looked away without so much as a glimmer of any emotion.

"I've heard from my son that you are...something else." Abbot spoke directly to me. "That you do not look like us anymore."

"I'm not like you." My hands curled into fists and Robin started to get antsy. "Turns out, I was never a demon." That got Zayne's attention and an emotion out of him. Surprise. "Yeah, I have some demonic abilities, but... Well, does any of that matter?"

"No," Zayne answered, shocking me. "It never mattered before. Not to any of us. It doesn't matter now."

There was a tugging sensation in the general vicinity of my heart.

"You said that you have a lead on the Lilin." Nicolai spoke up, always the peacekeeper of the bunch. "That it may be holed up with the Church of God's Children?"

Roth was eyeing Abbot like he wanted to rip the Warden's head off, and he would've, back on the night I had been captured, if I hadn't stopped him. "Yes. Layla and I are going to check it out and if the Lilin is there, we're going to need backup."

"That's why we're here," Dez responded. "You tell us what you want us to do. This is your show."

Abbot's shoulders hunched, and it was obvious that he wasn't happy with that decision. Roth looked smug as he said, "We need you all to stay close by. If things get hairy, you'll know."

"How is that?" Nicolai asked.

One side of Roth's lips curved up. "Nitro. Off."

My gaze shot to him as the tiny black cloud appeared before him. It dropped to the rooftop, and then rapidly pieced together, forming a tiny kitten.

Zayne shook his head. "What is it with you and runts of the litter?"

"Patience, Stony, patience."

Before Roth finished those words, the little ankle biter increased before our eyes. Frail shoulders expanding into powerful hunches. The back lengthened into thick muscles covered by sleek white fur. What started off as a soft growl turned into a menacing, reverberating snarl that raised the hair along the back of my neck.

Nitro looked like a panther, if panthers were white.

Goodness.

"Nitro will let you know if things get out of control," Roth explained. "It will be obvious."

I couldn't stop staring at the cat. It plopped its butt down, its pink tongue moving over its teeth. It looked hungry, and the Wardens looked very, very unhappy, especially when it coughed out what sounded suspiciously like a laugh.

Roth turned to me. "Ready?"

"Yep." The blade was tucked into my boot, just like Roth had his. We walked to the ledge overlooking the alley below. The fastest way down was to jump. Roth shifted quickly, tucking his wings back so he didn't knock me off the edge with them.

Knowing that all eyes were on us, I allowed my own shift to take place. My skin buzzed with the change, and it was like finally waking up after being asleep for days when it happened. My wings unfurled, arcing high above me, the feathers tickled by the wind.

Someone murmured an expletive behind us, and it sounded a lot like Abbot. I glanced at Roth and grinned.

"Meet you down there," he said, and jumped.

"Show-off," I muttered.

Instead of jumping, I sort of walked off the ledge and empty space immediately reached up to grab me. Gravity was a beast. The alley raced toward me, and I let my wings spread out, slowing the descent.

I landed in a crouch, propping up to find myself at eye level with an old man with a dirty, unshaven face.

"Holy mother," he gasped, stumbling back against the wall and then sliding down it, clutching his brown bag to his chest.

I winced as my wings folded in, disappearing. "Whoops?"

Roth chuckled, back to his human form, as he reached down, taking my hand. I sent the poor man an apologetic look, and then we hurried around the side of the building to the main street. My heart was thumping as we joined the thin crowd on the sidewalks.

"I hope that doesn't count as exposure," I said as we crossed the street.

He squeezed my hand. "I really think the Alphas have bigger problems to deal with right now." Then he shrugged. "And seriously, you should've seen the look on the man's face when he saw *me*. That was kind of funny."

I shook my head, but a little grin peeked through. Roth was in a far better mood than he had been immediately after the witches had left with Bambi. Distracting himself with what lay ahead was working for him and it was a strange thing to be grateful for, but I was.

"There it is," I said, two buildings down from the building housing the Church.

He arched a dark brow as he studied the four-story structure. "Have the windows always been like that?"

I nodded as a door to the building we stood in front of opened. A blast of music and laughter followed the young man out. His aura was a sea-moss green, swirling smoothly as he hunkered down in his jacket, heading in the opposite direction. "Yeah," I answered. "They've always had the windows covered from the inside so you couldn't see anything. It just adds to the shadiness, doesn't it?"

He snorted. "Remember the guy who threw holy water on you?"

I rolled my eyes. "Not something I'd forget."

"I really hope he's in there."

"Oh dear," I murmured.

"You know what I just thought of?"

I looked at him. "What?"

Some of the mischievous sparkle was back in his amber gaze. "I didn't get to deflower you in my Porsche."

"Oh my God." I gaped at him. "What in the world made you think of that right now?"

"It's called multitasking." He winked. "And I still plan on breaking that baby in, just so you know."

"You're ridiculous." Slipping my hand free, I started toward the building and the grin I was rocking faded like an old memory as soon as we neared the door. "Do you feel that?"

"Feels like home."

I ignored that, because I'd been to Hell, and Hell didn't even feel like this—like a gallon of oil had been dumped over our heads. Walking was like pushing through slime. It was thick in the air, a heavy evil that had to be what the witches had been talking about, and never in my life had I felt anything like this.

Roth edged around me, reaching the handle of the door. "Locked." He twisted sharply, like he'd done in the basement of the school when we'd been hunting down the source of a very rotten, demonic smell, snapping the lock while hitting it with a dose of not so heavenly heat. "And unlocked."

The moment he opened the door, the smell about knocked us back a good three feet.

"Oh my God." I smacked my hand over my mouth, clamping down on my gag reflex as I glanced around the dimly lit lobby.

"Jesus," muttered Roth, his lips peeling back in a grimace.

The scent was that of meat left out too long mixed with something I couldn't quite place. Worse than sulfur or a dirty back alley in the city. Carefully, I lowered my hand, trying to not breathe through my nose. If the smell was any indication, things were really, really bad here.

Behind the vacant receptionist desk, there was a huge banner hanging. Crudely drawn Wardens, who looked more like overgrown bats than gargoyles, were on either side of the words THE END IS NIGH.

"So cliché." Roth started around the desk, toward double,

windowless doors. "You'd think they'd come up with something new."

I followed, disappointed that the smell was getting worse. "But the end is *nigh*."

"You—" he glanced over his shoulder at me as he reached the double doors "—are adorable."

I would've smiled at that, but the doors had opened, and all I could do was press my lips together to keep from hurling all over Roth's back.

Candles were everywhere, casting a flickering, soft light throughout a large atrium-style room that had been converted into a place where sermons would be held, complete with pews and the chancel, a raised platform.

The pews weren't empty.

They were also the source of the wretched smell.

They were full of bodies.

twenty-two

I DREW IN A DEEP BREATH, AND WHILE I IMME-
diately regretted it, the stench was overshadowed by the horror of what we were staring upon.

Dozens and dozens of bodies were scattered throughout the
pews, some slumped over while others were still sitting up,
their heads fallen back, jaws slacked open. They were in various states of decomposition. For as much as I'd experienced in
recent months, never in my life had I seen anything like this.

"Good God," I said, horrified.

Roth stiffened as movement near the chancel drew our attention. It had been vacant moments before, but now a figure stood in front of the altar. I winced. It was the Lilin—and
he'd taken the form of Sam once more.

"I think this is appropriate," the Lilin said, spreading its
arms up at his sides. "I have a congregation of the dead."

"Most people would aim higher," Roth said, eyeing the
carnage with distaste.

"I am not most beings, now, am I?" It grinned slightly from
its elevated perch. "I've been waiting for you to come, sister."

"I am not your sister," I gritted out.

"Acceptance is the first step of recovery, or so they say." The Lilin walked to the edge of the chancel and crouched. "You're here to help me."

That wasn't so much a question, but I answered anyway. "No. I'm here to stop you."

The thing chuckled smoothly. "You cannot stop me. Neither can the Prince."

"I wouldn't put money on that," Roth retorted.

Milky white eyes drifted to Roth as the Lilin smiled mysteriously. "I guess we will see about that, won't we?" The Lilin's gaze found mine. "We need to free our mother. It is a travesty that a force such as she should remain chained. We are in this together and—"

"You can stop the sales pitch right there," I interrupted. "There is nothing that you can say that will sway me. You won't be able to free Lilith. Don't you understand that? Nothing will free her. After Paimon attempted to do so, extraordinary measures were put in place to prevent her from getting out."

"True," remarked Roth, rather smugly. "The Boss has her on lockdown. It's not going to happen."

"That is where you are wrong," the Lilin responded from its perch. "If I succeed in raising Hell to Earth, no one down there will be paying attention to Lilith. She will be the least of their worries."

Muscles locked up all along my back. "If you bring Hell to Earth, the Alphas will step in. They will wipe us all out, including you."

"It's not like they can throw a magic switch and then we're gone."

Roth sighed. "It has a point there."

"That's not helping," I said under my breath.

"The Alphas will fight us and we will fight back, even those who do not want to see Lilith free or for Hell to open its gates. They will fight," the Lilin continued. "As I will, and while we all are fighting to survive, the world will fall apart. If I cannot free our mother, then I truly have nothing to lose."

What Grim had warned me about was coming true, but it really wasn't a surprise. The Lilin really had no thoughts of its own. All it was concerned with was freeing Lilith, and if it couldn't have that, then it would settle for chaos and absolute destruction.

The Lilin rose fluidly. "You will see. In the end, you will have no choice but to help me."

The darkness along the wall, which had been still and unnoticeable at this point, suddenly moved. Thick shadows shifted and grew, slipping up and over the ceiling like a muddy oil slick. The stench of the room rose, but the evil in it became suffocating. There was the source of the darkness and we'd been standing in the middle of it the entire time.

"Wraiths," I gasped, stepping back.

They swarmed across the ceiling, like something straight out of a horror movie, and then dropped to the floor, among the benches.

But that wasn't all.

We could see the wall now, could see that there were several statues lined up. They looked like the stone gargoyles perched atop so many of the city's buildings, but cruder, more grotesque than the real thing. Some looked like goblins. Others were part lion and a few looked like birds. Not the happy, dove kind. More like pterodactyls. There were about twenty of the statues.

"They created them out of stone." The Lilin gestured at the bodies in the pews. "So bizarre. They used them as a reminder of the evil they so badly wanted to fight. Ironic."

A heartbeat passed.

The first row of pews shot up straight in the air, shattering apart and sending bodies in every direction. The second row followed and then the third, the fourth...

Boards were flying, along with pieces of those left behind. Each burst of pews was a crack of thunder.

"Somebody better call the Ghostbusters," Roth muttered. "Because we don't have time for this."

I would've laughed, wanted to, but a piece of wood winged its way in my direction. I dipped down, narrowly avoiding getting plowed over. The board smashed into the wall behind us.

I shifted immediately, welcoming the change. Roth did the same as he jumped, snatching a rather large piece of board out of the air. Snapping it in half, he tossed it down.

Sparks flew and flames rose from the farthest corner as the knocked-over candles started a fire among the debris.

Reaching down, I withdrew the dagger from my boot, and then started down the center aisle, toward the chancel. The wraiths didn't like that. They came at me. Shaped like humans, but no more substantial than smoke, they were tricky beasts to fight. One managed to get a hold of my hair, yanking my head back. I hissed as I twisted out of the wraith's grip.

The Lilin shouted something in an ancient, guttural-sounding language that meant nothing to me, but the wraiths responded. They pulled back, and then darted to the walls.

"Oh crap," Roth said. "It's about to get ugly."

I didn't have to wait long to see what he meant. The wraiths hit the statues, draping themselves over them like a blanket.

I didn't know what they were doing, but every instinct told me I wasn't going to like it.

The shadows pulsed, and then they disappeared, seeping into the statues, wiggling their way through the cracks and openings. Some wraiths remained near the ceilings, their forms twisting and trembling.

A great and terrible shudder worked its way through the building, scattering the broken boards and bodies, and the shudder turned into a groan cut off by the sound of stone grinding against stone.

Then the statues moved.

"What in the...?" I said.

Roth growled low in his throat as the things straightened and stretched, as if waking up from a slumber. The lion-shaped gargoyle threw its head back, letting out a deafening roar that was so realistic.

A goblin-like gargoyle pushed away from the wall. Only about five feet tall, its footsteps thundered as it raced toward Roth, cackling in a low-pitched voice.

Roth stepped to the side, spinning around. He grabbed the goblin's arm, and then shot to the ceiling. Arcing swiftly, Roth flew back down at a harrowing rate, slamming the goblin into the floor.

The floor dented as the stone creature shattered into large chunks, releasing the wraith. The black shadow poured out of the remains, knocking Roth back several feet.

My familiar shifted on my stomach, peeling itself off before I could stop it. Robin appeared, at first the size of a fox and then he grew, taking on the size of a Doberman, and boy, that was freaky.

Robin darted up the aisle, his overly large but sleek body

moving incredibly fast. He jumped, snatching the tail end of the wraith, dragging it back down. My mouth dropped open. I had no idea that familiars could touch wraiths, but Robin wasn't just touching. He was shaking his head like a pit bull with an evening snack, whirling the wraith from side to side.

The other statues converged on us, and in a minute, I lost sight of Roth. Knowing that the blade would do nothing against these things, I sheathed it back in my boot.

Shrieking from the ceiling, the pterodactyl-type gargoyle dive-bombed me, its beak opening as if it planned on swallowing me whole. I jumped to the side, but the bird twisted, and that's when I saw its tail. It caught me in the hip, knocking me over.

I hit the ground, my hands landing in something wet and sticky. I so didn't want to think about that as I pushed myself off the floor and stared through the curtain of my hair. The creature dived at me again, and I rolled onto my back. Using my legs, I pulled them up, and then swung them back down, popping up in a crouch.

The bird came at me again, but this time I was better prepared—I launched up and caught one of its wings. Tapping into the strength I'd always had in me, but never really used, never truly understood, I broke the wing near the small horn.

Screeching, the bird spiraled down to the floor, crashing into the destroyed pews. Picking up a board, I followed it to where it rolled to a stop, at the foot of the chancel. I raised the board and as the stone creature rose to its hind legs, I smacked the board into its head. Wood broke and stone shattered from the neck up. The rest of the statue toppled over as black smoke poured toward the ceiling, reminding me of that TV show Sam had gotten me addicted to.

Spinning around, I caught sight of Roth kicking one of the statues into the wall, and then twisting to catch the one behind him. He moved with brutal grace, destroying everything that came within touching distance of him.

Robin had cornered another wraith, so I turned to the raised platform, where the Lilin stood surveying the carnage. He smiled down at me, so much like Sam that I wanted to get up there and beat the ever-loving—

A statue slammed into me, throwing me several feet into the air. My wings expanded, stopping me from being thrown against the wall like one of Roth's statues. I hovered for a moment, spying the lion creature.

It was massive, its powerful muscles coiling and tensing as it stalked toward me, mouth open to reveal stone fangs.

That was one creature I did not want to get a hold of me.

Turning toward the Lilin, I landed on the chancel, and as I expected, the lion didn't come toward me. It backed away just as the double doors exploded open.

Wardens were here.

"Perfect," the Lilin said, its smile spreading.

I shot toward it, but the Lilin dodged me, jumping off the platform. Cursing under my breath, I followed. I made it two steps before Roth appeared beside me, grabbing my arm and spinning me to the left, out of the way of another goblin-looking creature.

"Thanks," I muttered.

"My pleasure." Roth shot up, and then drew back from the thickening cloud of smoke from the fire. "We need to get out of here before this whole place goes up."

Fire was licking its way up the walls, hungry as it consumed everything it touched. A section of the ceiling had already come down.

Stalking toward the Lilin, I stopped and dipped as another one of the possessed stone creatures made a run at me. Its meaty hands snagged my shirt, but I jerked back, breaking its hold. Spinning around, I kicked out, planting my foot into its chest and knocking it back.

Arms flailing, it fell back into the flames, but immediately came back out, this time on fire.

"Good God," I groaned, crouching down, and then jumping out of its grasp. Landing several feet away from it, I caught sight of Robin darting between the broken pews, chasing after a wraith.

The fiery creature veered off, distracted by Nicolai. The Warden easily avoided it, listening when Roth shouted instructions on how to break them apart. I turned back to the Lilin, seeing that it had reached one of the Wardens, intent on feeding. Out of the corner of my eye, I saw Abbot had one of the creatures by the neck.

Picking up speed, I raced up the aisle, aiming to power bomb the jerk, but it whipped around at the last moment, saw me and launched itself at me. There was no stopping the collision.

We smacked into others and hit the floor, rolling several times, coming to a stop a few feet from the fire, with the Lilin on top. It smiled down at me. "Give up."

"Not going to happen." Lifting my legs, I circled its waist and threw my weight behind the turn, flipping it off me. I moved, raising the dagger, seconds from plunging it deep into its smirking face.

Something crashed into me, knocking me to the side and

chasing the air out of my lungs. Rising up, I came face-to-face with the damn lion. Beyond it and the Lilin, I saw Zayne creeping up the center aisle, a dagger in his hand. Slowly I backed up, eyes on the disturbingly sharp claws.

The Lilin laughed. "Do you like my pet?"

"Do you like this?" Zayne growled, bringing down the dagger in a wide swoop.

The Lilin whirled and twisted at the waist, but wasn't fast enough. The dagger hit a few scant inches above the heart.

My body spasmed and the dagger fell from my fingers as an intense, breath-stealing fire exploded inside me. Screaming at the burst of sudden unexpected pain, I stumbled back and tripped over a leg—human or stone, I couldn't be sure—and I hit the floor. I tried to drag in air, but my lungs seized. I glanced down, saw that a line of red was bleeding through my sweater, just above my heart and closer to my shoulder.

What the...?

Roth spun in midair. His wide eyes moved from me to the Lilin, then to Zayne, who raised the dagger again. I pressed my hand just below my shoulder, stanching the flow of blood as I struggled to my feet.

"No!" Roth shouted, changing direction. "Zayne! No!" He hit the ground beside Zayne, slamming him in the shoulder and forcing him back several steps. He reached up, grasping the wrist that held the dagger as he stared into the bewildered face of Zayne. "Stop."

The Lilin choked out a laugh as it staggered to the side, coming close to the flames. Blood poured down its chest as it heaved for breath. "You kill me," it grunted out, "you kill *her*."

twenty-three

THE LILIN'S WORDS BOUNCED AROUND IN MY head, but there was little time to focus on them. The doors burst behind me and the fight spilled out into the lobby and the smoke became too dense to see or breathe. The fire raged out of control.

Zayne tore himself free of Roth as the Lilin backed into the smoke, disappearing from sight. I turned, doubling over as the burning sensation in my shoulder spread. I searched the mess for my familiar, panicked when I couldn't see beyond two feet in front of me.

"Robin," I called out, gritting my teeth against the pain.

He came out from the cloud of smoke, shrinking in size as he raced toward me. Jumping up, he hit my hand, and then took the form of my tattoo. Roth was suddenly beside me, wrapping an arm around my waist.

Zayne was on my other side, his face marked with confusion as he saw the blood on my shirt. We moved out of the room, hitting the lobby. There, Dez and one of the stone creatures were duking it out, going fist to fist until another stone gargoyle came through the doors, slamming into Dez's waist, throwing him through the window. Glass shattered, and then the fight was outside, in the street.

Nicolai was in front of us, his gaze darting back and forth. "What happened?"

"I don't know. I stabbed the Lilin and this happened to her. You need to shift into your human form," Zayne said as we stepped out into the fresher, cleaner night air. "Both of you. You stand out too much."

Roth shifted back before I did. It took a moment, because adrenaline was pumping way too fast in my system, but my wings folded in and when I lifted a hand, pushing my hair back from my face, I saw insanity.

People streamed into the streets from the bars and buildings nearby. In their panicked, terrified state, they probably couldn't tell the difference between the Wardens and gargoyles. All they saw was a brutal battle. Screams rose, as did the smoke. It now poured out of the building.

The fire had spread, reaching the top floors of the Church's headquarters and jumping to the roofs of the buildings next to it, giving the sky a burnt-orange tint.

"I'm okay." Pushing down the pain, I stepped away from Roth and Zayne. "Where's—?"

Before I could finish the question, the damn lion exploded out of the building. It had sprung itself into the air and now hit Zayne in his back. The two of them fell into a parked car. Metal crunched under their combined weight. They rolled, taking out the windshield.

"Stay out of the fight," Roth said, and I didn't get a chance to respond. In his human form, he ran over to where the lion had Zayne pinned on the hood.

Even in his human form, Roth was a force to be reckoned with. He gripped the lion's shoulders and hauled it back. Twisting, he tossed the creature.

A cab racing down the street slammed on its brakes, but not in time to avoid taking a direct hit. The lion slammed into the passenger-side door, tipping the cab up on its side even as the lion landed on its four stone paws.

That thing would not die.

Without warning, a hot gust of air blew into my back, and I turned, spying the stone creature that had been on fire. Disregarding the pain, I spun out before it could grab me.

Dez appeared, his wings stirring the ash settling around on the ground. He landed in a crouch, and then rose. With the epic kick of the century, he knocked the creature back into the building. Before I could so much as high-five him for that, another one slammed into him.

I turned, spying the Lilin as it stumbled out of the burning wreckage of the building, its face covered with soot. Our eyes locked, and then it pivoted, starting to run down the street. I wasn't even thinking as I raced after it.

Because it was injured far more than me, I imagined, I caught up to it. I launched myself at it, slamming my good shoulder into its back. The Lilin went down, me on top of it. It immediately bucked, but I wasn't having it.

I shoved my hand at the back of its head, forcing it down, but it fought me as I planted my knees on either side of its hips. It managed to lift its head. "Are you truly this stupid? You can't kill me without killing yourself. We are in this together."

My stomach dropped at his words. "That doesn't mean I can't beat the crap out of you!" I slammed its head back down and stars exploded behind my eyes, causing me to cry out. *"God,"* I grunted.

"Idiot." It wheezed out a laugh. "You have to learn everything the hard way."

Uncaring at this point if it hurt me, I cocked back my arm and slammed my fist into its ribs. I barely felt that new kiss of pain. I swung back to deliver another punch that was probably going to hurt me more than it, but that would give me a sick sense of satisfaction when a low grumble stopped me.

Looking over my shoulder, I sighed when I spotted the lion. "You. Again."

The Lilin reared up, knocking me off it. I hit my back, and was slow to get to my feet, my eyes fastened on the new threat. I was aware of the Lilin running off, but I didn't dare give chase. It didn't seem like any of these monsters had gotten the message that killing me killed the Lilin. The lion stalked me, its stone tail swinging. That tail hit another car, shattering a window.

Someone shouted, but I didn't know who the source was. The lion crouched, preparing to attack, and I knew this was going to seriously hurt. It launched into the air, and all I could see was its claws. Made of stone, they were huge. But suddenly, there was a massive Warden in front of me. Tall and broad, his golden hair was as brilliant as a real lion's.

The Warden took the direct hit in the upper body and staggered under the force of the attack. I gasped as he gripped the sides of the creature's head while the monster dug in with its claws, ripping through the granite texture of the Warden's skin, spraying blood.

With a shattering crack, the Warden twisted the creature's

head clean off. Dark shadows joined the crowding smoke, but the creature was down, finally.

The Warden turned to me, and terror seized me as I locked eyes with Abbot. The vibrant blue broke free as his skin started to pink, revealing the horror of the injuries, the ruthless extent of the damage.

"No," I whispered, stepping forward.

Abbot opened his mouth, but there were no words, just air bubbling through his torn neck. His legs caved under him, and I shot forward, trying to stop his fall. But with his weight and my injury, it was a useless endeavor. We both went down on the sidewalk. He landed on his back and I beside him.

There was so much blood.

I clamped my hands on his neck as I lifted my head, scanning the street as I screamed for help. I don't even know who I screamed for, but Roth finally emerged from the smoke, his steps faltering as he saw what was left of the lion creature and of Abbot. I screamed again, this time for Zayne and then for Dez, for Nicolai, because someone had to help him.

Someone needed to.

Roth stepped around Abbot's legs and knelt beside me, his hands reaching for mine. "What are you doing, Layla?" His voice was hoarse, and when I looked at him, I saw a bruise forming along his jaw. "What are you doing?"

I thought it was obvious. "I'm stopping the blood. I'm—"

"Layla." He shook his head as he wrapped his hands around mine. "It's too late."

"No," I said, glancing down at Abbot—at the man who had raised me, who had betrayed me, but had ultimately saved me. It couldn't be too late.

Abbot's eyes, once so vibrant and blue, were a dull shade

and fixed on…on nothing. There was no aura around him, no matter how hard I tried to see it. But I saw that the injuries were not limited to just his throat. His chest…

"Oh God. Oh. God, no."

Roth pulled my hands back, and I didn't fight him, because he had been right and there was no point. It was too late. My head rebelled at what I was seeing, at what had happened so quickly.

Out of the smoke and chaos, others were coming toward us. First Nicolai, and he had drawn up short, and then the one person I didn't want to see this, but that I was also too late to stop.

Zayne saw his father.

He fell to knees on the other side of Abbot, and he reached for his father, but stopped, his hands hovering over Abbot's still, ruined chest. He trembled. "Father?"

There was no answer. There never would be.

Time seemed to stop, and no one moved, and I heard no sound even though there had to be screams and shouts, sirens and flames crackling as the fire devoured the buildings. There was nothing but Zayne staring down at his father with horror etched into his face.

There was just nothing but Zayne.

I clambered free of Roth and crawled around Abbot. I came to Zayne's side, dipped under his wings and wrapped my arms around him. He shook so fiercely that my teeth rattled, but I held on, and when Zayne reached down and gripped my arms, he didn't pull mine away. He held on so he…so he wasn't alone.

Abbot was dead.

twenty-four

THE NEXT HOUR WAS A BLUR.

I remembered Zayne and Nicolai gently gathering up Abbot's body and getting him into a large SUV I wasn't even sure belonged to any of them. I remember climbing in with them, along with Roth. I remembered hearing sirens and seeing flashing blue and red lights as Nicolai navigated the crowded street full of destroyed cars and panicked people.

Then we were at the compound, a place I hadn't thought I'd ever return to, and there was Geoff and Jasmine and Danika. Each of their faces was marked with shocked horror as Abbot was carried out of the car and into the house.

But it was Morris who killed my heart.

It had been so long since I'd seen him, the Wardens' man of all work, and I had to stop myself from rushing over to him when he walked out of the kitchen, sadness etched into the deep grooves of his face. When he saw me, he smiled slightly, but it didn't reach those dark, soulful eyes.

Jasmine—practical, fast-thinking Jasmine—had grabbed a sheet and laid it out on the floor. Abbot had been placed upon it, and Morris had taken hold of the edges, wrapping them around Abbot, forming a death shroud.

Zayne remained by his father's side, his head bowed, and I remained close by, just in case he needed me. I wasn't sure if he had need of me or what I could do for him, but I'd do whatever I could. Roth and I were forgotten as the members of the clan drifted in and out of the room.

I learned when Dez phoned in that all the stone creatures had been destroyed and that he and the other Wardens were currently hunting down the wraiths the Lilin had created. From what I heard, they were also trying to do some damage control among the humans. Some of the people on the streets had seen the wraiths, and to them, wraiths would look like stereotypical ghosts…a level of exposure the Wardens didn't want to risk. Dez was going to have to do a lot of fast talking to convince everyone that hadn't been what they'd seen. Luckily, those who'd been at the scene hadn't been able to tell the stone creatures apart from the Wardens.

It was going to be a mess. It *was* a mess, and only time would tell how bad, but I doubted any of us was really thinking beyond this moment.

"Why don't you sit down?" Roth asked, his eyes full of concern.

I shook my head as I shifted my weight from one foot to the other. "I'm okay."

He looked at me and then to where Zayne was. I could tell Roth wanted to say more, but was forcing himself to stay quiet.

Finally, after what felt like forever, Zayne pulled the remaining folds of the blanket together, covering Abbot's face.

"Are you ready?" Geoff asked stoically.

Zayne pressed his hands into his thighs and stood. "Yes."

Nicolai stepped forward and the men lifted Abbot's body, carrying him out of the room. My heart started to pound and I knew they were going to take him somewhere more private, to prepare his body, to clean him up as best they could.

Wardens—when they died, their bodies did what any human body would do, but the process was faster for them. Within a day, there would be nothing really left beyond bones. That was why they burned their dead.

Hours had passed by the time Dez and the rest of the clan returned, and even though my legs, my entire body felt numb, I was there when Abbot was lifted up the hastily made pyre and I was there when Zayne carefully placed a lit torch at the feet of his fallen father. I was there to see Nicolai place his arm around Danika's shoulders.

I was there when nothing but ash remained.

When it was all over, Roth carefully placed his arm around my waist, startling me. It wasn't that I'd forgotten that he was there, but I was... I was simply out of it. Looking back, I'd probably be fascinated by the fact that the Crown Prince of Hell had borne witness to the ritualistic funeral of a Warden.

Roth guided me back into the house, but we didn't make it very far before Jasmine appeared in front of us. Sadness radiated from her every pore, but a look of steely determination had settled on her beautiful face.

"Come with me," she ordered, turning toward the stairs.

When I didn't move, Roth took matters into his own hands. Or arms. Turning to me, he thrust one arm under my knees and in the next breath, I was up off my feet and cradled against his chest.

"What are you doing?" I demanded.

"You've been on your feet this whole time and you were

injured." He started for the stairwell, behind Jasmine. "Don't tell me that you're fine. Let Jasmine look you over."

I started to protest, but he was already halfway up the stairs, and it hit me right then—everything that had happened in the last couple of days. Exhaustion grabbed hold of me and didn't let go. It dug in deep and I was weary to my very bones.

Jasmine stopped in front of what used to be my bedroom, and when the door opened, a wave of nostalgia smacked into me. I looked around as Roth walked me to the perfectly made bed and set me down. He lingered close, sitting on the other side.

Nothing had really been touched with the exception of the bed being made, because that seriously hadn't been me. My desk was still cluttered with notebooks, loose papers and books. The closet door was ajar, revealing the mess of clothing half dangling off its hangers and strewn about the floor, mixed among college applications.

It was too weird being back here.

I looked over at the window Abbot had once bolted shut and saw the dollhouse. My chest contracted, because I couldn't help but think of the past—of Zayne. In a fit of rage, I had destroyed the dollhouse, and he had rebuilt it back to its former glory. The dollhouse also reminded me of how Bambi had made it her home.

Tears clogged the back of my throat, but I didn't let them fall. Instead, I focused on Jasmine, who'd put various herbs and her bag of torture devices, otherwise known as a sewing kit, on the bed.

"Can we get the sweater off?" she asked, twisting her long dark hair back and securing it with a hair tie.

Reaching down, I tugged the ruined sweater over my head. I had a tank top under it, but even if I hadn't, I would've been too tired to care if I was showing off my goodies.

Roth took the sweater from me, tossing it to the floor, and then placing his hand on my shoulder. His eyes were fastened to my face.

Jasmine made a soft, clucking sound as she eyed the wound. "What happened?"

"I really don't know." I cleared my throat. "Zayne stabbed the Lilin and *this* is what happened to me."

"The Lilin was stabbed with an iron dagger," Roth added. "But it doesn't look like she has the symptoms of being stabbed with one."

Jasmine shook her head as she poured antiseptic on a cloth. "No. She would be very ill if that was the case. I'm sorry if this hurts." She placed the cloth against the wound, and yeah, it did sting, but I'd felt worse. "How have you been?"

"Okay." I didn't want to talk about myself. I glanced at the door and then at Roth. "Zayne...he'll be okay, won't he?"

Roth was slow to nod. "He has to be."

"He's right." Jasmine mopped up the blood on my shoulder and arm. "With his father gone, Zayne is in line to be the head of this clan."

My eyes widened. I hadn't even thought of that.

"He's too young to completely take over," she continued. "And it will probably fall to Nicolai to step in until Zayne is ready."

It was the end of an era and would be the beginning of another.

My body was present while Jasmine talked as she cleaned my wound, and yet, my mind was a thousand miles away it seemed. I couldn't believe what had happened. This outcome had never crossed my mind. I wasn't mentally or emotionally prepared for any of this.

"Good news," Jasmine said, drawing my attention. "The

wound is already starting to heal. I don't need to stitch it closed."

Thank God, because the last time I had that happen, I had to be held down. Jasmine smoothed some kind of cooling, minty-smelling salve on my arm, and then rose. "You should get some rest," she said. "It's late. I'm sure the clan will have no problem with you both staying here."

Roth raised both brows at that. "You sure?"

She smiled tiredly. "If I'm wrong, then someone will be up here to tell you to leave. Meanwhile, are either of you hungry? I can have food sent up."

"I'm fine." Roth looked at me. "You?"

"I'm good." I reached out, grabbing Jasmine's hand as she turned to leave. "Thank you."

"No thanks are ever needed." With that, she left the room.

Glancing down at my shoulder, I saw the glistening puckered skin. The wound was nowhere near as bad as it had originally felt.

"Want me to grab you a new sweater?" Roth asked, and when I nodded, he headed to my closet, returning with a thick chunky one that buttoned up the front. He was quiet as he took care of the buttons and then knelt, pulling off my boots.

As he kicked his own off, Morris appeared in the door, carrying two glasses. Both had orange juice in them, and that brought a watery smile to my face. He walked them over to the nightstand, and as always, he didn't say a word. When he turned, he reached out, cupping my cheek with a cool hand. The smile was back on his face and this time it reached his eyes. Then he patted my cheek and left the room, leaving the door half-open.

"That man...he is strange," commented Roth.

"He's wonderful," I immediately defended Morris.

Roth shook his head slowly. "I'm not disputing that, but…"

"But what?"

"I don't know. He just…gives me the creeps." Roth frowned. "And nothing gives me the creeps."

I made a face. "There's nothing creepy about him. Morris is the best and he's an old man—not exactly a threat to you."

"Like I said, I don't know how to explain it." Turning to me, he scrubbed his fingers through his hair. "Tonight has been…"

"A complete mess?" I scooted over, resting against the back of the headboard as I picked up the cup of OJ.

Roth sat beside me so we were shoulder to shoulder. He stretched his legs out. "Yeah, that about sums it up."

I took a sip and then another before setting it aside. When I looked at him, I saw that the bruise along his jaw was already fading, but I brushed my fingers around it. "Are you okay?"

His brows knitted. "Don't worry about me."

"I do."

"There's no need."

I sighed. "Roth."

"I'm fine," he said finally. "It doesn't even hurt."

"Good." I struggled to take an even breath. "Tonight… I don't even know what to think. I can't believe Abbot is gone."

He took a deep breath. "You know how I feel about that man, what he aided in doing to you, but I know he raised you." He slid his hand around mine and squeezed. "I know what happened isn't easy for you to accept."

Closing my eyes, I leaned back. "He died protecting me. I can't… God, I don't even know what to say. I was so angry with him before this, but in the end, he came through. I…" I stopped, opening my eyes. They felt wet, and when I spoke, my voice was hoarse. "I still loved him, you know?"

Roth brought my hand to his mouth and pressed a kiss atop it. "It's obvious that he still loved you as well."

"Yeah." I blinked my tears away and drew in a shaky breath. There was a pause. "Do you want to go check in on Zayne?"

I turned my head toward him, not as surprised by the thoughtfulness as I once might have been. "Yes, but I think... I think he probably needs a little bit of time."

"Probably," he murmured, reaching over and tucking a strand of my hair back behind my ear.

Forcing my thoughts to the newest problem we'd discovered, I pulled our joined hands into my lap. "The Lilin...it told me that we were in this together. You heard it say that. I guess we didn't realize how literally we should take his words."

Roth made a low, angry sound in the back of his throat. "I didn't see this coming."

"Me, neither," I replied drily. "But it makes sense. Part of me created it. As did a part of Lilith. Grim told me that we were joined, the three of us, but he failed to really go into detail about what that meant."

"Of course he did."

"That would've been good to know," I went on tiredly. "I mean, that's a pretty big detail. If we kill the Lilin, then it kills me. And I'm assuming that works both ways."

Roth's gaze turned intent. "There has to be another way. If there's not, we'll just find a way to keep it...out of trouble."

I arched a brow at that, because for one thing, I didn't think there was anything we could do to keep the Lilin out of trouble short of killing it. But even if we did manage to contain it while letting it live, where did that leave Sam? His soul would be lost, plus all the souls of the congregation the Lilin had taken out. Granted, those people were fanatics, but that didn't mean they deserved that kind of fate.

Roth's eyes shifted to the doorway, and I followed his gaze, my breath catching when I saw that it was Zayne. I opened my mouth but he spoke first. "Can I come in?"

"Of course." I pulled up my legs to give him room, but he lingered by the door, just inside the room. My heart ached for him, for everything. "Are you…?"

"I don't… I don't even know what to think." He shoved his hands into the pockets of his pants. "But that's not why I'm here. I wanted to apologize."

My mouth dropped open.

"I didn't know that when I stabbed the Lilin it was going to hurt you." His crystalline gaze met mine. "I would never hurt you. No matter what. I didn't—"

"I know. I know you didn't. I never once thought you'd do that if you'd known. We didn't even know," I insisted. "You don't need to apologize. That's the last thing you need to do right now. Seriously."

Some of the conflict eased out of his features. Not a lot, but some. "Do we know why this happened?"

Part of me wanted to tell him he didn't need to worry about this, but then I realized that he might be seeking to distract himself, and I didn't want to take that from him. I told him what Roth and I had just discussed.

"There's got to be a way to fix this," Zayne said when I was finished. "To separate you from the Lilin."

"But what if there is no way around it?" A tremor worked its way through me. "What if the Lilin and I are really joined, like we appear to be, and—"

"Don't say that." Roth's eyes brightened fiercely. "Don't even finish that thought."

"He's right," Zayne said, rubbing his hand over his chest. "There has to be another way. We just don't know what it is yet."

I wanted to believe that there was something else, but if we were connected, we were connected.

"We could check with the seer," Roth suggested.

Turning to him slowly, I stared at him. "The little kid?"

He nodded. "If anyone might know, it would be him. The key is just getting him to spill."

"The seer?" Zayne looked confused.

"The kid who kind of communes with, well, I don't know what he communes with, but he doesn't work for either the heavens or Hell." I paused, grinning slightly. "He likes to play 'Assassin's Creed.'"

"And he likes chicken," Roth added.

I snorted. "We can check with him tomorrow." A moment passed and I frowned. "He'll probably know we're coming."

Roth smirked.

My gaze flipped to Zayne. Shadows had blossomed under his weary eyes, and he looked… He looked lost.

"Layla, you know you can stay here." His shoulders tensed. "Both of you can stay here as long as you need. Okay? And if you leave—just be careful. I have… I need to go."

Slipping off the bed, I walked over to him. Before he could leave, I wrapped my arms around him. He stiffened, and then he turned in my embrace. Reaching down, he folded his arms around me. Against my cheek, he whispered in a gruff voice, "Thank you."

And then he let go and left the room, closing the door behind him.

I closed my eyes again, squeezing them shut. I don't know how long I stood there, but when I turned around, I made my way to the bed. Climbing in, I returned to the position I was in before, shoulder to shoulder with Roth.

"I don't think he knows," I said.

"Knows what?" Roth asked quietly.

I looked at him. "I don't think he knows how his father died. That Abbot was protecting me. He's already so—"

"Stop." Roth captured my chin, holding my gaze. "That guy that was just in here? I hate to say this out loud, but he's a good guy. He doesn't hate you. He never could. He might not like you right now, but that has nothing to do with his father. I don't know if he knows how Abbot went down, but if or when he finds out, he's not going to blame you. Because it wasn't your fault. And he knows that."

For a second I didn't know what to say. "I hate it when you're right."

Roth chuckled as he wrapped his arm carefully around me and held me close to him. My cheek found its way to his shoulder. So much had happened in a span of days that my head constantly buzzed with all of it. But in this second, right now, my head was quiet.

"I wouldn't have changed a thing."

I blinked as I lifted my head. "What are you talking about?"

"The offer I had Cayman make to the witches." He dragged his thumb under my lower lip. "Even if I'd known that they'd ask for Bambi, I still would've agreed if it meant saving you. I can only guess Zayne would feel the same about the way Abbot died."

"Oh, Roth…"

"I just want you to know that. Okay?" He leaned over, kissing my forehead. "I miss that snake. I'm always going to miss her, but if I had to do it all over again, I would. No questions asked. I'd do it all over again for you."

twenty-five

I REALLY WASN'T SURE HOW ZAYNE *AND* STACEY ended up in the backseat of the Mustang the following morning. Stacey had showed up first thing, moments after I'd stepped out of the shower, banging on the front door and demanding to be allowed in.

A huge part of me—okay, all of me—wished I'd been in the command room to see Geoff's face when *that* went down. In all our time as friends, Stacey had never been allowed at the compound before.

From what I gathered, the Wardens had refused to allow her entrance until Zayne appeared. Turned out she'd learned of my now-minor injury through Zayne at some point the night before, because neither Roth nor I had been answering texts.

The fact that she and Zayne were texting in the first place was a huge surprise to me. I didn't think they'd ever exchanged numbers before. Not that Stacey would've been against having Zayne's number, but I wasn't sure when the whole becoming text-buddies thing had happened.

Probably when I was in Hell.

Was that only yesterday? The day before? I couldn't keep track of the time anymore.

Right now, she was supposed to be in class, not that I could really take her to task on that since I hadn't stepped foot inside the school in what felt like forever.

Since Zayne had been in the room when Roth had suggested paying the seer a visit, he'd brought it up while Stacey was visiting me in my old room. She demanded to go with us, and after about a half an hour of arguing, I'd given up on trying to reason with her. I didn't want her anywhere near any of this, not even the seer, but as she had pointed out more than once, she was already knee-deep in it.

It was also good to see her animated and active instead of a washed-out ghost version of the friend I loved.

I was surprised that Zayne had joined us. He was quiet, his expression stoic. I didn't know how he was processing the grief of losing his father mere hours ago, but he was holding it together, and that strength was admirable.

When I'd seen Elijah die, I'd felt grief but it had been a different kind. With his death, I lost the potential of what could've been. Not that I ever fooled myself into thinking one day he would wake up and accept me as his daughter, but I'd mourned the loss...the loss of what never was. When Abbot died, I'd felt the loss of the only father figure I'd known, yet even though my grief was sharp, it was nothing compared to what Zayne must be feeling.

And my grief over Sam still didn't reach the heights of what Stacey had experienced. It seemed, that through all of this, I was just getting a taste of the consequences of what was happening, not the whole swallow.

I had a feeling that would change, though, very soon.

The ride to the seer's house was awkward, because it started with a trip to the local grocery store.

The Perdue chicken was tucked between Zayne and Stacey. The former was shooting daggers at the back of Roth's head anytime I glanced back at him. Roth was on his third round of humming "Paradise City," appearing oblivious to the death glare directed at him. I was trying to pretend like everything was dandy and totally not about seven levels of awkward, and Stacey looked like she needed a bucket of popcorn.

When we finally pulled up in front of the old home with its wooden fence and stone walls near the Manassas Battlefield, I was ready to dive-bomb out of the car.

"I think it's best that you two stay in the car." Roth turned off the ignition, and then twisted back, eyeing our tagalongs. "Tony is peculiar. We don't need to piss him off."

Zayne glanced at the chicken. "You have to bring him a chicken?"

"Eh…" Roth didn't answer.

"He's really a kid?" Stacey asked, glancing at the house. A curtain swayed across a window near the door. "Like a kid, kid?"

"Yeah, he's probably only nine or ten," I explained, reaching for the door.

"Geez," murmured Stacey, slowly shaking her head.

"You two going to be okay here?" I hesitated.

Roth snorted. "I'm sure they'll be just fine."

I shot him a look, and he turned an innocent stare on me while he reached behind him. "Someone hand me the chicken?"

It was Stacey who handed it over. "This is so weird."

"You have no idea," I muttered.

Roth waited for me on the other side of the Mustang, lightly placing his hand on my lower back. "You feeling okay?" he asked as we stepped through the gate and passed the neatly trimmed bushes.

"Just a little sore," I admitted, because saying I was 100 percent fine wouldn't be believable.

Dipping his head, he brushed his lips over my forehead before we climbed the stairs. I glanced back at the car and found that Zayne had not stayed inside as instructed. He was standing beside the car, his back to the house. He was right there, but looking at him felt like I was seeing a recorded image of someone. He was there but not.

The door opened before we knocked, drawing my attention. The faint blue aura faded, revealing Tony's mother. She was wearing a white cardigan this time, but the pearls I remembered were still clasped around her neck.

"I'm still not happy to see you," she said.

Roth raised a shoulder. "And I'd say I'm sorry, but I still wouldn't mean it."

Good Lord, not this again.

"Let them in," came the voice from behind the woman.

She stepped aside and there he was. First I saw the white glow around him, brighter than what clung to Zayne. A pure soul, totally rare. The urge I usually felt at seeing a pure soul was minimal, almost forgettable. The boy was all blond curls and had the face of a cherub. He was adorable—with the exception of the white pupils in the middle of his cobalt eyes.

Because those eyes were still freaky.

Tony glanced at the grocery bag Roth held. "Another chicken? Are you serious?"

"Hey. I hear Perdue is the best," Roth replied.

"And I hear Tyson is not that bad, either." Sighing, the pint-size seer gestured at his mom. "Take it."

The woman, who was probably well versed in the bizarreness, took the bag. "It's Taco Tuesday. This will have to wait."

"You bet it will." The seer motioned us to follow him. The house smelled of pine and apples, making me yearn for Christmas. "You know, you could've allowed your friends to come in. Instead they're out there, being all broody and probably creeping out the neighbors."

"They're probably the least creepy thing your neighbors have seen," Roth pointed out.

"Depends on what you think is creepy, eh?"

I smacked Roth's arm when he opened his mouth, obviously forming yet another retort; if I didn't stop him, he never would. He shot me a look, but Tony let out a very childlike giggle.

We followed him into the living room. There was a massive tree all decked out with ornaments with a mountain of presents already tucked under it. Another video game was paused on the TV, but this time it didn't look like a medieval game. There was a car and what looked like a police officer chasing after it.

Tony plopped down on a beanbag, and somehow he made that look like a throne. "I know why you guys are here."

"Of course," I murmured, sitting down on the couch.

He raised a blond brow as he glanced at Roth. "Just so you know, when you ended up chained in the fiery pits, I wasn't laughing like I predicted."

Roth's eyes narrowed at the reminder as he sat on the arm of the couch beside me.

"Maybe just a low chuckle of amusement," Tony added slyly.

"Are you sure it wasn't a high-pitched giggle of amusement?" replied Roth. "Since you haven't hit puberty yet?"

Oh dear.

Tony lifted a chubby hand and flipped Roth off.

"Ah, did I upset the wee, little baby—"

"Roth," I sighed, punching his leg lightly. "I can't take you anywhere."

"Not true." He winked at me. "I'm adaptable in any situation."

Tony propped his legs up on the coffee table, crossing them at the ankles. "While I think it's great that you two have obviously come to terms with what you both are and your feelings for one another, I have better things to do than watch you two—"

"Tony!" his mom's voice rang out from somewhere in the house. "Get your feet off the coffee table now!"

I pressed my lips together to keep from laughing as Tony rolled his weird eyes but did as he'd been told. His feet thumped off the hardwood floors. "You want to know how to kill the Lilin," he said, staring balefully in Roth's direction. "You know the rules. I cannot help one side over the other."

"Screw the rules," Roth ordered.

"Easy for you to say when it's not your life that will be on the line," the seer retorted. "The thing is, you both should already know the answer you seek."

"We know how to kill the Lilin," I said, scooting forward on the cushion. "Stab it in the heart or decapitate it, and we almost succeeded with a stab to the heart, but—"

"But you discovered a small complication?" He turned a

woeful stare on his screen, as if spending a minute away from his game was torture. "A fatal wound to the Lilin delivers a fatal wound to you."

I nodded.

"It's expected. A part of you was used to create the Lilin, just as a part of Lilith was used to create both of you," he continued, tilting his head to the side. Several blond curls flopped over. "All three of you are joined."

That had been said before, but no one had mentioned the fact that killing the Lilin would also kill me. That little tidbit had been left out. Not that I was entirely surprised.

"We need to know how to separate the two." Roth opened and closed the hand closest to me. "That's why we're here."

"And I know that." Tony barely dragged his attention from the paused game. "This conversation is wasting my time and yours."

"Do you not care? I know your stupid game is important, but if we can't stop the Lilin, you're going to die. Everyone is going to die!" I shot to my feet, wanting to grab the little seer and shake him, but—but there was a part of me that understood he wasn't being obtuse. We were the ones who were. Frustration pounded through me. "If we don't succeed, the Lilin will jump-start the end of the world. Even you warned us of this last time we were here."

"Last time you were here, I *saw* that there was a good chance for that to happen." His pupils were at once a brilliant white. "Now I *see* that it will not happen. You will stop it."

I tensed. "But—"

"You," he repeated, eyeing me intently, "will stop it. And you already know how. The story is over. The end."

Roth sucked in a shrill breath, but I think I stopped breathing for a second. What none of us wanted to acknowledge in the hours after we'd gone toe-to-toe with the Lilin was now smacking us in the face again.

Killing the Lilin meant killing myself.

"You're not helping us out here, bud." Roth's voice was calm, but anger and something else, something akin to desperation, were rolling off him, becoming a tangible entity in the room. "We need to know how to kill the Lilin without harming Layla."

"And as I've said, you already know the answer to that," Tony replied from his beanbag throne. "You just don't want to accept it."

I closed my eyes briefly. "So what you're saying is…vice versa. If we kill me, we kill the Lilin?"

"That's bullshit," Roth spat, and he was on his feet by the time I opened my eyes. "It's an unacceptable answer."

A look of remorse flickered across the young seer's face. "It's the only answer."

Roth started toward Tony, and I snapped my hand out, grabbing his arm. He breathed in deeply, his chest rising sharply. A second later, Tony's mother was in the room.

She held a casserole dish above her head, as if she was ready to pitch it at one of us. "I think it's time for you all to leave."

My grip tightened on Roth's arm. She was right. It was time to go, because we knew what the answer was. We'd known what it was before we'd even come here, or at least I had. Roth was still mad eyeballing the seer, so I tugged on his arm.

"Roth," I whispered. "Let's go."

He turned a sharp glare on me. "You're just going to accept that?" He threw an arm up toward Tony. "That there's no other way?"

"No," I said, and it wasn't so much a lie as it was an attempt to end this before we ended up wearing green-bean casserole. "But we're done here." When he still hesitated, I pulled on his arm again. "We'll figure this out on our own."

My words sounded weak to my own ears, but Roth finally relented. We started toward the front hallway, passing Tony's stern mother.

"Everything is for a reason," the seer called as we neared the archway to the foyer, and when I looked back, he was standing, his expression solemn and wise beyond his years. "Not one thing in this world happens without a purpose. Everyone's actions—those of the Prince and of your Wardens—have all been leading up to this. They've all sacrificed for you, for this. And it will not be in vain."

Stacey's face was the color of a piece of notebook paper and her dark eyes were wide. "No," she said, and then louder, "No."

Twisting around in the front passenger seat, I glanced at Roth. At his hands. His knuckles were bleached white from gripping the steering wheel. He hadn't said much since we'd returned to the Mustang. He stared straight ahead, a muscle ticking along his jaw as he drove us back to drop Stacey off at the high school.

"Is there literally nothing that can be done?" Zayne asked, his hands resting on the back of my seat. "Or is it just that the seer doesn't know what it will take?"

"I don't think there is a way," I replied, flicking my gaze back to Zayne. He didn't look just angry or confused, but more like a combination of the two. "It makes sense in a way, the fact that it's connected to me and both of us are connected to Lilith. Our blood created the Lilin."

"Maybe it makes sense to *you*," Stacey said, pulling one leg up and tucking it against her chest. "None of any of this crap really makes sense to me, but whatever. What are we going to do now? If we can't kill the Lilin…"

"If we don't kill the Lilin, we lose Sam. We lose all those souls that the Lilin has taken," I reminded her.

Her face contorted as she looked away, staring out the window as the lawns and homes gave way to walls. "I haven't forgotten that. I just…"

Zayne leaned back in his seat, rubbing his hands down his face. "There's got to be something. There's so many damn books in my…my father's study. I'll check them when I get back. I'll get Dez on it, too." Lowering his hands, he sighed heavily. "We're not giving up."

The fact that Zayne still cared enough about me to want to help eased a little of the burden I carried with me from hurting him so terribly. Then again, I shouldn't be all that surprised. There was probably a part of him that hated me, understandably so, but under it all, he was a good guy—a great guy.

"Did you hear me?" Zayne asked, drawing my gaze back to him. "We're not giving up."

"I know, but…but we're running out of time for Sam. And how much longer are the Alphas going to allow this violence to continue?" I was asking damn good questions. Ones that neither Zayne nor Roth could answer. "The Lilin took out an entire congregation of God's Children. And yeah, I'm sure they weren't on the big guy's favorite list, but it's only a mat- ter of time before the Lilin does something that can no longer be overlooked. It almost exposed all of us when it woke those gargoyles. How much time do we really have to figure out a way around this?"

"What are you saying?" Roth, finally speaking, barked out the question.

Startled, I looked at him. His eyes were trained on the road. "I don't know. Just that we...we don't have any time."

Roth lapsed back into silence, and then we were pulling up in front of the high school. Seeing it, after what felt like forever, triggered a mixed response inside me. Part nostalgia and part keen disappointment—I wasn't able to forget how much I'd looked forward to getting up every morning and going to school. Within those walls, I used to be able to pretend that I was normal. Looking back now, I saw how foolish that was, that childish urge to hide from what I was.

It wasn't something I could do anymore.

Stacey grabbed her backpack off the floor of the Mustang and climbed out. I followed, so that I could give her a quick hug. We couldn't linger, though. If any of the school officials saw me outside, that would raise a slew of unwanted questions we didn't have time for.

"You okay?" I asked when I pulled back from the hug.

Nodding, she brushed her overly long bangs out of her eyes. "Yes. No." She hitched up the strap of the bag farther up her shoulder. "Why are you even asking if I'm okay? You're the one who's virtually a Siamese twin with a psychotic demon. Don't worry about me right now."

"It's kind of hard not to."

"Or is it just easier to worry about me instead of yourself?"

I opened my mouth, but what could I say to that? It was boldly on point. Glancing at the thick clouds, I sighed. "I don't know what to think right now. I…" I trailed off, shaking my head.

Stacey reached out, grasping the sleeve of my sweater and tugging gently. "You know you're the sister I never really asked for, right?"

I grinned. "Yeah."

"And I love you, no matter what. You know that also. And you know how much it…it killed me to lose Sam." Tears filled her eyes, but her gaze was steady. "I can't lose you, too."

Her statement unnerved me. "Why do you think that's going to happen?"

"Because I know you," she replied, her voice hoarse. "Promise me you're not going to do anything stupid."

"Me?" I forced a laugh that sounded like dry bones rattling. "Not do something stupid?"

The joke did nothing to ease her mind. "You know what I mean. Promise me, Layla. I want to hear you promise me."

"I promise," I whispered.

As I parted ways with Stacey, I knew that my promise had done very little to reassure her. Truth was, the promise was one I never should've made. Because I had a lot of stupid left in me, and I knew what I had to do.

twenty-six

ROTH AND I HELPED ZAYNE AND DEZ SKIM through the ancient tomes that filled the floor-to-ceiling bookshelves in Abbot's study well into the evening. We were even joined by Danika and Nicolai once night fell. As we went from one dusty page to the next, I could hear the high-pitched giggles from Izzy and the shrill cries from Drake on and off all evening—clearly Jasmine was having a tough time wearing them out enough to get them to bed. By the time we called it a night, I hadn't actually seen the twins and we hadn't found anything of use.

Except I did come across a small creature called a Pukwudgie in one of the tomes, a tiny troll-like creature I'd heard about only once before, when Dez had brought Jasmine to our compound all those years ago. She'd been bitten by one and had been very ill as a result.

I still sort of wanted to see one with my own eyes.

Snow was falling by the time Roth and I left. We headed to the Palisades since it was closer than the McMansion, parking in the garage and bypassing the club down below. As soon as I walked into the loft, he called off the kittens. I watched them scatter about the room. One headed to the piano while the other two darted under the bed.

"Want me to get some food?" he asked, dropping his keys atop the bookshelf.

I wasn't really hungry, but I knew Roth hadn't eaten all day. "Sure."

"I'll go grab us some stuff," he said, instead of summoning Cayman like he normally would. "Anything in particular you want?"

Pressing my lips together, I shook my head and watched Roth start toward the door, stop as if he wanted to say something and then leave. Unease churned in my stomach. Asking about food was the most he'd said since we left the seer's house. Suspicion blossomed. What was he up to?

What was I up to?

Restless, I looked around the room, and then called for Robin. He peeled off my arm, a fox-shaped shadow until he hit the floor. There, his reddish-orange fur was twitching as he looked back at me, head cocked to the side.

He knew.

Of course he did.

Chirping, he pranced over to the open closet door, to the clothing he'd dragged off hangers and had fashioned a bed out of. I watched him curl his bushy tail close to his body, and then I walked to the roof entrance.

Cold air greeted me as I opened the door and climbed the narrow staircase. A fine layer of snow coated the empty pots and the canopy above the chaise rolled silently. All the trees were bare, but not dead. Life would be renewed in the spring, if mankind made it to the spring.

I made my way to the ledge and stared at the glistening lights of DC. A misty cloud formed every time I exhaled, but it was pleasant out here, above the noise of the city and the noxious fumes. Calm even. We were a handful of days away from Christmas, and we were running out of time.

We were out of time actually.

Although Zayne and Dez had planned to continue scouring the books for a way to end the Lilin or somehow incapacitate it, I doubted they would find anything. Besides, even if we could disable the Lilin, that did nothing for the souls it had consumed, nothing for Sam.

I took a deep breath, but it got stuck in my throat as a razor-edged panic rose like a ghost in the night, threatening to drag me under. Before I could give in to it, I felt Roth's presence. Swallowing hard, I pushed the fear down, all the way down, and faced him.

He stood just outside the door, the breeze ruffling his dark hair as snow peppered the strands and his eyes glittering like tawny jewels. "What are you doing up here?"

I shrugged a shoulder. "I don't know. It's kind of pretty, with the snow."

"And it's freezing," he commented.

"Neither of us is affected by that."

"I know." One side of his lips curved up. "I just felt like pointing that out." He paused. "You're not hungry, are you?"

"Not really."

An eyebrow rose as he walked across the roof. "Want to stay out here for a while?"

"Yeah. Yes. I do."

The half smile remained as Roth sat down on the chaise. The cushion he patted was protected from the snow, but only if the wind didn't really start picking up. I walked over to him, and when he extended his arm, I placed my hand in his.

Roth tugged me down between his legs, positioning me so that my back was pressed against his chest. His arms folded around me, and I closed my eyes, smacking any thought out of my head just so I could take the moment to enjoy the warmth of his body and the comfort of his embrace.

I don't know how long we sat there watching the snow fall silently before Roth spoke again, but the snow on the floor of the roof seemed to have thickened. "I've been thinking," he began. "About you in one of those really skimpy bikinis. The kind where the backside of the bottoms are really just dental floss."

"Oh my God." I laughed as I trailed my fingers over his hands. "Why am I not surprised by this?"

"Now. Now. Hear me out," he replied, resting his chin on my shoulder. I turned my cheek to him, waiting. "You wouldn't be the only one who would be wearing less clothing than what we've got on right now."

I really had no idea where this conversation was heading, but I was thrilled that he was talking and I was also willing to just—to just let it all go for right now, for these precious moments, to humor whatever was coming out of his mouth.

"Would you also be in a barely there bikini?" I asked.

I felt his lips curve into a smile. "You would not be able to control yourself if you saw something so amazing." He tugged me back into the V of his legs when I had started to twist toward him. "You'd treat me like a piece of meat."

"Oh really?" I laughed.

Roth leaned back against the cushion, bringing me along

with him so that we were stretched out as the snow continued to fall. "Uh-huh. So I would just be wearing swim trunks."

"Speedo?"

"Even I wouldn't wear a Speedo," he replied.

"How is a Speedo any different than me wearing what is basically dental floss?"

"It is. Just trust me on this." He tilted his head to the side so I could see his expression. "Anyway, the swim trunks and itsy, bitsy bikini would also involve a sandy white beach. You've never been to a beach, right?"

"Right." I bit my lip when he shifted so that his lips brushed the lobe of my ear, sending a shiver down my spine. "So what about this beach?"

"The beach would exist in a tropical area, where it's always warm and almost always sunny," he went on, one hand toying with the hem of my sweater, the other lazily roaming up and down my leg, from thigh to hip. "The beach would be a place far away from here."

"How far?" I whispered.

"As far as we want." One hand traveled up to my chin and his fingers guided my head back. "I was thinking along the lines of Turks and Caicos." He kissed my forehead. "I haven't been there." His lips coasted over my brows. "But I've heard of this place called Grace Bay." He dropped a kiss on each of my eyelids. "White sands. Water the color of turquoise." Then he kissed the tip of my nose. "Paradise, or so I'm told. We should go."

I smiled faintly. "We should."

His gaze met mine as he drew back. "I'm being serious. We can leave in the morning."

My smile started to fade. "What?"

"It will take nothing for me to get us a private jet. Just a few words spoken to the right person, and then we're on our way. It's a little too far to fly ourselves." His eyes searched mine intently, and I stiffened, because he really wasn't joking around. "We could be there by tomorrow night."

"Roth—"

"We can leave all of this," he pushed on, his hand cupping my cheek. "Let the pieces fall where they may, but you and I will be far from this—"

"There's nowhere we can go to truly escape this. The Alphas will intervene. The Lilin wants that, and even Grim has called it. They will bring about the end of the world. Hiding out at a beach isn't going to save us."

"We could try, dammit. We could try to survive," he insisted, his eyes flashing bright in the darkness. "Leaving here promises us at least a tomorrow—maybe even a week or a month, but staying here—what do we have?"

I sucked in a sharp breath. "What do you mean?"

"You think I don't know what's been going on in your head since you realized your life was tied to the Lilin's?" His hand curled around the nape of my neck as he leaned in, pressing his forehead to mine. "Dammit, Layla, I know..."

My eyes squeezed shut against the sudden burn.

"You're too good. You don't see that, but I do. You're *too* good, but I'm not." His voice hoarsened. "Let me be selfish enough for the both of us."

"What about Sam, Roth?"

"I don't know. I don't have an answer for that you want to hear," he admitted. "I'm sorry. You're my priority. Forget the rest."

I wrapped one arm around his neck, saying nothing as I

tucked my head under his chin. His hand remained at the back of my neck. "I know you think there is only one way out of this. You give up your life to stop the Lilin," he said, his voice thicker than before. "But I can't let you do that."

"I don't want to do that."

His other arm circled my waist as he shifted his head, his lips brushing my cheek as he spoke. "Then don't."

Roth made it sound so simple. The thing was, even he knew it wasn't that easy. If we left this place tomorrow, there was a good chance we'd have days, maybe even weeks or months before the Alphas stepped in and attempted to wipe us all out. But how could I seriously enjoy those days or weeks knowing that I turned my back on Sam... God, on mankind? What was happening was so much bigger than us, so much more important than what we wanted or desired.

His hand spasmed, and he forced out the words in a harsh whisper. "I'm terrified."

My heart turned over and then doubled up. Hearing him admit that was a shock to my system. I pulled back, meeting his gaze once more. "You're never scared."

"I'm not scared. I'm terrified," he repeated, threading his fingers through my hair. "I'm terrified of losing you and that there will be nothing that I can do to stop it."

There was a part of me that wanted to simply reassure him, but in this moment, all my defenses came crumbling down. The panic that rested in the pit of my belly expanded. Roth must've seen the fear in my eyes because he tugged me back to his chest.

"I won't let this happen," he said. "I'm the Prince. There has to be something I can do. I can go to the Boss."

But if there was something the Boss could've done, wouldn't

it have already been done by now? Or could the Boss even step in at this point? It didn't matter. As I clung to Roth, I knew, deep down, we really didn't have tomorrow. If I delayed what I needed to do, I would not only lose Sam and the other souls the Lilin had already taken, but I ran the risk of millions of lives being lost if the apocalypse was in fact set in motion.

I ran the risk of Roth doing something even more stupid than what I planned, and if I couldn't save myself, then at least I could save Sam. I could save the other souls. I could save the innocent people who would die because the end was coming. I could save Roth.

When Roth lifted my head, he opened his mouth to say something, but I didn't want there to be any more words between us. I closed the distance, kissing him. He tried to turn his head, but I grasped his cheeks, refusing to allow whatever words he wanted to speak to form on his lips.

And when the kiss wasn't enough, when he tried to speak again, I lifted up, planting my knees on either side of his hips. I pressed our bodies together, and when his mouth finally parted, my heart ached in the worst way, but he was kissing me back and it was scorching. His hands fell down my back, and his desperation amplified what I felt.

His muscles suddenly tensed, and then he was standing. I wrapped my legs around his hips. Our mouths were fused together and we stepped out under the snow. Wind picked up, tossing my hair around us.

I didn't think we'd make it back to the stairwell.

We barely did.

Once inside the narrow hallway, the door slammed shut behind us, and Roth turned, pressing my back against the wall. We were tangled in each other, our breaths coming in short pants as the hardest part of him was pressed against the softest part of me. The snow that had fallen on us had melted, dampening our skin and hair.

We kissed. We clung to each other, and the outside world went on hold once more. Right now, these stolen moments were just about us. Nothing else mattered then except how he felt and our love for one another.

"Hold on," he told me, and I wasn't planning to let go.

Roth captured my breaths with his lips as he turned, starting down the stairs again. He kicked the door shut behind us, sealing out the cold, and when he turned, he knocked into the piano bench, toppling it over.

We almost didn't hear it.

He carried me right to the foot of the bed, the whole time kissing me, drinking me in, and it wasn't enough. Not even when he nipped at the sensitive skin below my ear, dragging a heated sound out of me.

We parted long enough to get rid of everything between us, and that took longer than necessary, because we kept stopping…and we kept getting distracted each time a shirt came off or a button came undone. Our hands. Our fingers. Our mouths. Everything about us was greedy.

When my back hit the bed and I stared up at him, thinking was completely impossible. He consumed me, but I knew it went both ways, because his hand trembled as he touched me and his voice shook when he told me that I was beautiful; when he said that he loved me, over and over. His voice quaked each time.

What came next was simply him worshipping me and me repaying the honor. There wasn't a part of me he didn't explore, from the arch of my foot to the many valleys on the way to my lips. Our eyes and hands were locked as we started moving together. And when it was over, we lay together, his hand trailing over my ribs, to my hips, and then we started all over again. We exhausted ourselves in all the love we felt and we held off the shadows by sheer willpower until there was nothing left.

Sleep did not come for me afterward, even though I wanted nothing more than to snuggle into Roth and ignore everything, I couldn't. If I did, everyone I cared about would be lost, and countless, nameless innocent people would be caught in the cross fire. Knowing that I was the only thing that could truly stop this, walking away wasn't something I could live with. Besides, turning my back would only give us a few days, maybe only hours, because once the Lilin pushed too far, exposed too much, the Alphas would wipe us all out, and they'd been waiting oh-so patiently for a good reason to do so.

I had to do this. I knew that there was no other option, but as I watched Roth while he slept, what I was about to do cut deep into me. It *hurt*. A knot had formed in the back of my throat, a heaviness pressed into my chest and my eyes stung as tears filled them.

My fingers itched to touch him, just one last time, but I'd risk waking him by doing so. I settled for memorizing every beautiful angle of his face, from the sharpness of his cheekbones to the hard line of his jaw, only slightly softened by sleep. I committed to memory the thickness of his lashes and the natural arch of his brows. I looked my fill when it came to his full lips and I wished I'd get to see those dimples once more, or the way the tawny amber of his eyes would brighten when he looked at me. I yearned to thread my hand through his hair just once more, feeling the silky smoothness as the strands sifted through my fingers.

I ached to hear him say *I love you* one more time.

None of that was going to happen.

Squeezing my eyes shut against the rush of tears, I carefully rolled out of the bed and tiptoed to where my clothes were piled on the floor. In the quiet darkness, I dressed, grabbed the iron dagger off the piano, and then crept over to where Roth lay on his side, facing the space I'd rested on.

"I love you," I whispered, my voice choked. "I love you so much."

And then I did the one thing I never planned to do, but the only thing I could. I left Roth.

twenty-seven

AS I SORT OF EXPECTED, IT DIDN'T TAKE ME LONG to find the Lilin. I'd left Roth's loft through the rooftop exit and had taken flight, letting the cold wind ruffle my wings one last time.

It was almost ironic—this whole thing.

Roth had sacrificed for me. Zayne had. Even Abbot, in the end. All of them had given something up to keep me alive. Due to what the witches had given me, I'd gained immortality and for a sweet, short time, I'd had a taste of forever with Roth. And once I fully understood what I was, I'd been given unbelievable strength. My mere presence struck fear into the hearts of demons and Wardens alike. I'd become a force to be reckoned with, a total badass of a hybrid mess.

And ultimately, all those sacrifices and everything everyone had ever done had led up to this moment—when I would take all of that away. I wanted to laugh, but I had a feeling that it would be the crazy kind of laugh and I would break down, because I didn't want to die.

Because I wasn't that brave.

Because I wasn't this selfless.

I was just one girl with no other options, no other card up my sleeve.

Landing in Rock Creek Park among the thick, tall snow-tipped trees, I'd walked the trail, oddly calm. Okay. Maybe not calm. As I stared up at the moon breaking free from the clouds, I felt *nothing*.

I was empty—determined, but completely empty.

Only a few minutes passed before I heard a soft chuckle from behind me. The stake was in my back pocket, where I'd have easy access to it, but I left it there as I slowly turned around.

A light dusting of snow coated the ground and flurries drifted down to Earth. The Lilin was standing about five feet from me, and it looked like Sam again. Anger pricked at my skin. I *hated* it when that thing took on his image.

And it knew it.

The Lilin smiled at me from across the short distance. "Have you finally come to your senses?"

I raised my brows. "If coming to my senses is helping you free Lilith—"

"Our mother," it interrupted.

Ignoring that, I continued. "Then you're out of your mind. I will never help you free her, because freeing her would mean the end of everything."

"Not freeing her means the end anyway," the Lilin responded, taking a step forward. "Don't you understand that? I will continue stripping souls until the Alphas have no choice but to step in, until they eradicate every demon and Warden topside."

My hands tightened. "Why would you do that? You would be killed right along with the rest of us."

"Ah, yes, that's true, but I know Hell will not stand for the

Alphas going after all the demons. They will retaliate, and it will be Armageddon." The Lilin that looked like Sam smiled as if it was picturing a sunny day at the beach. "My death— your death—will be worth knowing that rivers will run with blood and these humans, these overgrown parasites, will die by the millions."

Absolutely thunderstruck by his words, I shook my head. "You're...a hundred percent certifiable."

"No. I just have nothing to lose. My life? This shell I'm using?" It patted itself on the cheek. "It's nothing. I have nothing to give up. And even if I did, I would do it for our mother. I would do anything to deliver her the revenge she deserves."

I blinked. "That's kind of sad."

One shoulder rose. "It is the truth."

Something sparked in my chest, and it tasted like hope. "It doesn't have to be. Don't you understand that? You have choices to make. You can stop what you're doing and try to make something out of this life you were given—"

The Lilin threw its head back and laughed.

"We have free will," I insisted, grappling onto anything that could somehow change its mind. "All of us, not just the humans, have free will. You can change. You can stop this right now. You—"

"Free will? You are naive, sister. There is no such thing. We are born with our fates clearly laid out in front of us. There is no changing that."

"You are wrong, so incredibly wrong." I wanted to stomp my foot to drive the point home. "Anyone can change their paths, including demons. Look at Roth. He never used to think free will existed, but when he made a choice to save me, he realized it did. Look at him!"

It grinned. "Ah, the Prince. I look at him and I see someone who was once great and feared by all, but who has become nothing more than the lackey of a stupid, silly little girl."

I clenched my jaw. "I'm not the one who's stupid, bud, and he's no one's lackey."

"Enough," it sighed. "Really. This conversation bores me. You know you cannot stop me. You have to have realized that by now. You can't kill me, because doing so would kill you. I am a part of you."

"You are nothing," I said, full of bitter venom.

It inclined its head. "If I had feelings, you might have hurt them."

As I stared at the Lilin, that tiny spark of hope flickered, and then went out. There would be no reasoning with it, just as Grim had said. Maybe if I had taken that approach from the beginning, there would've been time to try to change its mind, but there wasn't enough time to do that now, and it was too much of a risk to chance it.

The weight pressed farther down on my shoulders and my chest as the Lilin inched close to me. I held my ground, taking a deep breath. "What…what do you really look like?"

Surprise flickered across the face I missed so badly. "What?"

"You heard me. You're not Sam. You're not Elijah. I want to know what you really look like."

The flurries around us seemed to ease up as the Lilin studied me thoughtfully, the fine dusting of snow coating its dark hair. "What does it matter?"

I wanted to see its real face, just once, but that wasn't exactly the most convincing argument. "I don't know. Maybe… maybe it would help me understand you better."

Its eyes narrowed, and then it cast its gaze to the sky. It sighed dramatically. "You are so human."

When Roth said it, those words had been dipped in warmth and love. When those very same words came out of the Lilin's mouth, they were an insult.

The Lilin suddenly shot forward, stopping no more than two feet in front of me, its eyes pure black. "You want to see what I really look like?" it demanded. "You want that?"

"Yes," I whispered.

It smiled, and then it began to transform. Its entire body trembled, and then shook violently. I wanted to step back, because at this point, I sort of expected it to explode, but found myself unable to move as it shortened and became slimmer, as the brown hair gave way to hair so blond it almost appeared white. Bones snapped and refused again into different lengths. Its features contorted until I was staring into eyes that were a pale shade of blue, leached of almost all its color.

Sucking in a sharp breath, I felt like I was staring into the mirror. An exact replica of me stood there.

"I am you," it said, in my voice.

"No." My heart started thumping. "You are not me."

"I am. I've always been you." A small smile appeared, revealing just one side of its teeth, and all I could think at that point was—was that what I looked like when I smiled? God. "We are one and the same," it added. "We are no different. Do you understand that?"

A handful of months ago, a sight like this would've delivered a blow to my confidence. I'd have been shaken to the point that I wouldn't have been able to recover from it. Thinking that I was a part of something so cruel and evil would've crippled me.

But I wasn't the same girl now as I'd been then.

"This is some kind of trick." My voice was steady as I stared at myself. "How do you look like me? You haven't—"

"We are a part of one another," it replied, glancing down at itself. With a low giggle, it ran small hands down its sides and then across its front, then up.

Wow.

That was disturbing to see...myself kind of feeling myself up.

"You helped create me." Reaching up a hand, it started twirling a strand of hair around its finger. One pale brow rose. "We share the same blood."

"That's all we share, and I know this isn't your real form."

The smile turned coy as it raised one shoulder. "If you say so."

I drew in a deep breath. "You're a coward. You know that? You can't even show me who you really are."

"I am not a coward." The smile slipped from its face.

Mimicking its earlier movements, I shrugged a shoulder. "No wonder you can't show me what you actually look like. You don't see yourself clearly."

Cheeks flushing red, the pale eyes disappeared in a flood of black. The Lilin began to change form again. This time my mirror image was stretched like Gumby. As bones cracked, the icy-blond hair shortened to shoulders that were broader. The Lilin stopped trembling and what stood before me was something altogether familiar and yet different.

And I knew deep down this was really the Lilin.

The eyes were pools of black and the complexion pale. Cheekbones were high like mine, but broader and the tilt of the jaw was more masculine, the lips less full. The Lilin, in its true form was a male, was a head taller than me and a little broader, much slimmer than Roth or Zayne. It—he—was beautiful in a creepy sort of way, a fragile masculine sort of beauty that looked like it would shatter at any moment.

He looked like *Lilith*.

He looked like *me*.

If someone put the three of us in a room together, it would be obvious that we were related. Not until this very moment, staring at him, did I really see it. This creature…this thing truly was a part of me. We did share the same blood. It was my brother.

The knot from earlier returned to my throat and I wanted to cry. As stupid and useless as it would be, I wanted to flop down on the cold, snowy ground and cry, because I really was staring at something I was a part of—my own twisted flesh and bone.

"Are you happy now?" he asked, and his voice was deep.

I shook my head, blinking back tears. Roth's face formed in my thoughts, and I hoped with every ounce of my being that he could forgive me for this. "No. Not at all."

Confusion flickered across his face and then his expression evened out, turning bland. "I'm done with this foolishness."

"So am I."

Reaching behind me, I pulled the dagger out of my back pocket. I moved as fast as I could, faster than I ever had, and my brain was a vast, empty canvas as I moved. I didn't think, didn't register the return of bewilderment marking his features.

But then, in a split second, realization thundered through me as I stepped forward, thrusting the dagger into the Lilin's chest with every ounce of my strength.

I *was* brave.

Shock splashed across his features at the same moment pain exploded in my chest. The intensity of it was so jarring that

I let go of the dagger, jerking back. The pain was like fire, engulfing my chest and spreading into every limb. It was so much more powerful even than when the Wardens had stabbed me in the stomach, an intensity that was final. Wet warmth poured down my front. My heart beat, and then there was a sharp wrenching sensation from deep inside of me.

Black eyes were wide and his hands were pale as he gripped the end of the dagger. "What...what have you done?"

I wouldn't answer even if I could.

Because it was happening.

The wound in his chest lit up, pulsing with a blue-tinged light that seemed to come from within and the light spread rapidly, as if his skin had been peeled back. The light burst in flares of different colors, soft pinks and blues, and buttery yellows, and those lights, almost like little balls, shot straight up, disappearing into the sky above us.

Not lights, I realized dumbly, but the souls—the souls of everyone the Lilin had consumed. I knew in my heart of hearts that Elijah was among them, and so was Sam. I could almost feel him, I thought, almost hear Sam's chuckle and feel his hand brush over mine.

He was free.

I knew it.

There wasn't another heartbeat.

Our legs folded at the very same second, and we crumpled, folding like a paper sack. I didn't feel the ground stop my fall. I didn't feel anything. All I saw, through the darkness creeping into my vision, was the snow beginning to fall again, a tiny flake coasting to the ground.

And then I saw nothing at all.

twenty-eight

I DIDN'T REMEMBER CLOSING MY EYES, NOT even blinking. Yet somehow I was no longer lying on the cold ground in Rock Creek Park, but standing instead, and it was the park—but not during the night, or during the winter. Sunlight beat down through the leafy limbs and a warm breeze toyed with the hairs around my face.

What in the what?

My gaze dropped to the ground, and the Lilin wasn't there. Confusion pounded through me as I stared at the empty spot before me and then down at the front of my sweater. It was bloodied, as expected, but there was no pain in my chest. And this was the park in DC, but it also wasn't.

Something seemed wrong. Fragile. *Thin.* As I walked closer to a tree, I brushed my fingertips along its bark. Bits of it flecked off, turning to ash. I jerked my hand back.

"What have you done?"

Spinning toward the sound of the voice I'd only heard once before, I couldn't suppress the weird shudder at the sight of her—of Lilith. Dressed in the same barely there white gown

I'd seen her in last time, she looked different. Mainly because there was a splash of red coursing down the front of her dress, matching mine.

"How...how are you here?" I asked, glancing around. "Are you free?"

"Free?" Her pale eyes widened. "I will never be free because of you—because of what you've done. You've killed my son—you've killed me!"

Maybe dying made me a little slow on the uptake, but her response didn't answer my question. "I don't understand."

"How can you not?" She drifted toward me, her bare feet snapping out from under the long gown. "You killed him, knowing that would be the death of you—the death of me."

Okay. I had no idea that my actions would kill her. Nope. No one had filled me in on that. I'd assumed she was like a Twinkie, would survive a nuclear fallout.

"Where are we?"

Her blood-red lip curled up. "In the in-between."

"The what?"

"Are you pleased with yourself?" she ranted, ignoring my question. Her cheeks leeched of all color. "You think killing him—killing me—will change anything? Evil will still be evil. Hell will not cease to exist. Dark deeds will still be carried out."

"But it will...it will stop Armageddon," I said, blinking.

She scoffed. "For a while, but, child, do you know how many times the world has come close to being obliterated? The end is inevitable."

I closed my eyes, suddenly feeling woozy. "But it won't happen now."

"I've never been more disappointed in that which I created," she seethed, and when I opened my eyes, she was directly in front of me, a tall and terrible, beautiful apparition. "Does any of my blood course through your veins?"

"Yes." I swallowed, but it did nothing to easy the nausea.

Her eyes, the same color as mine, rolled. "Doubtful. I would have bred something more intelligent, with greater cunning and actual survival instincts."

I stepped back from her, forcing air into my lungs, but it felt like I was only getting a sliver of what I needed.

"To think that I have survived thousands of years, overcoming so much, to be taken out by the hand of my own daughter." She huffed. "And in so cowardly a way. But my son—he honored *me*. He worshipped *me*, as he should, but you ended him. You are no child of mine."

"I'm your daughter," I gritted out, focusing on her. "The daughter you left at birth. What in the Hell do you expect from me?"

"Loyalty?" she returned.

I stared at her, wanting to laugh in her face, but my lips felt strange. Numb. Cold. "You left me with the man who wanted to kill me."

"But he didn't, did he? Obviously not."

Shaking my head, I immediately regretted doing so. The world spun a little. "I had to stop the Lilin. There were too many people's lives at stake. Maybe you don't care about that. Maybe you've never cared about any of that, but that's where we're different." Legs weak, I leaned against the tree, but the moment my weight touched the trunk, it gave way.

Staggering to the side, I watched the great oak cave into itself, breaking apart in chunks that disintegrated into flakes.

It crumbled soundlessly. One minute the tree was a solid part of this world and the next it was gone.

"What's...happening?" I turned wide eyes on Lilith.

She pursed her lips as she eyed me with her chin raised. "You're dying. That is what is happening."

"I'm not dead now?"

"Yes and no. Your body has already grown cold, has it not? But you're not all the way dead. Not yet, but you will be soon." She waved her hands, gesturing at the trees. "As I've said, you're in the in-between. When you entered, the bond between us drew me here. When you perish, so will I. Creating you was the risk I took. We were joined, and you were destined for greatness. I thought you would be like *me*."

Now some of what Grim had said made sense, about the danger Lilith created for herself when she created me...naturally. But where was the Lilin? Why wasn't he here with us?

Then it occurred to me as I stared at my mother. I had a soul. She had a soul. The Lilin didn't. When it died, it ceased to exist. Not so for us.

I guessed none of that really mattered now.

"Destiny is bull," I said, my hands icy as I curled them against my palm. I couldn't feel them. "No one is destined for anything. We control our own fates."

"Obviously," she muttered with another roll of her eyes. "But look at you now, the road you've chosen. What do you know of life? Your entire existence was pointless."

Behind her, another tree gave way, falling into itself, breaking apart in a plume of dust, and then another and another.

"Not true." My legs shook, and I wasn't sure how long I could remain standing. "I know of friendship. I know of...of love. You know nothing of those things."

Lilith flinched and for a long moment she was silent. "That is not true. I did know of love, the purest kind."

"Is that so?" I whispered. The sun was gone now, the sky a mottled shade of violet and the grass a crispy brown.

"Yes." Her voice was quiet, faraway, and I realized then that I was no longer standing. I was on the ground, and I wasn't sure I was even there anymore. I knew I was slipping away, for real this time, into nothing and my eyes drifted shut. The last thing I heard was, "When I held you in my arms and you stared up at me, only a few minutes old, I knew the purest brand of love."

twenty-nine

WHEN I OPENED MY EYES AGAIN, IT SEEMED LIKE only a handful of moments had passed, and I felt out of it, like I'd fallen down some kind of rabbit hole. It took me a few seconds to realize I was staring up at snowcapped branches.

The sight was really...beautiful.

Tiny icicles had formed on the ends of the branches and the snow glistened in the sunlight like a thousand white diamonds. Was this heaven? I didn't think there was snow in Hell or that it would be this pretty. Then again, Roth had said that things were always pretty at first. I'd seen what he'd meant for myself. Pain sliced through my chest, as real as the blade I'd used to kill the Lilin. Roth. God. It hurt to think of him and what he must be going through.

My fingers were cold.

So were my toes.

Wait. My feet were bare? My gaze lowered down the length of my body and I could see the tips of my toes. The blue polish was chipped, and if I was dead and in heaven, I thought at least my nails would look like I recently had a pedicure.

Except my entire body was cold, way too cold. I exhaled and a misty cloud puffed before my lips. So, I was breathing and I was cold, and I was going to take a leap of logic and go with the idea that I might not be dead, dead.

Sitting up took effort. The branches surrounding me danced a bit as dizziness washed over me. Snow clung to my hair, to my eyelashes. The sweater I wore was the same one I remembered, stained with my blood. Gingerly, I reached down and tugged up the hem. I sucked in a rough gasp of air.

There was no wound.

Lifting my gaze, I let the sweater fall back in place as I looked around. My heart jumped in my chest. Realization kicked in. I stumbled to my feet, swaying unsteadily. I was on the observation deck of the tree house near the Warden compound. A barrage of memories rushed me. Escaping to the tree house when I was a child and got lonely, and the endless hours of Zayne lying next to me, shoulder to shoulder, as we counted stars. But how in the world had I ended up here?

Then I tugged on the collar of my sweater and I saw Robin's tattoo. He was curled around my shoulder, and his tail twitched as I studied him. He was here, too. But he hadn't been on me when I'd left Roth's place. Had Robin found me somehow?

I started to jump off the deck, but thought twice. My legs were shaking as I walked across the deck and ducked into the house. The climb down the tree was slow and the snow gave way under my feet when I hit the ground.

Following the path I'd walked so many times I could do it blind, I slowly made my way toward the house. Whenever my knees started to knock too badly, I stopped for a couple of minutes. Weakness invaded every cell. It was as I imagined having mono felt. All I wanted to do was lie down and nap, then take a longer nap. Except I needed to keep walking, because I... I didn't know if I was really alive or if this was some kind of weird afterlife or something.

When the crumbling retaining wall came into view, I almost dropped to my knees. As I dragged my gaze up and saw the mansion, I could barely catch my breath. The detail, down to the broken curb near the front doors, was too accurate to be anything but real.

The pavement was icy under my feet as I forced myself across the roundabout. I made it to the curb when the front door burst open.

Nicolai stood there, his handsome face pale as he stared down at me from the top of the steps. "Layla?"

My throat felt thick. "Hi?"

He didn't move, only seemed capable of staring at me, and there was a good chance that I was going to face-plant on the steps. An icy breeze rippled across the entryway, stirring the dark strands of his hair, tossing them across his face.

Then he moved.

I tensed and stumbled back as he came down their wide steps, three at a time. Within a heartbeat, he was in front of me, clutching my upper arms. His vibrant blue eyes were wide.

"We thought you were dead," he said hoarsely.

"I'm not?"

He shook his head. "No, little one. If you're standing here, you're not."

Confusion swamped me. "That's...good news."

Nicolai choked out a laugh, and my gaze wandered over his shoulder. I saw Geoff standing in the doorway, and Danika was halfway down the steps, her mouth forming a perfect O.

My gaze swung back to his. "I don't know what happened."

He nodded, and then stepped away so that he stood beside me, curving his arm around my shoulders. "Let's get you inside and we'll figure this out."

I didn't argue with him as he led me up the steps and into the blessed warmth of the house. Everything seemed the same as it had the last time I'd been here, right after Abbot had passed, except it felt like years since I'd crossed the threshold.

Nicolai guided me into the sitting room, the very same one I'd sat in so many times. He placed me on the couch. "I'm going to grab Jasmine."

I wanted to tell him that I was okay, but he was gone before I could say a word, and then Danika was there, draping a heavy quilt over my shoulders. I grasped the edges of the quilt with numb fingers. "Thank you."

She knelt in front of me, shaking her head. Her mouth opened, and then she rose quickly, backing off. Without even looking up, I knew why she'd retreated.

Zayne was there, on his knees in front of me. He shared the same awestruck expression that Nicolai and the rest of the Wardens wore. His mouth worked, but there were no words.

"Hi?" I croaked out again, proving once more that I was the lamest when it came to speaking in general.

"How are you here?" He grasped my knees, his grip tight as he leaned forward. The fresh winter-mint scent surrounded me, but it didn't fill me with yearning like it used to. No, now it was like being wrapped in a blanket of familiarity. It was bittersweet, still powerful, yet ultimately no longer the source of my longing.

"She doesn't know," Nicolai answered from the doorway.

Glancing up, I saw that he wasn't alone. Dez was there and Jasmine was brushing past them, heading straight for us.

"Did you...?" Zayne didn't take his eyes off me.

At first I thought he was talking to me, but it was Dez who answered. "Yes. A few seconds ago."

Before I could ask what they were talking about, Zayne said, "Layla, what happened?"

I cleared my throat, figuring it was time for me to actually string together more than a few words. "I don't know. I met up with the Lilin and I..."

"You killed him," he finished for me, his expression tensing. "You killed yourself, Layla."

"I had to, Zayne. It was the only way, but I'm not so sure if I succeeded now." I glanced at Jasmine as she sat beside me on the couch. "I really think I'm okay."

Jasmine smiled warmly. "I just want to make sure, all right?"

"The front of your sweater is covered with blood," Zayne reasoned. "Let her look. Please?"

Exhaling slowly, I nodded and let Jasmine check me out as Zayne rose stiffly. He seemed to lean toward me at first, but stepped away. There was a weight on his shoulders that hadn't been there before as he stood above us. I wondered if it was because he would take over the clan in a few short years, or because of what had happened with us.

"You killed the Lilin," Zayne said after a moment. "The Alphas told us that the Lilin was dead. They pulled back— no longer threatening to wipe out all of us. That's how we knew something happened—that something had to have happened to you."

Jasmine tugged the quilt closer around my shoulders as she

finished checking me out. "She's fine," she said to Zayne. "From what I can see. No wounds."

Zayne lifted a hand, scrubbing his hand through his hair. "When Roth showed up, we knew." His voice was rough, and my heart squeezed like someone had dropped it into a juicer. "He said you left in the middle of the night without him. I... I don't even know why he came here, what he thought we could do for him. He said that one of his contacts had confirmed that you...that you'd done it. Roth was..." His brows knitted together as he looked away. "We had a funeral for you, Layla."

My stomach dropped. "You did *what?*"

"You were gone. There was no body." Nicolai frowned from the doorway, and I suddenly felt like hurling because he was talking about *my* body. "But we knew you were gone and I...we had to give you that rite, after what you sacrificed."

Great guacamole, I had no idea what to think about that. I missed my own funeral! Well, if I'd been dead, dead I would've missed my funeral anyways. "That seems a little quick," I said finally.

Zayne stepped toward me, his expression severe. "Layla, it wasn't quick. You've been gone for six days. The funeral was two days ago."

"Six days?" My eyes widened. "It couldn't have been six days. It was just last night..." I trailed off, remembering what Roth had said about time moving differently down below. The disconnect had happened when I went down to see Grim. Though I didn't think I'd gone to Hell this time. I had a feeling I had been in something more like a waiting room of sorts. Time must've moved slowly then, too. I shook my head and cool, damp hair clung to my cheeks. "I thought I died. I was in this place and I saw—"

A commotion rose from the hallway, cutting me off. I looked up as Jasmine rose from the couch. A rush of warm tingles tiptoed across the nape of my neck. Nicolai turned and I saw Dez step to the side, away from the room.

"It's him," Dez said softly.

I was standing before I realized what I was doing, the blanket slipping off my shoulders. My senses started coming online, firing all at once. Shivers raced up and down my spine.

My heart stuttered, and then skipped a beat as a tall form parted the Wardens crowding the door. Messy raven-colored hair fell forward into ocher eyes that were deeply shadowed.

Wrinkles clung to the black shirt he wore. It looked like he'd slept in it for days, as did the dark jeans. The laces on his boots were untied. He was a mess, every inch of him, but he was still the most striking thing I'd ever seen.

Roth strode into the room, stopping halfway. His full lips parted, and I caught a quick glimpse of light reflecting off the metal ball. Our gazes locked, and it was like the world around us just slipped away. It was only him and me, and I didn't remember moving and I didn't see him move either, but in a heartbeat, I was standing before Roth, staring up at him.

"Layla?" His voice cracked halfway through my name. He reached out, clasping my cheeks with hands that shook. A shock jumped from his skin to mine.

Tears filled my eyes as I inhaled deeply. The sweet, dark scent of his settled over me. In that very moment, there was no lingering doubt in my mind that I was alive and this wasn't some kind of bizarre hallucination.

"I'm here," I whispered as the tears broke free. "I'm really here."

Roth's hands slipped off my cheeks, and then his arms were

around me. He hauled me up against his chest, onto the tips of my toes as he buried his face in the crook of my neck. He staggered back a step, and I guessed his legs had given out, because the next thing I knew, he was on his ass and I was straddling his lap, my knees on either side of his hips.

His entire body trembled as I wrapped my arms around him, holding him just as fiercely as he held me. We were so close I could feel his heart pounding and the rapid rise and fall of his chest. Tears ran down my cheeks unchecked, and I had no idea how long we sat like that, clinging to one another as Roth rocked back and forth ever so slightly. I couldn't get close enough. I wanted to burrow my way in, because this—*this*—I never thought I'd feel any of it again—his arms around me or his warmth or his unique scent. Only a tiny part of me had hoped that somehow, someone would let him see me after I passed on, but I hadn't been counting on it. I'd left to face the Lilin never expecting to experience this again.

Raw emotion expanded inside me, and it was almost too much, but in an odd way, not enough.

Roth jerked back, lifting his head. There was a sheen in his amber eyes, a glassy quality that tore at my heart. I'd never seen a demon cry, didn't even know it was possible, but I'd been wrong. Then my cheek was pressed against his shoulder again, and he was holding me so tight there was a good chance I'd turn into a squeak toy, but it would be worth it. There were no words between us. None needed to be spoken. Every action was drenched in what we felt for one another.

One of his hands traveled up the line of my spine, fisting around my hair at the nape of my neck. He dragged my mouth to his, and he kissed me. There was nothing soft about it. The kiss tasted of desperation and joy, of pain and relief, and of the bright rediscovery of tomorrow that had once been stolen away.

The kiss was the act of someone who never thought he'd have the chance to experience it again. I tasted blood and I wasn't sure if it was from him or me, but it didn't matter. Our tears mingled and our hands clutched at one another. He was so very much warm and alive under the clothes, and I was so very much here, with him.

Roth pressed his forehead against mine, and my hands trembled as I pressed them against his damp cheeks. He hadn't shaved and the rough bristle tickled my palms. "I love you," he said, and then spoke in a language I didn't understand before switching back. "I love you. I love you. I love you."

thirty

HOURS LATER, WE LAY IN BED, OUR ARMS AND legs tangled as night fell and snow continued to blanket the ground.

The trip back to the McMansion had been a blur. The Wardens had left us almost immediately, which was shocking. Things had most definitely changed if they were now willing to leave a demon and, well, whatever I was alone in their sanctuary, even if they were standing guard outside the sitting room.

No one stopped us when we left, and I hadn't seen Zayne. Only Nicolai and Dez had been visible when we exited the room. I was in no shape to fly the friendly skies, so we ended up having Cayman pick us up.

He'd been overly excited at the idea of playing chauffeur.

I lay on my side, the front of my body pressed against Roth's. I was curled around him and his hand slid up and down my spine in a continuous, smooth caress. Since the moment he'd walked into the sitting room at the compound, there hadn't been one second where we weren't touching one another.

And only a handful of seconds had passed between the moment we'd stepped into the bedroom and when our clothing ended up in a forgotten pile on the floor. Again, there had been little said between us, but what we felt for one another was expressed in each brush of our fingertips, sweep of our lips and in the way we moved against one another.

I wasn't sure how much time had passed after our hearts slowed and the fine sheen of sweat cooled on our skin.

The tips of his fingers followed the line of my spine. "I went to Hell looking for you."

I lifted my chin, peering up at him from when I was snuggled up against his chest. "You did? Roth, that was so dangerous. They could've kept you."

He looked down at me, dark eyebrow raised. "I thought you were dead. The last thing I was worried about was the Boss throwing my ass in the pit. And as it turns out, I was in such a pathetic way, the Boss took pity on me, and just tossed my ass out of Hell after telling me you weren't there."

Resting my hand above his heart, I felt it beat strongly before I spoke. "Still, it was dangerous."

"I was… I was desperate." His hand made another trip up my back. "I've never felt that before. I mean, when that asshole Warden stabbed you, I felt fear, tasted it for the very first time when you were in my arms and I thought you might die, but this was so much stronger. It was different. When I woke up that night and you were gone, I knew… I just knew what you'd done, and I wasn't even mad at you for it. I was too damn afraid to feel anger at first." He tipped his chin back, staring at the ceiling as he swallowed hard. "Some kind of missive went out from Hell. Like a freaking text message, saying that the Lilin was dead—actually, it was a text message. A group text message to every demon topside. I saw it on my phone when I got out of bed."

For some horrible reason, I had the urge to laugh. Hell sent texts messages—group ones at that? It kind of fit, since there was nothing worse than being on the receiving end of a group message—sort of like being held hostage. But nothing was fun about any of what Roth was telling me.

"The moment I read that text, I swear my heart stopped. I left the room and found Cayman downstairs. The look on his face confirmed it. You were gone and I... I couldn't deal with that. That's when I went to Hell, but you weren't there, and I thought...you'd gone *up there*. And that made sense. That no matter what ran in your blood, you would end up there." His hand stilled midway down my back. "But up there, you were totally out of my reach. Forever."

My heart broke when his voice cracked. "I'm a demon, Layla. I'm a selfish prick. Even though I thought you'd ascended to a place like that, I couldn't ever get to you. Never again. I wanted to be happy for that, but I couldn't. I couldn't deal. These six days you've been gone, I..." He cleared his throat as he lowered his chin. His eyes were open and there was that painful glossiness heightening the amber color. "There was nothing but anger and pain. It wasn't fair. Not for us. It wasn't fair, and when the anger finally faded away, I was dead inside, Layla. That's the damn truth. I was dead inside."

Tears blinded me. "I'm sorry. I did that to you and I'm so sorry—"

Roth shifted and suddenly we were both on our sides, facing one another and at eye level. The hand on my back ended up along the nape of my neck. "There is a huge part of me that wants to throttle you—old-school strangle you, but with love."

My brows climbed up my forehead.

"There's a huge part of me that wants to rage at you for making the choice that you made. There's a ginormous part of me that wants to shake you until you understand that you made a decision that broke me." His hand tightened at the back of my head. "You *broke* me, Layla."

Emotion clogged my throat. "I... I didn't have another choice."

Bright eyes fixed on mine. "And you know what? That's the part that killed me the most. You didn't have a choice. I get that. I got that then, and you know, there was a part of me that understood it the moment we spoke to the seer, but I didn't want to accept it. Maybe if I did then we could've faced this together. So you...you wouldn't have done it alone."

"No," I whispered, placing my hand on his cheek. "There was nothing that you could've done. You're not at fault for any of this."

His gaze searched mine as if he was looking for a hint of insincerity, and when he didn't see it, his eyes drifted shut. "The thing is, Layla, even though there are parts of me that feel that way, it does nothing to touch the elation of holding you in my arms, the thrill that comes along with feeling your heart beat and hearing each breath you take. That's what matters most."

Roth was giving me a pass. There was no doubt in my mind he wanted to lay into me, but he got why I had to do what I'd done and he was letting it go. He never ceased to amaze me with his very un-demon-like tendencies. He'd once said that people with the purest souls could be capable of the greatest evil, and I knew that worked both ways, especially when it came to him. I might not be able to see a soul around him and everyone might say he didn't have one, but at his core, he was better than most humans and Wardens I knew.

His lashes lifted as he slid his fingers out from my hair and followed the curve of my jaw to my mouth. He dragged his thumb along my lower lip. "I wish you hadn't had to be by yourself. You must have been so scared."

I'd been terrified, but I didn't think he needed to know that. "You couldn't have been there with me," I told him quietly. "You would've never allowed it to happen."

"True," he remarked. "What... How did it go down?"

I searched his face. "Do you really want to know?"

"Yeah. Yeah, I do."

Drawing in a deep breath, I moved my hand to his bare chest. "As soon as I left here, the Lilin found me. I guess he knew I'd come to him eventually, but to join him. And he's... He really is a he. I asked that he show me who he was. First, he shifted into me. Like I was looking into a mirror."

"You are nothing like that thing," Roth ground out.

My lips slipped into a small smile. "I know. He finally showed himself. He kind of looked like me, if I was a dude. It was weird. Maybe not, since he really was sort of my brother. I have a really messed-up family."

He snorted. "Shortie, that is one thing I can understand."

I arched a brow. "I stabbed him in the heart. He didn't see it coming." At that point, I left out the gory details surrounding the whole dying part. "I ended up in this bizarre, in-between place. I saw... I saw my mother again."

Shock splashed across his striking face. "What?"

"It really wasn't her. More like her spirit. All of us were

connected—are connected. When the Lilin died and I was dying, she was able to come to me." I paused, frowning. "She was kind of a bitch. Again."

Roth let out a surprised laugh. "I could've told you that."

I narrowed my eyes at him, but told him what Lilith had said to me. "She talked to me for a little bit, and then the world started falling apart around me. I thought I heard her say that she had loved me when she'd first held me as a baby, but I'm not sure. That really doesn't match everything else she said to me.

"Anyway, Lilith told me that I was dying and it felt like... It felt like I blinked and then I was in the tree house. It didn't feel like days had passed. Maybe minutes, at the most an hour or so. I didn't think I'd get this—a second chance. I'm still not sure how I did."

Pain flickered over his face, and it resonated within me. His voice was low when he spoke. "I never thought I'd see you again. That I'd spend an eternity wanting you—mourning you. I could've dealt with that if I knew you were alive and happy. It would've been hard. I probably would've spent a lot of time banging my head off a wall if you ended up with Stony." He paused. "And I probably would've also been a creepy stalker keeping tabs on you. I mean, I'm a demon. What does anyone expect? But as hard as that would have been on me, I could bear it because you would've been alive."

Turning my head, I kissed his palm. "This isn't some kind of dream or hallucination, is it?"

"I don't think so, but if that's the case, I don't want to wake up from it." His nose brushed mine as he spoke. "I could spend forever like this."

I bit down on my lip, knowing so much more still needed

to be said. "It was so hard leaving your bed—leaving you. I want you to know that. I didn't do it lightly. It hurt, Roth, and it was the hardest thing I'd ever had to do. All I could've hoped was that one day you'd forgive me and find some sort of peace, because I had to do it. I had to…"

"You needed to…save the world," he said softly. "And you did. Look at you, you little hero, saving mankind from the apocalypse."

"I guess I did." That felt weird to think, to believe in. I kind of felt like someone owed me a lifetime supply of sugar-cookie dough, my favorite thing in the world to eat. "This is going to sound terrible to admit, but when I…well, after everything happened and I was lying there, I thought that saving the world really wasn't worth it, because I—"

"I get what you're saying. You don't even need to finish the sentence, and no, it doesn't make you a terrible person. If I'd had my way, we'd be lounging in some far-off island as the world around us went to shit."

"No, you wouldn't have left."

A single dark brow rose. "You give me too much credit, Layla. That's exactly what I was planning. I was pretty much going to kidnap you and whisk you away. I figured we could survive, even against the Alphas, while drinking mojitos and getting a suntan. We'd try at least, and I was willing to watch the world burn if that meant being there with you to watch it. I wouldn't have sacrificed you. My…compassion for others, with the exception of you, does not run that deep."

He was being honest and he was a demon, so it wasn't really like I could fault him for any of that.

"So that was all with Lilith?" He smoothed his thumb along

my cheek. When I nodded, he frowned. "I don't understand. How did you get back here?"

"You mean how am I alive?"

His lips pursed. "I was trying to avoid saying that, so I didn't sound ungrateful or anything."

"I don't know how, Roth. I was wondering if you did something. Made another deal, maybe?"

"I tried. Went to the witches, but they said there was nothing they could do," he explained. "I did get to see Bambi. Well, Bambi peeled herself off that woman the moment I showed up. It was... I needed to see her then." He took a deep breath. "I didn't do this, Layla. Trust me. If I could gloat about saving you, I would be all over that, but this... I had nothing to do with this."

"Then who?" I whispered.

He gave a little shake of his head. "I don't know. Had to be a higher being. Maybe the Alphas?"

I snort-laughed. Real attractive, but I couldn't help it. "Doubtful. They hate me. They probably threw a pizza party in the clouds when they learned I was gone."

"Pizza party?" he murmured, the corner of his lips tipping up slightly. "More like a kegger."

"Thanks."

That slight grin grew a little more as he lifted his gaze to mine. "You know what? Doesn't matter. You're here. That's all that matters to me."

I wasn't sure if it did matter who saved me, but there was a part of me that still worried, because what if some random creature came to collect, like the witches had? I didn't like the idea of someone showing up to demand payment at any given time.

Unless it had been Castiel, because I was totally cool with him rising me up from perdition if that was what happened.

Roth guided my head back and he kissed me, lingering in a way that made my toes curl. "Right now, all I want to think about is the fact that you're here. That's all I can focus on." He caught my lower lip in a quick, delicious little nip. "If someone or something comes knocking one day looking for payback, we'll face it together."

Wiggling so our bodies were pressed close, I buried my face against his chest. "Together," I whispered.

"Together," he repeated. "Never again will you have to face anything like that alone. No matter what. I'm going to be glued to your freaking hip if need be."

For the first time since I woke up in the tree house, an acute tension eased out of my muscles and I smiled. Even during all the beautiful, hands-on welcome home Roth had given me, I hadn't *really* smiled. I'd done a lot of other things, but now, as he kissed the top of my head, all I could do was beam.

No matter what, we would face anything that came our way together.

Roth rolled me onto my back. Hovering over me with his weight supported on powerful arms, he grinned that one-sided grin that used to infuriate me to no end. But now it was a glimpse of the Roth I fell in love with; the Roth I was going to do my damnedest to spend *eternity* with.

thirty-one

"SO...WHAT'S IT FEEL LIKE TO DIE AND COME back to life?"

I shook my head as I frowned down at the cell phone. "You've asked me that question, like, three times already."

Stacey's snort echoed through the bathroom. "I'm asking every day I talk to you just to make sure nothing has changed and you're not going to turn into a zombie. I don't wanna have to go all Rick Grimes on your ass."

Rolling my eyes, I twisted the length of my hair in a top bun, and then shoved about a hundred pins in to keep it in place. "That's not going to happen, and I'd be a walker, not a zombie."

"Semantics," she replied. "Am I going to see you today?"

I nodded, and then realized, like an idiot, she couldn't see me. "Yeah, I think Roth and I were planning to swing by this evening. He mentioned something about picking up cheese fries."

Stacey and her mom, along with her baby brother, were still staying at her mom's sister's house. They hoped to be in a new home by spring, but her aunt's house was as nice as the McMansion Cayman had acquired.

"Have I told you lately how much I like Roth and all his good ideas?" she said.

Laughing, I picked my sweater up off the counter. "You like him because he brings you food."

"I'd like him even better if he acted like a real demon and turned my brother into a frog or something," she muttered.

As I dragged the thick sweater on over my head, Robin darted across my shoulder and ended up stretched out along my lower back. "I don't think Roth has the capability to do that."

"He could try," was her response, and I could practically hear the pout in her voice. Picking up the phone, I turned it off Speaker as I headed into the bedroom. I frowned as I spied one of the kittens curled up in a fuzzy little ball atop the scarf I planned on wearing. It was Thor.

Dammit.

A familiar pang of loss hit me in the chest as I cautiously approached the bed. I missed Bambi. After things had settled down a little, I'd remembered that Roth had mentioned seeing her. We'd reached out to the coven and surprisingly they'd allowed us to visit. Seeing Bambi had healed some of the hurting in my chest. I knew she was happy and she was okay, treated like a princess, but still, even though the apocalypse was averted, she no longer belonged to us.

"So…" Stacey drew the word out. "Are you getting ready to go talk to Zayne?"

I stopped a few feet from the bed, my brows knitting. "What? How do you know I'm doing that?"

"Zayne told me he'd texted you yesterday," she answered.

Thor lifted its head.

"I didn't know he told you that," I murmured absently, distracted by wondering how I was supposed to gain access to my scarf without shedding blood.

"It doesn't...bother you that Zayne and I talk, does it?"

"What?" I ignored the way the kitten's ears flattened. "No. It doesn't bother me. Why would it?"

"I don't know," Stacey murmured. "I just wanted to make sure."

I shook my head even though, again, she couldn't see it. "I think it's great that you're spending time with Zayne." And I really, truly meant that. Stacey had lost Sam, and Zayne had lost his father...and, in a way, he'd lost me. At least that was how it felt sometimes. "You guys are there for each other, and that's amazing. I just didn't know he told you about texting me."

"Good," she replied. "I'm happy to hear that, because it's nice... It's just good to have him around right now." There was a pause. "Is Roth going with you?"

I snorted. "Uh, no. If Roth went with me, they would spend the entire time trying to outsnark one another."

Stacey giggled. "You know, if it wasn't for you, I think they'd have an epic bromance."

Zayne and Roth bromancing it out? Doubtful.

"Well, I'll let you go, but call me when you get done and let me know how everything goes with Zayne. Okay?"

"All right. I'll talk to you soon." After saying goodbye to Stacey, I slipped the phone in my back pocket, and then took a deep breath. I may be one badass half demon, half Warden, half something else entirely, but these damn kittens terrified me.

Snapping forward, I grabbed the edge of my scarf and yanked hard as I jumped back from the bed. The little demonic ball of fur flopped onto its back, four paws sticking up at the ceiling. It just lay there, swirling its tail back and forth over the comforter.

"Sorry?" I said, backing away.

Thor turned its head toward me and meowed the most pitiful sound known to man. I almost started toward it, to make sure it was okay, but then I caught myself. "I'm not falling for that. You're fine."

The kitten's ears pinned back as it rolled onto its side. Then it popped onto its little paws and strutted across the bed, and I mean, it *strutted*, tail swaying and all. What an evil little turd.

Looping the scarf around my neck, I headed downstairs. I could hear Cayman talking in the kitchen, something about basting versus brining, and while I wanted to believe he was talking about a turkey, I wasn't willing to put money on it. I'd taken one step off the stairs when Roth walked through the entryway.

My heart did a cartwheel. The sight of him alone did that to me, and I doubted that would ever change.

As tall as Roth was, the height and breadth of his shoulders was striking enough, but throw in the work of art that was his face and eyes that shone like topaz jewels, he stole breath and hearts everywhere he went.

He was wearing a long-sleeved dark blue thermal and even with the studded belt, his black jeans hung distractingly low. As he reached up to scrub his fingers through his hair, pushing the choppy lengths off his forehead, the thermal rose and I was greeted with quite the glimpse of golden skin and those two little indents on either side of his hips.

Roth was grinning when I finally dragged my gaze to his.

"You keep looking at me like that, Shortie, and you're not going to be leaving this house anytime soon."

Heat flooded my cheeks as I toyed with the loop I'd made in my scarf. "I wasn't looking at you in any particular way."

"How many times do I have to tell you what a terrible liar you are?"

I wrinkled my nose at him. "Whatever."

He crossed the distance between us. Catching my hands, he pulled them away from the scarf, and then he started readjusting it himself. "You're leaving to go talk to Zayne now?"

"Yeppers." I eyed him cautiously. I knew he wasn't exactly thrilled with the idea of my heading off to meet up with Zayne, but he knew how much it meant to me, so he was basically—surprisingly—keeping his mouth shut about it.

"Robin's with you?" Fixing the scarf to his apparent satisfaction, which looked no different than how I'd done it, he then dropped his hands to my shoulders.

I nodded just as the fox's tail switched along the base of my spine. "On my back."

He frowned. "I still don't like that idea of you going out there. I can—"

"Roth," I said, stretching up and placing my hands on his chest. "I'm going to be okay. You know that. I'm officially pretty badass."

"I'm not questioning your badassery, but just because the Lilin is gone and the Wardens are playing nice right now, that doesn't mean everyone is puking rainbows out there."

Yuck. I could've done without the imaginary. "I know."

He studied me for a moment, and then sighed. "I'm being overprotective."

"Yeppers peppers."

His hands slid up my neck, eliciting a shiver from me. He cupped my cheeks. "It's hard not to be, at least for a little while."

"Understandable."

"Text me when you're done. I'll meet you." Guiding my chin down, he kissed my forehead, and I think he also kissed the top of my bun, which was really cute. "Okay?"

"Okeydokey." I was evidently in a rhyming kind of mood as I started to slip away, but he caught my hand and tugged me back. Badassery went right out the window, because I ended up pressed against his chest. "Roth—"

Circling an arm around my waist, he bent me backward as he lowered his head. Roth kissed me, and he...wow, he kissed me like we'd never done it before, like it was his first time learning the curve of my lips, and he took his time doing so. The kiss was *thorough*. My pulse raced as I melted into him, wrapping one arm around his neck as I clutched his arm with my other hand.

"Oh for the love of my innocent, virtuous eyes, could you guys not do that where I have to see it?" Cayman's voice carried from the kitchen doorway.

Roth lifted his head, and as he straightened, I watched in a daze as he grinned slyly at me. "Just want to make sure you don't forget me."

Cayman snorted. "I don't think she's going to forget that anytime soon."

So true.

Roth appeared rather pleased with himself. "Say hi to Stony for me."

I shot him a look, and he appeared completely unrepentant as he winked and then swooped down, kissing me once more before he let go. But there was a part of me that thought Roth wasn't being a jerk when it came to his request, and that alone was kind of amazing.

Cold grass crunched under my boots as I crossed the lawn, heading for *the* bench. The temps had jumped over the past couple of days, melting the snow, and the sun was out, and even though it was still chilly, people were out everywhere on the National Mall.

Sitting down, I immediately winced as the iciness from the wood seeped through my jeans and chilled my bum. I hunkered down in my sweater, squinting at the bright winter sun.

Humans milled about, heading for the museums, some sitting on benches playing chess, others out jogging and being all healthy. Did any of them know how close they'd come to the legit end of the world, like the trumpets blaring and rivers running with blood kind of end of the world?

I really didn't even have to ask myself that question, because I already knew the answer. Even with the gargoyles awakening and wreaking havoc and even with all those poor people who'd seemingly dropped dead on the streets, mankind seriously had no idea what a near miss they'd had with the apocalypse.

We'd saved the day. *I'd* saved the day, and they would never know.

Man, it was kind of like being Batman, but without the cool cape.

But if I were Batman would that make Roth, Robin, the Boy Wonder? Ah, no. I couldn't see him being down for that, but the thought made me grin from ear to ear.

The sound of footsteps drew my attention, and I looked up.

Zayne was a few feet away from me, one of his hands shoved deep in the pockets of his jeans and the other holding a square black bag. His shoulders were hunched, his chin dipped low. My stomach did a weird wiggle, not entirely pleasant. My familiar didn't affect my ability to see auras like Bambi had, but now I almost wished it did. That would be better than having to see how…how dull the glow around Zayne had become. The antique white of his aura was a constant reminder of what I'd done to him.

And it hadn't been the only thing.

My grin weakened a bit, but I didn't let it fade away, because despite everything, I was happy to see him.

"Hey," he said, and he smiled, but it didn't reach those vibrant eyes. God, I missed that smile, how he did it with his face—his *whole* being. "You came."

I gave a little shake of my head. "Of course I came. I told you I would."

"Yeah, you did." He sat beside me, placing the bag on the other side, and then shoved both hands in his pockets as he stared straight ahead. Several moments passed. "I just thought maybe you would've changed your mind…or something."

Understanding seeped in. "I wouldn't change my mind, and Roth would never ask that of me."

Zayne's head swung in my direction. He opened his mouth, closed it, and then tried again. "I… I like your hair like that."

"Oh." I reached up, gingerly poking at my bun. "I honestly didn't feel like doing anything with it."

"It's different." He glanced at me and then quickly averted his gaze. "Anyway, I wanted to see you, to tell you that I'm glad that you're okay. I didn't get the chance to tell you that when you showed up at the house. All of us were pretty shocked to see you." The longer he spoke, the more some of the awkwardness fell by the wayside. "When we'd heard that the Lilin was dead, well...we knew what that meant. I knew what that meant."

"I'm sorry," I said. I realized that I'd been saying that a lot, but I still meant it. I just wished I could say something else.

A quick grin appeared before vanishing. "I know you are. What you did was incredibly brave. Crazy, but brave. I'm not going to lecture you for it. I'm sure... I'm sure Roth has already done that." He paused, taking a deep breath. "You know, you can't doubt what you really are, anymore. Inside. You have to know. To make that kind of choice you made, you can no longer doubt your worth. I just... I just wanted you to know that."

I squeezed my eyes shut and let out a shaky breath. "I... Thank you." That was all I could say, because he was right. I knew what I was on the inside. Being a demon or a Warden didn't make me who I was. My decisions and my actions did. And I wasn't perfect—and I wasn't evil. I was just me.

A breeze tossed a strand of his blond hair across the chiseled line of his jaw. "Enough about me," I said, and Zayne chuckled. "What?" I asked.

He slid his hands out of his pockets as he leaned back against the bench, relaxing. "Layla-bug, you died and came back to life. Kind of hard not to focus on that."

At the sound of my nickname, I got a little giddy inside. "Okay. Good point..." I racked my brain for something to say and found it. "I'm going back to school next week. Roth and Cayman did their thing and the school officials think I've been out with mono or something. I can catch up and graduate on time."

"That's good." Sincerity clung to his voice. "What about college?"

I shifted on the bench. "I think I'm going to apply for spring semester—to some of the colleges around here, but once I'm done with school, I kind of want to travel." Thinking back to the conversation I'd had with Roth about seeing the world, I smiled. "I've never been anywhere and I want to see things—the beach, the mountains—a desert. I have time to do that. Lots of time."

"That's right. I don't know how I keep forgetting that you… you're not going to age or anything." His jaw tightened. "I think it's good, though—the whole travel thing. You'll have fun."

"Yeah." It was weird and something I honestly didn't obsess over, but I was forever going to look like this…unless someone managed to stab me in the heart or chop my head off. I really needed to change the subject again. "But really, enough about me. I want to know how you're doing with everything."

He raised one broad shoulder. "Taking it day by day, to be honest. A couple of the nearby clans are coming in, to scope everything out. It's nothing to worry about," he added when I tensed. "It's just procedural crap from what Nicolai and Dez have said."

"They've been a lot of help, haven't they?"

"Yeah. I've got a couple more years before I need to take over, and I know between the two of them, they will do things right. They're going to bring about some of the change that is needed, especially with how close Nicolai and Danika are getting."

I grinned, still liking the idea of those two together. "Change is definitely needed. Things have been a bit…archaic." If Danika had her way, and I couldn't see her stopping until she did, then the females of the clan would have a heck of a lot more choices in the future. "But aside from your responsibilities to the clan, how are *you*?"

His brows knitted together. "It's hard some days," he admitted quietly. "Talking to Stacey has been good. She...she understands, you know?" He paused while I nodded. "I know my father and I didn't see eye to eye on a lot of things toward the end, but he was my dad, and I loved him." He glanced at me. "He loved you. You know that, right? Underneath it all, he did care for you."

Recalling the conversation Zayne and I had after Abbot died, I nodded. "I know."

"I miss him."

I started to reach over to squeeze his arm, but halted halfway. I wasn't sure if he wanted that kind of comfort from me now.

Zayne must have caught the movement out of the corner of his eyes, because he half turned, picking up the black bag. "I brought you something."

My brows flew up. "You did?"

He nodded as he reached inside. "I thought you might be missing this."

Curious, I watched as his arm lifted and a raggedy, furry brown head came into view. I clasped my hands together, my mouth dropping open as Zayne pulled out an old, beat-up teddy bear that had seen better days. "Mr. Snotty," I breathed, reverently.

Zayne had given me Mr. Snotty the night Abbot had first brought me to the Wardens' compound. I'd only been seven and terrified of the winged creatures with their hard, stone-like skin and jagged teeth. I'd rushed through the house, found a closet and hid in it until Zayne had coaxed me out of it, offering a once-pristine teddy bear.

I'd loved that thing.

As much as I loved Zayne.

I took the bear, clutching it close as Zayne cleared his throat. "I know you're not a little girl anymore. Heck, I know if push comes to shove, you could kick my ass now, but I thought… well, you could always use Mr. Snotty. He belongs to you."

Tears burned my eyes as I buried my face in the top of Mr. Snotty's head and breathed in deeply. The scent of what used to be my home clung to the little bear, and I almost started sobbing right there. Hugging that bear, I wanted to go back in time just so I could get one more hug out of Abbot, before everything went downhill between us.

Blinking back tears, I lifted my face to Zayne. "Thank you. Thank you so much."

He closed his eyes briefly. "I miss you, Layla."

My chest squeezed like it was in a vise. "You don't have to," I whispered, angling toward him as I held the bear. And here we were, finally at the heart of the reason why we were sitting on the bench. "I'm right here. I miss you, Zayne. I want to be friends."

"I know. It's just… I'm not ready for that," he said, flipping his gaze to the sky. His chest rose with a deep breath. "I like to think that one day I will be. Well, I know I will. One day."

"I will be waiting," I told him. "I mean it. I'll be waiting for that day."

Some of the weight I carried around my heart eased as Zayne nodded slowly. Then he smiled as he looked over at me, really smiled that full-faced grin that I grew up adoring, and in that moment I knew that there really would be a "one day" to look forward to.

thirty-two

ZAYNE AND I CHATTED FOR A LITTLE WHILE
longer, and when it came time to leave, I was reluctant to
part ways. I didn't know when I'd see him again. I'd been so
close to jumping on him and hugging him like I did with Mr.
Snotty, but I knew it was still too soon for that.

Teary-eyed, I watched Zayne head across the lawn and I
hoped that "one day" became someday soon. I really did.

I gently placed Mr. Snotty back in the bag and when I stood,
I started across the lawn in the opposite direction, toward the
museums. I was going to text Roth soon, but I needed a couple
of minutes to sort through all I was feeling. I was happy that I
got to see Zayne and to know he didn't hate me, but I missed
him something fierce. I wished it could be the way it was before he and I had gone down that road, but I couldn't find it
in myself to regret any of what he and I shared. We needed to
experience everything we had for both of us to know where
we really stood with each other. Although I wanted to force
him to be my friend right now, I respected and cared for him

too much to not give him all the time he needed. In the mean-time, I could only be glad he had Stacey to talk to.

I cut through the benches and tables, focusing on taking deep and even breaths as the bag holding Mr. Snotty swung gently at my side. Out of the corner of my eye, I thought I spotted a familiar dark face. Stopping midstep, I turned to my right.

Morris sat at one of the wooden tables, his bushy brows furrowed in concentration. One fingerless gloved hand was balled under his chin and the other hovered over black and white chess pieces that were strategically placed on the game board.

I don't know what shocked me more—the fact I was seeing Morris out and about when I hadn't seen him at all since the night Abbot died, not even when I'd returned from the... well, from the dead, or the fact that he wasn't alone. Across from him sat a raven-haired woman. Dark, oversize glasses covered most of her face, but from what I could tell from her seated position, she was tall and slender, the tawny skin of her hand as it moved over the chess pieces was flawless.

Morris had friends? Lady friends? Lady friends who appeared much, much younger than him? Go, Morris...

The woman moved one of her knights, taking what I guessed was a pawn of her opponent's. As she scooped the dark piece, a thick cloud crept over the sun, blocking it out suddenly. Startled, I glanced up and frowned. It was so dark it was almost dusk.

An odd shiver curled its way down my spine as I lowered my gaze to them. The shiver spread its chilly fingers across my shoulders. Robin grew restless, sliding off my back and crawling to rest just below my ribs.

Morris glanced up, his soulful gaze finding mine. The skin

around his eyes crinkled as he smiled widely. I raised my hand as the sun broke free from the inky cloud and I wiggled my fingers at him.

This was weird.

He shifted his attention back to the chess game, and I had a feeling that I was dismissed, which I was oddly okay with. I didn't know what was going on there, but I'd started to walk past them, to the sidewalk when a soft, lilting hum caught my attention.

Every muscle in my body locked up as my skin tingled. The hum—I recognized it, would always recognize it. "Paradise City." The same song Roth constantly hummed, but this time, it was coming from a woman.

It had to be a coincidence, I told myself as I slowly turned back around. The amazingly on pitch tone was coming from the woman sitting across from Morris.

She stopped humming and her red lips curled into a half smile as she reached up, removing the shades. Then she turned her chin toward me, and I saw her face. The woman was shockingly beautiful. Every single feature perfectly pieced together. High, defined cheekbones, tiny nose and impossibly full lips, but it was her eyes that knocked the air right out of my lungs.

They were the color of two amber jewels…identical to Roth's.

"You know," she said, speaking in a voice that was thick like smoke, "he's always been my favorite Crown Prince."

My jaw unhinged, and I gaped at her like a fish out of water. *My favorite Crown Prince? My?* Was she…? Oh my God.

Oh my God! The Boss was a woman!

The woman tilted her head to the side and her black hair

slipped over her shoulder. "Ah, I can see the wheels turning in your little head. It warms my bitter heart to know that my Prince is with someone who is at least marginally intelligent."

There was a good chance my eyes were going to pop out, so that insult pretty much went right over my head. "You're..."

"I bet you can guess my name. Like that one song says, I do go by many." The sunglasses dangled from her fingers as she studied me. "Have you wondered why you're here, Layla?" When I started to glance around, she laughed darkly. "Not here, in this park, you little fool, but standing there with blood coursing through your body and your heart beating in your chest?"

Morris raised his brows again—whether at her latest insult or at the reminder of my near-demise, I wasn't sure—but he remained silent, as always.

"It was you?" I said after a moment. "You brought me back?"

She didn't answer immediately. "As I said, Astaroth is my favorite Crown Prince, but I will not raise the dead even for him. At least not without gaining something from it."

I shook my head. "I don't understand. If it wasn't you...?"

"Oh, it was me. And you're welcome." She slipped the sunglasses back on, but it still felt like she could see right into me. "But it was because of your mother."

If the wind had blown that second, I would've fallen right over. "*Lilith* saved me?"

"Lilith promised to never attempt an escape again if I saved you, and that was an offer that even I could not pass up. So I made her a deal, and here you are."

A thousand emotions swamped me, and my knees felt weak. Lilith saved me? Disbelief swirled, mingling with hope, elation and just more shock. Had she finally recognized me as her daughter and had done something redeeming? The bag started to slip from my fingers and I tightened my grasp.

And then it struck me.

If I had died, then Lilith would've died, too. There was no point for the Boss to make this deal unless...unless she had partly done it for Roth.

Holy cracker jacks, was the Boss capable of compassion? Oh man, the world had just turned upside down.

"Now, don't get all ooey and gooey inside, my dear. If you died, then she would've died. So did she feel a motherly bond for you or was she in the end, just saving herself? Perhaps she hopes that one day you will change your mind and free her. After all, then she wouldn't be escaping, now would she? Who knows? I really don't care," she said, raising one shoulder in a delicate shrug. "Neither should you, because you know what you should care about? The fact that besides the Alphas, I'm the only being that can undo Astaroth's existence with just a snap...of my two little, bitty fingers."

Both Lilith as my possible savior and the Boss being awesome forgotten, I felt my back stiffen and my eyes narrow as her threat smacked into me. Fury took hold and I had to use every ounce of restraint not to shift right there and freak some people out.

I didn't even recognize the voice that came out of me in a low growl that caused those walking nearby to give me a wide berth. "I may not be able to defeat you, but I know I can go toe-to-toe with you. So if you harm one hair on Roth's head, I will bathe in your blood and make a necklace out of your entrails."

Then I braced myself for some major whoop ass that was

probably going to bring the Alphas screaming down on us, and maybe I should've had Roth come with me today after all, because my little trip had suddenly taken a really bad turn.

But then Morris smiled and his shoulders shook silently while she tossed her head back and laughed loudly. Nothing about what I said was funny. Or at least I didn't think so. I glanced around, unsure of what was happening.

"I like you," she said once she stopped laughing. "I really do. You are deserving of the Crown Prince."

"Um…"

"And I can see that you and I… Well, I think we'll get along famously." She turned back to the game. "Visit whenever you like, but one last thing."

"Uh…"

She picked up a knight as she licked her lips. "Threaten me again, and I don't care what your mother has promised, what friends you have in high places, or what it will do to Astaroth—*you* will be wearing entrails as a necklace, but they won't be mine."

Alrighty then.

I wasn't stupid, so I knew when it was time to make an exit. I walked away from the table in a daze and it wasn't until a good five minutes later that I stopped in the middle of the crowded sidewalk to wonder out loud, "If that lady is the Boss, then what or *who* in the Hell is Morris?"

Instead of texting Roth, I ended up heading back to the house. I walked in through the front door, placing the bag that contained Mr. Snotty on the chair in the sitting room. As soon as I crossed into the living room, Roth was there.

Moving as quick as a shadow, within a second, his arms were around me and his lips were skating up the side of my neck.

Immediately, a soft sound escaped me as my blood heated. One of his hands found its way under my sweater and smoothed over my bare skin, sending a hot shiver through me.

"You didn't text me," he said to the space just below my ear.

My eyes drifted shut. "Huh?"

His deep chuckle warmed me. "You were supposed to text me and I was supposed to come to you."

"Oh. Yeah. That's right." I bit down on my lip when he kissed the space his lips had brushed against. Why hadn't I texted him? My eyes popped open. "Dammit. You're so distracting. I need to tell you something."

"Mmm. Tell me something." His other slipped down my back. "I'm listening."

I was having trouble breathing. "I can't talk when you're doing that."

"Doing what?" he said innocently.

"You know what." Reaching behind me, I caught his hand and pulled it away from my behind.

"It's not my fault you can't multitask," he said as he started walking me backward. He twisted us around and then sat, pulling me down in his lap so that I was facing him and my legs were shoved against the arms of the chair. "Now. I'm sitting. You're here in my lap, where I like you to be, and I'm listening."

"Okay." I blinked slowly while he grinned up at me.

He looped his arms around my hips loosely. "You met with Zayne?"

"Yes, but that's not what I wanted to tell you." As his brows drew down, I poked him in the chest with one finger. "I'll tell you all about that later. It was good chatting with him and all."

"But?" His gaze dropped to my mouth, and I had a feeling he was going to kiss me.

I needed to get this out before he ended up succeeding in obliterating my senses and it was hard enough when his fingers started moving along the band of my jeans. "But I think I met your mother, Roth."

His finger stilled as his lips parted. A dark look crept into his face, tightening the skin around his eyes. "My *mother*?"

"Yeah. You know, the Boss. She was at the Mall, and I heard her humming 'Paradise City.'" Everything came out in a rush at that point. "I turned around and there she was. And wow, she's really pretty. I mean, she looks a lot like you. Not that you're pretty. You're handsome and hot, really kind of beautiful and—"

"I get what you're saying," he interrupted. "And thanks. But just this once we should talk about something other than my hotness. Did the Boss say anything to you? Do anything?"

"Well, she told me that Lilith made a deal to never escape Hell and that was why I was saved, but that didn't make a lot of sense, because Lilith dead solves the problem of Lilith. I think she…she took the deal for you—the Boss. And she also said that you were her favorite Crown Prince." Crossing my arms, I frowned. "She also said that she could undo your existence."

His eyes narrowed. "Why would the Boss say that?"

"I…um, I kind of threatened her."

"You did?"

Biting down on my lower lip, I nodded. "I sort of told her that I'd bathe in her blood and wear her entrails as a necklace if she harmed you."

One corner of his lips twitched. "You did *what*?"

I lifted my chin. "I wanted her to know that I did not take kindly to thinly veiled threats against you."

Roth's face softened. "Oh, Shortie…you do me proud."

Blushing, I looked away as I rolled my eyes. "Whatever."

"I'm serious. You sought to protect me." His fingers curved around my chin and guided my eyes back to his. "I'm honored that you would do that. I'm sure the Boss wasn't too happy about that."

"Well, she kind of laughed…and then said she liked me. And then she basically told me I'd wear my own entrails if I ever threatened her again. It was weird. You never told me that the Boss was a female, and your mother. And I thought you called the Boss a he before. Or am I making that up? It doesn't matter."

Talk about crazy in-laws, dear Lord.

"A female?" He laughed deeply. "The Boss is whatever and whoever it chooses to be."

Now I was the one gaping at him. "What?"

He trailed his hand along my jaw, cupping the nape of my neck. "The Boss isn't my mother or my father. More like my *creator*, and for some reason recently, the Boss has favored looking like a woman who sort of resembles me, but the Boss is neither male or female."

I opened my mouth, closed it, and then opened it again. "Um…"

"Weird, right?"

"Yeah." My head hurt.

After a few moments, Roth frowned thoughtfully. "What was the Boss doing at the Mall?"

"She was playing chess—oh my goodness, I almost forgot!

She was playing chess with Morris! You know, Morris as in the chauffeur and jack-of-all-trades at the Warden compound. He was there with her." I rocked with excitement, causing Roth to get an interestingly strained look on his face. "Why was he with her? Why were they playing chess? Holy canola oil, they were playing chess! How cliché! Oh my goodness, what if he's—"

"I don't know what he is," he cut in.

My eyes were wide. "He never speaks and he's awesome with a gun and can break out some kung fu moves, but wait... I can't picture—" I lowered my voice "—*you know who* shooting a gun or using kung fu."

His lips were twitching again. "Yeah, tough to imagine the big guy upstairs needing a weapon or martial arts."

True. I deflated like a balloon with a pinprick in it. For a second, I'd thought I was onto something amazing. "But he has to be *something*."

"Anything is possible." His fingers eased the muscles in my neck as his gaze locked onto mine. "So about your mom..."

I tilted my head, giving him better access. "Your— I mean, the Boss told me that she made a deal to never escape if I was saved, and at first, I thought, wow, Lilith finally did something for me—her daughter—but then the Boss reminded me that if I had died, then Lilith would die, that Lilith knew that. She was basically saving herself." I shrugged. "So, I guess we know now, huh? How I came back. I'm still grateful. It doesn't matter how I got back, only that I'm here."

His expression lost its hard edges again. "You're right. You're here and that's all that matters, but here's the thing, Layla. The Boss... Well, the Boss has moments of great compassion and sometimes the Boss does everything possible to avoid taking credit for that." He leaned in, pressing his forehead against mine. "And Lilith could be the same way. Does something good and then hides it. Or maybe she was just saving her own ass, but you know what?"

"What?" I whispered.

He tilted his head, kissing the tip of my nose. "You'll never know the real reason, but you can choose to believe whatever you want about it. You don't have to make your choice now, but no matter what you decide to believe, it doesn't change who or what you are or how much you mean to me or to Zayne or to the other Wardens and Stacey. Even Cayman," he added.

"Even Cayman?" I laughed hoarsely.

He kissed the corner of my mouth. "Even him. None of that changes. That female—Lilith—if she did what she did to save you, that's great. If she did it to save her own life, then forget her. Either way, it doesn't change you."

I closed my eyes as I leaned into him, and he took my weight, wrapping his other arm around me. "You're right."

"I'm always right, Shortie."

"No, you're not." I grinned when he snorted. "But you are right now. It would be nice to know that Lilith cared for me and made a choice to save me, because I'm her daughter, but it doesn't really matter in the end."

"Nope." He kissed the other side of my lips. "Not at all."

"I matter," I whispered, and he rewarded my response with a direct smacker on the lips. "You matter. We matter." I got another kiss for that. "Zayne matters and Nicolai and Dez and all the other Wardens matter. Stacey matters. Even Cayman matters."

His lips curled into a smile against mine. "I wouldn't go that far."

"Shush it." This time, I kissed him.

Roth clasped my cheeks as he pulled back. "Are you okay?"

I knew he was asking not just because of what happened with Lilith, but also with Zayne, and I loved him so much for that—so, so much. "I'm okay."

"Ah, then you better hold on, Shortie."

"Hold on—" I squealed as he stood suddenly, and I did hold on, wrapping my legs around his lean hips and my arms around his neck.

"You got it." Then he kissed me again as he made a low sound deep in his throat that sent shivers all across me. His lips glided over mine again, nibbling and clinging to them until he deepened the kiss with a plunge of his tongue, and I felt the metal ball. Every sense fired in all directions, and it was explosive, and my heart fluttered, along with many, many other parts of my body. A familiar yearning surged inside me, and instead of sending fear skittering through my system, it shot darts of sublime pleasure through my veins.

"Don't stop holding on," Roth ordered, and dark sensuality deepened his voice. "I'm going to make you more than okay."

And he lived up to that promise.

Six months later...

A warm wind lifted my hair, tossing the pale strands across my face and stirring the tiny, sensitive feathers layering my wings. The moon was high and clouds were thick, a perfect night for flight.

I was perched on the roof of One World Trade, one foot

on the ledge, the other dangling off. My wings were arced high, keeping me from toppling right off. Down below, dazzling lights lit up the streets. I couldn't make out people, but I could see their shapes, a bunch of tiny blurs moving. Around me were other buildings stretching tall into sky, windows lit up while others darkened. None of them were as high as me.

Reaching behind me, I placed my hand flat against the building and closed my eyes. The sad and yet powerful history of rebirth and renewal that had taken place on this patch of land was hard not to feel, not to take a moment to recognize.

I had learned a long time ago that sometimes humans could be more evil than any demon rising up from the pits of Hell.

A sharp whistle drew my attention and my eyes opened as I let my hand fall back to the ledge. The whistle had come from somewhere on Wall Street, and a grin tugged at my lips. I stood slowly.

And then I took flight.

Wind rushed up, immediately catching my wings as they spread. Arcing up with closed eyes, I flew higher, and cold air swirled over my heated skin, down the center of my back and over my wings. It was just like Jasmine had described it when I opened my eyes. I stretched out my arm and I really thought I could possibly grasp the stars in my hand and tug them close to my chest.

Maybe I could even fly straight to the heavens, but I seriously doubted the Alphas would be too thrilled about that. The mere thought of knocking on their pearly gates brought a smile to my face as I allowed myself to spin like a little missile before I hit the part of the atmosphere where I could easily be clipped by a plane and would start to have trouble taking in oxygen. I knew if I went any farther, I wouldn't be able to breathe, but I also knew instinct would take over and my body would force me back down. I'd learned that the hard way last night.

One glance below and it was like the whole world was right beneath me. Buildings jutted out at me, like dozens and dozens of fists reaching up. Millions of people lived and breathed in an area that now appeared so incredibly small.

What an awesome view of New York City.

A torrent of wind smacked into my wings, but I spun out of the gust, and then swooped down. Tucking my wings back, I let myself get caught in an epic free fall. I picked up speed and for a moment, the rate at which I fell stole my breath, but there was no fear or panic, just an incredible rush of adrenaline and joy.

Halfway back to the city, I unfurled my wings, slowing my descent so I didn't pancake into the side of a building, because that would have been one heck of a way to end the night and my little cross-country jaunt.

Coasting over the city, I avoided the areas I knew the other Wardens frequented and glided back toward the financial district. The New York clan knew we were here. Dez had even phoned ahead, warning the clan he'd come from not to mess with us, but I didn't want to push our luck. Though I doubted I was enemy number one for them and we all had worked together half a year ago to stop the Lilin and the apocalypse, my partner in crime would always be another story—a very tricky story.

Slowing down, I landed in a crouch on the roof of what I thought was a bank. I'd just folded my wings back when a heavy form landed beside me, causing tiny pieces of stone to loosen from the ledge and fall to the ground. Arching a brow, I looked up.

Roth stood with his legs wide and wings spread. His skin was inky like onyx, shiny and hard. Bare-chested, he blended into the night around him. Or he would've if he hadn't flashed his fangs at me—and if the skull on the buckle of his belt wasn't bright white.

"Your hair," he said.

My eyes narrowed while I resisted the urge to reach up and see what he meant. "What about it?"

He grinned as he knelt beside me, quickly slipping back into his human form. "You look like you just rolled out of a Guns N' Roses video."

"Thanks for that."

"Possibly even the 'Paradise City' video."

"Better and better."

Leaning over, he kissed my temple and then my brow. "Freaking sexy as hell, though. Reminds me of what it looks like after I get my fingers in it and we're—"

"I get the picture." I laughed. "Totally know where you're going with that."

"What? I was going to say when we're waking up in the morning."

I snorted. "Oh, whatever."

His deep chuckle sent a shiver through me. "You know me too well."

That was true. Closing the distance between us, I gave him a quick peck on the cheek. "Did you see me?"

"Yes." He closed a hand around my nape, keeping me from pulling away. "I saw you kiss the stars."

My lips spread in a wide smile. I liked the way that sounded.

"Want to see me kiss my own personal star?" Yeah, that was cheesy, but even though I couldn't see his smile, I could feel it in every cell in my body. His closeness, his happiness and mine, practically had my body humming.

"Always," he murmured.

Tilting my head, I brushed my lips over his once and then twice. The hand along my neck tightened as I ran the tip of my tongue along the seam of his wonderful mouth. His lips parted, and I took the kiss deeper, and like every time, he tasted like dark, sinful chocolate, and like every single time, one kiss was never enough. There were more as we crouched on the ledge of a roof, sixty-some stories high, and I knew if we didn't come up for air soon, we would start to get greedy, first with our hands and then other parts of us.

That had also happened last night.

Pulling back, I let out the breath I was holding as I cupped his jaw in my hand while he made the most pitiful sound. I giggled in the minute space between our mouths. "Later," I promised.

The sound turned to a deeper rumble full of approval. Anticipation swelled, forming a hunger much greater than the one I lived with every day. "Later better come soon," he growled.

He slid his hand from my neck, down my back. Through the loose, thin tank top, I could feel his heat. "Tomorrow we leave? Canada next?"

I nodded. "Canada it is."

He said nothing as he rested his hand on my hip, and I was quiet as I stared out at the city down below. I was staring at my future while I crouched next to my eternity, and that was a wonderful, beautiful feeling.

I still hadn't picked out a college yet or decided on what I wanted to major in, but that was okay. I had time and I didn't want to rush a second of it.

"Is it later yet?" Roth asked.

Casting him a lingering look, I grinned as I rose fluidly, with a grace I never thought I'd ever be capable of. "Only if you can catch me."

Roth rose at once, capturing my hand before I could even take off, threading his fingers through mine. "Already did, Layla."

And so he had, a long time ago, when he strutted into a dark alley and took out a Poser demon. Truth be told, I really didn't even want to run.

This was love, and love could change people, even if that person was really a demon and the Crown Prince of Hell.

"I love you," I told him, and I told him that every day and I would tell him that over and over again.

Roth lowered his forehead to mine as he brought our joined hands to his chest, placing them above his heart. "And I love you," he said. "With every breath I take, I will always love you."

★ ★ ★ ★ ★

Jennifer L. Armentrout
and Harlequin TEEN
are thrilled to introduce
THE PROBLEM WITH FOREVER,
the first in a brand-new
contemporary young adult series.
Read on for an exclusive sneak peek!

one

THREE SUGARS.

Every single morning, Carl Newport dumped three huge
spoonfuls of sugar in his coffee. Well, when he thought no
one was looking, he'd add two more. For a man in his early
fifties, he was fit and trim, but he had one mean sugar addic-
tion. In his study, the home office full of thick medical jour-
nals, there was a drawer in his desk that looked like a candy
store had thrown up in it.

Hovering near the sugar bowl, he reached for the spoon
again as he glanced over his shoulder. His hand froze.

I grinned from where I sat at the huge island, an empty ce-
real bowl in front of me.

He sighed as he faced me, leaning back against the granite
countertop, and eyed me over the rim of his mug as he took
a drink of the coffee. His dark black hair, combed back from
his forehead, had started to turn silver at the temples, and with
his deep olive skin, I thought it made him look fairly distin-
guished. He was handsome, and so was his wife Rosa. Well,
handsome wasn't the right word for her. With her dark, exotic

features, she was very pretty. Stunning, really, in the way she held and carried herself.

I placed my spoon in the bowl, carefully so it wouldn't clang against the ceramic. I... I didn't like to make unnecessary noises. An old habit I'd been unable to break.

Glancing up from my bowl, I found Carl watching me. "Are you ready for today, Mallory?"

My heart skipped unsteadily in response to what felt like an innocent question, but was really the equivalent of a loaded assault rifle. I was ready in all the ways I should be. Like a nerd, I'd printed off my schedule and the map of Lands High, and Rosa had called ahead, obtaining my locker assignment, so I knew exactly where everything was. I'd *studied* that map. Seriously. As if my life depended on it. There'd be no need to ask anyone where any of my classes were. Rosa had even made the trip with me yesterday to the high school so I got familiar with the road and how long the drive would take me.

Today was the first time I'd be attending public school. Well, not the first time. There were times before, when I was younger, but I barely remembered them, so I didn't count them. Then there was the other time, after Carl and Rosa had taken me in, and that first day at middle school had been an epic fail.

That was four years ago.

But now I was ready. I *should* be ready.

"Mallory?"

I glanced up and gave a curt nod as I pressed my lips together and dropped my hands to my lap. I was totally ready.

Carl lowered his mug, placing it on the counter behind him. "You're sure you know the way to school?"

Nodding again, I hopped up from the barstool and grabbed

my bowl. If I left now, I would be fifteen minutes early. Probably a good idea, I guessed as I placed the bowl and spoon in the stainless steel dishwasher.

"And you have everything you need?" he asked, and as I straightened, he twisted his body toward me. Carl wasn't a tall man, maybe around five foot eight, but I still only came up to his shoulders. "Use your words, Mallory. I know you're nervous and you've got a hundred things going on in your head, but you need to use your words. Not shake your head yes or no."

Use your words. I squeezed my eyes shut. Dr. Taft had said that phrase a million times over, as had the speech therapist that had worked with me three times a week for two years. *Use your words.* Words flew through my head like a flock of birds migrating south for the winter. Words were never the problem. I had them, always had them, but it was the plucking the words out and putting a voice to them that had always been tricky.

I drew in a breath and then swallowed. "Yeah. *Yes.* I'm... ready."

And I had to be ready, because today was a big day. It went beyond attending a new school. If I had any hope of attending college next year like a normal, functioning person, I had to make it through one year of public school.

I had to.

A small smile tipped up his lips as he scooped a long strand of auburn hair back from my face. My hair was more brown than red until I stepped outside. Then I turned into a living, breathing crimson fire engine of redheaded awkwardness. "You can do this. I completely believe that," he said, dipping to place a kiss on my forehead. "*You* just have to believe that, Mallory."

My breath hitched in my throat. "Thank you."

Two words.

They weren't powerful enough, because how could they be when Carl and Rosa had saved my life? Literally and figuratively. When it came to them, I'd been at the right place at the right moment for all the wrong reasons in the universe. Our story was something straight out of an *Oprah* special or an ABC Family movie. Unreal.

Saying thank you would never be enough.

I hurried to the island and grabbed my book bag and keys before I broke down and started crying like a kid that just discovered Santa wasn't real.

As if he read my mind, he stopped me at the door. "Don't thank me," he said. "Show me."

I started to nod, but stopped myself. "Okay."

He grinned then, crinkling the skin around his eyes. "Good luck."

Opening the front door, I stepped out on the narrow stoop and into the warm air and bright sun of a late August morning. My gaze drifted over the neatly landscaped front yard that matched the house across the street, and was identical to every house in the Pointe subdivision.

Every house.

Sometimes it still shocked me that I was living in a place like this—a big home with a yard and flowers artfully planted, and a car in the recently asphalted driveway that was mine. Like I'd wake up and find myself back…

I shook my head, pushing those thoughts away as I approached the decade-old Honda Civic. Kept in great condition, the silver paint hadn't faded. The car had belonged to Rosa and Carl's real daughter, a high school graduation gift given to Marquette before she'd left for college to become a doctor, like them.

Except she never made it to college. An aneurysm. There one minute and gone the next, and there had been nothing that could be done. I imagined that was something Rosa and Carl had always struggled with... They saved so many lives, but couldn't save their daughter.

It was a little weird since the car belonged to me now, like I was somehow a replacement child. They never made me feel that way and I'd never say that out loud, but still, when I got behind the wheel I couldn't help but think about Marquette.

Before I backed out of the driveway, the reflection of my eyes in the rearview mirror snagged my attention. They were way too wide. I looked like a deer about to get slammed by a semi, if deer had blue eyes, but whatever. The skin around my eyes was pale, my brows knitted. I looked scared.

Sigh.

Relaxing my face took effort, and practically the entire twenty-eight-minute drive to Lands High, and the moment the three-story brick school came into view, beyond the baseball and football fields, all that effort went to waste.

My stomach twisted as my hands tightened on the steering wheel. The school was huge and relatively new. The website said it had been built in the nineties, and compared to other schools, it was still shiny.

Shiny and huge.

I passed the buses turning to do their drop-off in the roundabout and followed another car around the sprawling structure, to the mall-size parking lot. Parking wasn't hard, and I was a little early, so I used that fifteen minutes to do something akin to a daily affirmation, just as cheesy and embarrassing.

I can do this. I will do this. Over and over, I repeated those words as I climbed out of the Honda, slinging the bag over my shoulder. My heart pounded as I looked around me, taking in the sea of faces streaming toward the walkway leading to the back entrance of Lands High. Different features, colors, shapes and sizes greeted me. For a moment it was like my brain was a second away from short-circuiting. I held my breath. Eyes glanced over me, some lingering and some moving on as if they didn't even notice me standing there, which was okay in a way, because I was used to being a ghost.

But I wasn't supposed to be a ghost anymore. Christ—that was the whole point of being here. My hand fluttered to the strap of my bag and, mouth dry, I forced my legs to move.

First big step was joining the wave of people, slipping in beside them and focusing on the blond ponytail of the girl in front of me. My gaze dipped. She was wearing a jean skirt and sandals. Bright orange, strappy gladiator-style sandals. They were cute. I could tell her that. Strike up a conversation.

I said nothing.

Her legs were toned, as if she was a runner like Rosa. The girl in front of me had gorgeous legs. Mine were the equivalent of twigs, much like my arms. When I was younger, I remembered being told I'd blow away in a strong gust of wind. Not much had changed.

And I really needed to stop staring at her legs.

Lifting my gaze, my eyes collided with a boy next to me. Sleep clung to his expression. He didn't smile or frown or do anything other than turn his attention back to the cell phone he held in his hand. I wasn't even sure if he saw me.

The morning air was warm, but the moment I stepped into

the near frigid school, I was grateful for the thin cardigan I'd carefully paired with the tank top and jeans.

From the entrance, everyone spread out in different directions. Smaller students who were roughly around my height, but were definitely much younger, speed-walked over the red and blue Viking painted on the floor, their book bags thumping off their backs as they dodged taller and broader bodies. Others walked like zombies, gaits slow and almost roaming aimlessly. I was somewhere in the middle, moving at a normal pace, average.

But there were some who raced toward others, hugging them and laughing. I guessed they were friends who hadn't seen each other over the summer break or maybe they were just really excitable people. Either way, I stared at them as I walked. Seeing them reminded me of Ainsley. Like me, she'd been homeschooled—still was—but if she wasn't, I imagined we'd be like them right now, hopping toward one another, grinning and excited. Normal.

Ainsley was probably still in bed.

I took the stairwell at the end of the wide hall, near the entrance to the crowded cafeteria. Even being close to the lunch room had my heart thumping. I didn't even want to think about that right now, because I might end up in that corner again.

My locker was on the second floor, middle of the hall, number two-three-four. I found it with no problem, and hey, it opened on the first try. Twisting at the waist, I pulled out a binder I was using for my classes in the afternoon and dropped it on the top shelf, knowing that I was going to be collecting massive textbooks today.

The locker beside mine slammed shut and my chin jerked

up. A tall girl with tiny braids all over her head flashed a quick smile in my direction. "Hey."

By the time I got my tongue to form that one, stupid little word, she'd already spun and was halfway down the hall, and I was murmuring at air. Feeling about ten kinds of slow, I rolled my eyes and closed my locker door. Turning around, my gaze landed on the back of a guy heading in the opposite direction.

I don't even know why or how I ended up looking at him. Maybe it was because he was a good head taller than anyone around him. Like a total creeper, I couldn't pull my eyes away from him. He had wavy hair, somewhere between blond and brown, and it was cut short against the nape of his bronzed neck, but was longer on the top. I wondered if it flopped on his forehead, and there was an unsteady tug at my chest that made me think of a boy I used to know years ago, whose hair always did that—fell forward. A boy it kind of hurt my chest to think about.

His shoulders were broad under a black T-shirt, biceps defined in a way that made me think of someone who either played sports or did a lot of labor. His jeans were faded, but not in the expensive way. I knew the difference between name-brand jeans that looked well-worn and jeans that were simply old and on their last wear. He carried a single notebook in his hand, and even from where I stood, the notebook looked about as old as his pants did.

Something weird wiggled in my chest, a feeling of familiarity, and as I stood in front of my locker, I let myself think something I hadn't allowed myself to really consider.

I might actually know some of the people here. Kids I'd grown up with, slept in the same house with. Maybe they wouldn't remember me. It had been four years since I'd seen any of them, but I'd remember them and I especially remembered *him*.

★ ★ ★

Most of my classes were AP, and I blended right in, taking my seat in the back. No one talked to me. Not until before lunch, at the start of English, when a dark-haired girl with sloe-colored eyes sat in the empty seat across from me.

"Hi," she said, smacking a thick notebook on the flat surface attached to the chair. "I hear Mr. Newberry is a real jerk. Take a look at the pictures."

My gaze flickered to the front of the classroom. Our teacher hadn't arrived yet, but the chalkboard was lined with photos of famous authors. Shakespeare, Voltaire, Hemingway, Emerson and Thoreau were a few I recognized, and I probably wouldn't recognize them if I didn't have endless time on my hands.

"All dudes, right?" she continued, and when I looked back at her, the tight black curls bounced as she shook her head. "My sister had him two years ago. She warned me that he basically thinks you need a dick to produce anything of literary value."

My eyes went wide.

"So I'm thinking this class should be a lot of fun." She grinned, flashing straight, white teeth. "By the way, I'm Keira Hart. I don't remember you from last year. Not that I remember everyone, but I think I would've at least seen you."

Sweat covered my palms as she continued to stare at me from dark brown eyes. The question she was throwing out was simple. The answer was easy. My throat dried and I could feel heat creeping up my neck as the seconds ticked by.

Use your words.

My toes curled against the soft leather soles of my flip-flops. "I'm... I'm new."

There! I did it. I spoke. Take that, Dr. Taft. Words were

totally my bitch. All right, perhaps I was exaggerating my accomplishment since I technically only spoke two words and repeated one, but whatever.

Keira didn't seem to notice my internal dumbassery. "That's what I thought." And then she waited, and for a moment, I didn't get why she was looking at me so expectantly. Then I did.

My name. She was probably waiting for my name. Air hissed in between my teeth. "I'm Mallory... Mallory Dodge."

"Cool." She nodded as she rocked her curvy shoulders against the back of the chair. "Oh. Here he comes."

We didn't talk again, but I was feeling pretty good about the sum total of seven words spoken, and I was totally going to count the repeat ones. This was, by far, so much better than middle school. I'd made it through four classes, spoken to someone, and even though Mr. Newberry spoke with an air of pretentiousness that even a newbie like me could pick up on, I was floating on a major accomplishment high.

Then came lunch.

For the most part, I was a complete fail at it.

Nerves had twisted my stomach into knots, and even though I made it through the lunch line, all I grabbed was a banana and a bottle of water. There were so many people around me and so much noise—laughter, shouting and a constant low hum of conversation—that I was completely out of my element. Everyone was at the long square tables, huddled in groups. No one was really sitting alone from what I could see, and the smell of disinfectant and burnt food was overwhelming.

As I left the cafeteria, I thought my gaze drifted over Keira sitting at a half-full table. For a second, I thought she saw me, but I hurried out into the somewhat quieter hall and kept going, passing a few kids lingering against the lockers and the faint scent of cigarettes that surrounded them. I rounded the corner, and at the last moment, avoided a head-on collision with a boy not much taller than me.

He stumbled to the side, bloodshot eyes widening out of surprise. A scent clung to him that at first I thought was smoke, but when I inhaled, it was something richer, earthy and thick.

"Sorry, *chula*," he murmured, and his eyes did a slow glide from the tips of my toes right back up to mine. He started to grin.

At the end of the hall, a taller boy picked up his pace. "Jayden, where in the fuck you running off to, bro? We need to talk."

The guy I assumed was Jayden turned, rubbing a hand over his close-cropped dark hair as he muttered, *"Mierda, hombre."*

A door opened and a teacher stepped out, frowning as his gaze bounced between the two, and I figured it was time to get out of the hallway, because nothing about the taller boy's face said he was happy or friendly, and the teacher sort of looked like he wanted to cut someone.

I ended up in the library, playing Candy Crush on my cell phone until the bell rang, and I spent my next class—history—furious with myself, because it probably was Keira in the lunchroom and I could've approached her table. She seemed nice enough, but instead I hid in the library like a dork.

Doubt settled over me like a too-heavy, coarse blanket. What if I couldn't do this? What if I was always going to be this—whatever this was—for the rest of my life? Maybe school was a bad idea. College would've been different, less pressure to fit in, and I could've eased into it. My skin grew itchy by the time I headed to my final class, my heart rate probably somewhere near stroke territory, because my last period was the worst period ever in the history of ever, ever.

Speech class.

Otherwise known as Communications. When I'd registered for the school, I'd been feeling all kinds of brave while Carl and Rosa stared at me like I was half crazy. They said they could get me out of the class, even though it was a requirement at Lands High, but I'd had something to prove.

Ugh.

Now I wished I had employed some common sense and let them do whatever it was that would've gotten me excused, because this was a nightmare waiting to happen. When I saw the open door to the class on the third floor, it gaped at me, the room ultrabright inside.

My steps faltered. A girl stepped around me, lips pursing when she checked me out, but I wanted to spin and flee. Get in the Honda. Go home. Be safe.

Stay the same.

No.

Tightening my fingers around the strap of my bag, I forced myself forward, and it was like walking through knee-deep mud. Each step felt sluggish. Each breath I took wheezed in my lungs. Overhead lights twinkled and my ears were hypersensitive to the conversation around me, but I did it.

My feet made it to the back row and my fingers were numb, knuckles white, as I dropped my bag on the floor beside my desk and slid into my seat. Busying myself with pulling out my notebook, I then gripped the edge of my desk.

I was in speech class. I was here.

I'd done it.

Knuckles starting to ache, I loosened my death grip as I

glanced at the door, sliding my damp hands across the top of the desk. The first thing I saw was the broad chest draped in black, then the well-formed biceps. And there was that tired notebook that looked seconds from falling apart, tapping against a worn denim-clad thigh.

It was the boy from this morning, from the hallway.

More than curious to see what he looked like from the front, I raised my lashes, but he had turned toward the door. A girl was coming in behind him; the expression on her face said he gave great full frontal, but he seemed to be looking at someone out in the hall, and he laughed. The girl got all googly-eyed.

Tiny hairs rose all over my body. That laugh… It was deep, rich and somehow familiar. A shiver crept over my shoulders. *That laugh…*

He was walking backward, and I was rather amazed that he didn't trip over anything, actually somewhat envious of that fact. And then I realized he was heading toward the back, and holy crappers, there were two seats open, one on either side of me.

He turned at the end of the desks, stepping behind the occupied chair, and my gaze tracked up narrow hips, over the stomach, up and up, and then I saw his face.

I stopped breathing.

My brain couldn't perceive what I was seeing. It did not compute. I stared up at him, *really* saw him, saw a face that was familiar yet unknown to me, more mature than I remembered but still achingly beautiful. I *knew* him. Oh my God, I would know him anywhere, even if it had been four years and the last time I'd seen him, that last night that had been so horrible, had changed my life forever.

I couldn't move, couldn't get enough air into my lungs and

couldn't believe this. My hands slipped off the desk, falling limply into my lap as he dipped into the seat next to me, his gaze on the open door, and his profile, the strong jaw that had only been hinted at the last time I'd seen him, tilting as his eyes moved over the front of the class. He looked like he did back then, but bigger and everything more...more defined. From the darker brows and thick lashes to the broad cheekbones and the slight scruff covering the curve of his jaw.

Goodness, he'd grown up in the way I'd thought he would when I was twelve and started to really look at him, to see him as a boy.

My heart was trying to claw itself out of my chest as lips— lips fuller than I remembered—tilted up, and a knot formed in my belly as the dimple formed in his right cheek. The only dimple he had. No matching set. Just one.

Leaning back in the chair that seemed too small for him, he slowly turned his head toward me. Eyes that were brown with tiny flecks of gold met mine.

Eyes I'd never forgotten, never really stopped thinking or dreaming about, and never stopped worrying about.

The easy, almost lazy smile I'd seen a million times in person and in my head slipped off his face. His lips parted and a paleness seeped under the naturally tanned skin. Those eyes widened, the gold flecks seeming to expand. He recognized me; I had changed a lot since then, but still, recognition dawned in his features. He was moving again, leaning forward in his seat toward me.

Don't make a sound.

"Mouse?" he breathed.

Is Amanda being haunted by an evil presence…or has she simply lost her mind?

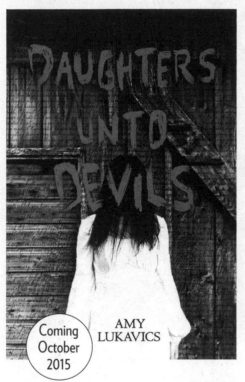

Secretly pregnant, 16-year-old Amanda wonders at first if her family's move to the prairie will provide the chance for a fresh start, but it soon becomes clear that there is either something very wrong with the prairie, or something very wrong with Amanda.

Coming October 2015

AMY LUKAVICS

GOD BLESS THE LITTLE CHILDREN

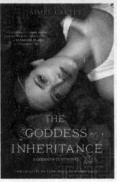